PRAISE FOR JANE HADDAM

NOT A CREATURE WAS STIRRING

"Vintage Christie [turned] inside out . . . *Not a Creature Was Stirring* will puzzle, perplex, and please the most discriminating readers."
—*Murder Ad Lib*

PRECIOUS BLOOD

"A fascinating read."
—*Romantic Times*

ACT OF DARKNESS

"Juicy gossip abounds, tension builds and all present are suitably suspect as Demarkian expertly wraps up loose ends in this entertaining, satisfying mystery."
—*Publishers Weekly*

A GREAT DAY FOR THE DEADLY

"Haddam . . . plays the mystery game like a master . . . A novel full of lore, as of suspense, it is bound to satisfy any reader who likes multiple murders mixed with miraculous apparitions and a perfectly damna-

MORE PRAISE FOR JANE HADDAM

A STILLNESS IN BETHLEHEM

"A high-quality puzzler."
—*Publishers Weekly*

"Classic mysteries are back in vogue, and Jane Haddam's . . . Gregor Demarkian series is one of the finest."
—*Romantic Times*

A FEAST OF MURDER

"Haddam offers up a devilishly intricate whodunit for fans of the classic puzzler."
—*Tower Books Mystery Newsletter*

BLEEDING HEARTS

"A rattling good puzzle, a varied and appealing cast, and a detective whose work carries a rare stamp of authority . . . This one is a treat."
—*Kirkus Reviews* (starred review)

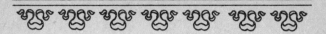

Festival of Deaths

JANE HADDAM

BANTAM BOOKS

New York Toronto
London Sydney Auckland

FESTIVAL OF DEATHS
A Bantam Book/December 1994

ISBN 0-553-56085-9

Published simultaneously in the Untied States and Canada

Bantam Books are published by Bantam Books, a division of Bantam Doubleday
Dell Publishing Group, Inc. Its trademark, consisting of the words "Bantam Books"
and the portrayal of a rooster, is Registered in U.S. Patent and Trademark Office
and in other countries. Marca Registrada. Bantam Books, 1540 Broadway, New
York, New York 10036.

PRINTED IN THE UNITED STATES OF AMERICA

RAD 0 9 8 7 6 5 4 3 2 1

Festival
of Deaths

Prologue

Friday the Thirteenth in New York

1

For DeAnna Kroll, the crisis started at three thirty in the morning on Friday, November 13, in the lobby of the Hullboard-Dedmarsh building at Twenty-fourth Street and Fifth Avenue in Manhattan. Actually, of course, the crisis had started much earlier—in another time zone, in another country—when a thick fog had rolled across the rump end of Great Britain and settled stubbornly in the hollows made by Gatwick and Heathrow airports. All flights in and out were canceled for hours, and remained canceled, even as DeAnna was getting out of her chauffeur-driven limousine onto the pavement in front of the Hullboard-Dedmarsh's tall glass doors, muttering under her breath about how she was going to go stark raving bonkers *permanently* if she had to spend one more *minute* listening to white people. Actually, the chauffeur-driven limousine wasn't DeAnna's idea, and she didn't usually categorize the problems in her life by the race of their perpetrators. Gradon Cable Systems insisted on the limousine for the middle-of-the-night runs

DeAnna made to headquarters. It was the only way old Bart Gradon could be sure he wouldn't be woken up personally because DeAnna was either stranded or (God help us) arrested. DeAnna got stranded because there wasn't a cab driver in Manhattan who wanted to pick up a six-foot-tall black woman with the curves of a Nubian fertility goddess and the shoulders of an NFL linebacker—at least not in the middle of the night. She got arrested because a certain segment of the New York City police force was convinced that no black woman could afford to wear that much Gucci suede if she wasn't turning tricks. DeAnna credited these arrests with having changed Bart Gradon's mind about all the really important things. Until he'd been forced to find a lawyer to get her out of jail before dawn, he'd be fond of arguing that racism didn't exist any more. DeAnna credited herself with having memorized his private phone number out of his executive assistant's private phone book in the less than four seconds it had taken that assistant to pop into Bart Gradon's private office bathroom and deposit a bar of gift soap on the Baccarat crystal soap stand.

As for white people, DeAnna Kroll usually got on quite well with them. She got on especially well with the long-term staff of *The Lotte Goldman Show,* many of whom she had known for over fifteen years. *The Lotte Goldman Show* had been DeAnna Kroll's own personal idea, back in the days when she was still living her job from day to day, convinced that any second now she was going to be fired and sent right back to where she'd started from. Unlike the other young women at the other desks crammed into the small square room called Programming and Development, DeAnna had not started in Rye or at Wellesley. She hadn't even started in school. She'd been sitting in a two-room apartment on 145th Street and Lenox Avenue, counting out the twenty-two dollars and sixteen cents left of her welfare check and wondering how in God's name she was going to feed the baby for the next two weeks, when she got word that she'd passed her high school equivalency exam. She had been eighteen years old. Her new baby had been eight months old. The baby who had provided the occasion for her dropping out of school had just turned three. There were people who made the kind of big leaps DeAnna had made in the years since who said they didn't remember any of it, it all went by in a blur. DeAnna thought they were full of shit. She remembered all of it, thank you very much, from her first job interview to her first apartment in midtown to the endless interview with the admissions director of the Brearley School, where she wanted to send her daughters. DeAnna remembered all of it and would just as soon forget.

The night doorman at the Hullboard-Dedmarsh was asleep in his chair. DeAnna pressed her face to the glass and rapped as sharply as she could with the edge of one of the gold rings on her right hand. On the other side of the dimly lit foyer, she could see a shapeless form stretched out on a leather couch. That would be the driver who was supposed to pick up the Siamese twins at the airport, and apparently hadn't. In the middle of the foyer there was a bright tall sign, with red letters on a white background, leaning on a rickety wooden tripod. The sign said,

---

MY SIAMESE TWIN IS
A TRANSVESTITE.

DeAnna swung cornrows over her shoulder and knocked again.

At the check-in station, the doorman stirred. On the couch, the driver turned just enough to make DeAnna think he was going to fall off. He didn't. DeAnna rapped for a third time and sent up a prayer that her chauffeur wouldn't decide to take off for parts unknown. On her way up, DeAnna had thought there would be places she could get to in this city that would be safe. Now she knew better.

The doorman jerked in his chair, unbalanced himself

and began to fall. The fall did what DeAnna's rapping had failed to do and woke him up. He saw the big black face staring at him from the window and leapt to his feet, imagining God knew what. DeAnna closed her eyes and counted to ten.

She had gotten to eight when she heard the sound of the key in the lock. She opened her eyes again and stepped back so that the doorman could let her in. Then she gave him a tight little smile—his name was Jack Pilchek, but she made a habit of not remembering it—and marched across the foyer to the couch where the driver was sleeping.

"Prescott," she said in her second-to-loudest voice. She saved her loudest voice for screaming fights with her younger daughter, who had just turned twenty and decided that she'd really much rather be a street person than a student at one of America's most expensive private colleges, but she wanted to be a street person in Reeboks. DeAnna hated Reeboks. She kicked the edge of the couch with her Gucci-shod toe and said, "Prescott, come, on, wake up, tell me what's going on here."

Prescott turned, stirred, sat up. His eyes were red and his face was lined. DeAnna thought he must once have been a fine-looking man, in that fine-boned Waspy way that characterized President Bush and the nonethnic presidents of Yale. She also thought he must once have had one hell of a drinking problem.

Prescott ran his hand through his hair and yawned. "Ms. Kroll. Hi. Sorry. Just a minute."

"Siamese twins," DeAnna reminded him.

"Right." Prescott blinked. "They weren't at the airport."

"You mean they weren't on their plane?"

"There was no plane for them to be on. It was canceled."

"Canceled."

"I talked to the woman at the reception desk. The— whatever. The airline."

"And?"

"And there's some kind of awful fog in London, so there aren't any planes leaving from there. There haven't been all night. Our night. I mean—"

"I know what you mean. Did you call Maria Gonzalez?"

"I tried. I called her office and I called here."

"And?"

Prescott shrugged. "No answer. No answer. No answer. So I came back here and Jack and I went looking around the building, but you're usually the first one here on tape days and Ms. Gonzalez wasn't, so we called you."

"Right," DeAnna said. She passed back to the check-in desk and tapped her long red fingernails against the laminated edge. Maria Gonzalez was the talent coordinator for *The Lotte Goldman Show.* She was supposed to discover the talent, book the talent, and make sure the talent got to the studio to tape. DeAnna supposed it was wrong to call Maria's charges *talent*, but she didn't have any other word for them. *The Lotte Goldman Show* had a problem format. People got on and poured out their most intimate secrets, their most exquisite pain. People cried and screamed and broke down into convulsive fits. People told other people how their lives had been ruined and how they needed something more than what they had to want to go on living. What most of them seemed to need was more and more sex.

And more athletic sex.

And more unusual sex.

And more ecstatic sex.

And—

For DeAnna Kroll, sex was a highly inadvisable activity prone to landing a woman with God only knew how many problems, not the least of which was a man who wanted more, but DeAnna Kroll was not a fool. Her original idea for *The Lotte Goldman Show* had been "Dr. Ruth with pizzazz." Her development of it had been somewhat eclectic, but her eyes had remained firmly on the goal. Sex, scandal, and celebrities, that was the ticket. That was how DeAnna Kroll had made *The Lotte Goldman Show* the most successful talk show in the history of television. One week a station in St. Louis had thrown Lotte up against Cosby and *Star Trek*, and Lotte had still pulled down a thirty-five share.

At the moment, Lotte was in danger of pulling down no share at all, because Lotte was in danger of having no show to tape for this afternoon. The Siamese twins were stuck in London. Maria Gonzalez—

DeAnna picked up Jack's phone and dialed Maria at home. The phone rang and rang and wasn't answered. DeAnna hung up and dialed Maria's office upstairs. There was no answer there, either. Then DeAnna wondered for a moment if she ought to be worried. Maria was a relatively new hire. She wasn't very dependable and she hadn't been working out too well. She was also very nearly as sex obsessed as the show's fans. She was probably asleep in some man's bed. Even so, New York being New York, it usually made sense to worry.

DeAnna rubbed her hands against her face. "Okay," she said, to nobody in particular. "We start from square one. Prescott?"

"Yes, Ms. Kroll?"

"I want you to go get Sarah Meyer. She lives on the East Side—just a minute, I've got the address in my book—Call her from the car and tell her we've got an emergency and then bring her here. Can you do that?"

"Yes, Ms. Kroll."

"When you get Sarah here, wait. I'm going to need you to do a few more things. Can you work overtime tonight?"

"It's this morning. Of course I can work overtime. I like the money."

"Good. Go get Sarah. We're going to have to think of something quick and then we're going to have to set it up. God, I've got to *think*."

"I've got to go," Prescott said.

"Go." DeAnna picked up Jack's phone again. Then she put it down again. She really ought to go up to her office. She really ought to make this next phone call in a private place. She really ought to get up close to Maria's files to see who it might be possible to get at the last minute. She really ought to do something about this screaming headache. Maybe there was nothing she could do about the headache. She was too phobic about drugs to take aspirin.

She stalked away from Jack's desk to the elevators and called back over her shoulder: "If Maria comes in, tell her I want to see her ASAP."

She stepped through the elevator doors and punched the button for the twentieth floor.

The next thing she had to do was call Lotte.

2

Lotte Goldman had come to the United States from Israel when she was nineteen years old. She had come to Israel from Germany when she was eight. That first trip was something she remembered in great detail, but it was like staring into a blinding white light. First there was the big black English car that had driven up to the back door of their house in Heidelberg. Then there was the thick brown blanket Lotte's mother had wrapped around her before laying her in the car's trunk. First there was Lotte's small brother David, whimpering in the dark. Then the door of the trunk came crashing down over their heads and Lotte had her larger hands around David's small ones, holding tight as she whispered, *"shh, shh, shh."* That was the fall of 1942, and if they had waited even a month longer it would have been too late. It had been too late for both of Lotte's parents, who had disappeared from the face of the earth, never to be seen or heard from again. All Lotte had left of them was a pair of photographs that said nothing to her at all. The stiff tall man didn't look like anyone she had ever known. The pretty woman with her wide face and gentle eyes was just another antique picture. The memory of escape had blotted out everything around it. It had obliterated all of Lotte's earliest life. David professed to remember, and she supposed that she believed him. She never could.

When the call came from DeAnna Kroll, Lotte was already awake, sitting up in bed, reading her way through a novel by Dorothy Cannell. Dorothy Cannell wrote murder mysteries of the humorous, rational sort, which was the sort Lotte liked. There had been very little reason and very little humor in her life. There had also been very little sleep. In the early days after the escape, Lotte had been unable to sleep because of nightmares. Then the world war had ended and the Israeli War of Independence had begun, and she had been awakened every night by gunfire and tears. Then there had been coming to America, and college and graduate school, and—it was thoroughly incredible how many things there were in life that could keep a person awake. Of course, by now, all those things had been eliminated. Lotte didn't have to worry about money any more. The show seemed to generate the stuff out of thin air, so that now in her old age Lotte was not just financially secure, but positively rich. She owned this enormous Park Avenue apartment and a house in the Catskills. She had a closet full of idiotically expensive clothes and a financial consultant who took her to lunch at the Four Seasons to discuss agressive strategies for capital maximization. Lotte didn't have to worry about David any more, either. He was a rabbi with a big congregation on the Philadelphia Main Line. He had a wife and three children and a black Persian cat. His wife kept a kosher home and invited Lotte to it at regular intervals. In fact, David's wife did better than that. Once a year, Lotte took the show on the road for a ten-city series of location programs. One of those programs was always filmed in Philadelphia during Hanukkah. When then happened, Rebekkah invited the entire cast and crew and really threw a party.

No, Lotte thought, there was really no worry in her life to keep her awake. She was just used to being awake. She went to bed late. She rose early. There was nothing she could do about it. She only wished she could convince DeAnna Kroll of that, because DeAnna Kroll always apologized too much when she called in the middle of the night.

The truth was, Lotte Goldman liked DeAnna Kroll very much. She had liked DeAnna Kroll from the moment the two of them met, in the back of a classroom at Columbia University, where Lotte was teaching a class on abnormal psychology. It had been an auspicious meeting if there ever was one. DeAnna had needed her score, as she put it, to make it necessary for Bart Gradon to promote her. She had been very direct about that aspect of the proposition. In return, Lotte had found herself being very direct about her side of it all. Her own honesty had astonished her. She had told DeAnna Kroll just how sick she was of psychiatry, and how much stupidity she thought it was. She had told DeAnna Kroll just how sick she was of Columbia University. There was something pinched and ungiving about the academic life that Lotte had never liked. On the day DeAnna Kroll had walked into her classroom, Lotte had just received her promotion to full professor, and it had left her in despair. The whole situation was crazy. It was very wrong to despise the good things life gave you when so many people had nothing at all. Lotte hadn't been able to help herself. It was not logical to be depressed about good fortune. Lotte didn't think she cared.

"Listen," DeAnna Kroll had told her, with a sharp wind coming through an open window at their backs and making them both shiver, "it probably won't work. But if it does work, there's no place it can't go."

Well, it had worked.

It had worked in spades.

And so had Lotte and DeAnna.

There was no accounting for it, but DeAnna Kroll was the closest friend Lotte Goldman had ever had, and she had a feeling that the compliment was returned. For some reason or the other, they fit.

When the phone rang, Lotte put down her book and picked up without a second's worry that what might be coming on the other end of the line was bad news about David or Rebekkah or the children. It was going to be DeAnna Kroll, and Lotte knew it.

"Don't tell me," she said, without bothering to say hello, "a saboteur got onto the set and blew it up. Bart Gradon saw yesterday's show and died of embarrassment. We have been invaded by representatives of the Moral Majority."

"The Moral Majority is out of business," DeAnna said, "and Bart can't be embarrassed. I don't know about the set. I haven't been down to the studio."

"You're not at the office?"

"Of course I'm at the office. It's four o'clock in the morning. Where am I supposed to be except at the office?"

"I could say in bed with a man, DeAnna, but that would serve no purpose. What is the problem?"

"The Siamese twins never made it. They're stuck in the fog at Heathrow."

"Heathrow." Lotte frowned. "Does the Concorde fly from Heathrow? Into New York?"

"It does, but it's no use. I was going to call you first thing I got up here, but I decided to do some checking first. Short of somebody on staff inventing the transatlantic equivalent of 'Beam me up, Scottie,' there's no way to get those two over here in time to tape."

"Ah," Lotte said. "What about Maria? What does Maria say?"

"I can't find Maria."

"It wasn't Maria who told you the Siamese twins would not be able to tape?"

"It was Prescott Holloway. He went to the airport and waited for hours then *he* tried to call Maria and he couldn't get her either. It's not a great night for getting people, Lotte, let me tell you. I've been calling the whole staff. I've gotten hold of maybe half of them."

"The other half probably have better things to do. You ought to get a better thing to do. You're going to leave it until too late."

"I had it too early. That's why I've got a twenty-three year old daughter and I'm only thirty-eight. Never mind the other one. The other one is giving me migraines."

"Your daughters will be fine," Lotte said. She meant it. She had known both of DeAnna's daughters since they were small children, and they seemed like very normal and psychologically healthy girls to her. They seemed especially psychologically healthy since she'd given up Freud in favor of feminism. "I suppose we'll have to think of something to tape a show on. We couldn't just let it ride for one day."

"No. We don't have enough of a lag."

"We ought to have enough of a lag. Most of the other shows tape at least a week in advance."

"Most of the other shows don't have our reputation for breaking news. You got anything you want to do?"

"I don't have anything that would constitute breaking news," Lotte said drily. "I have a few things that are fairly provocative."

"Such as what?"

"Such as those women I told you about. I went to their support group. The women whose husbands won't perform cunnilingus."

There was a pause on the other end of the line, and

Lotte smiled to herself. In one of the odder divisions of labor on *The Lotte Goldman Show,* it was Lotte herself who checked out support and self-help groups and twelve-step programs for possible guests. DeAnna had tried it and found herself to be too conspicuous, and neither Lotte nor DeAnna trusted anyone else on the staff to do the initial work. Once Lotte had found a group she thought had possibilities, she put Maria Gonzalez on the case, or whoever had Maria's job at the moment. Talent coordinators never seemed to last long on *The Lotte Goldman Show.*

"Ah," DeAnna said on the other end of the line. "Cunnilingus."

"You have to admit it's provocative," Lotte pointed out.

"I know it's provocative," DeAnna said, "but I thought we had reservations. I thought we'd decided that these women were Looney Tunes."

"Of course they're Looney Tunes. If you want my private opinion, I think the leader of that particular group is a full-blow delusional schizophrenic with better-than-average coping mechanisms. But that's not the point. This is an emergency. We have to do something very quickly. Isn't that right?"

"You've been dying to have these people on, haven't you? You've just been dying to."

"Something like that," Lotte admitted. "I think I can see myself, leading the discussion. How many calls do you think we can get about the explicitness of the language?"

"How explicit do you want to be?"

"Do you really want to know?"

"No," DeAnna said. "Let me think. We've got to have the husbands. That's the key."

"You're right. The husbands. It would be very good if one of them got on and said that he wanted to perform cunnilingus on his wife, but she would not let him."

"It would be better if one of the wives had never had

an orgasm. It's really too bad we just can't hire actors for these things."

"Someday we should go on the program ourselves," Lotte suggested, "and talk about how easy it is to do without sex and what a relief. Then we should cancel the program and take off for the south of France."

"I can't take off for the south of France," DeAnna said. "Sherleen would never forgive me. They don't have street people there."

"Yes, they do, DeAnna, I have seen them. But the street people are not black."

"Maybe Sherleen could get interested in being French. Never mind. I've got to make some phone calls. Cunnilingus."

"Cunnilingus," Lotte said solemnly.

"Would you mind coming in about an hour early? You probably won't get to do anything but sit around, but at least I'll be able to stop worrying about having everything in place, and if I can get hold of these people we can do a quick extra format run-through. Though why we do any format run-throughs at all is beyond me. Australian Aborigines know our format well enough to duplicate it."

"I'll be in an hour early," Lotte promised. "Go do what you have to do and stop worrying. Everything will be all right. Everything always is."

"Everything is always all right because I worry myself to death," DeAnna said. "Never mind that, either. I'm going to get off the phone. I've got to make one more stab at finding Shelley Feldstein. Cunnilingus."

"Cunnilingus," Lotte repeated, for what must have been the third time. The phone went to dial tone in her ear, and she put the receiver back into the cradle.

The Dorothy Cannell novel was lying open on her knees. Lotte picked it up, stuck a stray piece of paper from the night table into it, and put it aside. Her cigarettes were on the night table, too, a habit she had started early and been unable to break. She took one out of her silver cigarette case and lit up.

DeAnna would go out and set up a program on cunnilingus, and they would run it, and it would rate well. Lotte knew all that to be true. She also knew that the older she got, the less interested she seemed to be in any of the things they did programs about. Sex was like eating and sleeping and shopping and all the rest of it, something people did over and over and over again, something that didn't seem to get anyone anywhere. Just where Lotte wanted sex to get people, she didn't know. She didn't know where she wanted to get herself. But there it was.

She swung her legs out of bed and stretched.

Today she would go into the office early and that would break up the time. This afternoon she would have lunch with DeAnna at Viva Tel Aviv, and that would be a positive pleasure. This evening she would take a call from her brother, David, who would tell her it made no sense to keep kosher when she could never remember to observe Yom Kippur. Tonight she would be up too late, too restless to sleep.

Really, life would make a great deal more sense if she could spend a great deal more of it unconscious.

3

Sarah Meyer was asleep when Prescott Holloway called, but she wasn't surprised to be wakened in the middle of the night, and she was even less surprised to be wakened by the company driver instead of her own boss. Sarah Meyer was only twenty-six years old, but she already had the world figured out, and she didn't like it. She didn't like much of anything. Sitting up front with Prescott on the way into the office, feeling cinched and strangled by her seat belt, it occurred to her that she had a right to complain. She'd had a right to complain months ago, when the job she'd wanted—the one she'd slaved for, in fact, the one she *deserved*—had gone instead to the outsider Maria Gonzalez. Sarah had known what all that was about, and she still did, and nobody was going to talk her out of it. The least Lotte could have done was to give Sarah the job as Maria's assistant—but that hadn't happened either. Nothing ever happened the way Sarah wanted it to. Nothing ever had, not even when Sarah was in high school in Scarsdale, not even when she went away to college at Barnard, never. Written down on paper, Sarah's life looked perfect. Witnessed in living color, it was a mess. Sarah didn't even have a roommate any more. Her last one, a snippy little bitch from Baton Rouge, had packed up and moved out back in August. Sarah was not in the least bit interested in finding someone else. Whoever she did find was sure to be a first-class pain in the ass. Whoever she did find was sure to be pretty.

Sarah rode all the way into the Hullboard-Dedmarsh building without saying more than "hello" to Prescott. She marched through the lobby to the elevators without saying more than "hello" to Jack. Since Prescott and Jack both knew her well, neither one of them tried to start a conversation. Sarah was in a bad mood, and when she was in a bad mood she was nasty. When she was in a bad mood she was *ugly*, even uglier than usual, and she knew it. That was Sarah's stock in trade. She was ugly.

When the elevator doors closed, Sarah looked up at the car ceiling and sighed. She was tired and she was cranky and she felt even fatter than she really was. Her face felt like pudding. For years, she had told herself she would win out in the end, that the process was simple, that if she followed all the rules it would work out just like all those Beverly Cleary young adult novels she borrowed from the library. There would be her sister, Linda, pretty and brainless, knocked up at nineteen and sentenced to a life of diapers and drudgery. There would be Sarah, with an Ivy League diploma under her arm, marching off to the glamorous world of television. Or art. Or something. The problem was, Linda had indeed gotten married at nineteen, but she hadn't been sentenced to drudgery, because she'd married a student at the Harvard Medical School. Now the student was the most successful plastic surgeon in Westchester County, and Linda had maids. Sarah had one room on the Upper West Side and a closet full of mark-downs from Lerner's. She had also stopped going out to Westchester to visit Linda, because Linda always did the same thing. She played matchmaker. And it didn't work.

The elevator doors opened to the twentieth floor, and Sarah stepped out to find DeAnna Kroll pacing back and forth in front of the receptionist's desk, reading off a piece of crumpled paper and swearing to herself. Sarah could just imagine what the paper was. She could just imagine what the mess was like. She'd never trusted Maria Gonzalez herself. She'd never liked Maria's assistant, either. Maria's assistant was an olive-faced girl from Guatamala named Carmencita Boaz. Carmencita spoke perfect English in a lilting accent that sounded like wind chimes, and Sarah hated her.

Sarah trundled across the lobby, the thick mounds of her hip bulges straining against the spandex of her leggings, the heavy swelling globes of her breasts bouncing and shaking under the sheer rayon of her tunic. Sometimes she wished that she were black. Black women were allowed to be fatter than white women. It was true. You only had to look at DeAnna Kroll to tell.

DeAnna must have sensed movement in the foyer. She put down the piece of paper and looked up. When she saw Sarah, she nodded and folded her arms across her chest. Sarah was ready to spit. With anybody else, *Ms*. Kroll would at least have smiled and made a welcome.

"Sarah," DeAnna Kroll said. "I'm glad you're here. I'm having the devil's own time finding anybody."

"I was home," Sarah said.

"Yes. Well. Do you know what this is all about?"

"The Siamese twins never got here from London and now we don't have a guest for the show and you can't find Maria Gonzalez anywhere," Sarah said, as if she were reciting it, which she was, in a way. This what what Prescott Holloway had told her when he called to wake her up, and what she had worked so hard not to talk about in the ride down in the car. It was hard to talk about it even now. Maria Gonzalez was nowhere to be found. Oh, it figured. It really figured.

But DeAnna Kroll was going on. "I did find Carmencita," she was saying, "and I got Itzaak Blechmann just before he got into the shower, which was luck. But I still haven't found Shelley Feldstein, and I haven't the faintest idea how to start looking for Maximillian Dey and I need all of them, I really need all of them. Lotte will be coming in by five."

"Dr. Goldman? Why?"

"Because I'm paranoid," DeAnna Kroll said. "Because I'm climbing the walls. Because we've never missed a taping. I need you to get on the phone to the husbands."

"Husbands," Sarah repeated.

"Right. We're going to do the cunnilingus show Lotte's been talking about forever and a day. I mean, why the hell not? We don't have anything else. And I can promote it. I need you to get on the phone and line up the husbands."

"What about the wives?"

"I'll take care of the wives. As soon as you get an agreement from one of the husbands, send Prescott over there right away to pick him up. I don't want anybody getting cold feet. Do you have Prescott's car phone number?"

"In my book," Sarah said. "Of course I do."

"Well, good. Then get going. Oh, and I need as many of the husbands as you can line up. I've got a list of six of them I put on your desk. If we get too many we don't have to use them all. If you finish early, come find me and

I'll give you something else to do. God only knows, in a situation like this, there's more than enough to do."

"Right," Sarah said.

"Try to be pleasant," DeAnna Kroll said. "I mean, these guys are going to be doing us a favor, for God's sake. And they're going to be embarrassing the hell out of themselves, even if they don't realize it. But it's your job not to let them realize it. Until it's too late. Right?"

"Right," Sarah said.

DeAnna Kroll looked doubtful. She always looked doubtful when it came to Sarah, and Sarah resented it. Sarah set her face into its best grown-up pout and waited.

"Well," DeAnna Kroll said after a minute. "That's it. I guess we both better get to work."

"Right," Sarah said again.

"Right," DeAnna Kroll repeated. Then she looked helplessly right and left, shrugged, and turned away in the direction of the inner offices.

Sarah watched her go until she was out of sight around the corner of a plasterboard hallway, and then she followed, slowly, moving between the thin walls hung with pen-and-ink drawings from the early days of television like a small rolling ship moving through the Strait of Magellan. When she got to the place where DeAnna had turned, she stopped and looked, to make sure DeAnna was gone. Then she went straight on to the very back of the suite, where Maria Gonzalez and Carmencita Boaz had their offices.

DeAnna Kroll had said that she had been able to get in contact with Carmencita Boaz, so Sarah didn't think she had much time. She didn't think she was going to have much luck, either, but she never had much luck. What luck she did have consisted in this: Maria Gonzalez had already gotten into enough trouble on her own today; she didn't need any help from Sarah. Sarah could concentrate on Carmencita Boaz alone.

Sarah stuck her head into Maria's office anyway, just

to wrinkle her nose at the bank of photographs in clear plastic frames that littered Maria's desk and the Lucite vase of red silk flowers that graced the top of Maria's file cabinet. It was all so unprofessional. Maria was so unprofessional. Maria came to work every day in flowing skirts and wild hair. Sarah backed out into the hall again and went into Carmencita's office, which was not so enthusiastically feminine but was still feminine enough. Carmencita didn't have as many photographs, only three or four, of her parents back in Guatamala City and her ten-year-old brother in his uniform from Catholic school. Carmencita didn't have any flowers, either, just a small sparkly geode from the Museum of Natural History that Itzaak Blechmann had given her for her last birthday. Itzaak was always hanging around Carmencita's door, trying to think of something to say, trying not to look like an idiot. Sarah didn't know how Carmencita put up with him.

Sarah closed the door behind her and looked around the room, at the clear surfaces of the desk and the file cabinet, at the clean windows, at the bare walls. A lot of people in television kept very messy offices, with weeks-old doughnuts molding in drawers and papers strewn across the carpet. Maria and Carmencita kept their offices the way their mothers probably kept house. That could be a good sign. Sarah went to the file cabinet and looked under "Cunnilingus," but couldn't find anything. She couldn't find anything under "Oral Sex," either. Maybe that made sense. Maria and Carmencita were both Catholic as hell. They went to Mass every morning before coming to work. They were both very modest, too, very prone to blushing and embarrassment. Maybe Carmencita couldn't look at a word like *cunnilingus* staring out at her every time she opened the top drawer of her file cabinet without calling for the smelling salts. Maybe the whole Lotte Goldman show was just too much for Carmencita to take. Sarah tried "Husbands and Wives, Marital Problems, Sex" and was presented with a bewildering array of genital dysfunctions, from impotence to fetishes. None of it was what she was looking for. She stood back and tried to think.

These were a group of women who felt devastated because their husbands refused to perform one of the trendier acts of physical gratification. They met once or twice a month to "feel their rage" and "honor their pain." If she was Carmencita, where would she file them?

Sarah went back to the cabinet and checked carefully through all the folders in the first drawer. She looked in "Divorce" and "Dissatisfaction" and "Communication" without success. Then she went on to the second drawer and tried "Frequency" and "Gratification." Under "Gratification" she found a set of papers titled "Serial Killers—What Do They Really Want" and marked across with red pen:

> PHILADELPHIA THIS YEAR.
> TALK TO GREGOR DEMARKIAN.

Sarah wondered uneasily what short of program a sex show could do about serial killers and then put that folder back. She was just about to go on to file cabinet three when she saw the tag on the last file in this drawer. *"Idiotas."*

Idiotas, Sarah thought.

That meant "idiots."

She didn't need to speak Spanish to figure that out.

Sarah reached for the file folder, pulled it out and put it on top of the cabinet next to the geode. She opened it and found all the prearranged permission agreements for Lotte's cunnilingus show. She closed the file folder. She smiled.

Prearranged permission agreements were very important to a show like the one they were doing—sometimes because of emergencies like this one tonight, but mostly because there was some stickly legal territory in developing what were intended to be mass-marketed, commercial programs about ordinary peoples' private lives. Lotte Goldman refused to begin any investigation on the feasibility of a topic before she had her permissions. It was one of the most important responsibilities of the talent coordinator's office to get those permissions and make sure they were easy to find. Tonight, of course, they would be even more important, because without them they'd have to drag the lawyers out of bed and get the signatures all over again before they even started to tape.

Sarah thought about taking the file folder itself and decided against it. Instead she took the permissions out, left the rest of the papers, and replaced the folder in the drawer. Then she folded the permissions into a thick paper square and put the square under her tunic. That was one advantage to being fat and lumpy. Nobody ever questioned the appearance of one more lump.

Sarah let herself out of Carmencita's office and into the hall. She was prepared with an explanation if anybody caught her, but there was nobody there. She walked down the hall and stopped again at the side corridor where she had seen DeAnna Kroll go after she first came in. DeAnna was nowhere to be seen, but Sarah could hear her. DeAnna had to be down at her own office or in Lotte's, if Sarah could judge from the echo. She was doing her patented bellowing act on the phone.

"Shelley, for God's sake," she was saying. "I've got a love seat. A love seat. I can't put any of these people on a love seat."

Sarah walked the rest of the way to the lobby, looked around at the emptiness again, and then let herself through a door at the side of the elevator bank that led to what they called the "back hall." The "back hall" wasn't actually in the back of anything—it certainly wasn't in the back of the building—but it was that kind of place, concrete and cold, dark and faintly foul. Sarah made her way around coils of wire and metal buckets and big cans of paint to the incinerator door at the back, and then she took out the wad of paper that was the permissions and looked at them.

This was an old building with an old-fashioned incinerator. A long chute went down to the basement where a fire was kept going at all times, and anything that fell into it got burned up.

When Carmencita couldn't find the permissions, there would be hell to pay, there really would be. DeAnna Kroll would go positively ballistic, and Lotte Goldman would smoke in the office.

Sarah looked at the wad of paper in her hand and unfolded it. Then she ripped it in half and in half again. Then she opened the incinerator chute and shoved the scraps down. At the last minute, she was seized by caution. It was a good thing. One of the ragged-edged pieces of paper had fallen out of her hand. It lay on the floor just next to her left foot, threatening to incriminate her. Sarah bent down, picked it up, and shoved it into the chute after the rest.

The world might be a genuinely awful place erected for the single purpose of making Sarah Meyer miserable, but there was no reason to let it get its way all the time.

No reason at all.

4

Shelley Feldstein had started out as a dresser of department store windows, and she had been pretty good at it— very good at it—at a very young age. She had started the way all dressers start, as the assistant to an assistant, in a second-rate store with delusions of grandeur. She had just graduated from the Rhode Island School of Design and had delusions of grandeur herself. Maybe they weren't such delusions. By the time she was twenty-four, she was chief dresser for her store. By the time she was twenty-six she was head dresser for Saks. By the time she was twenty-eight she was free lance, the single most successful dresser in Manhattan, the kind of person to whom stores paid thousands of dollars to do just one window. She was also married, pregnant, and bored to tears. If she had been born in another time and place, she would have quit working as soon as her baby was born. Having been born in this time and this place, that didn't seem right. It also didn't seem right to give up the money. In the year that she was pregnant, Shelley bought home over two hundred fifty thousand dollars, beating her husband's take from his job as a stockbroker by better than twenty-five grand. Fortunately, Robert didn't mind. What Shelley minded was the repetitiveness of it. Executives from Saks and Lord & Taylor and Altman's and Bergdorf Goodman would call her in and tell her they wanted something different, but they wouldn't mean it. What they wanted was what had come to be called a "Shelley Feldstein Look." Shelley Feldstein was sick of the Shelley Feldstein Look. It reminded her of the Villager skirt and sweater sets she used to wear in high school. It was that out of date.

Shelley Feldstein had been brought up to be what her mother called "a sensible girl." She had been taught the importance of things, like home and family, husband and children, security and responsibility. She had been taught the dangers of chasing after butterflies, especially when that meant giving up a good job or a good marriage when you didn't have anything else on the line. Shelley might have gone on forever, posing faceless black mannequins wearing Christian Lacroix in tableaux meant to resemble the Amazon rain forest, if it hadn't been for a set of very unusual circumstances. In the first place, Robert took her to Tavern on the Green for dinner, which he hated, because she loved it and it was her fortieth birthday and she had been feeling depressed. In the second place, Robert said something grossly insensitive and made her cry, which he had never done before in all their years together.

In the third place, when Shelley had gone to wash her face, she had met Lotte Goldman and DeAnna Kroll in the bathroom.

The reason DeAnna had not been able to get in touch with Shelley was because all but one of the ringers on the phones in Shelley's apartment were off. They were off because Shelley's four-year-old had turned them off, which was what he had taken up for a hobby over the last few months. Shelley had gotten up in the night with a headache and gone down to the kitchen for an aspirin, and it was there that DeAnna had found her. The kitchen phone was a wall phone. Jason couldn't reach it.

Shelley had had her meeting with Lotte and DeAnna five years ago. They had been five good years, in spite of the fact that she was making less money than she had been doing windows. They had been five years of excitement and adventure and very late nights. In fact, Shelley had gotten pregnant with Jason in the warm glow of the euphoria that had visited her after DeAnna made her offer.

Coming into the studio at quarter after four in the morning, carrying a black leather tote bag from Coach full of line drawings and lighting specifications, Shelley felt like a student again, not the forty-five-year-old mother of six. It even made her secretly pleased that the sets she would be dealing with were intended to house such—well, outrageous programs. Shelley loved telling people she worked for *The Lotte Goldman Show*. Not only did everyone watch it, everyone was shocked by it. When Shelley got a couple of glasses of wine into her, she told stories about what it was like to work with the woman who smoked a cigar with her private parts and the man who had had his balls tattooed. That second one really got to the men, turning them green, making their eyes bulge. It was wonderful.

What was not wonderful was this set left over from the Siamese twins, and Shelley knew it. She dropped her tote back at the door of the studio and walked to the center of the stage, looking at the love seat, looking at the wide-armed club chair Lotte was supposed to sit in for the interview. For one thing, there weren't enough places to sit. DeAnna had said something on the phone about four couples. For another, the ambiance was wrong. Ambiance was the important thing. People on the outside had no idea. The set of *The Lotte Goldman Show* might look simple to produce, but it wasn't, because *tone* was everything. Get the tone wrong, and you were likely to have the FCC down on your neck, screaming about obscenity.

Shelley walked around the love seat and the club chair. She walked to the middle of the platform and looked straight up into the lights. She frowned. Then she went back to the studio door and picked up the interoffice phone.

"DeAnna?" she said. "Can you come down here a minute? And can you bring Itzaak?"

"I can't find Itzaak," DeAnna said. "I've tried."

"He'll come in with Carmencita," Shelley said dismissively. "He'll give her five minutes and come in after. Never mind. Come down here and talk this out with me."

"But—"

Shelley hung up. None of them wanted to talk about sets. None of them thought consultation about sets was important. Shelley just had to make them do what they ought to want to do.

By the time DeAnna came in, Shelley had the love seat pulled off to one side and listing at the edge of the platform. She wasn't strong enough to drag it any farther. She had the club chair all the way off and onto the studio floor. All that took was a sharp shove with her hip. She needed Itzaak for the lights and Maximillian for the heavy lifting, but she was feeling much better.

'It's going to be fine," Shelley said, as DeAnna came across to the set. "I was a little worried on the way over here, because of the time frame, but it's going to be fine. Where's Max?"

"On his way," DeAnna said.

"Good. We need him to paint a new set of backdrops. Pearl gray, I think, or even navy blue with a white trim. Something conservative." Shelley looked at the bright yellow backdrops now on the set and wrinkled her nose. "These are all we'd need. I can hear the phone calls now. What color dress is Lotte going to wear?"

DeAnna made a face. "I don't know. Do you need to know right away?"

"I need to know before Max paints. We don't want to paint gray and have in her gray. Or navy blue and have her in navy blue. She'd fade into the background. What about the guests?"

"I haven't seen the guests. I don't even know if we have any guests."

"What does Maria say?"

DeAnna looked away. "Maria doesn't say anything. I can't find her."

"You've tried her beeper?"

"Of course I've tried her beeper. I've tried her apartment. I've tried everything."

"That makes the second time this month," Shelley said.

DeAnna shrugged. "The last time we didn't have an emergency like this one. It doesn't matter. Lotte isn't fed up yet. And when Lotte isn't fed up—"

"—nobody is fed up," Shelley said. "I know. But we have to do something about this, DeAnna."

"Right now, I only have to do something about this show. Carmencita's coming in. She ought to know what you need. We've never had any trouble with Carmencita."

"Right. Well. Tell her I need to know what everybody's going to be wearing and also if there are any problems I ought to plan for—if one of the guests is too fat or too thin or too tall or too short, you know what I mean, something really out of the ordinary. I usually do this myself in advance but—"

"Don't apologize."

"I'm not apologizing," Shelley said. "Get me Max. Get me Itzaak. Oh, and as soon as we set up, get me Lotte, if she's in, because Itzaak's got to light her and I've got to be sure—"

"I know," DeAnna said. "I know."

"Everybody knows everything around here," Shelley said. "We sound like a couple of mynah birds. Go back to your office. If you could remember to give the messages I told you—"

"I'll remember. You going to need anything in the way of props?"

Shelley looked the set over, seeing it in her mind the way it would be once it had been transformed, and shook her head.

"No props. Some water because they have to have it or they choke. That's all."

"I'll make sure Sarah knows about the water."

Sarah. At the sound of Sarah's name, Shelley shot a look of sympathy at DeAnna and caught DeAnna shooting one back. The two women smiled and looked away from each other. Sarah was the ultimate example of Lotte's "not being fed up yet." Everybody else on the show had been fed up with Sarah for years. At least, Shelley thought, she was better off than DeAnna. DeAnna had to put up with Sarah as an assistant.

Shelley sat down on the edge of the stage and said, "Go. I've got everything under control. Send me the guys when they come in."

"You really think Itzaak was with Carmencita?" DeAnna asked.

"Don't be ridiculous," Shelley said.

DeAnna sighed. "It's my personal opinion that most women—Christian and Jew; fat and thin; white, black, and green—need their heads examined."

Shelley laughed, and DeAnna went striding across the studio and out the studio door. Shelley turned around and looked at the set, going over the changes in her mind one more time, making sure she had it all down pat. It wasn't as easy to think on no sleep as it had been when Shelley was still at Rhode Island, but it was easier than she would have imagined. Middle age had turned out not to be such a boogeyman after all.

Shelley had gotten to her feet and started across the studio to get her tote bag when she saw the dreidel, and then she couldn't help herself. It was sitting in the middle of the set where it didn't belong. Shelley couldn't abide having things where they didn't belong. It was an ordinary dreidel, a small top with four planed surfaces on its sides and the surfaces painted with Hebrew letters, a toy for family gambling games during Hanukkah. Hanukkah was late in December this year, but the dreidels had started showing up at delis and newsstands at the beginning of November, and now everybody on the show had at least one. Shelley supposed half of everybody in New York had at least one, since fifty cents, and not a connection to Judaism, was the only requirement for ownership.

She picked this dreidel up and turned it over in her hand, murmuring the Hebrew letters to herself and the sentence they stood for. *Nūn, gīmel, hē, shīn,* the letters went, meaning *Nes gadol hayah sham*—"A great miracle occurred there." That meant the miracle of the one night of oil that had lasted eight nights and allowed the Maccabees to win a military victory over Antiochus, after Antiochus had tried to forbid the Jews to practice Judaism. Shelley had grown up in a decidedly secular family and married a decidedly secular man, but even she knew this much about the religion of her ancestors. Hanukkah, her grandmother used to say, is the one holiday even Communists are loath to give up. Shelley hadn't known what that meant, because all the people in her family were advocates of Freud, not

Marx, and wouldn't have known a manifesto if it showed up for dinner.

Shelley flipped the dreidel in her hand one more time, and then stopped. The dreidel was defective. Maybe that was why it was left on the floor. The *nūn* and *gīmel* and *hē* were all in their right places, but the *shīn* wasn't. Where the *shīn* was supposed to be was a different letter entirely, the letter *pē*. Shelley had to wrack her brains to come up with the name—she had taken exactly six weeks of Hebrew lessons when she was thirteen and then decided the enterprise was going to make her crazy—but she was proud of herself for doing it. She wondered why nobody had noticed the mistake until the dreidel was bought and brought here. Maybe the mistake hadn't been noticed even then. Maybe she was the first one to see.

She stood up and started back for the door, and then the lights above her head began to go on one by one. She squinted into the rafters and said, "Itzaak?"

"Ready to go," Itzaak said, in his thick Russian accent overlaid with an Israeli lilt.

Shelley dropped the dreidel into her pocket.

"I've got to get the new set together," she said. "Then I'm going to give you a lot of work to do."

5

All his life, Maximillian Dey had wanted exactly two things, and now, at the ripe old age of eighteen, he had one of them. The one of them he had was his residence not only in the United States, but in New York. Back in the little seacoast town in Portugal where he had grown up, New York was like Atlantis, considered to be fabulous at the same time it was considered to be fake. Maximillian sent his mother and his sisters chips of New York City sidewalk, just to prove that it was real. He sent them pictures of himself sitting in espresso bars in Greenwich Village and standing in front of the Christmas tree at Rockefeller Center. He did not send them detailed explanations of the geography of the city or the status of the five boroughs. Boroughs were something he hadn't known about himself until he landed in the States. Besides, for the moment, there was nothing he could do about the fact that he lived in Queens. Maximillian was only surviving out there by rooming with three other young men like himself in a two-bedroom place that needed a coat of paint. He had checked out rents in Manhattan and they were appalling: fifteen hundred dollars for one room and a Pullman kitchen on West Ninety-fourth Street near Amsterdam Avenue; eight hundred dollars a month for a smaller room and a hot plate in a decaying brownstone on a seedy back street in the Village. It was insane. It was only a matter of time. Maximillian Dey was much too young to believe in his own mortality, physical or metaphorical. He was sure that he would have his apartment in Manhattan and his furniture from Conran's and his season tickets to the Metropolitan Opera by the time he was twenty-two. In the meantime, he bought discount everything and fished copies of *The New Yorker* out of the office wastebaskets to read.

The other thing Maximillian Dey had always wanted was a wife. It was because of this want of a wife that no one ever had to wake him up to come into the studio in the middle of the night. Maximillian was always awake in the middle of the night. He was also always out. After-hours clubs, Greek *boîtes*, Israeli dance joints, Spanish folk music forums where everybody had to bring their own bottles—Max knew them all. He went easily, night after night, from the more conventional entertainments of the Queens singles bars to the more exotic precincts of what one of his roommates called "clean sex shows." He knew the only place in town where a man could see a stripper who just stripped and nothing else. He also knew practically every unattached young woman in the city, except the ones he wanted to meet, and that was the problem. When Max said he wanted a wife, that was exactly what he meant. He wanted a young Catholic woman who believed in virginity, looked like Farah Fawcett, and wanted to have at least eight kids. He wanted a woman who would stay home and look after the house and be proud of him if he made enough money to send all their children to Catholic schools. He wanted, in fact, exactly the sort of woman he would have married if he'd stayed in Portugal, but he never would have admitted *that*. If he'd stayed in Portugal, any woman he married would have gotten fat.

Maximillian carried a beeper because it made him feel important, and because DeAnna Kroll hadn't had the heart to turn him down when he asked for one. Almost nobody had ever had the heart to turn Maximillian down for anything. He had been a pretty baby and an even prettier child. He was a positively beautiful young man. He was tall and slender and fine boned and soul eyed. He had the kind of face younger women were drawn to and older women melted for. He was a case study in the proposition that beauty is its own excuse. God only knew, women were always making excuses for him.

When he first came in to the studio after being called, Maximillian did what he always did: helped Shelley Feldstein move things from one place to another. Then, when Shelley had what she wanted, he went back to the storeroom to see if there was anything else that needed to be done. Like everyone else on the show, he was somewhat cavalier about union work rules, which he could get away with because the Gradon Cable System was somewhat cavalier about just about everything. Nobody who worked for Gradon stood on ceremony. Max went to the storeroom and looked around for things that needed to be put away. People were always hauling down boxes or unearthing trunks and then leaving them in the middle of ev-

erything. Americans were remarkably disorganized in that
sense. Today, though, there was nothing. The storeroom
floor was clean and shiny. The charwoman must have been
in with the mop. The storeroom shelves were orderly.
DeAnna Kroll must have been here herself on one of her
housecleaning rampages. Max turned on the lights and
walked all the way to the back of the room, looked
around, looked at the ceiling, looked at the floor. Then he
sighed and started out again. He didn't want to go home.
He was much too revved up for that. His roommates made
him crazy. He didn't want to spend an hour or two in a
Greek coffee shop. When the shops got too crowded, the
owners didn't like you taking up space with a cup of coffee and the morning paper. This was where a wife would
really have come in handy. If he'd had a wife, he wouldn't
have had no alternative but to hang around feeling useless.

He was just about to leave the storeroom—to try the
back hall, to see if anything had to be done there—when
DeAnna Kroll came in, jumped a little at the sight of him,
and then began to look thoughtful.

"Max," she said. "I didn't think of you."

Max smiled politely. It was a kind of smile he had
learned early. It was usually very effective. "You should
think of me always," he said. "It is how I think of you."

DeAnna Kroll shot him a look that said she wasn't
having any—DeAnna Kroll never was; she was the closest
thing to an impervious female Max had ever met—and
told him, "You can solve a problem I've got. You can at
least solve half of it. Do you have a clean sweatshirt?"

"Of course," Max said. "I have a clean sweatshirt and
a clean shirt. In my locker. I always keep them there. This
job—"

"I know all about your job. Go wash up."

"Excuse me?"

"Go wash up," DeAnna insisted. "Go to the men's
room and strip to the waist—you're sweating like a pig; I
suppose Shelley's been running you ragged—anyway, go

wash up and put on a clean shirt and a clean sweatshirt and come meet me in the greenroom as quick as you can. That's where I've got the women."

"The women?"

"The wives," DeAnna said impatiently. "Oh, God, I don't know how we're ever going to survive this. There's a guy in Lotte's office threatening to tear the wall-to-wall. Will you get moving?"

"Yes," Max said. "Of course."

Max did get moving, too. He had been in the United States now only ten and a half months, and with the exception of the two weeks he had spent getting himself settled, he had worked all that time for *The Lotte Goldman Show.* He knew what Lotte was like. He knew what Shelley was like. He knew what Itzaak was like. Most of all, he knew what DeAnna was like. When she got into this kind of mood, it was best to give her more than she was asking for.

Max not only kept a clean shirt and a clean sweatshirt in his locker. He kept clean underwear, clean jeans, and clean socks in there, too. His work was heavy and sweaty and hot, but he liked to go out when it was over. It didn't leave a good impression if you went out covered with sweat. There was a shower stall at the very back of the bathroom in the back hall, meant for use by the men who came in once a month to exterminate cockroaches. Max had discovered it his second week on the job. He went there now and cleaned up as thoroughly as he ever did when he had a date. He even washed his hair. If DeAnna Kroll wanted him clean, she would get him clean.

Max was fast. It took him less than fifteen minutes to shower and change, although that meant that his hair was hanging wet in the office air-conditioning and threatening to give him a sore throat. He made sure the stiff points of his Oxford cloth shirt collar were opened to precisely the right angle and that his sweatshirt rode up close enough to his waist. He made sure his fingernails were clean. Then he went back down the hall in search of DeAnna.

The storeroom door was still open when he came to it. The lights inside were still on. Max stopped and looked inside at all the barren order and sighed. Then he shut the lights out—

PRESERVE ELECTRICITY,

said a sign in the locker room—and closed the door.

DeAnna was up at the other end of the corridor, standing half in the greenroom and half in the corridor, looking frazzled. When she saw Max she brightened up a little, but not much.

"Thank God you're here," she said. "I think I'm going to lose my mind. Do you happen to know where Maria is?"

"No," Max said. Maria was in many ways just the sort of woman Max was looking for, but she was too old. She had to be twenty-eight at least.

"I don't know why I would think you would know," DeAnna said, "but there's all hell breaking loose around here and I'm absolutely bonkers. Just absolutely bonkers. Why doesn't she remember to turn on her beeper?"

"She isn't wearing her beeper," Max said helpfully.

"What?"

"She isn't wearing her beeper. Or perhaps should I say carrying it. She carries it?"

"Never mind what she does with it," DeAnna said. "How do you know she doesn't have it?"

"It's the one with the little enamel rainbow on the back, yes?"

"Yes," DeAnna said.

"It's on top of the file cabinet in Mrs. Feldstein's office," Max said. "I saw it there myself, less than an hour ago, when I went in to put some things away Mrs.

Feldstein asked me to. It was sitting right there next to the little statue of the head of Einstein—"

"God*damn*," DeAnna said.

"I think perhaps she took it out of her pocketbook looking for something else and then forgot to put it back," Max said. "Women are always doing this thing. They carry so much in their bags, they pull it all out looking for the one lost thing and then they lose something else. I think this is true."

"I think I have a headache," DeAnna said. "The pre-arranged permissions are lost. Maria is lost. I've got a guy used to play end for Ohio State swearing he's going to break my bones. Never mind. You're going to do a favor for me, right?"

"Right," Max said loyally.

"Good." DeAnna stepped all the way into the hall and closed the door of the greenroom behind her. "In that room," she said, "I have six women. They are the guests who are going to be on the show we tape today—you know the Siamese twins couldn't come?"

"Of course."

"Good. So instead we've got these women, and we had to drag them out of bed in the middle of the night and then we had to get their husbands in here too and everybody is in a very bad mood, Max, let me tell you, everybody is in a very bad mood. Now normally it's Maria's job to see that everybody calms down and that nobody leaves—that's the important part, that nobody leaves—but Maria isn't here. I've got Carmencita in with the men—"

"This is not likely to calm them down," Max pointed out.

"If they try any of *that*, I'll break their heads. I want you to take care of the women. You think you can do that?"

"Possibly, yes. I am to calm them down?"

"You are to be sure they do not leave. No matter what, Max, it's important. You are to be sure they don't leave. If you can make them happy, that would be even better."

"I can, of course, only try," Max said.

"I can, of course, only wait for the lawyers, who aren't exactly in a sunshine mood this morning either. You're sure that was Maria's beeper you saw?"

"Oh, yes. Definitely."

"Wonderful. Marvelous. She could be in Alcapulco and the world is coming to an end. Get in there and be nice to the ladies, Max. I've got to see a woman about a shit fit."

"Excuse me please?"

"I've got to go talk to Lotte." DeAnna turned on her high pointy heel. A moment later she was chugging down the hall, her cornrows dancing, the flowing edges of her skirt and her jacket billowing in the wind. She looked like a swarm of angry bees that had developed a coordinated intelligence. Max would not have wanted to get in her way.

Of course, if it was up to Max, Maria Gonzalez would never have been given so important a job as that of talent coordinator. It was a position that carried too much responsibility to be left safely in the hands of a woman, and in Portugal they would have understood that. It was one of the great confusions of America for Max that American men were so thoughtless and easygoing about the things they let women do. It was as if they didn't think anything was really important. Max supposed that some of that might be due to how different American women were from women anywhere else in the world. Max didn't trust Maria Gonzalez with responsibility and he wouldn't have trusted any of the women he knew in Portugal, but he thought DeAnna Kroll was competent enough to run the world. Still . . .

Still. The only women he had to worry about now were the ones in the greenroom. He faced the greenroom door, reached for the knob, and hesitated. Then he knocked. He had barely stopped knocking when the door was opened and a round, plump face peered out, suspicious.

"Who are you?" the woman demanded.

Max bowed, the way he had seen it done in the old movies that played every Saturday night at the small tavern in his town. "I am Maximillian Dey," he said. "I have been sent to keep you company until the taping."

The small round face retreated behind the door, to set up a chorus of whispering. Then the door was drawn all the way open and Max found himself looking at six women, mostly middle-aged and mostly plump, but middle-aged and plump in a pleasant way. The tallest one—who was not the one who had originally opened the door—came forward and checked him out. The tallest one had a pimple the size of Mount Rushmore on her left cheek.

"He looks all right," she said. "He even looks—sensitive."

"Oh, he's European," one of the others said. "You could hear it in his voice. Europeans are entirely different."

"I'm sure he would never refuse to perform cunnilingus on his lady friend," a third one said.

Max bowed again. He didn't know what this *cunnilingus* was, but he was sure he would not refuse to perform anything for the woman he loved, except to change diapers or wash the dishes. As to these women—

—well, if this cunnilingus was something he was supposed to perform on *them*, they would probably let him know.

Itzaak Blechmann had had a difficult life—a very difficult life—and now, at the age of forty-six, he was beginning to come to terms with it. For many years he'd had only his dreams, screaming nightmares that woke him at two and three and four o'clock in the morning. His waking world had never seemed quite real. His present had never seemed to be as compellingly true as his past. After he had been allowed to leave the Soviet Union for Israel—after the deaths of his wife and his mother; after his left leg had been broken for the third time and finally rendered permanently deformed—he'd had trouble simply getting through the days. He wasn't depressed. It was one of the oddities—maybe one of the blessings—of his nature that he was never depressed and never despairing. In spite of everything that had happened to him, Itzaak found it impossible to think of life as anything but God's most wonderful gift. What he found troubling was practical thinking. How to make change. How to catch the bus. Which of the keys on the ring opened the door to the apartment. His mind and body seemed to be permanently stuck in crisis mode. His fright-or-flight response never came down out of high gear. He couldn't buy a loaf of bread and a chicken at the grocery store without becoming totally confused. That was why his best friend in Jerusalem had advised him to go to the United States.

"You can be just as kosher in New York as you can be in Tel Aviv," Abraham had told him, "if you're careful. And there's not so much . . . emergency there."

Itzaak Blechmann was not a hick. He hadn't been a hick when he was living in Jerusalem. He knew there were problems in New York City, problems with race, problems with poverty. Still, he understood what Abraham meant. In some ways, living in Israel had been very much like living in the Soviet Union. In the most important ways it had not, of course. Nobody in Israel was going to send Itzaak to jail for keeping kosher or going to shul. The Israeli government didn't send spies in the guise of rabbis or bug the walls of houses of worship. The two countries were as far apart as they could be, except for the fact that they were both constantly and unrelievedly in the middle of a crisis.

There were times when Itzaak would have liked to have been in the Soviet Union to witness the fall. There were times when he wished he knew much more about the history of the Arab-Israeli conflict and was on-site to investigate it further. Mostly, he was happy he had come to New York. Standing on a street corner in the dark when the whole of Manhattan seemed to be deserted was just as frightening as hearing the sirens go off in Jerusalem or listening to the sound of heavy boots coming up the stairs in Leningrad. The rest of the time things were calm. It had taken a while, but Itzaak had gotten used to ordinary life. He bought shoes and ate in restaurants without going into spates of mental paralysis. He read the papers in Russian and Hebrew and English without getting his languages mixed up. He played chess with friends without losing his concentration to worries he should have been free and clear of years ago.

Most of what he did, however, had to do with this job, and the three other like it he had for various other shows on the Gradon Cable System. Itzaak Blechmann had not been trained as a lighting engineer. He hadn't even been trained for the theater. He had agreed to try this because Lotte Goldman had agreed to give him a job. The job he'd taken had been as Lotte's lighting engineer's assistant. Itzaak hadn't known at the time that the man had already declared his intention to leave the show at the end of the taping year. In the long run it had worked out better than could be expected, and Itzaak had been launched. But that was six years ago.

Carmencita was new. Carmencita had been on *The Lotte Goldman Show* for less than a year. Carmencita was also a revelation. Itzaak Blechmann had known women in his life. He had been married. He had had his share of affairs in Jerusalem and New York. He had never in his life known anyone like Carmencita. Part of it was that she was young. Part of it was that she was exotic, with skin the color of poured gold and deep black hair and eyes so blue they made him think of sapphires. Itzaak didn't know where the blue eyes had come from, but he wouldn't have traded them for anything. He wouldn't have traded Carmencita for anything. She was far too young for him and far too Catholic, but he couldn't stop thinking of her and he didn't want to stop thinking of her and that's the way it was. Itzaak was in the grip of the greatest passion of his life, and it made him think the unthinkable. It made him think that he would die if he didn't marry this woman who was not a Jew.

Prison camps and exile, the judicial murders of two people he dearly loved, year after year of living in hiding—Itzaak Blechmann had done more than most people would ever be asked to do in the service of his God. It was as impossible for him to consider turning his back on the commandments of that God as it had become for him to consider giving up Carmencita.

Or vice versa.

Or something.

When Itzaak tried to think about Carmencita, he got muddled.

Itzaak had been standing just outside DeAnna Kroll's office when DeAnna had been screaming at Carmencita about the prearranged permissions. He had wanted to go inside to help, but he had known better. He had retreated down the hall to wait until Carmencita came out, so he could comfort her. But he had turned his attention away for a moment and missed her. Now he was sitting in his office with his feet up on his desk, his job done until the taping started, listening to the sound of her heels in the corridor outside.

"Carmencita?" he called out.

"I'm coming right to you," Carmencita said.

Carmencita was only five feet tall—which suited Itzaak, who was only five seven—and she wore very high spike-heeled shoes to make herself look taller. She stopped when she got to the door of his office and looked inside, smiling when she saw the coast was clear.

"I just wanted to make sure the dragon lady wasn't around," she said. "Whew. I had less trouble from the nun when my sister and I stole the money from the poor box to buy ice cream."

"She shouldn't yell at you like that," Itzaak said. "It's not proper."

"I ran down to Eidelhauer's and got pastries. You want something to eat?"

Eidelhauer's was a kosher bakery. Itzaak like to think Carmencita went there out of sensitivity to him, but she might not have. Lotte Goldman kept kosher, too. People who worked for the show got used to buying kosher when they wanted food for the office.

Carmencita handed him a Danish and perched on the edge of his desk. "I wish we knew where Maria was. It's making me crazy. She must have been the one who took the permissions out of my file. Nobody else would have bothered. I wonder where they are."

"They were very important?"

"DeAnna had to get the lawyers down here to get new ones. Not having them certainly caused a lot of trouble and cost a lot of money. I don't know. It just doesn't make any sense. Have you seen her?"

"I was with you," Itzaak pointed out.

"I know you were with me. You're a funny man, did you know that?"

"I wish I was. Then maybe you would laugh at my jokes."

"I don't mean that kind of funny. I mean funny. I mean you don't, well, you know. You don't act the way men act."

"I don't?"

"You know what I mean."

Itzaak blushed. "It's not that I don't feel it," he said. "It isn't that, if that's what you think."

"Of course that's not what I think. I think just the opposite. That's just my point."

"Do you want me to—to act like—ah—"

"Of course I don't. That's not what I meant either. I just wish—"

"What?"

Carmencita sighed. "Never mind," she said. "It doesn't matter. I have a good time when you take me out. Don't stop."

Itzaak thought he was as likely to stop taking Carmencita out as a crack addict was likely to stop doing dope, but that didn't seem to be a very delicate way to put it, so he didn't. He took his feet off his desk and leaned forward over the blotter. It was something to do.

"So," he said. "What about Maria? Has nobody seen her at all?"

"Not since we all left here this afternoon," Carmencita said. "I rode down with her in the elevator."

"And?"

Carmencita shrugged. "And nothing. We talked about this sale they're having at Macy's. Bathrobes and bath towels and things like that."

"She didn't say where she was going for the evening?"

"She wasn't going anywhere for the evening," Carmencita said. "She said she was going straight home and going to bed. She had to meet the Siamese twins here at three A.M."

"It seems like an odd time for anybody to be coming into the airport."

"It was. It was one of those chartered flights that cost a dollar ninety eight. I guess they aren't rich Siamese transvestites. Either that, or DeAnna was having one of her moods. Maria must have turned the ringers off on her phone and then slept through her alarm."

"Maybe you should go up there and get her," Itzaak said.

Carmencita nodded. "I suggested that myself, but DeAnna sent Prescott Holloway. I'm supposed to be soothing the savage breasts of the husbands before showtime. Except now they're all in with the lawyers and nobody wants me around. You want another Danish?"

"No thank you," Itzaak said. "I'm not so happy with you soothing the savages, as you put it. They sound violent."

"They're very sweet, really. They're just terribly hurt. I mean, most of them didn't even know their wives wanted—what their wives say they want. The women just went off and joined this support group and now here they all are about to go into worldwide syndication and it's humiliating. It's not embarrassing for the wives, you know, because the wives will be able to look important at cocktail parties for months after we air. But for the husbands . . ."

"I am sure you would never do such a thing to your husband," Itzaak said.

"I am sure that if I was a boss, I would never do something like this to my assistant," Carmencita said. "Oh, well. There's nothing but to see it out and hope for the best. I'm afraid I'm not going to be able to sit with you to watch the taping."

"Why not?"

"Because even if Maria is found, we're going to need two people to handle the guests. We can't herd them all together in a group. They fight."

Itzaak shook his head. "They're going to fight when they get home."

"They're going to get *divorced*," Carmencita told him, "but that's not my responsibility. I just have to make sure they get through the next three hours. Are we going out to breakfast after this is done?"

"We always go out to breakfast. I never want to miss going out to breakfast with you."

"Good." Carmencita hopped down off the desk, looked into the pastry bag again, and came up with a third cheese Danish. Itzaak was charmed. Three. *Three.* This was no hard-bitten American career woman with her mind on her diet. This was a lovely, life-celebrating creature who would one day be a marvelous cook.

"I think I'll go see if the lawyers are done with my gentlemen," Carmencita said. "Max is in with the ladies. They're behaving predictably. See you later?"

"See you later," Itzaak said.

"I'm really glad you're here. If it wasn't for you, I think I'd lose my mind."

Itzaak almost told her that she ought to lose her mind, she'd fit in a lot better on *The Lotte Goldman Show.* It was the kind of joke he knew he was supposed to tell and was so very bad at. She was gone anyway, out the door, down the hall, her heels clicking sharply even on the carpet. Itzaak wondered what it was they made the heels of women's shoes *from*.

At the last minute, he got up and went to his office door, to see if he could catch a glimpse of her walking away. He got Maximillian Dey and Lotte Goldman instead, although not in the same time or the same place. Max was coming out of the greenroom door looking a little green himself. Lotte was going in the direction of her office with a distracted look on her face. Itzaak didn't think he could blame her for being distracted. So far, it had been a mess of a day from start to finish.

Itzaak went back to his office, sat down at his desk,

and began to fuss with the things on his blotter. He didn't keep much—a picture of his wife and a picture of his mother, a little replica of the Israeli flag, a copy of the Torah—but what he had he treasured, and he didn't like the feeling he sometimes got that the things on his desk had been moved around in his absence. Nothing had ever been taken. He would have noticed that. He thought it was probably just the cleaning lady, polishing up. He didn't like it anyway.

Today, however, nothing was missing and nothing was moved, and Itzaak decided to take it as a good omen.

The rest of his day was going to go well, and so was Carmencita's.

7

Prescott Holloway had been born and brought up in the city of New York—in Brooklyn, in fact, so that he had gone to Erasmus High School, just two years behind Barbra Streisand—but no matter how hard he tried, he couldn't remember when The Change had happened. That was how he thought of it, as The Change, as if New York were a woman going through menopause and having some kind of fit. Prescott Holloway didn't know much about women. He didn't know anything about menopause. Even so, the metaphor seemed to fit. It even had an element of hope in it. Women went through menopause and came out the other side and were normal again. Maybe New York would do that, too.

At that moment, New York was what it had been at least since the election of the last mayor, and maybe before—meaning nuts in a totally nasty way. Prescott couldn't remember a time when New York hadn't been nuts. That was part of the city's identity. It was just that lately, lately . . .

That kid from Utah, chased through the subway tunnels to his death ...

That woman in Central Park ...

The Change.

What really made Prescott nervous was the car he drove. It was Bart Gradon's idea of the minimum necessary luxury for a major cable network, but Bart Gradon's ideas of minimum necessary luxury had been formed on Wall Street and the Connecticut Gold Coast. Prescott was parking at the curb outside something called the Bodega Santiago in a pearl gray Cadillac stretch, longer than two ordinary cars, complete with telephone, television, VCR, radio, compact-disk player, and bar. The streets looked empty enough—it *was* five o'clock in the goddamn morning—but trouble could come out of anywhere, anytime, and trouble had a mean face. Especially up here. Prescott looked up the street at the lighted storefront that was the public face of the local Pentecostal church. These days, the Latinos who weren't in gangs all seemed to be holy rolling, coming to Jesus in a whirling cloud of sweat and hair, screaming and writhing on the floor. The churches were as bad as the crack houses. They stayed open all night. Prescott could hear the hymn music from where he was sitting, faint and tinny but with a driving beat.

If Prescott had Maria Gonzalez's job, he would have moved downtown. He wouldn't have had anything to do with an ethnic neighborhood like this one, any more than he had anything to do with his old neighborhood back in Brooklyn. He lived off Times Square, in a fifth floor walk-up with the bathroom down the hall, just to be in the middle of everything.

Prescott turned the engine off and looked up and down the street again, up and down, up and down. He took his keys out of the ignition and opened the driver's side door. Not a single shadow moved. He made a set of New York City brass knuckles anyway: the sharp point of a key sticking up between each finger of his right hand, the bunched knot of ring and leather tab pressed against his palm. All the drivers he knew carried their keys like this, ready to scratch and tear at the face of anyone who got too close. He didn't know if anybody had ever actually tried the trick and made it work.

He pushed the lock button on the door and then slammed the door shut. Then he checked the numbers on the buildings across the street for 586. It was hard to read anything amidst the clutter of signs. It was harder because the signs were all in Spanish. There were no Korean grocery stores here. Bodega. Lecheria. Santeria. Prescott didn't know if he was getting that last one right, but he knew what it was. It was a store that sold voodoo magic.

Number 586 was right next to the storefront marked *Santeria*. Prescott made a gesture at it that was actually the Italian ritual for warding off the evil eye—although he didn't know that; it was just a gesture he had picked up in the old neighborhood—and walked up to 586's front door. It opened without complaint, but beyond it there was a vestibule, and at the other end of the vestibule was another door. That one, Prescott was sure, would be locked. He tried it anyway. He found out he was right.

On one side of the vestibule, the wall had been fitted with steel-case mailboxes and small round buzzers. The buzzers took the place of the fancy call-boards that graced the more expensive buildings downtown. The call-boards had two-way intercoms. These buzzers were connected to nothing but more buzzers upstairs. If you had an apartment in this building and somebody buzzed you, you either had to come all the way downstairs to find out if it was somebody you were willing to let in, or just buzz back and release the lock on the inner door. Prescott knew that somewhere in this building there would be a sign warning residents not to release that door without checking who was calling first. He also knew that residents would pay no attention to it. In a building like this, many tenants would be old women. Their legs would ache and their backs would creak. It would be much too painful for them to keep coming downstairs.

Prescott found the buzzer with Maria's name on it and pressed that one. From what he had heard in the office, he knew she lived alone. He pressed the buzzer again and waited again, not feeling much hope. If Maria had been home, she would have answered her phone. He pressed the buzzer for the third time. On the floors about him, he could hear rustles and moans. At this hour of the morning, the people who worked in the small factories in Long Island City would be getting up to go to work.

Maria didn't answer the buzzer this time, either. That settled it. Prescott looked at the bank of mailboxes again. Always pick a last name with a single initial, he thought. The spelled-out names were almost always names of men. The last thing he wanted at this hour of the morning was to wake a knife-wielding Hispanic crazy out of bed in a bad mood. Always pick a last name with a single initial, because those almost always belonged to women. Maria's mailbox said, "Gonzalez, M." Prescott found "Esposito, C." and pressed that one, long and hard.

Somewhere upstairs, a door opened and a man began to shout. Prescott crossed his fingers and pushed the button for "Esposito, C." again. This time he tried shorter bursts, on the assumption that if Esposito, C. was a woman who lived alone and had been asleep, he had already woken her up. He now had only to convince her she had heard what she thought she heard. The man upstairs began to swear again. Then the buzzer on the inner door sounded, and the lock disengaged.

Prescott let himself into the stair hall and looked up the wall. "Señora?" he called. "Señorita?"

A spate of furious female Spanish rained down on his head. Prescott started up the stairs.

"Señora," he said as he climbed. "I am looking for Maria Gonzalez. I have come from Dr. Goldman, who is her employer. Maria is supposed to be at work, but she is not there, and nobody can find her. I wish to make sure she is not lying in her apartment hurt."

Prescott said all these things slowly and clearly and as loud as he could. He had no idea if Esposito, C. could understand him and supposed she could not. He was slightly heartened by the fact that all the sound above him had stopped. At least someone was trying to listen.

"Señora?" he said again, as he reached the landing where the woman stood in front of her open door, a short round woman beginning to get old, careworn and suspicious. "Señora," he said again. *"Por favor."*

That was the extent of Prescott Holloway's Spanish.

The extent of Esposito, C.'s English was "Hello." She said it as soon as she saw Prescott in his uniform, and then she backed into her doorway and let out a yell. The yell brought a fat middle-aged man to the stair rail of the landing above them. He stood blocking out the stairwell light and looking Prescott over.

"What do you want?" he asked finally, in English not nearly as accented as it ought to be, considering how stereotypically immigrant he looked.

Prescott told him what he had told Señora Esposito on his way up.

"So how do we know it's true?" the fat middle-aged man demanded at the end of it. "How do we know you're not some kind of cat burglar?"

"In this neighborhood?" Prescott blinked.

"People have stereos in this neighborhood," the fat middle-aged man said. "They have VCRs. They have televisions."

"Sure," another voice said—young, this time, teenage and hostile, "we're all welfare queens in this building. We're all getting rich off the city of New York."

"Don't *all* of us spend all our money on crack," another teenage voice said.

Prescott shifted uneasily. This was what he didn't

need. Teenagers. Too many of the teenagers up here had nothing to lose.

"Look," he said. "I'm a chauffeur. I'm a driver. You can see for yourself. My car's parked right across the street."

"How do we know which car is yours?" the fat middle-aged man demanded.

"Just take a look," Prescott told him.

Downstairs, there was a *snick* of opened door and the soft slap of rubber-soled shoes on linoleum. A moment later, the door-*snick* sound happened again and somebody laughed.

"Oh, Jesus Christ," the someone said. "You should see it. Stretch caddy half as long as a football field. Only reason it hasn't been ripped off is that everybody's afraid it might be booby-trapped."

"Maybe it is booby-trapped," the fat middle-aged man said.

"Look," Prescott Holloway told the company at large. "All I'm supposed to do is check Señorita Gonzalez's apartment and make sure she hasn't fallen ill on the kitchen floor. That's it. Then I can go back to my boss and let her figure out what to do next."

"You got keys to the apartment?" the fat middle-aged man asked.

"Of course I don't have keys to the apartment," Prescott said. "I've got a credit card. If the door isn't bolted from the inside, I can get in. If it is, we know we've got trouble. All right?"

"She's not lying in that apartment sick on the floor or anything," said a young woman's voice Prescott hadn't heard before now. "She's not in the apartment at all. She didn't come home last night."

The fat middle-aged man seemed to make up his mind. He moved away from the stair rail and began coming down to Prescott.

"All right," he said. "We'll let you in. But we're going to be standing here watching you."

"Fine," Prescott said.

"We all know Maria," the fat middle-aged man said.

"I know her, too. I work in the same place."

"We're not going to let you take anything away."

"I don't want to take anything away."

The fat middle-aged man looked skeptical, but he motioned to Prescott to come forward, and the two of them started down the stairs to the floor below, where Maria's apartment was. Prescott was glad now that he had not tried to go straight to it when he was buzzed in. There were buildings where nobody wanted to know anything about anyone else, and then there were the other kind.

The fat middle-aged man stopped in front of a door marked "2B Gonzalez, M." and stepped back to let Prescott do his stuff. Prescott got his Citibank automatic teller card out of his wallet and slid it into the crack in the door. There were plenty of security doors now where the locks could not be opened with plastic no matter what, but this wasn't one of them. Prescott didn't think anything in this building had been replaced since 1959, except light bulbs.

The lock trembled, shuddered, jerked and sprung. Prescott pushed the door in and looked at the darkness.

"Shit," he said.

"Don't swear in front of the women," the fat middle-aged man said.

Then the fat middle-aged man reached an arm over Prescott's shoulder and a hand through the door, and Maria's small apartment was full of light.

It was full of everything else imaginable, too. It was full of feathers and scraps of cloth. It was full of pastry crumbs and chipped stoneware plates. It was full of shredded bits of ancient carpet and peeling strips of plastic lampshades.

The place had been trashed.

8

Carmencita Boaz heard about the destruction of Maria Gonzalez's apartment at ten minutes to six, and it bothered her, but she didn't have time to think about it. Later she knew it would bother her a lot, like so much about living in the city did. She had told Itzaak that her dream was to move somewhere small and countrified, like New Hampshire, and he had laughed, but she had meant it. There might not be much in the way of Hispanic culture in New Hampshire, but Carmencita wasn't sure she minded that. She'd had quite enough of Latin America when she'd been living in Latin America. Her New York neighborhood reminded her so much of Guatamala City, it made her want to cry. Carmencita didn't like cities at all, and she wasn't very fond of hot weather. She could just see herself in the New Hampshire countryside with the snow falling on her hair. She could see herself making maple syrup and apple cider and brining up a pack of children who could all say the Pledge of Allegiance without Spanish accents.

The six men who were supposed to be on the show today were sitting in Carmencita's office, looking dejected. A couple of them had come in breathing fire, but it hadn't lasted. Carmencita had known it wouldn't. The lawyers had gotten to them. The lawyers always did. There was something about hearing your most private obsessions spelled out in the language of tort law that took the starch right out of a man.

"It's worse than getting a divorce," one of the men complained, after it was over. "With a divorce, at least you know what it's all about. With this, it's like they just did it because they felt like it."

The sentiment might be expressed a little inarticulately, but Carmencita knew what the man meant. Carmencita was not a feminist. It was her private opinion that the women in this case were what her friend at her neighborhood branch of the New York Public Library would call "grade-A number one ball busters."

Ball busters was not an expression Carmencita Boaz used, except in the privacy of her mind. Nastiness was not a modus operandi she had been brought up to adopt. When she saw the women in the hallway, she was invaryingly polite. When she talked about them to Itzaak, she was blunt without being obscene. In Carmencita Boaz's background there were legions of nuns, nuns who had been her teachers, nuns who had been her aunts, nuns who had watched over her in playgrounds and at Mass, every last one of them repeating over and over again, "Carmencita, you must be a lady."

Carmencita checked her watch, looked over her dejected brood, and tried her best encouraging smile.

"We're going to go out to the set in just five minutes," she said. "We will seat you around a low coffee table, on which will be placed pitchers of ice water and glasses in case your throats get dry. We're going to try out a few seating arrangements—"

"Just don't sit me next to Darlene," one of the men said. "I'll break her neck."

"They always sit the husbands and the wives together," another said. "Don't you ever watch this show? The husbands and wives just sit there holding hands and calling each other the worst names—"

"I'm being accused of refusing to do something I never even heard of," a third man said. "I'm being accused of doing something I can't even pronounce."

"You don't think anybody watches this show," the second man said, "but you're wrong. All the wives watch it. And they talk to each other."

"Oh, God," the first man said.

Carmencita would have liked a drink of ice water herself. She would have liked a long talk with Itzaak, but Itzaak wouldn't be available. He'd be up in the rafters playing with the lights. She opened her office door and motioned the men to go through it.

"Let's get an early start," she told them. "It can't do any harm and you're getting much too nervous. You'll all be fine."

"Of course I won't be fine," the third man said. "I'll be the laughingstock of Port Chester, New York."

Since this was undoubtably true, Carmencita decided not to try to answer it. Instead, she made another falsely hearty gesture at the door, and was gratified when the men got slowly to their feet and headed in her direction. They looked like prisoners on the way to the electric chair, but then in a way that was exactly what they were. Carmencita got them into the hall in a ragtag cluster and headed down the hall for the set.

Sarah Meyer was standing at the set door, frowning. Sarah Meyer was always frowning. Carmencita paid no attention to her.

"DeAnna wants to see you," Sarah said when Carmencita arrived at the door. "I think it's supposed to be important."

Out on the set, single seats had been arranged in a half circle facing the benches for the studio audience. If everything was running on schedule, that audience would be down in the lobby, clutching their tickets and wondering out loud why *The Lotte Goldman Show* had to tape so *early*. Carmencita often wondered the same thing herself.

"I would like you to go down and take the seats on the left-hand side of the platform," Carmencita told her charges. "Start with the one farthest left as you face the stage from the audience. The gray chair in the middle is where Dr. Goldman is going to sit. Will you do that for me now, please?"

"Oh, shit," one of the men said.

The others drifted into the studio, and the complaining man followed. Carmencita knew why they taped so early. It was because they aired the same day. She just thought it was silly.

"What did DeAnna want?" she asked Sarah Meyer. "Did she say?"

"She didn't say to me," Sarah said. "All she said to me was go get a ream of typing paper from the storeroom and if you see Carmencita tell her I want her. She didn't even tell me what she wanted the typing paper for."

"Maybe she wanted to type."

"DeAnna doesn't type. DeAnna doesn't even answer her own phone."

"Maybe she wanted to make paper airplanes and shoot them out the window of her office at the traffic," Carmencita said. "I've got something to do right now. I'll find DeAnna when I'm done."

Sarah Meyer sniffed. "She's in there on the phone with the cops who are at Maria's apartment. She had to send Prescott all the way back up there and the cops are furious. He wasn't supposed to have left the scene at all. Do you think it will make the papers, because Maria is with *The Lotte Goldman Show*?"

"I think I don't have time for this conversation," Carmencita said. "Here comes Maximillian with the women, and you know what that means. Fights are likely to start breaking out any minute."

"I heard DeAnna talking to Lotte about it and they were really very mysterious. DeAnna was saying how Prescott was saying that nobody could have done it who didn't have a key, because the lock was locked when he got there and it was one of those old-fashioned locks that won't lock with the door open and then you can pull the door shut and there you are. It was the kind of lock you had to use the key to lock once you got the door closed."

"Maria lived in an old building."

"I told Prescott you had a key to Maria's apartment,"

Sarah said. "I remember her saying so. You have hers and she has yours. In case either of you gets locked out."

Carmencita turned on her heel and gave Sarah Meyer the first long, direct look she'd ever given her. She took in Sarah's lumpy weight and Sarah's formless features and Sarah's rash of blackheads along her chin.

"What," she asked, "is all this supposed to be about?"

If it was supposed to be about anything, Sarah wasn't saying. She gave Carmencita a little cat smile and backed away. When she reached the intersection in the corridors she turned and hurried away.

"*Come* on," Shelly Feldstein's voice said from somewhere inside. "Let's get going, Carmencita, we've got this run-through to do before we can let the screaming hordes up and we're running late."

"Right," Carmencita said.

"I'm going to change Lotte's chair to the black—no, not the black, she'll look like a hanging judge—to the navy blue one. I'm going to run. Are all your people ready to go?"

All Carmencita's people were ready to die of embarrassment. There was nothing she could do about it. She marched down to the platform and looked her men over. They hulked in their chairs, looking too big and too menacing by half. Shelley Feldstein either hadn't noticed or approved of the effect.

"Okay," Carmencita said. "Why don't we try sitting up straight?"

If Carmencita Boaz had been in the sort of position the men sitting before her were in, she would have told any silly woman who asked her to sit up straight to go straight to hell—except that she would have done it politely, of course. But North Americans were different. They didn't think like people in the rest of the world. Maybe they didn't think.

"Okay," Carmencita said again, and the men stirred in their chairs and did their best to sit up straight.

Up in the rafters, Itzaak whistled the first few bars of "As Time Goes By," to let her know he was watching over her, and Carmencita relaxed.

Whatever Sarah Meyer was up to, it was creepy. Whatever had happened to Maria Gonzalez's apartment, it was creepy, too. Carmencita could ride above it all, serene and confident in the benevolence of the future, because Itzaak protected her. That was the secret of their relationship. Itzaak protected her in a spiritual way, and as long as he was near her, she felt all right.

What she was going to do about that—what either of them were going to do about that—considering the problems they were going to have with religion and all the rest of it, she didn't know. She just knew that she would much rather think about Itzaak Blechmann than about what might have happened to Maria, and that was that.

Her charges were beginning to look like lumps of Silly Putty softening in the sun. Carmencita clapped her hands again, and they came to attention.

9

Down at the other end of the office suite, DeAnna Kroll was sitting in Lotte Goldman's office, sitting on the desk and smoking the first cigarette she'd had in two and a half years, looking frazzled. Lotte was sitting in her own desk chair and putting on the persona she would have to maintain in front of the cameras. It never ceased to amaze DeAnna just how good Lotte was at this. Lotte could commit a bloody murder at noon and be ready to go on the air as if nothing had happened by 12:02.

"You've got less than a minute before you're supposed to be on the set," DeAnna told Lotte. "You'd better get moving."

"I'll get moving when I finish my cigarette. Are those policemen coming here?"

"Later this morning."

"Whatever happened didn't happen here."

"We don't know that anything happened at all," DeAnna said. "Maria might have messed up the apartment on her own. She may have taken off for Acapulco. She might have been dealing drugs or robbing us blind or doing something else we don't know about."

"Maria was a very clean woman," Lotte said. "And if the police are coming here, we have to wait for them. I'm already exhausted."

"You can stretch out on the couch in my office. I'll send Sarah Meyer over to one of those boutiques on Third Avenue to buy you a pretty little afghan."

"Sarah Meyer will come back with a hair shirt."

"Come on," DeAnna said. "We're all set up. We've got an audience waiting. We're going to get a long day. Might as well at least start to get it over with."

"That's what I like about you," Lotte said, getting up. "You're such a comfort." She hesitated next to the desk, stubbing her cigarette out in the crystal ashtray DeAnna had given her for Christmas last year. "Dee," she said, "do you think something serious has happened to Maria?"

"It looks that way, doesn't it?"

"Yes it does. I hate to say it, but I'm glad it didn't happen here. Whatever it was. I'd feel responsible for it."

"I just feel guilty I was so damned pissed at her earlier tonight," DeAnna said. "Is all this a bunch of sentimental crap, or what?"

"It's a bunch of sentimental crap," Lotte said firmly. "Oh, dear. I've forgotten my flower. You know. The thing I wear to hide my microphone. I forgot to take it off after the taping yesterday and then I must have forgotten to put it back on when I left the apartment today—"

"Never mind. We've got tons of that stuff in the

storeroom. I'll get you something before we tape. Go on out to the set."

"I will. Are you sure you can handle all this business with the police by yourself?"

"Until they get tired of talking to me."

"Well, it if gets to be too much for you, send them to me."

"Right," DeAnna said, pushing Lotte toward the door.

Lotte Goldman was a dear woman, but she'd have about as much success at dealing with the NYPD as a worshiper of Kali would have had dealing with Savanarola. DeAnna pushed her out into the corridor and pointed her in the direction of the studio.

"Go," she said. "I'll go get you a flower."

"Yes, Dee, I am going."

DeAnna turned away and marched off in the other direction.

It was after six o'clock in the morning now and the office had started to bustle. The clerk typists wouldn't be in until nine, but all the private secretaries had started to arrive, used to keeping their bosses' hours. DeAnna passed women setting up coffee urns and putting out memo pads and yawning into makeup mirrors. She went by one young woman who was saying to another, "I can't handle all this women's lib shit. I'd rather be married."

There, DeAnna thought, was a woman who needed psychiatric help.

DeAnna got to the corridor the storeroom was on, walked down to the end of it and opened the door. She put her hand inside to turn on the light switch and got nothing at all. Somehow it figured that the light would go out in the one place she had to get something from with less than a minute before taping. She couldn't change the light bulb herself, not unless she knew where to find a stepladder, which she didn't. Somewhere in the building there was a janitor who would fix it for her, but that would take half an hour, and she didn't have half an hour. She went back up the corridor and stopped at the first secretary she found.

"Do you have a flashlight? The light's burned out in the storeroom and I have to get something quick."

The secretary was a young black woman named Marsha, who carried one of those tote bags that looked as if it was big enough to move furniture. She contemplated the idea of a flashlight for a moment. Then she nodded, plunged into her bag, and came up with two.

"This one is really tiny." She held up something that looked like a pen but flashed on and off by some mechanism DeAnna couldn't determine. "This one ought to be all right."

The second flashlight was the standard-issue detective-story variety. Deanna took it and said, "Call maintainence. We'll still need somebody to fix that light."

"On the phone right away," Marsha said.

DeAnna went back to the storeroom, wondering what else Marsha kept in that bag. Tuna fish sandwiches. Hand grenades. The Hope diamond.

The storeroom door had swung closed. DeAnna pushed it open again. Then she switched the flashlight on and went inside. It was incredible how dark a room was when it didn't have any windows. Even the light from the corridor didn't do much to help.

The silk flowers were in a box on a shelf on the left-hand side near the back. DeAnna had seen them herself less than a week ago, when she had come in here searching for Liquid Paper after everybody else had gone home. She trained the flashlight on the shelves and found boxes marked "ball point pens" and "felt tipped pens" and "paper clips."

"Shit," she said under her breath. Then she moved even deeper into the room, wondering how far back it went, there was no way to tell in all this gloom. She swung the light around to see if she could find the back wall and get her bearings, and then she stopped.

It was only a glimpse, really, a split second where everything had been suddenly, terribly, irretrievably wrong, but a glimpse was enough. Once she'd seen she couldn't go back to the point where she hadn't seen. She could do anything but swing the flashlight back, and stop, and contemplate.

She contemplated long and hard.

She thought about the show, and how it could be disrupted.

She thought about Lotte, and Lotte's blood pressure, and Lotte's peace of mind.

She thought about her old neighborhood and all the things that used to go on there, the things she used to accept as a matter of course.

She wondered if she was getting soft.

She was looking straight into the smashed face of Maria Gonzalez, and she wanted to curl right up and die.

PART ONE

*Sex and
the Single Demarkian*

ONE

===

1

In the years since Gregor Demarkian had come back to Cavanaugh Street—come back from Washington, D.C., and a job with the FBI; come back from professional life and nine-to-five identity; come back to sanity—he had gotten used to the fact that even minor holidays would be celebrated around him with an hysteria worthy of the fall of the Bastille. Major holidays, like Christmas and Easter, would be occasions for all-out war. For the second Christmas Gregor had spent on Cavanaugh Street, Donna Moradanyan, his upstairs neighbor, had wrapped every light pole and mailbox in a four-block area with red and green metallic paper. This was Cavanaugh Street and Gregor accepted it. But Cavanaugh Street was an Armenian-American neighborhood and therefore dedicated to the Armenian Christian church, and Gregor had accepted that, too. Long ago, Armenia had been the first country on earth to make Christianity a state religion. Lately, Armenia seemed poised to become the most fervent example of re-

ligious revival in the newly liberated countries of Eastern
Europe. On Cavanaugh Street, the response was subtler
but undeniable. Even old agnostics like Gregor showed up
at church on Sunday, and a surprising number of young
people—raised to be secular children in a secular age—
weren't agnostics at all. Father Tibor Kasparian kept them
all moving in the direction he wanted them to go. He
called that direction "pure Christianity." "The first duty of
a Christian in the working out of his salvation is to sanctify the world," Tibor said, in the thick accent he had
brought with him from so many countries Gregor couldn't
remember them all. Then he proceeded to sanctify the
world by finding a religious meaning in Presidents' Day.
Gregor had gotten used to finding out that Tibor had discovered deep Christian significance in the Congressional
Proclamation that had established Arbor Day. Gregor had
even gotten used to the fact that as soon as Tibor had discovered such significance, he wanted to do something
about it. What Gregor hadn't gotten used to—what he
hadn't even considered the possibility of—was a
Cavanaugh Street celebration of Hanukkah.

"Hanukkah is a Jewish holiday," he had pointed out
to Tibor that morning, picking his way through the books
piled in columnar stacks on Tibor's living room floor to
get to the one halfway clear seat he could see. The seat
was only halfway clear because it had both of Tibor's
present reading projects on it: Judith Krantz's *Scruples
Two* and *An Investigation into the Mathematical Nature of
Time* by George Gamow. Gregor picked them both up and
balanced them gently on the shortest stack of books on the
end table. Those books were all in the Cyrillic alphabet.
Armenia no longer used the Cyrillic alphabet. Gregor had
seen a report on that on the evening news a few months
ago. Armenia now had an American-born foreign minister,
too. It was enough to give a man a headache. Gregor
checked out the rest of the books on the end table—some
Greek, some ancient Greek, some Latin, some French and

Passions of the Sea by Lisetta Farnham—and then turned his attention to Tibor himself, who was trying to bring overfull cups of bad black coffee in from the kitchen. "Hanukkah," he said again.

"Yes, yes," Tibor told him. "I know, Krekor, I know. But it makes sense. And I am not a bigot."

"I never said you were."

"Well, Krekor, it would not have been outrageous if you had thought it. There is the Armenian record on anti-Semitism."

Gregor was curious. "How is the Armenian record on anti-Semitism?" he asked.

"Appalling."

Tibor had reached him with the coffee. Gregor reached out for a cup and managed to spill only a drop and only on the floor. This was good, because he was due in less than an hour at a lunch in downtown Philadelphia with a friend of his from the old days at the Bureau. He took a sip of the coffee and nearly choked. He put his cup down on the end table and waited for Tibor to seat himself. Tibor kept tripping over the hem of his cassock.

"So," Tibor said, when he'd finally sat down. "I have told you, Krekor, Rabbi Goldman, David, he was my sponsor when I came to America?"

"You've told me, yes," Gregor said. "As an inducement to going on his sister's television show."

"The television show. Yes. Well, Krekor, David asked me to ask you and so I asked. That is not what I wanted to talk to you about today. You know the television show will be here in just three days?"

"You've told me."

"Yes, well, Krekor, it would be good if you could help us to clear this up before then. The graffiti, if you understand what I am saying."

"No," Gregor said.

"Don't you ever watch the news, Krekor? It is a terrible trial talking to you sometimes. I bring up what everybody knows because it has been on television for a week, and it is as if you have been on Mars. The graffiti was on a synagogue in the—I don't remember the street—here in Philadelphia where there is a neighborhood of Hasidim. The Hasidim are—"

"I know what the Hasidim are. Who."

"How am I supposed to know what you know?" Tibor shrugged. "Never mind, Krekor. You can imagine what kind of graffiti it was, and now everybody is upset. And it is not that they should be blamed for it, Krekor, because the graffiti was very foul. But the worst of it is that the police have arrested nobody for this."

"Do they know who did this?"

"Yes and no."

"What does that mean?"

Tibor fumbled around in his pockets and came up with a crumpled sheet of paper. He got up, leaned over yet more stacks of books, and passed it to Gregor. "That is the name of the organization which claims responsibility. I had David write it down for me because I have a hard time remembering it. This is perhaps psychological."

"Perhaps," Gregor said drily.

"The important thing here is that the police know what the organization is but they don't know who is in it. You see the problem? Have you ever heard of them, Krekor?"

What was written on the piece of paper was

WHITE KNIGHTS, DEFENDERS OF RACE AND FAITH

Gregor put the paper on the end table and sighed.

"I haven't heard of them," he said. "I don't have to have heard of them. Groups like this crop up constantly. We had an entire section at the Bureau devoted to nothing but keeping track of them."

"There is perhaps such a section at the Bureau now?"

"No perhaps about it. Of course there is."

"Well then," Tibor said. "Krekor. You go today to have lunch with an agent of the Federal Bureau of Investigation who is a friend of yours. He may have friends of his own in this special section. He may be able to . . . help us out."

Gregor picked up the crumpled paper again, stared at the name printed on it in such precise letters, and put it down again. "How long ago did all of this happen?" he asked Tibor.

"A little over two weeks."

"Two weeks. Do you know if the police got any physical evidence at the scene? Anything to link the act to any specific person?"

"I told you—"

"I know they don't know the names," Gregor insisted, "but they might have blind evidence that could eventually be definitive. Hair. Fingerprints. Even singed or torn skin."

"Ah," Tibor said, impressed. "I don't know."

Gregor tapped his fingers against his knee. "Well," he said, "I suppose we can ask. It's always possible they're sounding more pessimistic than they have to. In cases like this, though, the police tend to want to deliver hope if they possibly can. You do realize, if the police don't have anything of the kind I'm talking about, even if we do find out who was responsible, the police aren't going to be able to arrest them?"

"Not enough evidence?" Tibor asked dejectedly.

"Not enough evidence and too far from the commission of the crime. If this had come up within, oh, twenty-four hours or so—if you'd talked to me and I'd talked to the Bureau and the Bureau had come up with a couple of names that fit, all in the first twenty-four hours, then there might have been a chance to dig up a witness or find some new evidence, but now—"

"You make it sound so hopeless," Tibor said.

"It is hopeless," Gregor told him.

"Does that mean you will not ask your friend at the FBI for us?"

"Of course I'll ask my friend at the FBI. But you and your friend Rabbi Goldman have got to understand that what I'll be delivering, if I deliver anything, is a chance to catch these idiots the *next* time they do anything."

"The next time," Tibor said, shocked.

"This still doesn't explain to me why Cavanaugh Street is celebrating Hanukkah," Gregor said. "Donna came downstairs this morning and planted a neon menorah in my living room window."

"The menorah," Tibor said, leaping to his feet. "I forgot. Donna brought me one this morning and I have not yet put it up."

"Tibor—"

"I will only be a minute, Krekor. It is important. It is a gesture of solidarity."

"Right," Gregor said, but he supposed he understood. Tibor was always whipping the residents of Cavanaugh Street into a frenzy of solidarity for somebody or the other: starving children in Ethiopia; oppressed students in China; the homeless who filled the shelter run by a consortium of volunteers from Holy Trinity Armenian Christian Church, Holy Rosary Roman Catholic Church, St. Thomas Episcopal Church, and the Becker Street African Methodist Church. Tibor was a devotee of good causes. Gregor could hardly fault him for that. As for this latest enthusiasm—why *shouldn't* Tibor show his solidarity with the Jewish community of Philadelphia and the Philadelphia Main Line? Why shouldn't he? The only thing that worried Gregor Demarkian was what form this solidarity would take. The neon menorahs were interesting enough, but Gregor knew Cavanaugh Street. It would never in a million years end there.

Tibor came back from the front hall and tripped over a few books again, the hem of his cassock flapping, the sparse hair on his head bouncing as he flailed.

"There it is. All done. Now I have only to work on my voice. You will be home next Saturday, Krekor?"

"Far as I know."

"Good. You will come to our block party. I want everybody in this neighborhood at our block party. Lida Arkmanian is even now learning to cook kosher food."

"What?" Gregor said.

Tibor wasn't listening. He had finished his coffee and wanted to get more. He had come to that point in the conversation where he did not want to discuss anything more with Gregor Demarkian. That was why Gregor was suspicious. Gregor got suspicious when anybody on Cavanaugh Street told him that something they were about to make him do would be—well, not a complicated mess.

Block party.

Kosher food.

Right.

On any other day of the year, Gregor would have stopped and insisted on being told exactly what was going on. On this day, he was in danger of being late for a very important lunch. He got out of his chair and made his way back across the obstacle course of books, wondering when Tibor got the time to read like this when he spent so much time making Gregor Demarkian's life resemble one of the wilder plays of Ionesco. Gregor stopped at the door to the entry and called out,

"Tibor? I'm leaving."

"Have a good lunch," Tibor called back.

"Tibor?"

No answer.

Gregor went into the entry, got his coat from the closet and headed out the door.

When Tibor refused to talk to him at all, God only knew what kind of insanity was going on.

2

Later, Gregor Demarkian would tell Bennis Hannaford—his immediate downstairs neighbor; the woman half the magazines in America insisted on calling his "constant companion" and that half the people in America thought was his lover (Gregor had once told Tibor he'd as soon take the Tasmanian devil for a lover, it would be calmer)—that the hardest thing about his talk with Tibor that morning was not telling Tibor why he was having lunch with his "friend from the FBI." Tibor Kasparian was probably the man Gregor had been closest to in his life. Gregor's father and older brother had both died when Gregor was very young, and he had no distinct memories of either. Then there had been college and graduate school, the army and the Bureau. Men made close friends in places like that, but Gregor hadn't. Gregor had made a close friend in his wife. She had been enough for him as long as she was alive. It was after she died that Gregor had come back to Cavanaugh Street and found himself at loose ends. It was in coming back to Cavanaugh Street that he had met Tibor. It all got very complicated. Gregor Demarkian had grown up on Cavanaugh Street in the days when it had been an Armenian-American ghetto, the kind of place all its residents wanted to escape for the greener grass of the Philadelphia Main Line. He had come back to a Cavanaugh Street transformed, but not quite. The buildings had been spruced up and gutted and remodeled and rearranged. The tenements had been changed into townhouses and floor-through condominiums with twelve-foot-high ceilings and marble fireplaces and Anderson windows in brownstone frames. The people on Cavanaugh Street, however, had not changed at all. Lida Arkmanian bought her clothes at Saks these days and covered them over with a chinchilla coat, but she still went at cooking as if she could bring about world peace with it and worried about everybody's grandchildren. Hannah Krekorian took her vacations in the Bahamas these days, but she still talked a blue streak and lusted over love and romance the way a cat lusted after fresh fish. People were so much the same, Gregor sometimes found himself stopped dead in confusion, as if he had wandered into a costume party that refused to come to an end. Surely any minute now Lida would trade in that chinchilla coat for a cloth one from Sears, and Sheila Kashinian would confess that all those diamond rings were just paste. Surely any minute now Gregor's own mother would come trundling up from Ohanian's with a soft reed basket under her arm, carrying a plucked chicken and two cups of bulgur to make for tonight's dinner. Of course, Gregor's mother was dead now and Ohanian's had become Ohanian's Middle Eastern Food Store. Gregor put flowers on his mother's grave every Christmas Day and Ohanian's sold prepackaged filo leaves to tourists from Radnor for twelve ninety-nine a pound. It should have been enough to cause a case of terminal disorientation in anyone, but it wasn't, and that was the problem. Gregor Demarkian's loyalties were here. For the rest of his life, they would be.

What Gregor had had a hard time not telling Tibor that morning was what he was having lunch with his "friend from the FBI" for. Gregor kept putting the phrase—"friend from the FBI"—in quotes, because it belonged in quotes. Don Elkham was not strictly a friend of his, although Gregor described him that way, for want of another term to use for him. Gregor and Don had known each other since their first day of training at Quantico, and followed each other through the ranks at the Bureau ever since. The difference was, while Gregor had ended up chief and originator of the Department of Behavioral Sciences, Don had gotten stalled along the way. Of course, Gregor was retired now, with no standing at all. There was no reason for a man like Don Elkham to be jealous of a Gregor Demarkian who had demoted himself into nothing but an amateur. Even so, the jealousy was there. Gregor had felt it coming over the phone when Don had called.

What Don had called about was what he insisted on referring to as "a little criminal anomaly in New York." What he meant was that one of the staff members on Rabbi David Goldman's sister's television show had been murdered in Manhattan last month and there was enough strangeness around the case to get all the law enforcement people a little nervous. Gregor had wondered out loud what that had to do with the FBI, but the explanation had turned out to be less than sinister. Don Elkham was a station agent in Philadelphia. His best buddy from the army was the police lieutenant handling the case in New York. Everybody knew about the connection between Lotte Goldman's brother David and Father Tibor Kasparian, and between Father Tibor Kasparian and Gregor Demarkian.

"It's all over the place that you've been asked to be on *The Lotte Goldman Show*," Don had said on the phone, "and it's like Chickie said. Put two and two together, and it sure as hell is hot, the Armenian-American Hercule Poirot is going to be all over this case as soon as *The Lotte Goldman Show* hits Philadelphia."

"If you call me the Armenian-American Hercule Poirot one more time," Gregor said, "I'll hang up this phone."

"Chickie said I should call you up and ask you to lunch and talk it over with you," Don said. "Just to see what you're up to."

"I'm not up to anything. This is the first I've heard of any murder."

"It won't be the last. Chickie will see to that. I'll meet you at Café Blasé at noon on the first."

Chickie was the name of the police lieutenant in New York.

Café Blasé was one of those vaguely French restaurants that decorated all its food with flower petals, so that a perfectly respectable piece of fried chicken breast arrived at the table looking as if it had been drowned with Ophelia. Gregor had been there once or twice and he didn't like it. With another agent, he would have suggested another restaurant. With Don Elkham, he decided to let it slide.

He nearly slid himself, getting out of the cab in front of Café Blasé. December was never a good weather month in Philadelphia, but this December had been especially cold and wet. There were patches of slick brown mud at every curb. Gregor steadied himself against a mailbox and headed into the restaurant, going through the door just behind two young women in their twenties in thigh-high skirts and geometric hair. Sometimes these days, he felt as if he were in a time warp.

Don Elkham was sitting at a table in the bay window closest to the hostess's stand. Gregor gestured to the hostess and she let him through with a nod. The two young women looked bored.

Gregor went over to the table where Don was sitting and sat down himself. Don did not rise. Don had never had his manners too firmly glued on.

"Sorry I'm late," Gregor said. "I got here as soon as I could."

"Held up by the lovely Miss Hannaford," Don said. "Gregor Demarkian finds his debutante."

"Miss Hannaford likes to be called Ms."

"Well, that's a surprise. I can't imagine you falling for a women's libber."

Exactly what Don Elkham was supposed to know about who Gregor Demarkian was or was not likely to "fall for" was a mystery to Gregor Demarkian, since the only woman Don had ever seen him with was his Elizabeth, and she had hardly been a case in point against Gregor's falling for "women's libbers." The waitress came up and Gregor ordered himself a glass of Burgundy. He didn't much like wine, but he had to do something.

Don ordered himself a martini, which had to mean this was his day off. If it wasn't, he was asking for trouble.

"So," Don said. "What do you think? About the murder on *The Lotte Goldman Show*?"

"I don't think anything about it," Gregor said. "I told you on the phone. All I've heard about it, I've heard from you."

"Your friend Father Kasparian hasn't told you anything about it?"

"Father Tibor. And no, he hasn't."

"How about Father—uh—Tibor's friend. Rabbi Goldman?"

"I've met Rabbi Goldman exactly once. It was at a food fair in central Philadelphia. I complimented him on his wife's latkes. In spite of what you might think, I have not been spending every waking moment of every day of the last month consorting with people who are related to people who are involved in your friend's murder case. I am a little surprised that I hadn't heard about it at all. With television people involved, there's usually a bit more publicity."

Don Elkham was chewing on a breadstick. "The publicity was squashed," he said through a mouthful of crumbs. "The official line is that it was an ordinary mugging."

"I thought you said the circumstances were strange."

"They were. The woman—her name was Maria Gonzalez—the woman's apartment was ransacked, gone over real good, and by somebody in a hurry. Place was trashed. Body wasn't there, though."

"Where was it?"

"In a storeroom at the studio where they tape *The Lotte Goldman Show* in New York."

"Dead, I take it."

"Bashed on the side of the head hard enough to cave the skull in. But there's more. She wasn't there all the time."

"She wasn't in the storeroom," Gregor said.

"That's right. There were people in and out of the storeroom from about four o'clock in the morning on, and she definitely wasn't there all that time. She was found around six, maybe six thirty. I'd have to look at the paperwork. I don't remember."

"It doesn't matter," Gregor said. And that was true. Since nobody had asked him to investigate this case, and since he had no intention of investigating this case, he didn't need to be picture perfect about details. His curiosity could be satisfied by broad strokes. "It was a while, and she wasn't there to begin with. I'm not an expert on skull bashing, you know. My expertise was always poisons."

"She didn't have anything to do with any poisons."

"What about dope?"

"Not a trace. Not in her apartment, not in her office, not in her body, not in the storeroom."

"What about other things? Cash? Jewelry? Credit cards?"

"She was an immigrant from somewhere in Central America. She lived in a heavily Hispanic neighborhood that was also heavily poor. She made less than five hundred dollars a week. She didn't have any cash. She had about a thousand dollars in a savings account and a little over two hundred in checking. She had a pair of gold earrings. She was wearing them when she was found. She had a rosary made out of turquoise. It was found in her apartment. She had a Visa card with a clean balance. It was missing. Along with her wallet."

"Did you check the records?" Gregor asked. "Deposits and withdrawals?"

"We checked. No big deal."

"It does sound like a mugging, doesn't it? Except for the business with the body. I take it, from the way you've been talking, that she wasn't actually killed in the storeroom."

"She was not."

"In her apartment?"

"Nope."

"Any idea where?"

"I could say nope again," Don Elkham said, "but it would be redundant. You see what Chickie's problem is here. He can't just write it off as a run-of-the-mill mugging. It just won't fit. He went through that whole building—the building where the body was found—just on the off-chance she was killed somewhere on the premises, but no luck. He went through the building where her apartment was, too. He didn't find anything, but what if he had? It still wouldn't spell mugging. Not with the corpse traveling around like Marco Polo."

The waitress came up with their drinks. Don took his martini and gulped it. Gregor took a sip of his Burgundy, decided it was as bad as the food was going to be, and put his glass down. Then he watched Don take a second gulp and wondered just what was going on here.

"I thought," he said, after Don had put down his glass, "that you were going to ask me to stay out of this, assuming anybody involved ever asked me in. But you don't seem to be."

"It isn't necessary," Don said.

"What do you mean, it isn't necessary? Because the problem is in New York and I'm here?"

"No, not because of that. You travel. That's how you got in all the magazines. The Armenian-Ameri—never mind."

"Good."

"The thing is," Don said, "Chickie doesn't care. If you're involved or not, I mean."

"They why set up this lunch?"

"Because he doesn't want to be left in the dark, that's why. He doesn't want to wake up one morning and find out you've solved his case for him and your picture is all over the Daily News and he hasn't got the faintest idea what's going on. He doesn't want to look stupid in front of a bunch of television reporters."

"So what does that mean?" Gregor asked. "What am I supposed to do?"

Don Elkham shrugged. "Do anything you want. You will anyway. I'll give you Chickie's number if you decide you want to play it ethical for once. Of course, I wouldn't want to get in the way of the greatest amateur detective since Sherlock Holmes, which is what you are according to *Life* magazine last I heard, but still—"

But still.

Gregor thought it was going to be a miracle if he got out of this restaurant without breaking Don Elkham's neck.

TWO

1

There is a point in the progress of celebrity when a man goes from being famous on occasion—when he has a new book published; when the law firm or the government agency he works for takes on a particularly important case—to being famous all the time. Gregor Demarkian had passed that point somewhere in the middle of investigating a murder at a convention of nuns. At least, he had passed that point in Philadelphia. It was possible that in New York or Los Angeles, he would be able to go for weeks at a time without anyone calling him up to ask for his favorite recipe for chocolate fudge brownies or his favorite prediction for who would win the World Series. Gregor didn't know, because he hadn't been out of Philadelphia since last Christmas, when he and Bennis had taken Tibor on a short "vacation." Even then, he reputation had been pushing the line. It was now impossible for him to go anywhere where there had been the smallest amount of public violence without the local papers speculating that he had

been called in to "consult." He was beginning to think
there wasn't a town in America that didn't have at least
one unsolved, nonroutine murder on its police blotter, just
waiting for the ministrations of the man the *Philadelphia
Inquirer* had dubbed "the Armenian-American Hercule
Poirot." In Philadelphia the situation was worse, because
the situation was less focused. The *Philadelphia Inquirer*
had stopped expecting Gregor to leap into the middle of
any case that took its fancy. If Gregor didn't say he was
working on a solution to a murder, *The Inquirer* left it to
the Philadelphia police. What *The Inquirer* did do was
publish any picture of Gregor it could find—and there
were a lot of them, because once the word was out that
The Inquirer was paying, there were dozens of paparazzi
manqué willing to pop their flash bulbs and bring back the
trophy. Over the last few months, *The Inquirer* had published pictures of Gregor coming out of a restaurant, going
into three different branches of the public library, and running to catch a bus. When there was the reasonable resem-
blance of an excuse, the paper got more elaborate. When
Gregor had volunteered (as a result of Bennis's threat that
she'd play Axl Rose tapes in his ear if he refused) to serve
as a draw at the annual Armenian Street Festival to benefit
the Society for a Free Armenia, *The Inquirer* had published a solid page of pictures of Gregor getting pies
thrown at his face. *Philadelphia* magazine had gone one
better. It had published a full-page, full-color print of
Gregor after a pie had caught him square on the nose. That
was the same issue of *Philadelphia* that had contained the
information that Gregor's favorite food was Sara Lee's
chocolate fudge cake. This did not happen to be true—
Gregor didn't like packaged cake of any kind, and if he
had he wouldn't have admitted it; Lida Arkmanian would
have murdered him—but it resulted in exactly 4,678 Sara
Lee fudge cakes being delivered to Gregor's door, six by
messenger.

The nonsensical pictures of Gregor published in *The*

Inquirer appeared on what used to be called the "Society Page" and was now called "Lifestyles," and it was a picture from the "Lifestyles" page that was tacked to the bulletin board just behind the cash register at Ohanian's Middle Eastern Food Store when Gregor came in after his lunch with Don Elkham. Actually, it was well after. Lunch had been predictably terrible, and Gregor had felt the need to walk it off. He'd done some shopping and some reading at the library and some wandering around near the historic monuments before deciding it was time to get home. Now it was dark and wet and cold and he was carrying an unwieldy package full of new ties in tie boxes. Why they couldn't just fold ties into little lumps and put them in a bag was beyond him. The picture on Ohanian's bulletin board was of him standing around at intermission at a performance of the Philadelphia Philharmonic Orchestra. Bennis was at his side looking like a bird of paradise. He was in his brown suit looking like a lump. He rang the bell on Ohanian's counter, readjusted the tie boxes in his arms, and sighed.

"Mary?" he called out. "Michael?"

There was a rustle of curtains at the back and a young boy stuck his head through to the front.

"Oh, Mr. Demarkian. Just a minute, will you? I've got a little problem here."

The head disappeared behind the curtains again. Gregor put the tie boxes down on the counter. The head belonged to Joseph Ohanian, also known as Joey, who was just sixteen and supposed to be away at school at Deerfield. What he was doing home, Gregor didn't know.

The curtains rustled for a third time and Joey came out, looking hot and frazzled. "Boxes," he said with exasperation. "Dozens of boxes of canned stuffed grape leaves. Can you imagine that? My mother would eat canned stuffed grape leaves about the time she'd eat cyanide. She says we've got to stock 'em for the tourists."

"Where is your mother?"

"With my sister and everybody else in the neighborhood. Over at Bennis Hannaford's getting ready to watch that sex show."

"What?"

There was a crash from the back room, and Joey winced. "Just a minute," he said, and disappeared behind the curtain again.

Gregor left the ties where he had laid them down and went to the back of the store to get some cheese from the refrigerated compartment. While he was back there he picked up a can of smoked oysters and a jar of marinated artichoke hearts. With bread and pastry from the front, he could have what Bennis called one of his "perfectly awful dinners"—and nobody would bother him about it, because they would all be down at Bennis's watching "that sex show."

He wondered what sex show.

He put the oysters and the artichokes and the cheese down on the counter and watched Joey come back out through the curtains, more flushed than ever.

"A loaf of pideh," he said. "And about a pound of bourma."

"A *pound*? Are you having company, Mr. Demarkian?"

"If I were having company, I'd get two pounds."

"Bennis Hannaford told my sister Mary the other day that you really have to watch what you eat from now on because you're beginning to look less like Harrison Ford than like James Earl Jones, except of course you're white, but Mary said she thought James Earl Jones was the sexiest man in movies, so Bennis said—"

"I thought you were supposed to be away at prep school," Gregor interrupted. "Don't you go to Deerfield? Weren't you there last year? Don't tell me the school year hasn't started yet?"

The pideh were piled in a pyramid under the bulletin

board with Gregor's picture on it. The bourma were in a glass-fronted display case to the left of the cash register. Joey got the pideh first, put it in a paper bag, and put the bag down next to Gregor's other things. Then he went to get the bourma.

"I'm sorry if I put my foot in it," Gregor said. "I hope you haven't been expelled or something worse."

"No," Joey said. "I haven't been expelled. It's just that I've been thinking."

"About what?"

"Well, about places like Deerfield. They're not fair, are they? I mean, it's all well and good to say I got in because I worked hard and I'm smart—I mean, I did and I am—but that's not the point, is it?"

"What is the point?"

"Well," Joey said, "the point is, it wouldn't matter how good or how smart I was, if my parents didn't have the money, I couldn't go. And it's a lot of money, Mr. Demarkian. Almost fifteen thousand a year."

"Are your parents having money trouble?"

"No, no. Not at all. That's not what I mean."

"What do you mean?"

"I mean if they were having money trouble, or if they were poor, you know, because they just were or because they'd just immigrated to this country, you know, if it was something like that, it wouldn't matter how smart I was, I would never be able to go. You were smart. You didn't go to Deerfield."

"That was a different era. If you don't go to Deerfield, where do you go?"

"Well, my parents keep saying there are lots of good private schools in Philadelphia if I want to commute, you know, but they're missing the point. I want to go to public school, you know, like a regular person. But the public school I'd have to go to from here is—uh—you know— like it's dangerous. There have been a couple of shootings. That kind of thing. And so—"

"Joey," Gregor said patiently. "Where are you going to school?"

"I'm not," Joey said.

"You're not," Gregor repeated.

"I'm taking a year off," Joey said. "I can do that. I'm sixteen. Legally, I don't have to be in school at all."

"Wait a minute," Gregor told him. "Let's work this out. Last year you were at Deerfield. Right?"

"Right."

"This year you didn't want to go back to Deerfield. Right?"

"Right."

"You wanted to go to the local public school."

"Right."

"Which is the kind of place where students shoot each other."

"Yeah. Right."

"And when your parents wouldn't let you go to this public school, you decided to take a year off."

"You got it."

"Fine," Gregor said. "What's her name?"

Joey started, and then he began to blush. "Ah," he said. "Well. Gee. How did you figure that out?"

"Is she Armenian?" Gregor asked.

"Armenian from Armenia," Joey said. "Sofie Oumoudian. She came over with the first batch of refugees Father Tibor sponsored. She's really very—"

"Does she have parents?"

"She lives with her aunt. Her father died when she was six and her mother died in the earthquake. In Armenia. A couple of years ago. You remember. Anyway, uh, she really is a very unusual person. Very beautiful, but not in an American way. Small and round instead of tall and thin, but it fits her. I don't know. And very gentle. And very courageous. She had to be very courageous because she's very religious, and back in Armenia when she was growing up, being religious—"

"Stop," Gregor said.

"Sorry," Joey said. "Look. I know that public school is dangerous. Sofie had her wallet stolen at knife point three times last year. I can't just let her—"

"Let me tell you something else you can't do," Gregor said, "you can't defend her from the kind of person who would stick her up at knife point in a school hall-way because that person almost certainly belongs to a gang and almost certainly is taking cocaine and almost certainly doesn't give a damn whether he gets hurt or not, but you do and that will get you killed."

"So what am I supposed to do," Joey asked, "let her get killed?"

"No," Gregor said, rubbing his temples. "Let me think. Is Sofie the only student we have from the neigh-borhood at that school?"

"There are seven of them," Joey said. "They're get-ting slaughtered."

"I can imagine. All right. Let me talk to Father Tibor. We'll think of something."

"I keep trying to get Sofie to drop out, but she won't," Joey said. "She says education is important."

"She's right. What are you doing now that you're not getting any? Just hanging around the store?"

"Oh, no. I'm working at the Holy Trinity Armenian Christian School. As a teacher's aide. For free, you know. As a volunteer. I do the alphabet and teach basketball to the kindergarten and first- and second-grade boys."

"Wonderful," Gregor said.

"It is," Joey said brightly. "And Sofie—"

"Let me go find Father Tibor," Gregor said again. "Package me up and I'll get moving."

"Sure. But you know, Mr. Demarkian, if you want to find Father Tibor, you shouldn't go over to his place. He's at Bennis Hannaford's, too."

"Watching a sex show?"

"Old George Tekamanian couldn't get up the stairs

without help and Mrs. Arkmanian called him an old goat and said she wouldn't be party to raising his blood pressure and what would his grandson Martin say if he got overexcited and died at something like this and then Old George said—"

"Never mind," Gregor said desperately. "I get the picture. I'm in a little bit of a rush."

"If you really hurry, you'll get there just in time," Joey told him. "The show is due to start in two minutes."

2

The tall brownstone where Gregor Demarkian now had the third-floor floor-through apartment had once been a tenement, but it had been gutted and remodeled and turned into condominiums long before Gregor had come back to Cavanaugh Street to live. As a symbol of the transformation of the neighborhood, however, it was fairly weak, and that in spite of the fact that each of the four apartments had its own marble fireplace. Many of the other tenements on the street had been gutted and turned into single-family townhouses, like Lida Arkmanian's. Lida Arkmanian's upstairs living room window looked directly into Gregor's living room window. Lida Arkmanian also had a downstairs living room window (and, therefore, a downstairs living room), but that was the kind of thing that made Gregor feel a little dizzy. Lida Arkmanian with two living rooms and eight thousand square feet. Old George Tekamanian with a closet full of shirts from Ralph Lauren Polo. Sheila Kashinian with three mink coats. They had all been so poor growing up, and so isolated. They had all been so convinced that nothing much was ever going to change.

Gregor left Ohanian's and walked up the street, stepping carefully because the pavement was beginning to ice up. All around him were signs that Donna Moradanyan had been at work. The front of his own building was wrapped in green and red ribbons with a glowing menorah in every window that faced the street. The front of Lida Arkmanian's building—which Donna would have decorated—was more deliberately Christmassy, with bells and angels and cherubs nestled into clouds that seemed to be attached to the brownstone facing a fairy wish. Up the street a little farther, Donna had gone more deliberately Jewish, with glowing menorahs everywhere and a few Stars of David thrown in for good measure. Judiasm being a religion that placed a great deal of stress on the commandment *Thou shalt not make unto thee a graven image*, there weren't a lot of symbols for Donna to use, but she had done her best. Gregor saw the set of open scrolls one of the yeshivas downtown used to symbolize the Torah and a couple of Israeli flags. Donna was one of those young women young men of Gregor's day would have called "a game girl." He stopped at the steps to his building's front door and contemplated the multicolored tinsel with which she had hung the scraggly evergreen bush that grew against the banister. She had topped it off with another Star of David.

Gregor went up the steps and let himself into the foyer of the building, not even bothering to reach for his key chain. There was a lock on this door. All four of them had keys to it. Gregor was the only one who thought they should be using those keys. The rest of them—even Bennis,-who was a sophisticated woman and ought to know better—just left the door unlocked and went in and out as if they were living in the crime-free pastures of an Iowa farm. Gregor checked out the wreath on old George Tekamanian's door—evergreen and holly berry and a lot of shiny tinsel—and then looked over at the mail table. It was empty, meaning that Bennis had picked up her mail along with her own and taken it upstairs. Gregor sometimes wondered if she steamed open the envelopes with official-sounding return addresses on the envelopes—Federal Bureau of Investigation, Archdiocese of Colchester, New York State Department of Corrections—but he'd never had the nerve to ask her.

He climbed the stairs to the second-floor landing, shifted his grocery bags from his right arm to his left, and knocked on Bennis's door. Old George Tekamanian had the apartment on the ground floor of this building. Bennis had the apartment on the second floor. Gregor had the apartment on the third floor. And Donna Moradanyan and her two-year-old son, Tommy, had the apartment on the fourth. Donna decorated the doors to all of them. Bennis's door had a big silver bell with red metallic ribbon tied into a bow on the top. Donna knew better than to stick Bennis with anything religious.

Gregor knocked again, louder this time. The door opened and Sheila Kashinian stuck her bleached-blond head through the crack.

"Oh, it's you," she said, when she saw Gregor. "We were wondering where you were. We were only doing all this for your sake."

"Doing all what for my sake?"

But Sheila had already retreated into the apartment. Gregor left his grocery bags on Bennis's hall table and went straight into the living room. The living room was crammed full of what had to be all the women and half of everybody else in the neighborhood. Lida Arkmanian and Hannah Krekorian took up the couch, and Sheila in her high stiletto heels and overwhelming jewelry took a perch on one of the couch arms. Old George Tekamanian had the club chair. Father Tibor Kasparian had the red canvas director's chair Bennis usually used for work. Bennis and Donna were sitting cross-legged on the floor. There were other people there, too—Gregor saw June and Mary Ohanian crammed together into a kitchen chair pushed off to one side—but Gregor was already tired of taking inventory. He got the point. He stood at the back of the room and watched while Bennis's oversize television screen went from temporarily black to brilliant blue, showcasing a sprightly older woman in a tweed skirt and pearls.

"Help! He's killing me," the old woman said chirpily. "Women who say their husbands have penises that are just too big to handle. Next, on *The Lotte Goldman Show*."

"Penises," Hannah Krekorian said thoughtfully. "Do you think that's possible? That one could be too big?"

"I've heard of women being too big," Lida Arkmanian said. "But maybe that's more of that chauvinism they're always talking about. I mean, that you hear the bad things about women but you never hear the bad things about men."

"If that's chauvinism, there was none of it in my mother's house," Sheila Kashinian said. "You should have heard her and my aunts go at it."

"We did," Lida Arkmanian said. "We used to hide under the table and listen to all the old ladies talk."

"Those old ladies were younger than we are now," Hannah Krekorian said.

"Oh, do you remember the story about the woman who took a lover and then when she went to bed with her husband her husband could see her lover's image in her eyes?" Sheila Kashinian was practically squealing. "And first he killed her and then he killed her lover and it was a big mess but it was in Armenia—"

"I think your Aunt Helena used to make those stories up," Lida said.

"Maybe she did," Sheila said. "But they were good."

"I remember the story about the woman who had sex with her donkey," Hannah Krekorian said.

Gregor didn't want to hear the story about the woman who had had sex with her donkey. He didn't want to watch the commercial for designer perfume that was now flashing across the screen. He moved farther into the room and asked them, "What is it you think you're doing here? What is that thing?"

Bennis Hannaford stood up. "It's *The Lotte Goldman Show*. You know, the one you're supposed to be on next week."

"I can't be on a show about—about—"

"Well, you won't be, will you?" Donna Moradanyan asked him. "You'll be on one about serial killers."

"What's a show like this going to say about serial killers?" Gregor demanded. "Ted Bundy's ten favorite sexual fantasies? Richard Speck's—"

"That's the phone," Bennis said, jumping up. She raced into the kitchen, picked up, and pulled the cord as tight as it would go, so that she could stand in the doorway to the living room and watch what was happening on the television screen. The commercial was over and *The Lotte Goldman Show* had come back. The chirpy older woman was sitting in an artfully arranged crowd of middle-aged people, not one of whom looked to Gregor like he or she could manage to get excited enough to produce a heartbeat, never mind a sex life.

"We've got it on right now," Bennis said into the phone. "The production values are marvelous. I had no idea it was such a class act."

"Today, we are going to investigate one of the most explosive secret sexual dysfunctions of our, or any other, age," Lotte Goldman said. "We're going to look into the trials and tribulations of men who have been just too well endowed by nature, and the trials and tribulations of their wives and lovers. I want to warn you right now that some of the things you are going to hear on this program will be painful to listen to. I want to warn you as well that some of the language will be explicit. This program is not for the squeamish. And that said, I would like to introduce you now to our guests, who have each and every one of them courageously agreed to come here today and discuss this problem publicly, to bring it out of the dark closet in which it had been hiding and expose it to the light of day."

"I wonder if they'll have pictures," Sheila Kashinian said.

Bennis Hannaford waved the phone receiver in the air. "Lida, come here, it's for you. It's Rebekkah Goldman."

"She wants the address of the place with the kosher philo," Lida said, standing up. "I'll be right there. I don't want to miss any of this."

"You won't have to, Bekkah has it on too."

Lida stepped over Donna Moradanyan's shoulder and reached for the phone. "We are out of kimionov keufteh," she said. "There's another bowl I left in your refrigerator. Put them in the microwave and heat them up."

"I was a virgin when I was married," one of the women on television was saying. "I never saw one before I saw his. But when I did see his I had sense enough to be terrified."

Bennis disappeared into the kitchen.

Gregor decided to disappear into the kitchen after her.

He had to do something, because he didn't want to listen to what was going on on the television any longer. He looked at Tibor and old George Tekamanian, and saw that they both looked a little sick. All the women looked fascinated.

Gregor went around through the foyer again and got into the kitchen through that door. He found Bennis pulling bowls out of her refrigerator and tasting the contents of each one. She seemed to have enough bowls to throw a party for forty people. He pulled out one of her kitchen chairs and sat down.

"Bennis," he said. "What's going on out there?"

"Nobody wanted to watch their first Lotte Goldman

show alone," Bennis said. "They said they were afraid of what it would be like."

"They *said*?"

"It's the kind of thing you do in college," Bennis explained. "I mean, what's the point in watching something like that alone? You want to talk about it. You want to get embarrassed in public."

"Right," Gregor said.

"You can serve the enguinar chilled," Bennis said, "in fact, I think you're supposed to. Honestly, they should know better than to leave me alone with the food. Stop looking so green. You'll do fine."

"What's that supposed to mean?"

"On the show," Bennis said. "You'll do fine. You give great television. I've seen you."

If anyone in this crowd was going to see reason, Bennis was. What that said about the crowd, Gregor wasn't willing to contemplate.

"Bennis," he tried, in his best-modulated, most rational voice, "I can't possibly go on a show like that. I can't possibly. You must see that."

"Why?"

Bennis Hannaford was five feet four inches tall and weighed about a hundred pounds. She had thick black hair that floated like a cloud around her head, features so perfectly even and so well defined they could have been drawn by Dante Gabriel Rossetti, and not a wrinkle on her face in spite of the fact that she was thirty-six (no, almost thirty-seven) years old. She looked like an angel, even in worn jeans, a long-gone-shapeless turtleneck, and one of her brother's ancient flannel shirts. Only Gregor knew how truly implacable she was.

"Bennis," he said. "I have a reputation to consider. I make the newspapers a lot."

"I know."

"What will they say if I go on a show like that?"

"That you kept your dignity the whole time."

"I won't keep my dignity the whole time. I'll shout at somebody."

"Don't."

"How could I help it?"

"Gregor, everybody on Cavanaugh Street is counting on you. It's going to be only the second excuse they've ever had to watch that thing. And this Lotte Goldman person is going to be counting on you, too. Bekkah Goldman told Lida Arkmanian that Tibor told David that you said you would—"

"Think about it," Gregor said. "That's all I promised to do. Think about it."

"Well, then just think yes. Really. It'll be easier than you think. And you won't have to disappoint anybody."

"Bennis—"

The kitchen door on the living room side swung open and Lida came through, carrying the phone away from her ear.

"Here," she said, thrusting the receiver at Bennis, "hang this up. I have to get back out there. The woman in the pink dress was just describing the way her husband was so big, he punctured the inflatable doll they got him to relieve his stress."

"I'll be right there," Bennis said.

"Bennis," Gregor said.

But Bennis was gone, out there with the rest of them, thinking God only knew what, and Gregor knew it was no use.

That was his biggest problem on Cavanaugh Street.

He didn't know how to turn anyone in the neighborhood down.

He didn't know how to say no to women he had known as girls and old men he had known as strapping, bass-voiced pillars of the church.

He didn't know how to say no to much of anybody.

At least they fed him right.

He got a stuffed artichoke out of the bowl of enguinar and munched on it, imagining what he was going to do if Lotte Goldman asked him to describe the sexual practices of John Wayne Gacey.

A chorus of excited squeals rose out of the crowd in the living room. Gregor Demarkian winced.

THREE

1

For Lotte Goldman, the ten weeks the show spent touring America, taping in two-week sprints in five different cities, were an adventure. The first two weeks were always spent in Philadelphia, so she and anyone else from the show who wanted to could celebrate the first night of Hanukkah at David and Rebekkah's. After that, the migration might be for anywhere. In past years, Lotte had gone to Seattle and San Francisco, Phoenix and Tulsa, St. Augustine and St. Louis. She had found a good kosher restaurant in each one and lots of little things to bring home to her niece and nephews. Lotte got tired of being cooped up in New York. She got especially tired of doing nothing but going from her apartment to the studio and back again. When she had been younger, it had been different. Newly arrived in the city, Lotte had claimed every spare moment for discovery. She had gone to the Empire State Building and the Museum of Modern Art and the Brooklyn Botanical Gardens and the zoo. Even once she'd started her long climb to what would turn out to be success, she made time for herself. In those days, she would survive on two hours of sleep just to make sure she had time to hear *Aida* performed by Maria Callas or see the El Greco exhibit sent over by the government of Spain. It was after Lotte got successful that she got dull. Taping, researching, interviewing, talking to the press: it didn't sound like it should take so much time, but it did. The week after the show got its first forty share, Lotte went out and bought a Filofax, and she'd been addicted to it ever since. Things to do. Places to be. Phone numbers to remember. Lotte seemed to be busy all the time at the same time she seemed to be doing nothing at all.

"So take an afternoon off every once in a while," DeAnna Kroll was always telling her. "I would if I could."

Actually, DeAnna wouldn't and couldn't any more than Lotte wouldn't and couldn't. The real difference between DeAnna and Lotte was in how much Lotte loved leaving time. Part of that was temperament—DeAnna liked where she was now; she was suspicious of change of principle—but part of it was the nature of traveling reality for *The Lotte Goldman Show*. In that reality, Lotte rode to Philadelphia in the very front seat of whatever vehicle they were using to get there, and DeAnna did all the work.

The work DeAnna was doing this morning was the work she usually did just before they left for Philadelphia: supervising the loading of eight sofas, fifteen armchairs, twenty straight-backed chairs, twelve carpets, and ten coffee tables onto a moving van. The moving van was necessary because Shelley Feldstein refused to go anywhere without her back-up sets. "What if they don't have anything suitable?" Shelley demanded, every time DeAnna suggested that there were plenty of furniture stores in every town they were scheduled to stop in. "What if Lotte has to tape a show on suburban prostitution with her set all in *red*?"

As a rationale for dragging the volumic equivalent of

the contents of a small house all the way across the country and back again, this didn't make much sense, but no one could talk to Shelley about it. Shelley got hysterical. Lotte didn't remember when she and DeAnna had finally given in. Getting out of the cab now in the crisp December air, feeling the little rush she always felt being out in the city at night, it seemed to Lotte that they had been leaving this way forever. She knew it couldn't be true. Shelley hadn't been with them forever. Lotte couldn't remember what it had been like before. DeAnna probably could. She could probably remember the year, day, hour, and minute when Shelley had insisted on taking the furniture for the first time.

The cab driver took off from the curb in a squeal of brakes, as if he were trying to prove something, and Lotte went around the back of the moving van to find DeAnna. She was standing on a marble-topped coffee table in a pair of skin-tight black leather leggings and a black leather tunic encrusted with flattened bullets. She had her feet in four-inch stiletto heels the color of burnished moonlight. The moving man she was talking to looked a little shell-shocked. He was young and uniformed and obviously unused to be told what to do by a woman. Lotte thought he was certainly unused to women like DeAnna Kroll, assuming there were women "like" DeAnna Kroll. DeAnna had traded her cornrows this evening for the world's most outrageous Afro. It billowed out from her scalp like a wiry mushroom cloud with a mind of its own.

"The coffee tables have got to be wrapped in cotton," she was saying. "If they're not wrapped in cotton, they might get scratched, just faintly scratched, on the tabletops. If they do get scratched, no matter how minorly, my set designer is going to have a psychotic break. You got it? You wrap them in cotton, Shelley doesn't have a psychotic break, I don't have a bad day, everybody is happy."

"But Ms. Kroll—"

"I don't want to argue about it," DeAnna said. "I

don't want to argue about anything. I just want you to do it."

"But Ms. *Kroll*—"

"*Do* it."

"Come talk to me," Lotte said, over DeAnna's shoulder. "It's cold and you need a break."

The moving van was backed up to the loading door at the rear of the Hullboard-Dedmarsh building. Lotte had gone there because she knew she would find DeAnna just where she had found her and because she knew it would be a good place to talk in private. The rest of the cast and crew would be meeting in the front, where Prescott Holloway and his limousine were scheduled to pick them up. Lotte got DeAnna far enough from the moving van so that the young man began to relax and then said, "Well, I have done what we discussed. I have started it. What about you?"

"I've done what we discussed, too," DeAnna said. "I've got a friend at CBS News."

"And?"

"And he's legit," DeAnna said with conviction. "Absolutely legit. There's no hype about it."

Lotte felt her muscles begin to unkink. It was hardly credible, but Lotte thought she had been tense ever since she found out that Maria Gonzalez had died—or at least ever since the police investigation had started, when it became more and more clear that whatever had happened had not been a standard-issue mugging. Lotte had met her share of murderers—nobody could have been living in a major city in Germany in 1942 without coming in contact with those—but all the murderers she had met had been murderers for abstraction, the sort of people who bayed for blood over matters of mistaken principle or the illusion of religion. Murderers like that Lotte had always dismissed as essentially insane. Something went wrong with their blood chemistry and it was infectious, that was the trouble. The trick was to catch the disease early, before it could spread.

Insanity was how Lotte explained routine mugging murders, too. The murderers took drugs that made them temporarily insane. This thing with Maria Gonzalez was very different. That a man or a woman could murder someone they actually knew, someone they had talked to, someone they had eaten lunch with and taken messages for—it was horrible. That was what Lotte had told David on the phone. Horrible. David had told her she was naive. The Nazis had murdered people they knew, people they had talked to, people they had eaten lunch with and taken messages for and sometimes even gone to bed with. All murderers are alike.

There was a low concrete restraining wall at the edge of the short driveway leading to the loading door. Lotte sat down on it, got out her cigarette case, and lit up.

"So," she said. "Tell me. What did your friend mean by legit?"

"He meant big-time legit," Lotte said. "This Gregor Demarkian was an FBI agent. He did work on kidnappings for years, and he was good at it so he got assigned to Washington and the sensitive political work, problems with Senators and Congressmen and that kind of thing. Anyway, one day around, I don't remember, 1977 or 1978, he started helping some people in Oregon and Washington with these murder investigations they had, string of young girls, looked like it was the same person. The FBI isn't supposed to handle murder cases except in national parks or on Indian reservations, because murder isn't a federal offense, but they got around it that time because there were two states involved, Demarkian supposedly told the director at the time that he was investigating a man who was carrying on an interstate commerce in murder. If you see what I mean."

"Very clever," Lotte said.

"Yeah, Lotte. I know. He is very clever. He tracked this guy for Oregon and Washington and a couple of other

states, and because of the help he gave them the guy finally got caught, and that was Ted Bundy."

"Ah," Lotte Goldman said, sitting up a little straighter
and nodding. "Mr. Bundy. I've heard of Mr. Bundy."

"Everybody's heard of Mr. Bundy," DeAnna said
drily. "He's the most famous serial killer since Jack the
Ripper. Anyway, that's how Demarkian got what he
wanted. Bundy escaped from jail—a couple of times—
ending up rampaging across the Florida countryside,
Demarkian gave the police down there some help and they
ended up convicting Bundy—and then Demarkian went to
the powers-that-were and told them that if the FBI had had
the procedures in place to deal with someone like Bundy,
someone like Bundy would never have been able to do the
kind of damage he did."

Lotte thought about this. "As a thesis, it's dubious."

"Of course it's dubious," DeAnna agreed, "but it's
like I said. Demarkian got what he wanted. Which was a
special department of the Federal Bureau of Investigation
that does nothing but track serial murderers."

"He founded this department?"

"You got it."

"And he headed it?"

"For ten years," DeAnna said. "He was good at it,
too. He was involved in all kinds of famous cases. He got
his picture on the cover of *Time* magazine. He was a real
big noise."

"Why did he stop?"

"His wife got some really nasty form of cancer and
he took a leave to look after her," DeAnna said. "Then
when she died, I guess he just didn't have the heart for it.
My guy at CBS said that people were saying at the time
that Demarkian looked depressed enough to be suicidal.
They were really worried."

Depressed enough to be suicidal when his wife
died—*that* spoke well for him. Lotte was amused at herself. Here DeAnna was, rattling off a string of credentials

and professional accomplishments, and the first thing she says to make Lotte feel she will be able to trust this man is that he was depressed enough to be suicidal when his wife died.

"I'm getting to be an old Jewish person," she told DeAnna. "I ought to be a grandmother, the way I think sometimes these days. What about the things we have read about? The murder in Vermont? The one this past May at the convent—"

"I'm getting to that," DeAnna said. "Them, I guess. He does a lot of that sort of thing."

"He's a private detective?"

"Nope. Doesn't have a license and tells anyone who asks that he doesn't intend to get one."

"Then how can he take on these investigations?"

"By the simple expedient of not charging for them. Not that money doesn't change hands, mind you. There's a rumor going around that right after Demarkian cleared up a murder at the chancery up in Colchester a couple of Easters ago, John Cardinal O'Bannion directed some Catholic charitable funding organization he's head of to donate twenty-five thousand dollars to some cause Demarkian's pet priest is involved with—"

Lotte nodded. "That would be Father Tibor Kasparian. David's friend. Did you check into these private investigations, or whatever you're supposed to call them? You're sure he really did the investigating?"

"Oh, yeah. He's got letters of thanks from police departments all over the place, including one from the police department in Bryn Mawr, Pennsylvania, which I was actually able to check out. I talked to the guy he worked with on the Hannaford case. The guy couldn't have been more impressed."

The cigarette was burned to the filter. Lotte dropped it on the ground, smashed it out with her foot, and took another from her case.

"That settles it then," she told DeAnna. "He's just the person we're looking for."

"I agree."

"Now our only problem is convincing him he wants to interest himself in our problem. Did your person at CBS News indicate that this would be difficult?"

"I didn't ask him if it would be difficult."

"David says Father Tibor Kasparian says Mr. Demarkian is not always anxious to be involved. Ah, I wish he were coming to us instead of us going to him. I wish he were coming to New York." Lotte took a deep drag on her newly lit cigarette. "I can't help thinking it would be so much more convenient. We'll ask him to help us and then what? All the evidence will still be here."

"Maybe," DeAnna said.

"Ms. Kroll?" the young man from the moving van called out. "What about sofas with marble arms? Do they get wrapped in cotton too?"

DeAnna looked up and shook her head. "Duty calls," she said. "Are you going to be all right?"

"I'm going to be fine."

"Go in the front and entertain the troops. Next year I'm going to rent a U-Haul and get Max to load it. You sure you're all right?"

"Fine," Lotte said again.

DeAnna turned away and started heading back to the moving van. "We'll get Demarkian in on it and everything will be just fine," she said. "You wait and see."

Lotte Goldman sighed.

She didn't know if getting Demarkian in on it would make everything "just fine," but at least it would be doing something.

2

The police showed up at Itzaak Blechmann's door ten minutes before he was intending to leave for the Hullboard-Dedmarsh building. They were the same two policemen who had come before, twice before, with their badges held out and their faces set like bad clay models in a kindergarten class. They reminded Itzaak of the policemen he had known in Leningrad. All policemen were the same, he told himself. All governments are the same. Law and order can mean only one thing: a license to commit terror.

When Itzaak saw the faces of the two policemen through his peephole, his stomach heaved so badly he thought he was going to throw up right there on the floor. He had to put his head against the doorjamb and close his eyes and count to ten before he could open up.

The taller of the two policemen was thick and ham faced and vaguely lewd, so that everything he said sounded obscene, even something as simple as "Can I have a glass of water?" The shorter of the two was mostly bald and called the taller one "Chickie." Itzaak didn't like the idea of a grown man people called "Chickie." He wouldn't have liked it even if the grown man had been a civilian. The idea of a policeman named "Chickie" made him start to sweat.

Itzaak had his two suitcases packed for the tour and piled next to the door. Chickie and the other cop looked at them as they came in. Itzaak had been getting his coat out when they buzzed. He still had it in his hand. He put it over the suitcase and then went into the living room, where the cops had already sat down.

The two of them always came in and sat right down, without asking. Itzaak had the idea that this was not permissible in the United States, but he didn't know for sure, and he couldn't see what he was able to do about it. The one called "Chickie" was sitting in his BarcaLounger, his favorite chair in the world. The other one was sitting on the sofa.

Itzaak took a straight chair from his dining room table—his dining room was part of his kitchen; it was that kind of New York apartment—and sat down in it. The two cops looked at him as if he were a performing flea who had just done something terribly clever.

"Well," Itzaak said. "Well. Here you are again."

"That's right, Mr. Blechmann," the smaller cop said. "Here we are again."

"I take it you're not going to be here for long," Chickie said. "Since you're packed and everything."

"I am leaving on the tour," Itzaak said. "With the rest of *The Lotte Goldman Show.*"

"Ah," the smaller cop said. *"The Lotte Goldman Show."*

"My leaving has been cleared with the police department," Itzaak said. "Just like the leaving of everyone else who works on the program."

"Cleared," Chickie said. "Oh, we know it's been *cleared.*"

"I don't know what you're doing here," Itzaak said.

The one called Chickie had been staring at the ceiling. The other one had been staring at the floor. Now they looked at each other and nodded a little. Chickie reached into the pocket of his jacket and brought out a stenographer's notebook. His jacket was a badly cut brown tweed. Policemen here were like students in Leningrad in this one respect: their clothes always looked as if they had been modeled on creatures from another planet.

Chickie looked through his stenographer's notebook. Itzaak reminded himself that there was no Leningrad any more, there was no Soviet Union, and since he had done nothing wrong nothing wrong could be done to him.

Chickie stopped at a page covered with blotted-ink scrawl. "We checked it out," he said. "With Immigration and Naturalization. We checked out your green card."

"What is there to check out about my green card?"

"We checked it out to see if it was legitimate," Chickie said. "You know. The real thing. Not forged."

"Of course my green card is legitimate. I have been in the United States for six years."

"There are people, been here twenty years, their cards aren't legitimate," the smaller cop said.

"I am already taking citizenship classes." Itzaak felt himself go stiff. His head especially went stiff. It went so stiff he couldn't think straight. "If I pass my test, I will take the oath this coming Fourth of July."

Chickie looked through his stenographer's notebook some more. "We checked out your Social Security card," he said. "That turned out to be legitimate, too."

Itzaak didn't answer this. He thought anybody who faked a Social Security card had to be crazy. You had to pay all that money to the Social Security administration. How would you get it back if your Social Security card was faked?

Chickie was checking through his notebook again. "We tried to check out your background in—Leningrad, did you say?"

"It's St. Petersburg now," Itzaak said. "It was Leningrad then."

"Well, things seem to be a little confused over there. We can't seem to get anybody to give us a straight answer about anything."

"Like about why you were in jail," the short one said.

"And what you were in jail for," Chickie said. "Did you know we knew you had been in jail?"

"It was on your application at INS," the short one said, "but we didn't need that. We knew anyway."

"You can always tell when a man's been in jail," Chickie said.

"He walks funny," the short one said.

"Your application at INS said you'd been in jail for *political* reasons," Chickie said. "It said you'd been in jail for your *religion*."

"I am a practicing Jew," Itzaak said, stiff, stiff, paralyzed. "At the time, Leningrad was not a good place to be a practicing Jew."

"Well, I'll tell you, Isaac, we were thinking about that. We surely were. I mean, it stands to reason, doesn't it? If you'd been in jail for, say, murder, you wouldn't tell the INS *that*."

"I was not in jail for murder."

"Funny about your being a practicing Jew," Chickie said. "We got one of those in the department. Wears one of those little hats just like yours."

"Yarmulke."

"Yeah, yarmulke," Chickie said. "Thing is, he doesn't have a Spanish girlfriend just like yours."

"A Catholic girlfriend," the short one said.

"He wouldn't even talk to a Catholic girl," Chickie said. "So it kind of makes me wonder."

"Just like we wonder about which Catholic girl your girlfriend really was," the short one said.

"*You* say it was Carmencita Boaz," Chickie said.

"But it could have been either of them," the short one said.

"Look at it this way." Chickie slapped his notebook shut. "Your super saw you with a Spanish woman. That was it. The people in Carmencita's building, they never saw you at all. So it makes us think, if you see what I mean. It makes us curious."

"Because if your girlfriend was Maria Gonzalez instead of Carmencita Boaz," the short one said, "you'd probably be in a lot of serious trouble right about now."

Itzaak Blechmann did not believe that the people in Carmencita's building had never seen him. He thought they were protecting Carmencita's reputation, because he came late and stayed all night sometimes. He didn't blame them for thinking he and Carmencita were doing all sorts of things they weren't actually doing. What else would they think? He too wanted to protect Carmencita's reputation. He wanted to protect Carmencita more than anything. Now it appeared that he couldn't even protect himself.

"I never spoke more than politenesses and business to Maria Gonzalez in my life," he said helplessly. "She did not like me. And she was very devout."

Chickie put his notebook back inside his jacket and stood up. "That's all we came out here about. We just wanted you to know the way we were going these days. We just wanted you to know."

"We thought you might have some kind of comment you wanted to make," the short one said.

"Or some information you wanted to supply us."

"Or some suggestion you might want to make."

"Or something," Chickie said. "I'm convinced of it. One of these days, you're going to give us something."

"No," Itzaak told him. "I'm not going to give you anything. I don't have anything to give you."

The two policemen were on their feet. They left Itzaak sitting in his chair and walked to the door, side by side, as if they'd rehearsed it.

"Bye," Chickie said, when he'd gotten the door open and let his partner out into the hall. "See you when you get back from your tour. You have our card if there's anything you want to tell us."

"You can call us any hour of the day or night," the short one piped up from the hallway.

"If you lose the card, we're in the phone book," Chickie said. Then he went out into the hall, too, and closed the door after him.

Itzaak sat in the chair he had been sitting in and closed his eyes. He had to stop sweating. He had to start breathing well enough to get up and walk. He had to start thinking again and he had to do it soon, because things were worse than he'd thought they were. For a moment there, they had almost gotten close.

He got out of the chair and went to his bedroom. He picked up the phone he kept on the night table and dialed Carmencita's number. The phone rang and rang and rang, but no one answered. Carmencita must have already left to go downtown.

Itzaak went back out to the front door and got his coat off his suitcases and put it on. He wouldn't have a chance to talk to Carmencita in private now until they were at the hotel in Philadelphia. Since he didn't dare talk to her in front of other people, he would simply have to wait.

In the meantime, he thought he was going to get an ulcer.

3

Moments later—just as Itzaak locked his apartment door and started for the lobby to find a cab—Maximillian Dey got off the Lexington Avenue local at Fourteenth Street in a crush of people who all seemed to be dressed up to go to a biker's convention. The men wore fringed leather vests and no shirts—in this cold!—and ragged jeans and lace-up boots with metal-tipped spikes on the soles. The women wore torn net stockings and very short skirts and peasant blouses and high-heeled ankle boots. There was a heavy-metal club just south of here, and Max supposed they were heading there. It was a little early for that kind of thing, but in the city you never knew. Most of the men were old and most of the women were much too young and much too fat. Max could never get over just how fat Americans were, at every age. He expected it in the old, but in the young he looked for leanness. He wondered what caused it, and came to different conclusions. Diets, that was his conclusion of the month. Americans were fat because they went on so many diets. He'd watched a girlfriend of his go on a diet once, and after about three days it had made him so crazy he was ready to eat the refrigerator. Whole.

The stairway to the street was to his left. He let himself be pushed along by the crowd. It was moving faster than he wanted to. He reached the steps and started up at his usual measured rate. He was pushed first from behind and then from the side, so that he fell forward and then around and nearly broke his back. He shouted in the general direction of whoever it was might have pushed him, but he couldn't really tell. Everyone was milling around and the light was very poor. He was still moving up the stairs. There was no way to stop himself. He faced forward so he wouldn't stumble again and almost immediately felt an elbow in the small of his back, someone hurrying him forward. The push catapulted him upward and into the air. He stumbled on the top step and fell to his knees. The crowd would have run him over if he hadn't braced himself against a trash can.

"For Christ's sake," he said to nobody in particular. "What are you trying to do to me?"

He might as well have been talking to the Ghost of Christmas Past. There was nobody there to hear him. The biker people had disappeared. The street was deserted for a block and a half in either direction. Even Union Square Park looked empty.

And then it hit him.

"Goddamn," he said into the air, loud enough to convince anyone who might hear him that he was a certified crazy. "God*damn*."

He reached into his back pocket for his wallet and came up empty. His wallet was gone.

He had had it when he left his apartment. He remembered checking the hundred dollars in it twice and then tucking it back there.

He had had it when he got on the subway. He remembered the side of his hand knocking against it as he looked through his other pockets for a token. He kept everything in the world that was important to him in that wallet, and now what was he going to do?

He turned in the direction of Fifth Avenue and started walking, quickly and angrily, and the inside of his head took up a litany.

He was going to have to replace it all.

Replace it *all*.

And it was going to cost a hell of a lot of money that he just didn't have.

FOUR

1

Gregor Demarkian always took Father Tibor Kasparian seriously. He did what Father Tibor asked him, and he investigated what Father Tibor thought was worth investigating—with the exception of a possible permanent union between Gregor and Bennis Hannaford, which Gregor thought of as Tibor's single symptom of mental illness. Since the graffiti on the walls of Rabbi David Goldman's colleague's synagogue had nothing to do with Bennis Hannaford—she'd dated a Reform rabbi once and gone to her best-friend-from-college's oldest son's bar mitzvah, but beyond that she'd never had anything to do with synagogues—he started looking into it as soon as he got a free minute. It turned out to be more complicated than he had expected. Gregor called a friend of his at the Philadelphia office of the Bureau, who referred him to a mutual acquaintance in Omaha, who turned him around and sent him to a man all three of them had known at Quantico who was not in Washington, D.C. The man in Washington,

D.C., was on vacation. Gregor left four or five messages and then gave it up. The man would be back from Florida when the man got back from Florida. There was nothing Gregor could do before then.

The man's name was Ira Ballard, and he got back from Florida—at least to the extent of answering Gregor's calls—on the day Gregor and Tibor were due to have tea with Sofie Oumoudian and her aunt. The call came in at nine fifteen in the morning, while Gregor was standing in front of his closet, contemplating ties. None of his ties were going to do, he could see that. They were all either too loud or too wide. Tibor had already warned him that Sofie and her aunt were "very pious" and "very conservative," meaning they were really old-time Armenian, meaning God only knew what. At least Gregor knew his suits would do. Gregor had always been a terrible stick-in-the-mud about suits. Bennis had tried to talk him into buying anything from a houndstooth check to a jacket with wide lapels, but he had remained loyal to his 1950s organization man classics. The only concession he had made was in price. While he was still at the Bureau, he bought his suits at Sears. Now that he was retired, with decent if not spectacular money in the bank and nobody to worry about but himself, he let Bennis steer him to J. Press. J. Press was also good for plain white button-down shirts, of which he had a dozen. The ties were Gregor's own fault. He simply couldn't pick ties. He was hopeless.

Gregor and Tibor were due at the Oumoudian apartment at eleven o'clock. Gregor had started fussing through his closet at eight. When the call came in, he had all his ties laid out on the bedspread of his big double bed, and he was close to despair.

"I keep seeing your picture in the paper with this woman who looks like Elizabeth Taylor at twenty-five," Ira Ballard said, when Gregor picked up the phone. "What gives?"

"She's thirty-seven," Gregor said, "and nothing gives.

To put it the way she puts it, we hang out. Hello, Ira. I hope you had a good vacation."

"I never have a good vacation. I hate the heat. Nancy loves the heat. Every year she points out that we do it my way fifty weeks out of fifty-two, the remainder ought to be hers. So I hate the heat but I go to Florida. Is this some kind of emergency?"

"I wouldn't call it an emergency, exactly, why?"

"Five calls from you. One from Jack in Philadelphia. One from Fred Hacker in Omaha."

"Synagogues," Gregor said, "and anti-Semitic organizations. Nothing out of hand. Not yet."

"Right," Ira said. "Well, that's the name of the game. Not yet."

"It should be 'not ever,' " Gregor said. "Just a minute. There's something I have to do here."

The something Gregor had to do was pick up the ties. He was sick of looking at them. He put the phone between his ear and his shoulder and scooped the ties into both hands. Then he dumped them on top of his dresser. Jumbled up there in a pile, they looked like knotted snakes. He retrieved the phone and said,

"Ira, give me another minute, I'm going to change phones. It'll only take a second."

"Go right ahead."

Gregor put the receiver down on the bed. Then he went out to the kitchen, picked up the receiver there, and laid it down on the kitchen table. Then he went back to the bedroom and hung that receiver up. By the time he got back to the kitchen, he felt like a damn fool.

"You know what somebody should invent?" he asked Ira. "A gadget that would hang up a phone in the bedroom while you were talking in the kitchen. If you know what I mean."

"What anti-Semitic organization?"

Gregor got his kettle off the stove and filled it with water. He put it back on the stove and turned on the heat.

"Let me get my notes here," he told Ira. "You've got to understand, I'm giving you all this third hand. I haven't talked to the rabbi whose synagogue was involved. Not yet, anyway."

"Who have you talked to?"

"Another rabbi. Man name of David Goldman. He—"

"The David Goldman whose sister has that sex show?"

"You know him?" Gregor was surprised.

"I don't know him personally," Ira said, "but I know of him. He used to be all over the place down here before the Wall fell. He used to sponsor people who wanted to immigrate from the Soviet Union."

"I think he still does," Gregor said. "In a way, that's who I came in contact with him. He sponsored the man who's now my parish priest."

"Funny. I thought he made a point of sponsoring Jews."

"Maybe he just makes a point of sponsoring people who have been persecuted for their religion. Whatever. I've talked to Rabbi Goldman, but I haven't talked to the rabbi whose synagogue was involved, so take what I've got with that in mind. Oh, and I checked into the police reports. They're useless."

"They often are." Ira Ballard sighed. "Christ, Gregor, what are you going to do? The cops have fifteen murders a week to solve and some asshole to chase who gets his kicks driving by apartment buildings and spraying their windows with machine gun fire, they don't have a lot of time left over for spray paint. In spite of the fact that a little preventive medicine—"

"Ira."

"Never mind," Ira said. "Shoot."

The kettle was shooting steam and wailing in a high-pitched whistle that threatened to turn into a shriek. Gregor dumped a teaspoon of instant coffee in the bottom on a mug and poured water over it. The instant coffee was freeze-dried, and it foamed.

"The incident happened on the twenty-third of November at Temple Beth-El in Philadelphia proper, meaning not on the Main Line," Gregor said. "I'm sorry. You probably didn't need to be told that. Around here it's sometimes necessary. Temple Beth-El is the cornerstone of an Hasidic neighborhood, there's been trouble up there before—"

"With this same sort of thing?"

"Nothing so focused," Gregor said. "Nothing religious, certainly. A few smashed windows. A few overturned trash cans. That kind of thing."

"That kind of thing can be everything or nothing."

"Yes. I know. On the twenty-third, though, the attack was focused. Sometime in the night, the entire street facade of Temple Beth-El was sprayed over in phosphorescent paint. With the usual kind of thing. A lot of obscenities. 'Go back to Israel' with 'Israel' misspelled. 'Hitler was right.' That kind of thing."

"Any signature?"

"Definitely. 'White Knights, Defenders of Race and Faith.' "

"Mmm," Ira said.

"The police did try all the usual things," Gregor told him. "Nobody in the neighborhood had seen anything. Nobody had heard anything, either—"

"That could be fear," Ira put in quickly. "Sometimes, if the neighborhood is heavily populated by people who have immigrated from countries where there is a lot of officially sanctioned anti-Semitism, people are afraid to talk. They think the police are in collusion with the people who are tormenting them."

"Well, fear or ignorance, it doesn't matter now," Gregor said. "Nobody was willing to admit seeing or hearing anything. The rabbi at Temple Beth-El was working late in his office that night. His office is on the first floor, directly across the street from the synagogue's front door. He worked until midnight and then he went to bed. So whatever happened had to have happened after midnight."

"If we were dealing with anything but an Hasidic neighborhood, I'd want to put it later than that," Ira agreed. "Was there any precipitating incident that you know of?"

"What do you mean, a precipitating incident?"

"It could be anything at all," Ira said. "It could be really remote. We had a bunch of these guys in Oakland, went on a spray-paint rampage after that Israeli guy won the Nobel in medicine last year."

"Why?" Gregor was thoroughly confused.

Ira was exasperated. "How could I know why? Because they have IQs in the single figures, Gregor, that's why. I'm not kidding. I've been in this job, what now, seven years, maybe, and you know what I've found out? The guys who pull this shit are dumb. Not mentally retarded, Gregor, *dumb*. Stupid. It's incredible. We pulled this one guy in here, he's set fire to a black Baptist church in Tupelo, Mississippi. That was maybe the tenth church he'd set fire to, in maybe the third state. So we haul him in here and we ask him what in damn hell he thinks he's doing, and do you know what he tells us?"

"No."

"He tells us he's got to stop the black people from taking over the Christian churches before they feed poison to any more women and turn the women into feminists, which they won't stop doing because—"

"Wait," Gregor said.

"It doesn't make *sense*," Ira snorted. "These things never make sense. You listen for more than twenty minutes and your brain turns to mush."

"Oh," Gregor said.

"You ever read *The Protocols of the Learned Elders of Zion*?"

"No," Gregor said.

"It's the original anti-Semitic conspiracy theory. You could get better intellectual coherence from *The National Enquirer*."

"Oh," Gregor said.

"Never mind." Ira sighed again. "I could go on and on like this all day. These assholes would be funny if they weren't so dangerous. What was the name of your guys again?"

"White Knights, Defenders of Faith and Race," Gregor repeated. "Are you sure about the 'guys.' Aren't there women involved in these things?"

"There are women in the Klan," Ira said, "and on the fringes of most of the other organizations, yeah, but they don't lead any of them. For one thing, most of these groups are chauvinist as hell. They get to the part where St. Paul says wives should be subject to their husbands, and they don't bother to read the rest of the passage."

"I see."

"Anyway, women don't go out and spray paint people's synagogues," Ira said. "They've got more sense. Just a minute now. Let's see what we've got on the White Knights."

Gregor's coffee mug was empty. He put the kettle back on to boil and listened to the tapping of keys on a computer keyboard. The water boiled in no time at all. He'd drunk his first mug of coffee quickly. The water in the kettle was still hot. He dumped another teaspoon of instant coffee into his mug and watched while the hot water made it foam.

On the other side of the line, Ira had started to grunt. "Philadelphia," he was saying. "Philadelphia, Philadelphia. I don't have anything on them in Philadelphia."

"You mean they're not known to operate in this city?" Gregor asked.

"I mean we've never had any reports on them from the Philadelphia office. But you know that. You called the Philadelphia office."

"That's right."

"This is a very minor league group, Gregor. Tiny. These people are nobody important."

"They're important enough to have spray-painted this synagogue," Gregor pointed out.

"Spray paint doesn't make them important," Ira said. "Never mind. I know what you mean. Look, last April these people had a convention of sorts down in Kisco, Oklahoma. In a trailer park, no less. With beer. God, it's incredible. Anyway, I've got a notation here, we've got a file report on this thing. We must have had an agent there. I could talk to him and see what he has to say. And I could look up the file report."

"Would you?"

"Sure. We're having a reasonably slack time around here. That's why I could take a vacation. What are you going to do? Get the names and then stake them out?"

"Something like that."

"Best way to go about it. Of course, you can't if you're official. Not unless you've got some way to cover your ass—"

"Claim you had an informant?" Gregor suggested.

"Oh, that's good," Ira said. "That's very good. You always were good. I can get back to you in about two hours, how about that?"

"I'll be out. Why don't you try this evening? Or tomorrow morning, if it's more convenient."

"I'll interrupt your dinner. It's too bad the lady isn't more than a friend, Gregor."

"No it's not."

"You must be getting old."

Gregor heard a click in his ear. Ira had hung up. He hung up himself and went back to his coffee. Why was it, he wondered, that everything in his life that started out simple ended up complicated?

Through the kitchen doorway, he could see the menorah Donna had left him, perched in the window, plugged in and glowing. Sometimes he got so tired of symbolic gestures, he could scream.

2

Tibor came to pick him up for the walk to Sofie Oumoudian's apartment at quarter to eleven, and by then Gregor had managed to give himself what was nearly a nervous breakdown about his tie. He had also started to resent the hell out of Tibor and his cautions. If Tibor hadn't insisted, over and over again, on just how pious, devout, old-fashioned, European, and traditionally Armenian these two women were, Gregor would never have gotten so nervous. He had also begun to wonder just how accurate Tibor's description really was. After all, Sofie Oumoudian had managed to attract Joey Ohanian, and Joey was hardly a pious, traditionally Armenian young man. In fact, he was something of a rip. Gregor thought Joey would put up with a certain amount of shyness and sexual standoffishness for the sake of romanticism, but there would be a limit. The limit would probably have something to do with the back-seat of Joey's brand-new, shiny black Chevrolet sports car, his parents' gift to him on his sixteenth birthday, when they still thought he would finish out at Deerfield without giving them any problems.

Tibor arrived in impeccably correct dress, his cassock cleaned and pressed. That was one of the virtues of a religious uniform. It was appropriate everywhere. Tibor looked Gregor up and down once or twice and apparently didn't find anything wrong with him. Either that, or he decided it wasn't worth saying anything.

"I've brought pastries," he said, holding up a white box that had obviously come from Ohanian's. "It is customary to bring something. Do you know what you are going to say?"

"In a way," Gregor said.

"The aunt's name is Helena," Tibor told him. "She is in the church often and long. She lights candles and leaves offerings. I think there is family back in Armenia."

"You think?"

"She doesn't talk to me much."

One of the difficulties yet to be untangled in the wake of the fall of the Soviet Union was the position of the churches and their clergy. The Russian Orthodox Church had been thoroughly infiltrated by the Communist government, and it was generally assumed that the heirarchies of the smaller eastern churches had been infiltrated as well. In occupied Armenia there had actually been two churches, the official one and the one operating underground. Tibor had been part of the church operating underground. Of course, Helena Oumoudian would assume that any priest operating out in the open the way Tibor was now would be suspect. She hadn't been in the United States very long.

To get to the Oumoudians' apartment, Gregor and Tibor had to leave Cavanaugh Street and walk two blocks north, into territory into which Gregor had never before ventured. Tibor, whose motto was "if Christian behaved like Christians, we wouldn't need a welfare state," had a wider acquaintance with the blocks that surrounded their Armenian-American enclave. When the first immigrants had come in the wake of Armenian independence, Tibor and Lida and all the others had done their best to find places on Cavanuagh Street itself, just as they had founded the Holy Trinity Armenian Christian School to teach children who knew no English and had to learn in a hurry. After a while, though, there got to be too many immigrants. Cavanaugh Street was a small place. That was when Lida and Hannah and Sheila and Bennis had started buying up real estate on the fringes, hoping to export what Cavanaugh Street was to any other part of Philadelphia they touched.

That they hadn't quite succeeded was obvious as soon
as Gregor and Tibor got more than half a block north.
There were some signs of Cavanaugh Street on these
blocks—Donna Moradanyan had been out, scattering
bright foil paper and Christmas ribbons and glowing menorahs in her wake—but the brownstones looked mean
and dispirited and the streets were full of litter. Children
sat on stoops in the cold, dressed in thin sweaters, without
coats, their feet shoved into unraveling sneakers and innocent of socks.

The Oumoudians' apartment was in a looming building with grime on most of the windows that faced front
and a coating of something like sand on the steps that led
to the tall front door. Once upon a time, this brownstone
had been a single-family house. Now it was cut up into
apartments for people who had no time or energy or
money to maintain it. Gregor and Tibor went into the vestibule and rang the buzzer under "Oumoudian." The vestibule made Gregor even more depressed than the street
had. There was a bright silver bow on the Oumoudians'
mailbox—Donna Moradanyan again?—but no other decoration of any kind. The floor was dirty and the walls were
cracked.

"This is a mess," Gregor said under his breath.
"Maybe we should ring again. I don't think they heard
us."

"They heard us," Tibor told him. "Someone will be
down in a minute. It is a mess."

"Maybe we can come over here next week and clean
this vestibule up," Gregor said. "What could it take? A
couple of hours and twenty dollars worth of ammonia?"

"You don't think we should agitate for the landlord to
clean it up himself?"

"I think we should do that, too. I think we should get
him for neglect. Are there laws like that?"

"I don't know," Tibor said.

"There ought to be." Gregor pointed at the bright silver bow. "I'm surprised Donna didn't tell us. She must have been here."

There was a sound of footsteps coming down stairs on the other side of the door. Gregor and Tibor looked through the fire glass at a young girl in an unfashionably long dress coming toward them. Her hair was piled on top of her head in a pair of braids, and that was unfashionable, too, as was the fact that her face was clean of makeup. Unfashionable or not, Gregor had no trouble discerning what had first attracted Joey Ohanian to Sofie Oumoudian. The girl was lovely.

She came to the door, opened it up, and stood back to let them enter.

"We are very honored to have a visit from two such distinguished men," she said in an Armenian Gregor could just about understand. "We are afraid we will not be able to offer you the hospitality which you deserve."

"We need no hospitality," Tibor replied, in an Armenian just as formal, "except the grace of your company and the company of your aunt."

"My aunt and I have no grace," Sofie said, "but if it is the will of God we will please you." Then she looked from one to the other of them, broke into a wide smile and said in English, "There. We have gotten that over with. Now Aunt Helena can not fault me for being rude. Hello, Father Tibor. How do you do, Mr. Demarkian. Joey Ohanian has told me very much about you."

"Joey Ohanian had told us a lot about you," Gregor said.

Sofie blushed. "He is nice, Joey Ohanian. He gives me much help. And I need help. You can tell, my English is not good. You will come upstairs?"

"That's what we're here for," Gregor said.

"We will be honored," Tibor said. "Krekor, please, mind your manners."

"I never had any."

"Aunt Helena won't notice. She's been running around

for a week, like a—I can't remember—like a—now I have it—yes—like a chicken with its head cut off. Because the priest and the famous man are coming to the apartment together. She even got the tea glasses out."

"Tea glasses," Gregor marveled. "I haven't seen tea glasses since I was a boy."

"She has beautiful holders for them," Sofie said, "what do you call them, like the holders they have here for ice-cream soda glasses, but not exactly. I remember. A zarf. My English is very bad. Joey told me about the zarf. In Armenian there is another name for them and in Russian there is another name for them yet. It's quite confusing. My grandmother's are made from sterling silver, brought all the way from London before World War One."

"How did your grandmother manage to keep them?" Tibor asked. "What with the Turks—"

Sofie Oumoudian laughed. It was a beautiful laugh. It sounded like music. Gregor thought that if Joey Ohanian wasn't in love for good, he was a damn fool.

"There is a story in my family that when the Turks came, my grandmother was so anxious to save the tea glasses, she had my grandmother bury her in the root cellar along with them and after it was over it took the village three days to get her out. My aunt Helena says that any time anything terrible happens to Armenia, it falls square on the heads of the Oumoudians. That's why we came to America. Aunt Helena said God was telling us to move."

The second-floor landing was as dirty and neglected as the foyer, but it was a little brighter, because the door to the Oumoudians' apartment sported a wreath the size of a child's inflatable swimming doughnut. This Gregor was certain was the work of Donna Moradanyan, because he had seen her making it—and five or six others like it—on her kitchen table less than a month before. Donna had made two kinds. One had cherubs and bells and silver Christmas trees. The other had menorahs and Stars of David. Bennis had taken one of the kind with menorahs on it.

The Oumoudians had received a more conventional Christmas one. Gregor had no idea what somebody like Rabbi Goldman would think of a Hanukkah wreath.

"Before we go in," Sofie said, "do you mind if I ask you a question?"

"Of course not," Gregor told her.

"It's about this visit of yours. Which is because of Joey. It is also because of—of my wallet being stolen?"

"More than once," Gregor reminded her. "At knife point."

"Yes," Sofie said. "I know. Well. And I know I should have told Aunt Helena the truth, you see, but I did not. She thinks I had my pocket picked. She is an old woman, do you understand?"

"I take it you don't want us to tell her the truth," Gregor said.

"You can tell her the truth," Sofie said, "but I would appreciate it if you would tell her in such a way that she will not want me to stop going to school. I very much want to go on going to school. In Armenia, when I was growing up, we had the European system, and at eleven we took our examinations and those of us who did not pass them were not put in the classes to go on to university. But here, I have talked to a counselor at the school, and she says that there is no problem. If I want to go to a university, I can take new tests, and if I pass them there are places where I can get the money. And so—"

"Sofie?" a voice said from the other side of the door. "Why are you so long in the hall?"

Sofie blew a stream of air into the bangs that hung over her forehead. "Of course, I would like a lot of things," she said. "I would like a skirt as short as the ones the other girls wear. I would like to go to the movies with Joey without a chaperon. Maybe none of these things are possible."

"I think we can at least manage to keep you in school," Gregor said.

"Although perhaps not *that* school," Tibor amended.

"Sofie?" Helena called from the other side of the door again.

Sofie put her hand on the knob. "She has put on all her lace and taken out her cane," she warned them. "You'd better be prepared."

FIVE

1

The dreidel was stuck in the thin plastic bag the cleaners had put over Lotte's favorite rose tweed jacket. DeAnna Kroll took it out and looked at it. *Nūn, gīmel, hē, shīn. Nes gadol hayah sham.* "A great miracle occurred there." It was amazing what you picked up just hanging around people. DeAnna could remember years in her life—in her *adult* life—when she hadn't known a lot of words in English, never mind being able to reel off a sentence in Hebrew, never mind being able to recognize four letters in a different alphabet. There had been years in her adult life when she hadn't even known there were other alphabets. There had never been a time when she hadn't known about room service, though. Before she'd been able to afford it, she'd dreamed about it.

"Go to your own room," she told Maximillian Dey, who was still standing in the middle of hers. "I want to get some rest. Once we start working, we won't stop again until Hanukkah."

The room in question was the one DeAnna always took in the Sheraton Society Hill, which was her favorite hotel in Philadelphia, mostly because the room service was unbelievable. The room was full of stuff—Lotte's clothes, so she didn't have to bring them all the way out to David's; props for the show; her own luggage—but the bed was clear and the phone was in plain sight and she had a copy of *Vanity Fair* in her totebag. If she could only get Max out of here, she could be in heaven. She just didn't feel right about throwing him out on his ear. After all, he'd helped her get all this stuff up here. His job was to move the show, not the executive producer.

He was standing in the middle of the carpet, his hands in the pockets of his jeans, scowling fiercely. With Max, fierce never looked too fierce. There was something about his face that was much too young.

"It is a terrible thing," he was saying, as he had been saying, over and over again, since they left New York. "One minute I am on the subway, the next minute I am on the sidewalk, and there it is. There it is not. It is gone."

"Right," DeAnna said.

"It is as I have tried to tell you," Max said. "It is a terrible thing. It is an outrage."

"I know."

"Everything I have is gone. Everything."

"I know."

"My money. One hundred and two dollars."

"Do you need money, Max? We could get you some money."

"Thank you. I do not need money. My green card, it is also gone."

"You told me."

"And my pictures of my sisters and my mother that I carry all the time. That they sent me from Portugal."

"It's a shame."

"What will I do now if I want their pictures with me? Write to Portugal to get others?"

"That's an idea."

"What will I say to them, my mother and my sister? That my wallet is stolen? They will think this city is full of thieves."

"It's not this city, Max. We're in a different city now. And they're both full of thieves."

"I could tell them I have lost the pictures, but then they will think I am careless. They will think I no longer respect them. I will get a letter from their parish priest."

"Because you lost a couple of pictures?"

"There it is not like here," Max said. "There we believe in honoring our mothers. Especially our mothers. The wallet was made of real leather. I bought it in Manhattan. It cost me twenty-six dollars I should not have spent."

"Of course it did."

"It is the only grace that I am too poor a man to have a credit card. I have finally found the virtue in poverty all the nuns talked about."

"Is there a virtue in starvation, Max? Because I'm really hungry here. I'm really hungry."

"In my wallet there was also my library card and my membership card for the Museum of Natural History. It is a scandal, I tell you that. It is an outrage."

It is an outrage, DeAnna thought, sitting down on the bed and picking up the dreidel. Sometimes she wondered what it was like, living in a place where even poor people were innocent. Sometimes she wondered if she would have done the things she had done here if she had been there. *Here* meaning the United States. *Here* meaning a place where poor people were definitely not innocent, not even as children, because they lived in a sea of dope and prostitution and firearms and crime. Then she reminded herself that there were probably no black people in Maximillian's village in Portugal, and from what she'd heard about Africa she wouldn't be happy there, either. Then she told herself she was tired, which was true. When she was tired she always wandered off into the metaphysical, getting melodramatic about her inability to solve the age-old questions of the universe. Good and evil. Wealth and poverty. Black and white. When she wasn't tired she concentrated on four orders of shrimp cocktail and a bottle of Montrachat.

Maximillian was still standing in the middle of the room. For some reason, when he looked sad he also looked very thin. In spite of all the swearing he did in Portuguese, he was still a boy, and frail.

"Listen," DeAnna said. "Have you got a room in this hotel?"

"Not in this hotel. Across the street. With Prescott Holloway and the man who drives the truck."

"Fine," DeAnna said. "Why don't you go over there and lie down for a while? Why don't you order dinner in your room and charge it to the show—"

"I can't charge it to the show, as you put it—"

"I'll call over and give them a credit card number to bill it to. Go ahead. Go relax. Tomorrow morning, everything's going to start to go crazy. You're going to be throwing furniture around for Shelley. We're going to have that Demarkian man in—"

"The detective," Max said shrewdly. "Everyone is saying you have brought him here to make a secret investigation into the death of Maria Gonzalez. He will catch her murderer and we will not have to talk to that foul man from the police department again."

"If Gregor Demarkian makes an investigation into the death of Maria Gonzalez, there'll be nothing secret about it," DeAnna said firmly. "Seriously, Max. It's ten thirty. We have to be over at WKMB at four thirty. Which means we all have to get up at four or whenever. I've been up since three o'clock in the morning. You have to be exhausted."

"I am angry," Max said, "therefore, I am not exhausted."

"Well, I am. Exhausted, I mean. Go over and get some rest and let me get some, too. Have a couple of drinks on me."

"I cannot have a couple of drinks," Max said. "In this state the drinking age is twenty-one."

"Oh, dear."

"It would not matter if I had my wallet," Max said. "In my wallet I have a driver's license that says I am twenty-one."

"You don't drive."

"I do not have the driver's license to drive."

"Just a minute," DeAnna said.

DeAnna kept most of Lotte's luggage as well as her own. Lotte went out to stay with David and brought only an overnight bag, so as not to burden Rebekkah with the need for too much storage. It wasn't just jackets and dresses from the cleaners, hung up on a moving rack. It was suitcases and boxes of files. For some reason, no matter who helped her bring these things upstairs, it was Lotte's stuff that ended up piled on top of DeAnna's and not the other way around. DeAnna threw Lotte's Coach weekender to the side and found her own Louis Vuitton double-zip. This was how you knew both she and Lotte had come from nowhere and ended up with money. They both bought ridiculously expensive suitcases.

DeAnna opened the side pocket of the double-zip and came up with a bottle of Glenlivet Scotch. She didn't much like Scotch and she especially didn't like Glenlivet, but she always got a Christmas present of the stuff from the women in the typing pool, and she didn't want to hurt their feelings. She handed the bottle to Max and said, "There. Go drink that."

"Thank you," Max said. He shoved the bottle into the pocket of his jean jacket. "Thank you very much."

"Get a little smashed and get some sleep," DeAnna said.

"If you don't mind, I will share this with Prescott and the truck driver," Max said. "If I tried to drink all the liquor in a bottle of this size, I would be very sick."

DeAnna didn't care if he shared it with a pet rabbit and a stray cockroach, as long as he went somewhere else before he got started. She pushed him gently toward the door.

"I'll see you at four thirty in the morning at WKMB."

"Four thirty. WKMB."

"Don't be too hung over."

"I am never hung over. I am a man."

DeAnna pushed him into the hall. "I am a woman, and no one ever lets me get any sleep," she said. "Go, Max. I'll see you tomorrow."

He was out in the hall. DeAnna gave him another gentle shove, just to make sure. Then she retreated into her room and shut and locked the door. For a moment, she was afraid he would knock and insist on talking some more, but it didn't happen. She heard him say something under his breath, and then he was gone.

DeAnna went back to the bed, sat down again, and picked up the phone. She had the room service menu in this hotel memorized. She knew exactly what she wanted. She was going to order enough food for a family picnic and eat until she passed out.

She picked up the dreidel and spun it, watching it whir like the top it was across the polished surface of the night table.

There were always a lot of dreidels around for Hanukkah, but this year there were millions of them.

The situation was ridiculous.

Carmencita Boaz was glad that Shelley Feldstein did not keep kosher. Carmencita had nothing against keeping kosher. Itzaak kept kosher and she accommodated him, as she accommodated him in everything. If it had been Itzaak she had been intending to have dinner with tonight instead of Shelley, Carmencita would have found some place that served kosher food and gone to it, even if it took a cab ride halfway to the Ohio border. Since it was past ten thirty and she was tired and hungry, though, she was just as happy that she and Shelley would be able to eat right here in the hotel, with no need to go out into the awful weather. Carmencita wouldn't have thought that the weather in the United States could get much worse than it got in New York, but she would have been wrong. This was her first trip to Philadelphia, and it was a shock. Cold. Wet. Slush. Muck. It bothered her that there were so many fewer decorations here than she remembered from New York, both in her old neighborhood and in the streets around the Hullboard-Dedmarsh building. Her neighborhood was so Hispanic, it took celebrating Christmas as its cultural birthright, and said so whenever city officials began to make grumbling noises about the separation of church and state. The people who occupied the buildings around the Hullboard-Dedmarsh, and who occupied the Hullboard-Dedmarsh itself, were mostly Jewish and entirely determined not to let the Christmas spirit overwhelm their own. They decorated for every Jewish holiday on the calendar except Yom Kippur. Of course, Carmencita told herself, there were probably neighborhoods in New York that were even more barren than this one was, and neighborhoods in Philadelphia that could put her New York paragons to shame. It was just that she had seen what she had seen, and she couldn't very well change her opinion until she'd seen something different.

The Sheraton Society Hill was built around a courtyard, with restaurant seating right in the middle of the big open space. Coming out of the elevators, Carmencita saw Shelley sitting at a table, looking over the notes she had written on a yellow legal pad. Shelley was Carmencita's vision of what it meant to be a Real New York Lady. Her pen was sterling silver and from Tiffany's. She kept her yellow legal pads in a thick black leather writing folder that had been bought at Mark Cross. Shelley's clothes made Carmencita want to cry. It wasn't that they were good. Carmencita believed that if she worked hard and did right, she would have the money to buy good sooner or later. It was that Shelley's clothes were so obviously suited only to a woman who was tall and spare, instead of small and round like Carmencita herself. Carmencita didn't know if there were sophisticated clothes for five-foot-tall, hourglass-figured Spanish women. Somehow, she doubted it.

She made her way around a large potted plant and up to the table where Shelley was still hunched over her notes, oblivious. When Carmencita sat down, Shelley looked up and blinked.

"Oh," she said. "There you are. I have this almost worked out, I think."

"Good," Carmencita said, "one less thing to worry about. I have been upstairs, pacing back and forth, worrying that I have forgotten something."

"All you have to remember is to get Mr. Demarkian on the set on time. Do you have the permissions yet?"

"No, I don't have the permissions. There is a great deal wrong with this plan, Shelley, if you ask me. Things that should have been worked out back in New York have not been worked out. As far as I can tell, this Mr. Demarkian isn't even sure if he wants to go on."

"Rebekkah said he'd go on," Shelly pointed out. "Rebekkah is never wrong."

"You're probably right." Carmencita sighed. "Still. I sometimes think I should not be doing this job. Someone with experience should be doing this job. I should be doing the job I was hired to do originally."

Shelley cocked her head. "DeAnna was going to make a suggestion to you. Did she make it?"

"About what?"

"About making Sarah Meyer your assistant. That still wouldn't get you back to doing the job you were hired to do, as you put it, but Sarah's been around for quite a while. She might know things that could help you."

"If she did, she wouldn't tell me," Carmencita said sourly.

"There is that."

"When Itzaak and I talk about who might have murdered Maria Gonzalez, who might have had a motive, the only one we can come up with is Sarah Meyer. She didn't like Maria. And she doesn't like me."

"She's just jealous, that's all." Shelley waved this off. "I don't know what to do about Sarah. Lotte doesn't know what to do about her, either. How do you tell a person that she's killing herself with her own attitude?"

"I don't tell her anything," Carmencita said. "She snaps at me, and I'm half out of my mind all the time now as it is. Not that I don't appreciate the vote of confidence. Not that I don't appreciate the promotion, either. But even so."

"You're doing a fine job. A better job than Maria was doing, if you want to know the truth. At least you don't turn off your beeper every time you have a date."

"Mmm," Carmencita said.

"What's that *mmm* supposed to mean?"

Carmencita shrugged. "Maria always said she didn't turn off her beeper. Not on purpose, at any rate. I don't think she was trying to put herself out of reach. I think she was just bad with machines."

"Maybe. And, of course, that last night—" Shelley shuddered. "That last night. Do you think Gregor Demarkian will agree to put on his suit of armor and ride to the rescue?"

"I don't see how he could," Carmencita said reasonably. "Maria was murdered there, and we're here."

"I know. But anything would be better than that police detective. Or whatever he is. That awful man."

Carmencita agreed that he was an awful man. "He bothers Itzaak all the time, and it's just not right. Itzaak has his head full of images of the old Soviet Union and the secret police. He can't handle it."

"I don't think our friend Chickie likes Jews."

"Whatever it is he doesn't like, he ought to keep a better lid on it. It's bad enough having the police around every minute of the day, and Maria dead."

"And the one time something happens that we need the police for, they're not there." Shelley laughed. "Poor Max and his wallet."

Carmencita dismissed Max and his wallet. She dismissed Itzaak, too, in her mind, because if she started thinking about Itzaak she would never get anything done. She was feeling very guilty about Itzaak right now. He had asked her to have dinner with him on the bus, and he had been very insistent. She had already agreed to have dinner with Shelley, and it was a dinner to work, so she said no, but she wished she hadn't had to. When Itzaak got that insistent, he always had something to tell her that he considered important.

She had brought her briefcase down with her from her room. It was not a very good briefcase. She had picked it up cheap in a pawn shop on the edge of Harlem, but it had been cheap even when new. She got out the file she'd labeled "Demarkian—Details." Before she'd taken over Maria's job, she'd had no idea how many particulars there were to gather on every invited guest. What Lotte didn't need, Shelley did, and what Shelley didn't need, Itzaak did. Carmencita kept expecting to see someone rush into her office, waving papers in the air and declaring an emergency, demanding to have the guest's blood type the day before yesterday. It would have made as much sense as some of the things people did ask for.

The particulars on Gregor Demarkian that Carmencita had for Shelley Feldstein were height, weight, hair color, eye color, waist circumference, and shoe size. She also had a measurement she didn't usually take, but that she'd come across accidently and immediately seen was important. The measurement was of Gregor Demarkian's chest. Carmencita had found it in an ancient copy of *People* magazine, in a story about a murder Demarkian had solved during a Fourth of July party at the summer home of a movie star. That was a little intimidating, that was. That Gregor Demarkian went to Fourth of July parties at the summer homes of movie stars.

Carmencita pushed the detail sheet across the table until it was right under Shelley's nose.

"Chest measurement," she said. "That's what I wanted you to look at."

"Very big," Shelley nodded. "Yes, it is. We'll have to be careful with that. If we aren't, he'll make Lotte look like a China doll."

"I'm not worried about Lotte," Carmencita said. "If she looks like a China doll, it's just fine, at least according to DeAnna, that is. It was the first thing I worried about when I saw the measurements. He is so big. Lotte is so small. But we don't have to worry about that. DeAnna said."

"What do we have to worry about?"

"Herbert Shasta."

"Herbert Shasta?"

"He's the other guest. We were supposed to have four

of them. Serial killers, I mean, but we couldn't get the prison system to go along with it. You should have heard what the warden at the Florida State Penitentiary said. Anyway, all we got was Herbert Shasta, who was called the Allegheny Apache until the Apaches complained. Mr. Shasta used to murder very fat women and—um—commit acts on their dead bodies."

"Oh," Shelley said. "Well."

"Yes. Well. This is the problem. Mr. Shasta, you see, is very small."

"How small?"

"Five feet one inch tall. And slight."

"How slight?"

"One hundred and twenty-five pounds."

"One hundred and twenty-five pounds. I weigh more than one hundred and twenty-five pounds."

"Lotte weighs more than one hundred and twenty-five pounds," Carmencita said. "There are twelve-year-old boys who weigh more than one hundred and twenty-five pounds."

"Oh, dear," Shelley said.

"It would have been better if we could have gotten one of the other ones," Carmencita said. "There was a man in Texas who killed only women with red hair. He was six ten and built like King Kong. He would have been good. There was a man in Chicago who preferred Asian women in white jeans. He was six two and fat. He would have been good, too."

"Don't these guys ever kill anyone but women?"

"Of course they do. But we didn't ask them to be on the show, because the show is called—"

" 'Sex and the Serial Killer,' yes, I know."

"Mr. Demarkian is going to be sitting on that stage looking like a gorilla," Carmencita said. "He's going to make this Mr. Shasta look sympathetic. If we don't do something."

"Well," Shelley said with determination. "We'll just have to do something, won't we?"

"'We'll have to do something for more reasons than you know," Carmencita said, "because you see, when Mr. Demarkian shows up at the studio tomorrow, he's going to get something of a surprise."

"What kind of a surprise?"

"He doesn't know yet that Mr. Shasta is going to be on the program."

Shelley Feldstein cocked her head and grinned. "You know, Carmencita, I think you're going to make a world-class talent coordinator."

"If I don't get killed between six and noon and tomorrow morning," Carmencita said. "Can you fix this?"

"I don't know if I can fix it, but I can certainly help. Here comes the waitress. Think of something that you want to eat."

Carmencita didn't really want anything to eat, but she thought it would be impolite not to have something, so she ordered a chef's salad. Carmencita was the kind of person who ate when she was nervous and wasn't much interested when she was not, and now that Shelley seemed to be taking this little problem in stride, Carmencita was calmer than she'd been since she climbed into the limousine in New York.

Now if she could only think of some way to resolve all her problems with Itzaak, life would be perfect.

3

For Sarah Meyer, life would only be perfect if she woke up one morning and found out she was someone else. Dorothy Hamill. Madam Curie. Michelle Pfeiffer. Her own sister. Sometimes Sarah thought it would be enough to be herself, but transformed. Taller. Thinner. Smarter. Prettier. Something.

Tonight, she thought it would be enough if she could just get through Shelley Feldstein's door without anyone seeing her do it. It was taking forever when it shouldn't have taken any time at all. Sarah Meyer had never breached a lock with a credit card in her life. She wouldn't have known how to go about doing it, and she wouldn't have bet on her ability to carry it through even if she had known. When she wanted to get into somebody's room, she did it the easy way. She knocked. She tried the door to see if it was open. She used the key. The keys to the doors in this hotel were the electronic kind, that were programmed by computer and that you put into a slot and then pulled out quickly to get the knob to turn. Sarah had taken Shelley Feldstein's key out of Shelley Feldstein's purse's sidepocket when they were both heading downstairs in the elevator, and then when they reached the lobby Sarah had pretended to have forgotten something in her room and gone back up. Every woman Sarah had ever known carried her hotel key in that outside pocket of her purse if her purse had one, because every woman Sarah had ever known was more worried about being able to reach the safety of her room without delay if she was being followed than she was about someone stealing her key. If Shelley Feldstein had proved to be an exception, Sarah had backup plans.

The problem was, Sarah was no good at using electronic keys, her own or anybody else's. She pushed them in and pulled them out and grabbed for the knob, but it took her half a dozen tries before she got there in time. The mechanism didn't give you very long before it froze the door shut again. Sarah put the card in the slot again, pulled it out again, grabbed for the knob again. The little light on the jamb stayed green for a tantalizing few seconds and then switched again to red. The door remained locked.

"Damn," Sarah said under her breath. "Damn, damn, damn."

"Do you need some help with that?" someone said from behind her.

Sarah turned around to see a tall Hispanic man in a hotel uniform. She saw the napkin draped over his arm and realized that he must be from room service. DeAnna Kroll getting her shrimp, Sarah thought, and stood away from the door a little.

The man took the key card out of her hand. "Here," he said. "These are very tricky. A great many of our guests have trouble with them."

"Why do you use them?"

"It's cut our burglary rate by forty percent," the man said simply. "You can't do better than that." He shoved the key card in, pulled it out even more quickly, and grabbed the doorknob. It turned easily and the door swung open.

"There," he said. "You're in."

"Thank you," Sarah said.

"You've got to pull the card in and out very fast. Once the light goes green, the mechanism starts counting. Even though the card is still in the slot."

"Oh."

"You've only got five seconds to get the door open. Five seconds from when the light goes on. Remember."

"I will," Sarah said.

"Have a good night," the man said.

He turned away from her and started hurrying toward the elevators, keeping the arm with the napkin over it at an odd angle to his body. Sarah waited for him to turn the corner and then reached for the light switch just inside Shelley's door.

Have a good night, the man had told her.

Well, Shelley thought, she had every intention of having a good night, and with Shelley downstairs talking everything on earth over with Carmencita, she was going to have plenty of time to have a good night in.

And it figured, really, about Shelley and Carmencita.

Shelley had always been on the side of the enemy.

When Sarah had first broached the idea of taking over the job Maria Gonzalez eventually got, Shelley had told her not to be ridiculous.

SIX

1

Usually, when *The Lotte Goldman Show* wanted to bring a guest to the studio, it sent a limousine with Prescott Holloway driving. In Philadelphia, however, it saved Prescott Holloway to do personal errands for Lotte Goldman and DeAnna Kroll and sent a local driver. On this day, Carmencita had forgotten to make arrangements with local drivers—she really should still have been an assistant, in spite of her instincts—and Prescott had to go out after all. Gregor Demarkian didn't know anything about any of this. He knew only that it was five o'clock in the morning, that the weather was even more awful than it usually was at this time of year in Philadelphia, and that the neon menorah in Lida Arkmanian's ground-floor parlor window was blinking on and off. It was blinking on and off with a regularity that suggested it was supposed to blink on and off. It reminded Gregor of those churches in northern Florida, carved out of cinder-block ranch houses or nestled into the hollow shells of what had once been low-rent bars, topped by neon crosses that flashed like the signs of Las Vegas casinos. Churches like that had always made Gregor vaguely ashamed of Christianity. It had been his impression that Judaism was allowed to keep much more of its dignity.

Bennis was standing next to him in the foyer of their building when the limousine drove up. When it was safely parked at the curb, she grabbed him by the arm and pulled him out on the stoop.

"Let's go," she said, "before you lose your nerve."

"Where's Tibor?"

"He'll be here in a minute."

From the stoop, Gregor could see down Cavanaugh Street to Holy Trinity Church fairly clearly, in spite of the fact that there was a slight fog. As he watched, Tibor came out of the alley at the church's side that led to the rectory apartment at the back and came toward them at a brisk trot, the hem of his cassock waving. Gregor wondered what he was going to make the viewing public think of when the camera panned *The Lotte Goldman Show* studio audience. Of course, Tibor wasn't going to be the only clergyman present or even the only one in uniform. Gregor had laid down a few rules about this television appearance of his. One of them was that there had to be a reasonable number of people in the audience who were on his side. Rabbi David Goldman had promised to be there (in mufti). So had Father Ryan (in a Roman collar) and Father Yorgos Stephanopoulos (in full Greek Orthodox regalia). Gregor harbored the secret hope that all Lotte Goldman's planning would come to naught, the show he was supposed to be on would collapse, and what they would tape today would be a full hour of Lotte asking the priests about the sexual repercussions of wearing funny clothes.

The driver got out of the limousine just as Tibor reached it. The driver looked first at Tibor and then at Gregor and then walked up to the stoop where Bennis was standing.

"How do you do," he said, holding out his hand. "I'm Prescott Holloway."

"Bennis Hannaford," Bennis said.

"Father Tibor Kasparian," Tibor said.

"I'm Gregor Demarkian," Gregor said, and then wondered if it was customary in New York for limousine drivers to shake hands with the people they drove. Prescott Holloway looked like one of those men of whom it is said that they have "once seen better days." Maybe he was just trying to maintain his old sense of self-respect in the day-to-day grind of a job that had to be very difficult on the ego.

Prescott Holloway was opening the street-side passenger door of his limousine and helping Bennis in.

Father Tibor climbed into the car after Bennis. Gregor followed Father Tibor, waving away Prescott Holloway's offer of help.

"I'll be fine," he said. "I've gotten in and out of these things before."

"There's a television in this one," Father Tibor said, as Gregor settled himself into the rumble seat, "but not a VCR as there was in the one Bennis rented last year. Do you think there is a difference because of that, in the amount of money the car costs to rent?"

Prescott Holloway was just sliding in behind the wheel. "Actually, this car isn't rented. It belongs to *The Lotte Goldman Show*. We brought it down from New York."

"Does the show usually bring its own limousine when it travels?" Gregor asked.

"It depends on where it's traveling to," Prescott Holloway told him. "We brought two down here to Philadelphia, because Dr. Goldman would rather drive than take a train and she hates small planes. And, of course, if we drive we can do anything we want to the schedule, we don't have to depend on somebody else's departure times."

"It still sounds expensive," Bennis said.

"It's only to cities that are close. Philadelphia, of course. And Boston when we go there. And places in New Jersey and Connecticut. After we leave Philadelphia this year, everybody but me is going to get on a plane. Next stop, Kansas City."

"It's too bad that you don't get to go," Bennis said.

Prescott Holloway shrugged. "I got as much travel as I ever wanted when I was in the army. When the show goes on the road like this, I get to play backup driver for Mr. Bart Gradon himself, which means I get paid a great deal of money to do practically no work. It's a living."

"I suppose it is," Bennis said.

"Look at this," Father Tibor said. "In the window of Lida Arkmanian's front parlor. They are watching us."

Bennis took out a cigarette and lit up. "Of course they're watching us," she said. "They're all watching us. They probably set their alarm clocks to make sure they didn't miss us when we went. I wish we'd go."

"We'll go," Prescott Holloway said, shifting the limousine into gear.

That was the first Gregor realized that the car had not been turned off while it stood at the curb. Prescott Holloway had gotten out and handed his passengers in with the motor humming every minute. Surely that couldn't be safe? Bennis took a long drag on her cigarette and tapped her ash into the little silver cup imbedded in the armrest.

"Are you all right?" she asked him.

"I haven't had enough sleep," he said. "My mind has started to think it's in a *Columbo* episode."

"What?"

The car was pulling away from the curb, into the street, into the fog. Gregor closed his eyes and shook his head.

"Never mind," he said. "Never mind. I just seem to be going senile."

2

The first thing Gregor Demarkian noticed about the people at the WKMB studio where *The Lotte Goldman Show* was taping was how tense they were. The next thing he noticed was how many of them had not been born in the United States. Gregor did not jump to that kind of conclusion easily. He understood that children born and brought up in certain Hispanic neighborhoods in New York and Los Angeles spoke English with an accent as thick as that of anyone growing up in San Juan. It was getting to be a Stateside regional variation. In spite of being Hispanic, however, the young man who met them at the door of Studio C was definitely not American born and bred. He had the wrong kind of Spanish accent. The older man who was climbing through the beams above their heads hadn't been born in the United States, either. Gregor could recognize that accent anywhere. It was Russian.

The young woman who had brought them up from the street, Ms. Carmencita Boaz, also had the wrong kind of Spanish accent, but they already knew all about her. She had told them everything she needed to know as she was bringing them up in the elevator.

"People who don't work for Dr. Goldman don't realize what a wonderful person she is," Ms. Boaz had said. "They don't realize how compassionate and fair she is in every dealing she has. They see her on television and they hear her ask the questions that must be asked—because, of course, she is very professional, Dr. Goldman, that is why she has been so successful—but they hear her on television and they think she is tough."

Gregor saw Bennis and Tibor shoot glances at each other. He heard Bennis cough.

"All you have to do is look at our staff to see she isn't like that at all," Carmencita was going on. "Dr. Goldman is in the business of giving lifetime chances, really. To me. I came from Guatamala. I could have ended up working in a typing pool somewhere. To Itzaak. He had to escape from the Soviet Union back when there was a Soviet Union. His life was nearly destroyed. Even to Maria Gonzalez."

"Maria Gonzalez?" Gregor said.

"The one who died." Bennis sounded shocked.

Carmencita Boaz opened the door to Studio C and shrugged. "It is very bad that Maria was killed, yes, but that doesn't change the way she was hired. Dr. Goldman was an immigrant, you see. She understands immigrants. She looks after us."

"Only immigrants?" Gregor asked curiously.

A shadow seemed to cross Carmencita Boaz's face. "There are others, like Sarah Meyer, I suppose. But Sarah is none of my business."

Gregor was about to ask Carmencita Boaz what she meant by that, when the young man came to the door, hesitated for a moment, and then seemed to stagger. Gregor realized he was carrying a chair on his back. The chair was small enough to be mostly hidden when the young man faced front, but heavy enough to tilt him off balance. As Gregor watched, he dropped the chair and fell down hard on his rear end.

"Ouch," he said. It was a very Latin *ouch*.

Carmencita Boaz clucked her tongue. "Look at you, Max, you've come all apart again. You're all over the floor."

She meant the contents of Max's pockets were on the floor. Gregor leaned over and retrieved three dollar bills, a green card and a plastic wallet calendar with a picture of a naked woman on one side from the floor. He handed them over to Max and thought that the young man looked more than a little hung over.

"There you go," he said.

"Is this the detective?" Max said. "The one everybody says is going to investigate the death of Maria Gonzalez?"

"What?" Gregor asked.

Max stuffed the things Gregor had given him back into his pockets. "I could use a detective. I could use a very private detective who worked only for me."

Carmencita Boaz grabbed Gregor firmly by the arm. "No more of that," she said. "Max had his pocket picked just before we left New York, and he's been obsessed with it ever since."

"No," Max said. "It's not about that."

"Mr. Demarkian is due in makeup," Carmencita said firmly. "Aren't you supposed to be taking that chair someplace?"

Max looked at the chair for a minute and then picked it up again. "Shelley wants the blue chairs now. Is this believable? They're all the way downstairs in the truck."

Max staggered under the weight of the chair one more time and lurched past them out the door of Studio C and toward the elevators. Carmencita kept her hold on Gregor's arm and steered him—and in consequence Tibor and Bennis—across a floor crisscrossed with cables to another door at the back. It gave Gregor a chance to look at the set, which was nothing more than a platform with a few chairs and a coffee table on it, and a plain Sheetrock back wall holding up a small square painting of water lilies in a blond wood frame. Did it really matter what color the chairs were on a set like this?

The door at the back led to a corridor lined with Sheetrock that looked as if it had never been painted. There were no decorations of any kind hung on it. At the very back was a room with a glass wall looking out on the corridor. Through this glass wall Gregor could see a room furnished with cheap green couches and canvas director's chairs. Past the bad furniture was another door, also open.

Through it, Gregor could see the kind of high-tech padded chair favored by dentists and beauticians.

"Right in here," Carmencita Boaz said, shooing them in toward the director's chairs. "You may have makeup put on your face or not, Mr. Demarkian. It is your decision."

"Not," Gregor said definitely.

"I do have to tell you that makeup can make a large difference in the way you are perceived by a television audience. If you remember the stories about the presidential race between Richard Nixon and John F. Kennedy—"

"I *voted* in the presidential race between Richard Nixon and John F. Kennedy."

"Yes," Carmencita said. "Well. I should tell you that other guests may decide to be madeup just as you have decided not to. This decision on their part may have an impact on the way the television audience perceives—"

"—the other guests," Gregor finished up for her. "I know. Why do you sound like you're reading me my *Miranda* rights?"

Carmencita looked startled. "Oh," she said. "Oh, no. I did not mean anything like that. I am very sorry if I have been offensive."

"You haven't been offensive," Gregor said. "It's just that—"

"Now there are these papers that have to be signed," Carmencita interrupted him. She seemed to pull the papers out of nowhere, as if she had them up her sleeve. "For legal reasons, as you must understand, we cannot begin taping until we have your permission to tape. If you would sign on the third page and initial in the lower right-hand corner of every previous page."

"I'll have to read this," Gregor said cautiously.

Behind him, Bennis Hannaford snorted. "You've already read it," she said. "You've read it three times. I've read it twice. If you'd signed the one they sent you at the apartment, you wouldn't have to go through all this now."

"Maybe we should talk this over some more."

Carmencita was holding the papers in the air with one hand and a pen in the air with the other. Bennis grabbed both and held them out to Gregor.

"Sign the stupid thing. You can't get all the way to this point and back out. I'd kill you."

"I would also kill you," Tibor said. "Just before David Goldman killed me."

"Which would happen just before Rebekkah Goldman killed David. Gregor, you just can't do these things at the last minute. You just can't."

Gregor took the papers and pen out of Bennis's hands, initialed the lower right-hand corner of each page, signed on the line on the third page, and handed the whole mess back to Carmencita Boaz. She visibly relaxed.

"Well," she said. "There."

Gregor wondered what would have happened if he hadn't signed, but in a way he knew the answer to that question, so he didn't have to ask it. Tibor would stop speaking to him. Bennis would start yelling at him. Women up and down Cavanaugh Street would knock on his door for weeks, wanting to know why he had disappointed them in this terrible way for no reason at all. He doubted if *The Lotte Goldman Show* would have folded or that Carmencita Boaz would have lost her job, but he wasn't unaware that the suggestion that both things might happen if he did not cooperate had been floating in the air since he first shook hands with Ms. Boaz. He didn't really mind. Carmencita was undoubtedly paid to suggest such things.

"Well," she was saying again. "I will have some food sent down for you. Some coffee and some fruit. One of you would prefer tea?"

"I would prefer tea," Tibor said.

"Fine. That is fine. Some fruit and some tea and some pastry, then. We will need Mr. Demarkian on stage in about fifteen minutes, for lighting. That will be Mr. Demarkian alone."

"Of course it will," Bennis said. "I'm not going on television."

"I mean Mr. Demarkian without Dr. Goldman or the other guest," Carmencita corrected. "We will light again with all of you together in half an hour."

"Wait," Gregor said. "What other guest?"

Carmencita was backing toward the door. "Fifteen minutes," she repeated. "Only fifteen minutes. There's nothing to worry about at all."

"I'm not—" Gregor said.

Carmencita was already out the door. As her heels hit the hard floor of the corridor she began to move faster, so that she looked a little like those backup reels the silent movies had used to buy cheap laughs in the days before all that audiences wanted to see was one more bucket of blood in *Rambo LXVII*.

"Fifteen minutes," she said again.

Then she turned on her heel and ran down the rest of the corridor to the studio door.

3

The food came just as Carmencita Boaz said it would, in less than five minutes, on a big silver cart, with Tibor's tea in an elegant pewter pot nestled in a tiny electric blanket. The problem was that it was brought in by the sourest young woman Gregor had ever met, who introduced herself as Sarah Meyer and made it clear that bringing tea and oranges was far more menial work than anything she should have been doing. Her body language was so explicit it practically screamed. When it wasn't shouting about how shamefully she was underemployed, it was shrieking her dislike of Bennis Hannaford. Even Tibor noticed that,

which meant it must have been blatant indeed. Gregor noticed that Bennis didn't seem to mind. It occurred to him
that Bennis must have elicited a fair number of such re-
sponses in her time.

Bennis poured Tibor a cup of tea and handed it to
him. It was black and evil looking and made Tibor smile.
Then she poured Gregor a cup of coffee and handed it to
him. What she got for herself was another cigarette, long
and slim and taken from the sterling-silver Tiffany cigarette case her brother Chris had given her for her birthday
a few years back. Bennis never took cigarettes from that
case. She had a crumpled paper pack of Benson & Hedges
Menthols in the pocket of her skirt. Gregor could only
conclude that she had taken a dislike to Sarah Meyer equal
to the one Sarah had taken to her. Bennis was pulling out
all the stops.

If Sarah Meyer had noticed the bit with the cigarette
case, she gave no indication. She was looking over the
fruit on the cart and fiddling with a grapefruit knife. She
fiddled long enough for Tibor to finish his cup of tea and
hand the empty china back to Bennis for a refill. She fiddled long enough for Tibor to get his refilled cup and for
Bennis to finish smoking. Then she put the grapefruit
knife down on a butter dish and said to Gregor, "Look. I
know I'm not supposed to bother you. I'm only a secretary. I'm not supposed to bother anybody. But I want to."

"Bother me?" Gregor asked, confused.

"Ask you some questions. Necessary questions. Like
about what you're doing here."

"I'm appearing on a television show about serial killers."

Sarah Meyer looked disgusted. Don't hand me this
sort of crap, her look said. People have been handing me
this sort of crap for all my life. Gregor saw Bennis get out
another cigarette—from her regular pack this time—and
begin to look thoughtful.

Sarah Meyer had gone back to fiddling. She had a

white paper doily this time. "Everybody around here is saying you've been hired to look into the murder of Maria Gonzalez. Is that true?"

Gregor shook his head. "You can't hire me to look into anything. Nobody can. I don't hire."

"He doesn't investigate crimes for money," Bennis explained.

"You investigate crimes," Sarah Meyer insisted. "I've seen the magazine articles. You investigate crimes a lot."

Gregor nodded. "I do some consulting, that's true. But I don't charge for it. I'm not a professional."

"Are you doing some consulting here, about Maria?"

"Not yet."

"I don't understand."

Gregor's coffee was gone. He got up and poured himself another cup. "Nobody," he said carefully, "in any way connected to the death of Maria Gonzalez or to the investigation into the death of Maria Gonzalez, has asked me to consult with the investigation."

"But you know about it," Sarah insisted.

"I know about it."

"Did you read about it in the papers?"

"No," Gregor said. "I was informed about it first by an acquaintance, and I have heard a fair amount about it from Father Tibor here and from Rabbi David Goldman, who is—"

"Lotte's brother, I know." Sarah looked doubtful. It softened her fat face. "I just don't understand it. I really don't. Usually when the rumors are this strong, there's something to them."

"Maybe there is something to them," Bennis suggested. "Maybe Dr. Goldman intends to ask Gregor to consult, but she hasn't gotten around to it yet."

"Maybe," Sarah said, still looking doubtful.

"No matter what anybody intends," Gregor told them, "I have not as of now been asked and I do not as of now know much of anything about the case. Except that Ms. Gonzalez's wallet was stolen."

"What?" Sarah said. "Oh. Yes. Well. Maybe. Maria was always leaving things around places, if you know what I mean."

"No," Bennis said.

"She was really terribly disorganized," Sarah expanded. "I mean, it's a really bad trait to have in a talent coordinator, but there you are. She was always leaving things around and misplacing files and forgetting to switch on her beeper. It was a constant problem for everyone."

"I'm surprised she got the job in the first place," Gregor said. "I'm surprised she kept it."

"Oh, that." Sarah waved it all away. "That was just prejudice. Lotte likes to have pretty people around her and Maria was pretty. So is Carmencita. That's why she got promoted after Maria died."

"Ah," Bennis said.

"Carmencita is even worse than Maria was," Sarah went on. "She forgot to order the local limousines. That's why Prescott Holloway had to come down and get you this morning, and that meant Prescott wasn't out getting Lotte, and you can imagine the headaches that caused. Maria would at least have remembered the local limousines."

"That's good," Bennis said.

"This really isn't a very good place to work if you aren't physically perfect." Sarah sniffed. "Look at Max. He's supposed to do heavy lifting and cart the sets around and all that, and he can barely lift the stuff without giving himself a hernia. But he looks like someone who could have sat for Michaelangelo, so there you are."

"Mmm," Gregor said.

"I think she's prejudiced against Americans, too," Sarah said. "That's why she hires so many foreigners, right off the boat and everything. It's very discouraging, working for Lotte. It's enough to make me depressed."

"Why don't you quit?" Bennis took a long drag on her cigarette.

Sarah put the paper doily down and stood up straighter, getting ready to go. "They found Maria's body in the storeroom at the studio in New York," she said, "except it didn't make any sense, because people were going in and out of that storeroom all morning. DeAnna and Carmencita and Max. It wasn't until it was practically time to tape that anybody found a body."

"Maybe there wasn't a body for anybody to find," Gregor said.

"Maybe. But it's bothered me ever since. Doesn't it bother you?"

"No," Gregor said firmly.

"Listen," Father Tibor said. "Somebody is screaming."

"I think it's just machinery going wrong someplace," Bennis put in.

But Bennis was wrong. It was a high-pitched piercing wail and it went on and on forever, steadily and without a break, but Gregor had heard screams like it before.

Gregor was pretty good at following sound. He'd had to do it often enough in his life. He'd spent all those years on kidnapping detail. He could tell right away that the sound wasn't coming from the studio.

The corridor went to the left of this door as well as straight ahead. Gregor went left and listened as he walked, making sure the sound got louder and louder, sharper and sharper. It had begun to waver, but that was to be expected. The human voice can only do so much before it begins to fail. All along the corridor, people had come out of their offices. They stood frozen in their open office doors, not knowing what to do. Gregor went past them without saying a word and came to a stop in front of a door marked "Men."

"In here," he told Bennis Hannaford, who had come to a stop behind him. "You stay out."

"Like hell I will."

"You can't go barging into a men's room."

Of course, Bennis could most certainly go barging into a men's room. She'd done it before and she would undoubtedly do it again. Gregor didn't have the time to argue with her.

He pushed the door open and stepped into a room that seemed to be tiled on the walls, floor, and ceiling. He went around a gray metal privacy barrier and looked into the main room. The first thing he saw was a row of ornately painted urinals taking up one entire wall. The second thing he saw was the body of the boy called Max, spread out under a window at the far end, its face smashed into pulp.

The third thing he saw was a grossly pathetic small-time serial killer named Herbert Shasta.

Herbert Shasta was screaming like a stuck pig.

PART TWO

I Am Curious,
Demarkian

ONE

1

Bennis Hannaford sometimes gave Gregor Demarkian detective novels to read, leaving little piles of paperback books on his kitchen table when he wasn't looking, wrapping up half a dozen hardcovers in red foil and a bow and putting them under his Christmas tree. Since Bennis was a puzzle addict and not a devotee of the real, Gregor had been introduced to every master detective from Sherlock Holmes to—he couldn't remember to who, because he hadn't read them in order. What he did remember was that all these fictional detectives shared the same attitude toward the police, and it was negative. Even his favorite, Nero Wolfe, considered the professional law enforcement community a pack of mental defectives who had somehow gone into competition with him in the solving of unusual murders. Gregor couldn't understand it. In his experience, the professional law enforcement community was made up of wonderful people—and not only because he'd once been part of it. There had been exceptions, but Gregor thought most of the policemen he had met were smart. They knew what they were doing. They were rarely squeamish about doing it. They had access to a lot of very helpful high-tech equipment. Best of all, they had the authority. That was why Gregor was always happy to see the police in situations like this one. They had the most important kind of authority of all, the right to make people get out of the way and keep them there. By the time the police showed up at Studio C of station WKMB that morning, Gregor would have sold his soul for the ability to tell DeAnna Kroll to go to her room and stay there—and make it stick.

Meeting DeAnna Kroll was the second thing Gregor did after finding Max's body. The first thing he did was to grab Herbert Shasta by the coat collar and drag him out into the hall, shaking him as he went.

"Who does this man belong to?" he bellowed. "Who does he belong to?"

He didn't mean *belong to*, of course. Slavery was illegal and he knew it. He had no doubt, however, that the person he was looking for would know exactly what he did mean. And he was right.

It took no time at all for a short, compactly built middle-aged woman in a prison guard's uniform to come tentatively out of one of the doors farther up the corridor. She saw a large, angry man manhandling her prisoner and hurried toward them.

"Wait," she said. "Wait. You can't—"

"There's a dead man in there," Gregor Demarkian said, pointing at the men's room door.

The middle-aged woman blanched. The people leaning out their doors, watching the show, got very quiet.

The middle-aged woman's name was Karen Schell. It was on the thick black plastic name tag pinned to her uniform jacket above the breast pocket.

"Oh," she said. "Oh, God. Did he—"

"I don't think so," Gregor said.

"No?" Karen Schell looked confused.

Herbert Shasta was blubbering. "His face was smashed in. It was terrible. His *face* was smashed in."

"I was in the bathroom," Karen Schell said, blushing.

Gregor dumped Herbert Shasta on the floor where Karen Schell could get him. He tried to remember how Herbert had murdered his victims, and couldn't. In the jargon of the trade, Herbert had not been "one of his." Thank God. He looked up to see Bennis and Tibor at the back of the crowd, looking on. Bennis was trying to move forward. Tibor was holding onto the back of her shirt so that she couldn't. Gregor motioned to them both.

"Go call the police," Gregor said. "Don't call nine one one. Call the chief of police. Tell Tom Reilly you're calling for me and ask him to send me John Jackman—"

"John doesn't work out of Philadelphia," Bennis said quickly. "He works out of Bryn Mawr."

"He came back. I'm sorry, Bennis. I forgot you knew him. But he's the best the Philadelphia police force has and I know him. And with a case like this, the politics are such—"

"That you can get anybody assigned you want," Bennis finished. "That probably isn't exactly true, Gregor."

"Call Tom Reilly."

"Do you think they'll ever actually carry out a death sentence in the Commonwealth of Pennsylvania?"

Bennis spun around and walked away. Gregor sighed. Once, a long time ago, one of Bennis's crazier siblings had murdered their father, been arrested by John Jackman, been convicted by the state of Pennsylvania, and sentenced to die. This sibling was still not dead, because in spite of the fact that the Commonwealth of Pennsylvania had a death penalty, it never seemed to be enforced. For Bennis's sake, Gregor hoped that in this case it would not be. He didn't have time to think about it now.

"We've got to guard the door," Gregor told Tibor. "We have to make sure nobody goes in or out."

"I'm going to go in and I'm going to come out," a voice said, from way up the corridor, in the direction Bennis had gone.

The crowd that had begun to clog the passageway parted, and Gregor saw a tall black woman striding in their direction, looking as if a Sherman tank would have been insufficient to block her path. Gregor had to supress a smile. The woman was magnificent. Really. She was a vision in corn rows and flapping yellow silk, a carnival of necklaces and bracelets and dangling earrings, a symphony in silver and gold. She came to a stop two inches from where Gregor was standing and looked him up and down.

"Are you Gregor Demarkian?"

"That's right," Gregor said.

"I'm DeAnna Kroll. Get out of my way. I'm going to take a look at what's in there."

"Nobody's going to take a look at what's in there. Not until the police arrive."

"Even the police aren't going to take a look at what's in there unless I tell them to. Mr. Demarkian, I am the executive producer of this show. Nobody farts on these premises without asking my permission. Get out of my way."

"No."

"All right."

Gregor Demarkian was a very large man. He had been trained at Quantico by some of the finest experts in physical intervention in the world. He had also been sitting behind a desk for ten years before he went on leave to care for Elizabeth and had been retired for over three years since Elizabeth died. What DeAnna Kroll did was a moldy old trick taught to volunteer suicide counselors at walk-in street clinics, but Gregor didn't see it coming. One moment, DeAnna Kroll's hands were on his arms just below the shoulders. The next, Gregor was standing at the side of the door while DeAnna strode through it. He couldn't help himself. He admired the woman. He caught the men's room door before it shut completely and followed her inside.

When he got there, he found that she had stopped just where he had at first, at that spot where you come around the privacy barrier and get a full view of the rest of the room. The boy called Max was right where Gregor had left him, under the windows against the far wall. He was just as dead.

"Oh, God," DeAnna Kroll was saying. "Oh, God. Max. What a god-awful thing to happen to Max."

"Don't get sick here," Gregor told her. "Don't do anything here. The less there is to confuse the issue for the police—"

"Did that son-of-a-bitch do it? Shasta?"

"I don't think so."

"Why not?"

"Because like most serial killers, Mr. Shasta has a fairly fixed modus operandi. He wasn't my case, so I'm not sure of all the particulars, but I do remember he likes fat women, not thin boys. And he kills with an ice pick to the back of the neck. Not a blunt instrument to the side of the head."

DeAnna blanched. "Don't they just go crazy sometimes, these guys? Don't they just go on rampages?"

"Some of them do. But it's usually the psychotic ones that get that way—"

"Killing fat women with ice picks isn't psychotic?"

"I meant delusional," Gregor said patiently. "Some of these people hear voices and see visions. Most of them don't. And none of them goes on a rampage, as you put it, unless his cycle is played out."

"What does that mean?"

"It means that most of them get faster as they go along. At first they kill once every few months. Then it's once every month. Then it's once a week. Then—"

"Wonderful," DeAnna Kroll said. "Just wonderful.

Everybody's going to think it was Shasta who did it, aren't they?"

"Let's just say that unless the Philadelphia police find some very good hard evidence, any first-year law associate worth the paper his degree is printed on could use Mr. Shasta to get anybody but Mr. Shasta off."

"The police aren't going to be worth shit," DeAnna Kroll said. "You. That's who I want. You're going to find the hard evidence."

"Ms. Kroll—"

"This way," DeAnna Kroll said.

She gave Max's body one last look and then went back out to the corridor, slapping the door open with the palm of one hand and dragging Gregor after her with the other. The strength in her hands was phenomenal. Gregor knew men who had worked for years with hand grips and hadn't got as strong as this. When they were both out in the corridor, DeAnna stopped and looked out over the crowd. It was now so thick, it had to include people who hadn't been in the studio when the fuss had started. The grapevine must be all wound up and chugging along. DeAnna stuck her free hand on her hip and shouted. She did not have a gentle voice.

"Now listen to me," she boomed. "I want every last one of you out of this hallway. Out. Back in your offices. Back to work. No exceptions. Do you hear me?"

"Not Tibor," Gregor said.

DeAnna looked down at Father Tibor Kasparian, hovering anxiously at Gregor's free elbow. "You can stay," she said. "But the rest of you have got to go. Now. Right away. We'll call you when the police get here."

"Nobody should use the men's room," Gregor reminded her.

"Oh, shit," she said under her breath. "Okay, people," she shouted. "The men's room is off limits. Absolutely off. Use the women's if you have to and post a lookout. Or something." She lowered her voice again. "Christ. This feels like camp."

"I can't guard this room," Tibor said. "I am too small."

"When Bennis comes back she can help you," Gregor told him.

Tibor gave him a reproachful look. "The person I am most in need of guarding this room against is Bennis, Krekor. You know that."

DeAnna dropped Gregor's arm and rubbed her face with her hands. "Come on," she said. "Now we have to go do the hard part. Now we have to go talk to Lotte. And *explain* things."

That was the first time Gregor realized that he had not seen Lotte Goldman, not even once, since he set foot in Studio C of WKMB.

2

Gregor Demarkian knew nothing about television, cable or broadcast, national or local, network or syndication. He had no idea whatsoever how television people did things. Maybe it was customary for the star of a show to hide from her guests until it was time for the taping to begin. Maybe it was customary for the executive producer of a show to treat her subordinates as if they were new recruits to the United States Marine Corps and she was a drill sergeant. Maybe anything. Gregor let himself be dragged along, into new corridors and unknown territory. DeAnna Kroll was a force of nature. Like typhoons and tidal waves, nothing that got in her way was left standing.

"Here we are," she said, stopping in front of a plain door. Gregor was a little disappointed. He'd expected to see a star pasted on it. DeAnna knocked loudly and called out, "Lotte?"

"Come right in," a soft, thickly accented voice said. "I have been waiting."

DeAnna Kroll opened the door and pushed Gregor through it. "I came as fast as I could. That friend of his went off to call the police."

Lotte Goldman's office—or dressing room, or whatever it was—was far less alien territory than the rest of the studio had been. For one thing, it reminded Gregor a little of Cavanaugh Street when Donna Moradanyan had been at work on it. Lotte Goldman might only be occupying this space for a couple of weeks. She might have taken possession of it only a few hours ago. She had already taken pains to decorate it. A carved wooden menorah sat on the desk with nine unlit candles standing in the holders. The candles were white and sleek and slim, like abstract impressionist swans. At one side of her desk, Lotte had a book stand of the kind usually sold to hold large dictionaries. Open on top of it was an ornately illustrated book—illuminated, in the medieval sense—that promised to tell "The Story of the Victory of the Maccabees." Gregor's Jewish history was sketchy, but he knew that Hanukkah was the holiday that commemorated the miracle of a single jar of oil that had been only enough to last for one day but that had lasted for eight. After that, he got a little confused. He made a mental note to ask David Goldman to explain it all to him before the season was over.

On the window that looked out on the gray Philadelphia morning, Lotte Goldman had a bouquet of evergreen branches tied with a bright green ribbon. Since it was not a wreath, Gregor supposed it was suitably removed from the celebration of Christmas not to be offensive. Lotte had been standing next to this bouquet when Gregor and DeAnna walked in. She crossed the room to her desk, put her cigarette down in a glass ashtray, and held out her hand.

"Mr. Demarkian," she said. "I am Dr. Lotte Goldman."

"How do you do," Gregor said.

"We really don't have a lot of time to be polite,"

DeAnna said. "The police are likely to be here any minute."

Lotte Goldman picked up her cigarette and took a nice, deep drag. "I heard it was Max," she said slowly, "Max dead in the bathroom. Sarah came by—"

"Sarah would," DeAnna said.

"—and said that his face had been smashed in. Just like Maria's."

Gregor cleared his throat. "Dr. Goldman," he said carefully, "I think, at this point, that it might make sense not to jump to conclusions. It's possible, of course, that you're correct. That the two deaths are similar and therefore in some way connected—"

"Similar," DeAnna Kroll said.

"DeAnna found the body of Maria Gonzalez," Lotte Goldman said.

"And similar isn't the word for it." DeAnna had grabbed Lotte's cigarette pack and taken out a cigarette to light herself. "Identical, that's what I'd call it. Exactly the same kind of wound on exactly the same place on the head. And the cheekbone smashed—Lotte, I'm sorry."

"No," Lotte said. "Don't be sorry. We have to tell him. If we don't tell him, what good will he be able to do us?"

"We could get the New York police to tell him."

"Pffut." Lotte waved this away. "You remember the New York police. That awful man. That anti-Semite. He is only interested in annoying Itzaak."

"Itzaak is our lighting man," DeAnna explained. "He immigrated here from Israel and to Israel from the Soviet Union—"

"I know somebody who did the same thing," Gregor said.

"Yeah. Well. Lots of people did the same thing. Before the Soviet Union fell, anyway." DeAnna sighed. "Lotte's right. This guy in New York is just—well, he is just, that's all. Going on and on about how Itzaak might be an illegal alien."

"Is Itzaak an illegal alien?" Gregor asked.

"Of course not," Lotte said. "David was his sponsor. I know all about how Itzaak got here. This man in New York is just—"

"A bigot," DeAnna said definitely. "The bodies did look alike, Mr. Demarkian. I'm not saying that just to get you involved in this."

Gregor thought it over. "What about the body of Maria Gonzalez? Wasn't that in a closet?"

"It was in the main storeroom in our studio in New York," Lotte said. "But the police told us the body did not start out there, and I think they were right. There were people going in and out of that storeroom for hours before the body was discovered."

"Before *I* discovered the body." DeAnna made a face. "And before you ask, the answer is no. There was no place to hide a body in that storeroom. If it had been there, somebody would have seen it."

There was a stiff, formal little chair in front of Lotte's desk. Gregor sat down on it. "Think back about it. About the studio where the body was found in, say, the hour before it was found. Was the studio crowded?"

"Not crowded," DeAnna Kroll said. "There were people around."

"In the last half hour it was getting very full," Lotte corrected. "Some of the secretaries had started to come in."

"But it wasn't as crowded as it would have been once the regular day crew arrived," DeAnna put in.

"What about in comparison to right here, right now," Gregor asked them. "Was it as crowded as this?"

"Oh, no." Lotte shook her head. "Here you have our people and also the regular people from WKMB. This studio is connected to six others and four of them are in use.

In New York, we have only the one studio and the one crew to service it."

"A station like WKMB rents studio space," DeAnna explained. "In the off hours, which these are. They're not really used for anything but a show like ours or the local news. So here you've got us, and people from WKMB, and the renters."

"If what he wants to know is if it would have been easy for the murderer to move Maria's body into the storeroom," Lotte said, "the answer is no."

Actually, Gregor wasn't worried about how Maria Gonzalez's body had been moved into the storeroom. He could think of a dozen ways that could have been done, by the right kind of person with a good grip on his nerves. He was more interested in the timing of this murder and what that said—combined with the murder of Maria Gonzalez and assuming the two had been committed by the same murderer—about this murderer's state of mind.

"It's as if he likes crowds," Gregor said. "It's as if he were a magician used to working in danger of exposure. I saw this boy, this Max—"

"Maximillian Dey," DeAnna said. "He was from Portugal."

"Yes. Well, I saw him when I arrived. He was carrying a chair and complaining about having his wallet stolen."

"He had his pocket picked on the subway in New York," Lotte said. "Just before we came down here—just before. He was on his way to meet us when it happened."

"Why was he moving a chair?"

"Because Shelley Feldstein's crazy," DeAnna said. "She kept changing the set. She's our set designer. She was worried that you were going to look too menacing, you know, being as—uh—tall as you are. Next to Lotte and—um—"

"Mr. Shasta," Gregor said.

"Yeah," DeAnna said. "Exactly."

"Where would Mr. Dey have taken this chair?" Gregor asked them. "Is there a storeroom here, too?"

"There is, but he wouldn't have taken the chair there," DeAnna said. "It wasn't a chair that belonged to WKMB. It was a chair that belonged to us. We brought it from New York."

Gregor raised his eyebrows. DeAnna shrugged.

"I told you Shelley was crazy. She really gets into the stuff. Of course, she's also good."

"She's the best in the business," Lotte said.

"Any day now, she's going to start free-lancing and we're not going to pay enough to stay on her schedule." DeAnna was glum. "Doesn't that figure?"

"Back to Maximillian Dey," Gregor told her. "Where would he have taken that chair?"

"To our truck," DeAnna said. "It's parked downstairs. There's enough furniture in it to set up a couch franchise."

"Fine. He would have taken this chair all the way down to street level to the truck, and then what?"

"He'd have left that chair in the truck and gotten whatever chair it was Shelley wanted and brought it up," DeAnna said.

"Did he do that?"

"Did he do what?" Lotte asked.

"Did he bring the new chair up from the truck? Did he even get the old chair down to the truck? Do either of you know?"

DeAnna and Lotte looked at each other. "No," they said.

"Of course," DeAnna ventured, "Shelley didn't come to me to complain. So I suppose he must have at least—"

"At least what?" Gregor asked.

"I don't know," DeAnna admitted. "Shelley being Shelley, you'd have to ask her. Maybe Max brought the old chair down and the new chair up and that's why she didn't complain, or maybe she had her mind on something else."

"Mr. Shasta arrived just a little after Mr. Demarkian did," Lotte reminded DeAnna. "Perhaps her mind was taken up with him."

"Perhaps everybody's mind was taken up with him," DeAnna said. "What a weird little man."

"Can you think of any reason why anybody would have wanted to kill Maximillian Dey? Any harm he might have done anyone? Any information he might have it might have been dangerous for him to know?"

"Maximillian Dey was less than twenty years old," Lotte Goldman said. "The only harm he ever did anyone was the heart palpitations he gave girls his own age the first time they saw his face. And as for information—"

"He moved furniture," DeAnna said flatly. "Anything he knew, everybody else knew."

There was a knock on the door. Lotte Goldman dumped the burned-to-the filter stub she was holding into the ashtray and reached for another cigarette.

"Come in," she said.

Sarah Meyer stuck her head through the door and looked them all over.

"The police are here," she announced. "There's a big black guy looking for Gregor Demarkian."

3

His name was John Henry Newman Jackman, and he was not what most women would describe as "a big black guy," in spite of the fact that he was both big (six two, two hundred and ten) and black. When women looked at John Henry Newman Jackman, they tended to get specific. The first time Gregor had ever seen him—when Jackman was a rookie cop assigned to a serial killer task force Gregor was coordinating—Gregor had wondered in awe how he ever managed to get anybody to take him seriously. John

Henry Newman Jackman had the most physically perfect face Gregor had ever seen, on anybody, male or female, black or brown or red or yellow or white or green. It was so perfect it was almost an abstraction, The Human Face As Intended, as if God had decided to do it right just once so that everybody would know how it was supposed to be. Bennis always said that standing in front of John Jackman was like standing in front of a painting in a museum—but when John and Bennis were together, Bennis never looked to Gregor like museums were what she was thinking of.

All that was years ago, Gregor told himself firmly, and Bennis Hannaford's love life is none of my business. He turned the corner into the main corridor and was pleased to see that John was not only there but doing him proud. Usually, the police turned up at the scene of a homicide in a haphazard and uncoordinated fashion. The uniforms got there and called for the rest of the necessary personnel. The medical examiner's people and the fingerprint men and then evidence baggers and the homicide detectives all drifted through on no particular schedule. From what Gregor could see, John had organized this foray the way a general would organize a battle. The door to the men's room was open and guarded by a man in uniform. The evidence men were standing in the hallway, holding onto their equipment and waiting their turn. The medical examiner's people were already with the body. John Jackman himself was just coming out of the men's room, scratching his head.

"Gregor, for God's sake, what is this? I expected the queen of England, at least."

"Not the queen of England," Gregor told him. *"The Lotte Goldman Show."*

"What did you say?"

"The Lotte Goldman Show," Gregor repeated.

"Oh, shit."

"There's a minor league serial killer named Herbert Shasta in one of the rooms down there," Gregor pointed over his shoulder, "and before the show left New York they seemed to have had a murder that was just like this one, and that's only for starters—"

"You're giving me a migraine."

"—and Bennis is around somewhere—"

"Ouch."

"So I think we'd better talk."

John Henry Newman Jackman heaved out a sigh that would have done credit to Moses going up the mountain to collect the Ten Commandments for the second time.

"You're right," he said. "We really had better talk."

TWO

1

Hanukkah is also called the Festival of Lights, and because of that Rebekkah Goldman took the liberty of bathing her own house in lights, even though they were what other people would call Christmas lights. The house was in Radnor, in a "good" neighborhood that was not really expensive. Expensive houses in Radnor tended to run to eight thousand square feet and cost two million five. Anyone driving by would have thought Rebekkah was just another Christmas decoration enthusiast. She had lights strung around the pillars on her front porch. She had lights strung wound around the evergreen bushes that made up the hedge that bordered the road next to her front yard. She even had lights on her roof. She also had a Star of David, solid and glowing, at the end of her driveway, but Lotte thought that was rather funny. The Star of David would have had to have been the size of the Liberty Bell to have had any effect against that background of electric twinkles. It was a good thing that the members of David's congregation were Conservative and not Orthodox, with leanings that sometimes drifted toward Reform. At any rate, they didn't mind. David and Rebekkah's children did mind, but in another way. They wanted more lights, not fewer, and if they were going to have Jewish decorations they wanted one of those big electric menorahs the delis had downtown. Like all children, they were less interested in symbolism than they were in ostentation.

Like most women getting on in years, Lotte Goldman was exhausted at the end of an ordinary day. At the end of a day like this—Maximillian dead, God help us, and the police, and Itzaak getting hysterical and confusion everywhere—she felt as if her bones had turned to chalk. She felt it even sitting in David and Rebekkah's living room, which was the one place on earth where she was truly comfortable. It always came as such a surprise to her to realize she was old. In her dreams, she was still no more than eight and still in the trunk of that car. Waking up in the morning, she always headed for the bathroom of the first apartment she had ever had in New York, when she was in her twenties and had so little money she had to choose between toothpaste and bread.

David and Rebekkah wanted to hear everything that had happened. David had been on the phone to his friend Father Tibor Kasparian for an hour, but now he wanted to hear it all again from Lotte's mouth. The problem was that no one wanted to discuss it in front of the children. The children were all still very young, because Rebekkah was still young. David told Lotte once that he thought he'd done it on purpose, married this woman who had not even been born on the night he left Germany, who had not been born in 1948 when the War of Liberation was going on in Israel, who had not been born in 1957 when David had fallen in love for the first time. Lotte told David it was a damn fool thing to be guilty about. Rebekkah was a beautiful woman who had given him beautiful children and he was lucky to have her.

Rebekkah finally got the children in bed at nine thirty. They were supposed to be tucked in an hour earlier than that, but with Lotte in the house they were more than a little overexcited. They were also not stupid. Lotte didn't know why adults thought children didn't listen to what was going on on the evening news. With the television blaring through the house the way it did and their own aunt's name mentioned right there in the leader. Abraham, especially, wanted to know all the details. Abraham was twelve and convinced of his capacity to understand far more than any adult ever could. Lotte also suspected him of watching her show on afternoons when Rebekkah was out at the store or meeting with one of his teachers. Abraham didn't have to be in bed by eight thirty, or even by ten, but he was supposed to be up in his room "reading or resting," as David put it. Lotte assumed he would creep downstairs at just the right moment and eavesdrop.

Lotte waited until all the children were upstairs, even though she thought it would be useless, and then brought her coffee into the kitchen and sat down at the kitchen table. This was one of those oversize houses that had been built in the 1980s, with too much closet space and a kitchen the size of Fort Ord. The kitchen opened onto a family room with a cathedral ceiling and a fieldstone fireplace. Even with the homey touches Rebekkah was so careful to add to every room in her house—the photographs of children and other family in silver frames; the souvenirs of the last trip she and David had taken to Jerusalem—Lotte felt she had nothing to anchor herself to. Lotte needed the walls to be closer to her, like plaster skin.

David and Rebekkah came down together, having said their good nights. When Rebekkah came into the kitchen, she picked up a plate full of cake crumbs that had been left on the counter next to the refrigerator and put it in the sink for the maid to find in the morning. Rebekkah had a maid to clean but not a woman to cook or a nanny for the children. She didn't trust anybody to be as kosher as she was herself.

"Bram is absolutely livid," she said, chucking a cake-encrusted fork into the sink after the plate. "I suppose we should stop treating him like such a child."

"We'll stop treating him like such a child after his bar mitzvah." David dropped into a chair across from Lotte at the kitchen table and reached for the coffee pot still waiting at the table's center. His cup was still waiting for him, too. Rebekkah was smart enough to know that it made no sense to clean David's coffee cup before David was ready to go to bed. Lotte always wondered how David managed to sleep after drinking all that caffeine. "So," David said. "I talked to Tibor. He says things are a royal mess."

"Tibor would never say 'royal mess,'" Rebekkah chided.

"I suppose 'royal mess' is as good a description of it as any," Lotte said. "But it's not as big a mess as the other one was, back in New York. At least this time we have help."

"Do you mean Gregor Demarkian?"

"I mean the police," Lotte said firmly. "I do not know how to describe to you what the police were like back in New York. This man here seems both honest and intelligent, and that's a relief. Not that it will help either Max or Maria."

"Maybe the police in New York were right." Rebekkah slid into a kitchen chair herself. "Even if they weren't honest or intelligent. Maybe it was an ordinary mugging—"

"I've told you why it could not have been—"

"Yes, Lotte, I know, but hear me out. You did tell me there wasn't any rape, didn't you?"

"Yes, Rebekkah. Yes, I did."

"I know you did. And I've been thinking about it, Lotte. I've been thinking about it ever since we talked last month. And it just doesn't make sense any other way."

"But how does this make sense?" David demanded. "Maria in New York. This boy Max in Philadelphia—"

"But we don't know that," Rebekkah insisted. "A blow to the side of the head—"

"The same kind of blow to the same side of the head," Lotte reminded her.

"All right," Rebekkah conceded. "But it's not exactly a fine Italian hand. And if you don't accept a pair of muggings and a pair of coincidences—"

"More than a pair," David said.

"—then you're stuck looking for a motive." Rebekkah was stubborn. "And that's where the conspiracy theories you two are hatching lose me. The motive. Who would want to kill Maria Gonzalez? Or Maximillian Dey?"

David poured himself another cup of coffee, poured it carefully, poured it slowly. Lotte watched in fascination as he shoveled four teaspoonsful of sugar into it.

"The motive," he said carefully, "may not be anything any of us would take as sane. That man who was there today—"

"Herbert Shasta," Lotte said.

"Herbert Shasta." David nodded. "He's only one of a tribe, from what I understand. There are hundreds of people like him out and around."

"What you're trying to say is that somebody on Lotte's show is a psychopath. Sociopath. Whatever you call them these days." Now Rebekkah was mulish. "I say that's impossible. The people on that show live in each other's pockets. If someone was that far off, the rest of them would know."

"I don't think that's true," David said. "Look at Ted Bundy."

"So look at Ted Bundy." Rebekkah threw up her hands. "Ted Bundy is one man, and he's very unusual. Look at the rest of them. Look at Charles Manson. Look at Jeffrey Dahmer. Look at David Berkowitz, for heaven's sake. They were all at least a little off and everybody knew it."

"But Rebekkah," Lotte put in, "it really is impossible. Two deaths like this, with everything so close."

"All right then. Tell me. What was the motive? Is it somebody who just doesn't like Spanish people? Then you've got another nut. What else could it be?"

"I don't know," Lotte said.

"I don't know either," David admitted.

Rebekkah got up from the table. "I'd be willing to go along with this if either one of you could think of just one thing—just *one* thing—that doesn't make these two deaths look like coincidental muggings. Just one thing. A fingerprint. A tire track. Something."

David winced. "Rebekkah wants the strange case of the dog that didn't bark in the nighttime."

Lotte looked down at her hands. A fingerprint. A tire track. Sherlock Holmes marching around in circles with a magnifying glass. There *was* something.

"Wait," Lotte said.

The coffeepot was empty. Rebekkah was rinsing it out, so that it didn't stain. Sterling silver was something else she took care of herself.

"Wait," Lotte said again. "I remember."

"Remember what?" David asked her.

They were both looking at her the way her television audience looked at her, expectant. Lotte felt the way she felt when she had to announce that the subject of today's program is "Is Broccoli an Aphrodisiac?" thereby disappointing everyone. But there was nothing to do now but get it over with.

"I remember," Lotte told them, "the dreidel."

2

Shelly Feldstein was not a superstitious woman, any more than she was a religious one. She believed in science and mathematics, physics and chemistry, PBS and the *New York Times*. Her unconscious but unshakable take on serial murderers was that she would know one if she ever saw one and have sense enough to run like hell. Her very conscious take on the present situation was that a couple of admittedly bizaare coincidences were being used in the relentless effort at self-agrandizement being perpetrated on the citizens of the United States by one Gregor Demarkian. Shelley had only met Gregor Demarkian for about a minute earlier that day, when DeAnna Kroll had introduced them and Shelley had shaken the great man's hand. He hadn't looked like such a great man to her and she hadn't liked him on any level. She hadn't expected to. Shelley Feldstein hadn't met Gregor Demarkian before this morning, but she'd heard about him. What she'd heard she didn't like. Shelley was a woman who believed in institutions. Significant scientific discoveries were made in the well-funded laboratories of government research facilities or university departments. Great literature was written with grants from the NEA. Crimes were solved by the police. Why the police chose to put up with G. Demarkian, Shelley would never understand. Shelley made a point of never having anything to do with anybody who was even so much as fifteen pounds overweight, if she could help it. Fat was an infallible indicator. Anybody who let himself get fat had to have something wrong with his character.

Shelley put up with Sarah Meyer because she was stuck with Sarah Meyer, just the way everybody else was. Shelley had discussed Sarah's weight with Lotte and been told her to mind her own business. Lotte was very European that way. Europeans didn't understand how important it was to bring the natural appetites under control.

Sarah didn't seem to care. Shelley had asked her down to the bar to take some notes. As soon as she'd gotten there, Sarah had ordered a turkey sandwich with mayonnaise and a glass of diet Coke. Shelley supposed the diet Coke was a step in the right direction, but the sandwich was something else. She hated to see fat people eat.

"You should have had a salad," she said to Sarah, unable to help herself any longer.

"I don't like salads," Sarah told her. "And besides, I can't eat them with one hand and take notes with the other."

"I'm sure we could break for fifteen minutes to let you eat a healthy dinner."

"I don't want to eat a healthy dinner. I don't like healthy dinners. And there's nothing unhealthy about a turkey sandwich."

"Mayonnaise is nothing but fat."

"You're not my mother, Shelley. You're not even my boss. If we're going to finish this memo, we ought to get on with it."

Shelley knew that if she had been the boss, instead of Lotte, Sarah would never have been hired. DeAnna Kroll might never have been hired, either. Shelley would have run a much tighter ship.

Shelley picked up the notes she had brought down from her room and turned a little to the side, so that she wouldn't see Sarah when she accidentally looked up.

"Carmencita is doing her best to find us another serial killer, but at this point we can't count on her being successful. Especially as long as there's a chance that Herbert Shasta—ah—"

"Offed Max," Sarah said helpfully.

"Whatever. You ought to be much more careful of the

language you use, Sarah. You'll never get anywhere really important if you sound like an illiterate street urchin."

"It's all because of my disadvantaged background," Sarah said sweetly. "Because I went to Wellesley instead of to Hunter."

"Lotte still wants to use Gregor Demarkian on a program," Shelley said, "whether or not we can get a serial killer for him to debate with, but that's going to have to wait, too. At least until the investigation is over. What we've decided to do is to go on tomorrow with what we were always going to go on tomorrow. The shoe fetishists."

"Marla Maples's manager was accused of being a shoe fetishist," Sarah said. "Did we get him?"

"No. We have three men from the Shoe Lovers Liberation Army and four from Shoe Fetishists Anonymous."

"Are they going to be anonymous?" Sarah asked.

"Of course they're not." Shelley was exasperated. "None of these people are anonymous anymore except for the real addicts, the alcohol and narcotics people. And even some of them like to go on television. These are shoe fetishists."

"So?"

Shelley shrugged. "Lotte never goes to support groups unless she knows the people in them are ready to talk. She's got ways of finding out. She's good at it."

"Lotte found Maximillian in a support group," Sarah said, "did she ever tell you that? She found him in a support group in Queens. It was supposed to be very funny."

"A support group for what?"

"A settlement house kind of thing, you know. Where people went to get help with their English and tell each other how to apply for jobs and things like that. Lotte went because the same social worker who ran that group ran one on self-esteem for dwarfs—"

"I remember that show."

"—and Lotte got to the place early and there was

Max. It was right after Bill Rachetti quit to move to Florida."

"I ought to move to Florida," Shelley said. "God, it's awful about Max. It was awful about Maria."

"And bad luck is supposed to come in threes," Sarah said.

Sarah had finished her sandwich and gone to work on the potato chips that came with it. She ate them daintily and with deliberation, as if pointing out to Shelley how much she enjoyed each one.

"Let's get back to the show," Shelley said. "We're going to need a split stage. I'm going to want Max—well. It won't be Max, will it? I'm going to need someone to toss furniture for me at five A.M."

"WKMB will supply somebody. They do when our guy is sick."

"You better call them and tell them our guy is more than sick. Five A.M. We've got about thirty pairs of shoes in boxes in the truck. I'll need them all. I'll also need a wider than usual coffee table to put them on. And a cloth. A white tablecloth. Do we have one of those?"

"I don't know," Sarah said. "I didn't pack the truck."

"If we don't have one, we're going to have to get one. The shoes won't show up against the wood grain of the tables we've got. Maybe WKMB has a different kind of table. Ask."

"Now?"

"As soon as we're done here."

Sarah flagged down the waitress. "I'm going to be up all night the way this is going."

"Do you really think you ought to order dessert?"

"I'll have a hot fudge brownie with chocolate ice cream," Sarah told the waitress. "And yes I do think I ought to have dessert."

"It's your life." Shelley shrugged.

"It was Max's life this morning, wasn't it? Dragging things around for you and getting himself killed."

"What was that supposed to mean?"

"I mean nobody ever saw him come up after he took the chair downstairs," Sarah said. "I heard the police talking about it. And that Mr. Demarkian. Max left the studio to take a chair downstairs for you, and that was the last anybody saw of him until he turned up dead."

"And?" Shelley insisted.

"And nothing. But it's true. They were all saying how strange it was. I mean, you could hardly miss him, could you? He'd have been carrying something heavy. He was supposed to bring up the blue chairs. But he didn't."

"That's true," Shelley said. "He didn't."

Sarah leaned far across the table, so that in spite of the fact that she couldn't see Shelley's face—Shelley was still turned away—she could breathe down the side of Shelley's neck.

"Do you know what else they thought was strange?" she said. "You. You didn't complain. Max just left the studio and disappeared, and you didn't say a thing."

"I was busy."

"You were busy putting the sets together, but you couldn't do that without Max, could you? You should have been hollering the place down."

"Is this your own bright idea?" Shelley asked coldly.

Sarah shook her head. "It was Demarkian's. At least, that's who I heard talking about it. And talking about you."

"Demarkian is a fraud."

"He solved that murder the nuns had a few months ago," Sarah said. "And he solved the murder of Donald McAdam back around Thanksgiving."

"He horned in on a perfectly legitimate police investigation and made himself look good to the media," Shelley said sharply.

"Lotte and DeAnna have asked him to look into the deaths of Maria Gonzalez and Max Dey. Officially, you understand. For the program. He's going to be a consultant."

"Lotte and DeAnna need to have their heads examined."

"Demarkian said figuring out where Max was after he left the studio with that chair is the most important part of this case. I heard him. He said figuring out where Max was then is the key to everything."

"That's just wonderful. I hope he finds what he's looking for."

"Oh, he will. Gregor Demarkian always finds what he's looking for. That's the point of Gregor Demarkian."

The waitress had arrived with Sarah's hot fudge brownie. Shelley watched horrified as it was lowered onto the table at Sarah's place, a mountain of whipped cream and chocolate sprinkles and maraschino cherries. It looked like an illustration from that children's game Candy Land, where every move brought players in closer contact with sugar. Sugar. Shelley was nauseated by the very thought of sugar.

"My God but that's disgusting," she said.

Sarah shoved an overflowing spoonful of whipped cream and sprinkles and cherry into her mouth.

"I'll tell you what's disgusting," she told Shelley. "You. You're disgusting. The things you do. The things you think you can get away with."

"What are you talking about?"

"Nothing you have to worry about, you think."

"Sarah."

"You shouldn't leave the evidence lying around where people can find it," Sarah said. "You shouldn't think everybody's as blind as a bat. You shouldn't think everybody's as dumb as your husband, either."

"What are you talking about?"

This time, when Sarah dug her spoon into her hot fudge brownie, it came up dripping with ice cream and fudge as well as whipped cream and sprinkles. Sarah shoved the entire mess into her mouth—and it all got in there, Shelley noted, all of it, the woman had an enormous mouth—and grinned.

"Under the circumstances," Sarah said, swallowing, "considering who's dead and everything, and who you've been sleeping with, and how one thing might relate to the other, I think it would be a really good idea if I went and told all this to Gregor Demarkian."

It was like having a hot flash. It really was. Shelley had never had a hot flash, but she was sure that this must be what it was like. The world going red. Getting up out of your chair and onto your feet and not remembering doing it. She was going crazy.

"You little *bitch*," she said.

Sarah made another attack on her hot fudge brownie. "He was sleeping with Maria, too. On and off. I'll bet Gregor Demarkian would like to know that, too."

"Why don't you just rent the electronic billboard in Times Square and announce it on that?"

"They're both dead," Sarah said pleasantly, "and nobody knows why. Maybe this is why."

"If it is, you're being very stupid, Sarah. If it is, you're asking to get your head smashed in."

"I won't get my head smashed in. I'm too careful to get my head smashed in. You should have been more careful."

"Maybe I'll just kill you right here."

"Maybe you won't."

"You shouldn't lie to people, Sarah. Max wasn't sleeping with Maria Gonzalez. He tried and she turned him down. She was a good Catholic virgin. He told me."

"Maybe he was just trying to make you feel better. On account of your—advanced age."

The little pile of scrap paper that constituted Shelley's notes was still lying on the table. Shelley snatched them up and shoved them into her blazer pockets.

"You little bitch," she said again. "If you ever, ever spill this slime to anybody I'll kick you right in your fat ass."

"I'll sue," Sarah said happily.

And that, Shelley thought, as she steamed across the atrium to the elevator bank, was the problem with the twentieth century.

In the days of Ruth and Naomi, she could have cleaved Sarah's head with a meat ax and had a halfway decent chance of being considered justified.

3

In the days of Ruth and Naomi, Prescott Holloway would have been a desperado. He felt like a desperado now, walking the dark streets of a city he barely knew, looking for something he couldn't put his finger on. It had been a long hard day and tomorrow would be a longer one. With Max gone, they would call on him to take up the slack. There would be slack to be taken up, too. Prescott knew that staff from WKMB were supposed to take over if Max was ill or incapacitated, but he also knew that Shelley Feldstein's idea of taking over and WKMB's were not identical. It would be just like it was back in New York. When Max got tied up, Prescott got put into play. Prescott didn't mind it. It broke up his day.

What he wanted to break up his night was a drink, or a couple of them. He wouldn't have minded more of that Scotch Max had had the night before. What else he wanted was a woman, but he wasn't expecting to find one. Prescott's ideas of safe sex had nothing to do with AIDS, but he followed them inflexibly nonetheless. So far, they'd kept him from getting arrested and they'd kept him from getting rolled. If he walked fast enough on a night like this, he could keep himself from getting mugged, too.

Muggers didn't like him. He walked too quickly and he looked too mean.

The sound of the heels of his cowboy boots on the pavement was like drumbeats.

It made him feel as if his possibilities were infinite.

THREE

1

The headline in the *Philadelphia Inquirer* wasn't bad—

POLICE INVESTIGATE GOLDMAN
SEX SHOW MURDER

—but the subhead was even more embarrassing than usual, and all the way down to the Ararat that morning, Gregor Demarkian complained about it.

" 'Demarkian at Scene,' " he said to old George Tekamanian, who had decided at the last minute to have breakfast out and grabbed Gregor's arm for support in the process. Old George Tekamanian was in his eighties somewhere, one of the last remaining members of Gregor's mother's generation on Cavanaugh Street. The other two were maiden lady sisters in their early nineties who lived in an apartment on the ground floor of Hannah Krekorian's townhouse and claimed to be able to read crystal balls. Old George could remember when this neighborhood was so poor, the city didn't like to pick up the garbage more than once or twice a week. He could remember when Lida Arkmanian's townhouse had been a tenement carved up into fourteen one-bedroom flats. He could remember when people on Cavanaugh Street routinely lived in one-bedroom flats, in spite of the fact that they had four children and a grandmother living with them. Gregor could remember all these things, too, but unlike old George he was doing his best to forget them.

The subhead of the *Inquirer* story said: PHILADELPHIA'S POIROT FINDS BODY. At least it didn't say "Philadelphia's *Armenian-American Hercule* Poirot." Gregor wasn't sure that made a difference.

" 'Demarkian Finds Body,' " he told George, steering the old man carefully across the last intersection between their brownstone and Ararat. "That would have been all right, too. I'm not asking for anonymity."

"You are getting upset over nothing," George said. "*Tcha*, Krekor, you are being ridiculous. It is a compliment they are paying you."

"It is a boost in the advertising revenue they are paying themselves," Gregor said. "It sells papers."

"Well, then."

"Well, then, nothing. I wasn't put on this earth to sell papers."

"You should learn to walk faster, Krekor. I don't understand how you can poke along the way you do and not freeze solid in this cold."

The answer was, of course, that Gregor couldn't. He couldn't walk as fast as old George—who positively creeped along in his apartment, but picked up speed as soon as he hit a pavement; it was Gregor's vanity that old George had to be guided anywhere or helped along any street—and he was freezing. It was early in the morning and a gray day in mid-December. The first day of Hanukkah was this coming Sunday and Christmas was five days beyond that. Cavanaugh Street was as decorated as it was going to get. Donna Moradanyan had even managed to plant her gigantic red-and-silver bow on the flagpole that stood in the courtyard in front of Holy Trinity Church. The courtyard wasn't much more than a wide place in the sidewalk and the flagpole had been paid for by Howard Kashinian, who hated the bow, but that was all part of the coming of the Christmas season, too. Gregor wondered what life was like at this time of year for David Goldman and Rebekkah. Was Hanukkah just as crazy? Did the craziness come for some other holiday at some other time of year? Maybe David and Rebekkah always had calmness and sweet reason, the way the angels in heaven were supposed to have when they weren't fighting territorial wars against Lucifer and his minions. Gregor wasn't entirely sure he believed in God, but he did believe in saints, and Rebekkah Goldman was definitely one of them.

David Goldman was a lucky man. Gregor looked through Ararat's front window and found him sitting over coffee with Father Tibor Kasparian, in the floor-level cushioned booth on the platform. Gregor hated the floor-level cushioned booth. It was very hard for him to get down on the ground like that and get up again. Tibor, on the other hand, loved it. It was what he remembered from before he came to the United States. From what Gregor could see, David Goldman at least didn't seem to mind.

"Come on," Gregor said to old George, grabbing him by the sleeve. He grabbed one of the wooden bars that crisscrossed Ararat's new front door—solid mahogany, no more plate glass and textured aluminum here—and opened a passage for the two of them to go inside.

"Hi," Linda Melajian said as they approached the front desk. "Father Tibor and his friend are waiting for you. At least they're waiting for Mr. Demarkian."

"It's all right if I come along," old George said. "Nobody cares what they say in front of me. They just assume I'm senile."

"If you want the kosher menu, you've got to tell me

now," Linda said. "We can do it, but we've got to warn Mama in advance."

"Kosher?" Gregor said.

Linda grabbed a couple of menus and hurried over to Tibor's booth. "I wish we had a low-fat menu to serve you," she told Gregor. "Honestly, hasn't Bennis learned how to nag you? Your weight is a disgrace."

Gregor's weight was absolutely nothing compared to the weights of the really big master detectives, like Nero Wolfe. Gregor would have told Linda this, except that he knew it wouldn't do any good. The denizens of Cavanaugh Street liked to live in murder mysteries except when they didn't want to, and when they didn't want to always seemed to start about the time they brought up the problem of his weight. Gregor didn't think his weight was that much of a problem. He was only carrying an extra thirty pounds. And he was a big man.

He got down on the floor, planted his rear end on a cushion, and slid in behind the table next to Tibor. Old George popped down with all the grace of a fifteen-year-old gymnast and slid in next to David Goldman.

Gregor introduced old George to David and then asked them, "What was Linda talking about, the kosher menu? Since when does Ararat have a kosher menu?"

"Since I came down here to visit about two weeks ago," David Goldman said. "Usually I wouldn't put anyone to that kind of trouble, but there's one thing I've found out. It's an *exceedingly* bad idea to decline hospitality in this neighborhood."

Linda Melajian came back to the table, and Gregor ordered waffles with bacon and coffee. Old George ordered scrambled eggs, bacon, sausage, hash browns, grits, extra butter and tea. Gregor shook his head.

"Well," he said. "Here we are. I hope this is worth the trip, Rabbi. I told you over the phone that I don't really know anything yet—"

"You don't know anything until you see the lab reports," David Goldman said. "Yes, yes, I understand. I really didn't come here to pump you for information. It really is something Lotte told me last night that I wanted to tell you."

"Lotte can't tell you herself," Tibor said, "because she's busy this morning taping."

"They had to show a rerun yesterday," old George put in, "because they couldn't tape your show."

Linda Melajian came back with a tray of tea and coffee. The tea and coffee came in tall pots, with empty cups on the side. Old George filled his cup half full of tea and half full of cream.

"You know," Gregor said, taking his coffee black in reaction to old George's extravagances, "there's one thing that's confused me, from the very start of this. You're a rabbi."

"That's right," David Goldman said.

"I understand there are different kinds of rabbis—"

"I'm Conservative. That's a little less strict than Orthodox, but much more strict than Reform. And, of course, I'm much, much less strict than the Hasidim who had so much trouble here with the graffiti."

"All right. But you're a religious person. From what I understand from Tibor, you're very deeply religious. And your sister—"

"Does something very public and very embarrassing?" David asked.

"Well, it's certainly public. Do you mean to say you're not embarrassed?"

"Of course I'm embarrassed." David Goldman hooted. "So is Rebekkah. The day Lotte did the show where she had the five guys on who could only make love on carousels, Rebekkah threatened to hide in the closet for a week."

"But you're willing to help her with those shows," Gregor said. "You're willing to intercede with Tibor to get me to agree to appear on one."

"Of course."

"Of course?"

David Goldman poured himself another cup of coffee. His coffee pot was marked with a red dot. Did this mean it was kosher? Would there be a difference between kosher coffee and the other kind?

"Look," David Goldman said, "the first clear memory I have of Lotte is from when I was three and we were leaving Heidelburg. That's where we lived, in Germany, during the war. Anyway, we're both lying in the trunk of a car, covered with a blanket, and she has her body completely over mine, completely, so that if the car gets stopped someone might see her in the trunk but they won't see me. It wouldn't have worked, of course. I know that now. But at the time she made me feel extremely safe."

"How old was she?"

"Eight," David Goldman said. "Later, when we were living in what was at first Palestine and is now Israel, all during the war and then the War of Independence later, when we were very poor and there was very little food, I always had more than most people, because Lotte always gave me half of hers. And I never went without a blanket, because Lotte always found me one. And later when the fighting was momentarily over and Lotte came to the United States, the first thing she did after she got her graduate degree was bring me over and put me through the rabbinical program at Yeshiva University. Of course, Lotte is an atheist."

"I had noticed that," Tibor said sadly.

"Everybody notices it," David Goldman said. "But there used to be a joke in Yiddish when I was younger. A young man comes back from a sojourn in the big city and marches up to the rabbi who taught him for years in his small town and says, 'Rabbi, my entire life is changed. I no longer believe in God.' The rabbi shrugs his shoulders and says, 'That's all right. God still believes in you.' Well, that's how I feel about Lotte. God still believes in her. And will go on believing in her, in spite of the fact that she probably gives Him ulcers."

"Besides," Tibor said, "the Good Lord's ulcers may not be so critical as you think. Lotte Goldman is at heart a very conservative woman."

"Conservative?" old George Tekamanian said.

"She always comes down on the side of very traditional morality in the end," Tibor said. "She talks about these crazy things, but she does not approve of them."

Linda Melajian leaned over and put down a plate of waffles in front of Gregor. Then she began unloading heaping plates in front of old George Tekamanian.

"Good God," Gregor said. "What do you think you're doing?"

"It's my grandson Martin and my granddaughter-in-law," old George said. "They are coming this afternoon to bring me food and make sure I have a healthy lunch. I do not know why it is, Krekor, but food that is healthy for you always seems to taste awful."

2

Gregor didn't know if healthy food always tasted awful. He made it a matter of principle never to eat self-consciously healthy food. He didn't know if Lotte Goldman was in her heart a conservative, either. From what he'd seen of her show, he thought she was a nut case. What he did know was that everybody seemed to need a break, himself included. In spite of the fact that David Goldman had come down here specifically to tell Gregor Demarkian something relevant to at least one of the cases of murder that had occurred among the people associated with his sister's television show, he wasn't ready to talk.

The situation made Gregor Demarkian a little antsy. He was not a sociable man, in the ordinary sense of the term. He spent almost every morning of his life these days having breakfast in the Ararat with Tibor, but the two of them read their respective papers and made comments on the world in general. They didn't have "conversations" of any formal kind. Even Gregor and Bennis didn't have conversations of any formal kind. When he went down to visit her, or she came up to visit him, they talked about his work or hers or Cavanaugh Street, but mostly they talked about each other. Gregor knew everything about Bennis's latest Zed and Zedalia novel. That was what Bennis did for a living. She wrote fantasy novels full of knights and ladies and dragons and unicorns set in the imaginary countries of Zed and Zedalia, which would have been ridiculous if she hadn't been making so much money doing it. Gregor knew that Ulrich of Rolandia was about to kidnap the evil Queen Allisandra to harness her magic powers for his unjust aggressive war against the Crown Prince of Zed. He didn't know anything at all about the young man who had taken Bennis to dinner last week and didn't want to know. Bennis knew all about Gregor's last case—he always filled her in when the cases were over; he didn't want her trying to be an amateur detective, but he did like to hear her comments once the coast was clear—but nothing about his visits to Elizabeth's grave. Gregor didn't know if that was all right with her or not. Sometimes he worried that he didn't do more talking to Bennis in the way men usually talk to women they are close to because he was afraid to. What would he talk about, if Bennis insisted? The fact that they now spent more time with each other than most people who were married? The fact that except for one minor technicality, they might as well be married? On 'second thought, that technicality wasn't so minor after all. What was also not minor was the fact that he seemed to have wound his life around an extremely rich, extremely pretty, extremely impetuous, relatively young woman on whom he had no real hold at all.

That was the kind of thing he thought about, early in

the morning, when he was not thinking about cases or the excruciating things the *Inquirer* was saying about him or the problems that had to be cleaned up on Cavanaugh Street. That was why he didn't like to take time off for these little relaxations. Besides, once he was on a case he liked to get on with it, and this case especially struck him as urgent. Sometimes the feel he got for the thing was that the main murder had been committed and any violence that followed would essentially be panic. That had to be taken into consideration, but in cases like that it was sometimes possible to calm the murderer's mind, so that nothing new would happen while you were nailing the evidence to put him away for the old. Sometimes the feel was more electric. That was the feeling he had here. He couldn't shake the conviction that he was in the middle of an ongoing endeavor, and that if he didn't do something quickly it would be no time at all when he would find another corpse in his lap.

Tibor and David were discussing soup kitchens. They both participated in the running of one in the center of Philadelphia. Actually, Temple B'nai Shalom and Holy Trinity Church participated, along with half a dozen other churches in the area. It was one of those nondenominational, interfaith efforts that made the six o'clock news every once in a while on a slow day when the anchors wanted to look compassionate.

"It's the schizophrenics who worry me," David Goldman was saying. "Your idea is working very well with the temporarily displaced, but there's just nothing you can do about the schizophrenics. They get disoriented."

"What are they talking about?" Gregor asked George.

"Homeless people." George tucked into his second order of hash browns. "There are homeless people and then there are homeless people."

"There are the hard-core alcoholics," Tibor said, "and you have to watch them, Krekor, because they will take the food and hide it in their clothes and go out on the street and sell it to get money for bad wine."

"There are also people who are just down on their luck," David Goldman said. "That includes some of the bag ladies. Tibor here put a process into place—"

"I had an idea," Tibor objected. " 'Put a process into place.' What kind of talk is that?"

"Tibor set up a housing bank," David Goldman said. "The churches and Temple B'nai Shalom each adopt between one and six of these people at a time—"

"We do six," Tibor said, "because if we really need money I talk to Howard Kashinian and to Bennis. With Bennis, I ask. With Howard, I threaten."

"We do six, too," David Goldman said. "We find them an apartment, sometimes two of them together, give them the security deposit and a month's rent, help them get a job or deal with the government agencies—"

"But we can't do it with the schizophrenics," Tibor said, "because they get confused and then they wander off. These people are not integrated, Krekor. It is a terrible thing. And the insane asylums will not have them."

"We don't have insane asylums in America," David Goldman said. "We call them psychiatric hospitals. Or mental institutions."

"Insane asylums," Tibor said.

Gregor poured his cup full of coffee again. "I think," he said, "that it's time to get back to business. It's not that I want to rush you or anything—"

"Of course you want to rush us," David Goldman said. "You're a busy man."

"Krekor is not busy today," Tibor protested. "He has only to go with me for lunch to see Helena Oumoudian."

Gregor could have said something about having a life that stretched beyond the confines of Cavanaugh Street, but he didn't, because he didn't know if it would be true. Instead, he drank half the coffee in his cup and put the cup back into the saucer with inordinate care. He'd seen serial killers use delaying tactics like this as soon as they were brought in for questioning. It bothered him to think he might have picked up something from them besides a lot of professional pain.

"When you called last night," he said, "you said that your sister, Lotte, had figured out—"

"Not figured out," David Goldman said quickly. "It was something she'd found. Actually, she found one of them and Shelley Feldstein found the other. And it was strange."

"They found these things around the body of Maximillian Dey?" Gregor asked.

"Oh, no," David Goldman said. "They'd have mentioned it. It was nothing like that."

"They found them around the body of Maria Gonzalez?"

"They didn't find them around bodies at all," David said. "That's the point, you see. There's no way to know if they're connected. There's no way to know if they're important at all."

"If *what* are important at all?"

David Goldman hesitated, looking as if he'd dearly like to go back to his discussion of the homeless. Then he plunged his hands into the pockets of his jacket and came up with a double handful of dreidels. Dreidels, Gregor thought, blinking in astonishment. Ordinary wooden dreidels. He watched in disbelief as David Goldman looked through the piles and singled out two he apparently liked better than the rest.

"There they are," he said. "The strange ones."

"Strange ones," Gregor repeated. "Rabbi Goldman, those are dreidels. You can buy them on any street corner in Philadelphia at this time of year."

"In New York, too," David Goldman said. "But you can't buy them like these two. Look." David grabbed a third dreidel from the pile and began to turn it slowly. "*Nūn, gīmel, hē, shīn,*" he recited. "That's for *Nes gadol hayah sham.* 'A great miracle occurred there.' The miracle of the oil, you know."

"All right," Gregor said.

"Now look at these." David grabbed one of the two he had pushed out front. "*Nūn, gīmel, hē, pē. Nes gadol hayah poh.* 'A great miracle occurred *here.*'"

"I don't understand," Gregor said.

"Here," David Goldman insisted. "Here. In Israel. These two are Israeli dreidels."

"Israeli dreidels?"

"Shelley found the first one in the carpet on the stage at the studio in New York, before Maria Gonzalez's body was found but after she was dead, I'm sure, since I think the police said she'd died hours before. Anyway, it was just there, and Shelley picked it up and looked it over and thought it was defective. Then she gave it to Lotte."

"And Lotte knew what it was," Gregor said. "Because Lotte had lived in Israel."

"Well, a lot of people who haven't lived in Israel would know what it was," David said. "It's not a state secret. It would depend on how tied into the community they were, or their parents were. Shelley came from a rather heavily assimilationist family."

"Lotte didn't tell the New York police about this dreidel? And Ms. Feldstein didn't either?"

"There was nothing to tell. I mean, it was getting to be the time of year. There are dreidels all over the place, especially in New York."

"But this one?"

"Well, plenty of people who work for Lotte's show have been to Israel. And Itzaak Blechmann lived in Israel after he left the Soviet Union."

"What about the second one?" Gregor asked.

David Goldman poured himself more coffee and nodded vigorously. "It was the second one that stuck in Lotte's mind," he said, "because if there were two there should have been three, you see."

"No," Gregor said.

"I'll get there. Lotte found the second one in her temporary office yesterday after the police had left. She says she almost didn't realize what it was, because by now there really are dreidels all over the place and they're small and they just go wandering away—I live in a house with children, Mr. Demarkian, I can attest to the fact that they wander away—so she almost didn't look at it. And then she did."

"And it was one of these Israeli dreidels."

"With the *pē*, yes, and not the *shīn*."

"And there should have been three?"

"You can see why she didn't tell the police about it," David Goldman said. "It was in her office. There wasn't anything about the death of Max that was connected to a dreidel. What could she have told the police even if it had occurred to her. Why would it have occurred to her?"

"I don't know," Gregor admitted.

"I'll tell you now, I don't see why it would be significant, either," David Goldman said, "but when you were talking to us yesterday, you and that police detective—"

"John Jackman."

"You both said we should bring up anything at all that we found strange. And here this is. Lotte thought the dreidels belonged to Itzaak, but he says they don't. He says he didn't bring anything of that kind to the United States at all. And I think he might be telling the truth."

"Why?"

"Because he's very religious," David Goldman said. "He isn't the kind of person who would use even something as religiously insignificant as a dreidel as a souvenir. If he wanted to bring a souvenir from Israel, he would have brought an Israel flag or one of those snowballs with the parliament building in it."

"Why should there have been three of them?" Gregor was desperately trying to get back to what he still dimly thought might be the point.

"Because they're sold in sets of three," David Goldman said triumphantly. "Oh, I don't mean every dreidel in Israel is sold that way. Of course it isn't. But all the kiosks have sets of three all during the Hanukkah season, because tourists like to have more than one to bring home. And the sets are cheaper than buying the same number of dreidels one by one. But that's why the second one stuck in Lotte's mind, you see. You find one, you don't think anything of it. You find two, under the circumstances, you naturally start wondering where the third one is."

"Could I get one of these dreidels here?" Gregor asked David Goldman. "In the United States?"

David shrugged. "I wouldn't say it would be impossible, but I would say it wouldn't be easy. One of the import houses might have them. But why bother? It's not as if these were the big, ornamental kinds, you know, three or four times the ordinary size and carved into special wood and whatnot. These are the little wooden ones you see everywhere. And an importer who was very religious, as I said about Itzaak, might not want—"

"Yes, yes. Bear with me for a minute, please, Rabbi. I might be able to get one of these here, but it would be difficult, so the chances are that these two came from Israel."

"That's right."

"Meaning that whoever they belong to—assuming it's one person—had been to Israel."

"Or been in contact with someone who had been in Israel, yes."

"But he wouldn't necessarily have to be Jewish," Gregor said.

"Oh, no," David Goldman told him. "Lots of people buy dreidels, even in the United States. Children like to play with them. Adults sometimes just like to have them. And of course, with a certain kind of gentile, especially a certain kind of American gentile—"

"The kind that not only does not believe in God," Tibor said, "but that has no respect for religion—"

"Yes," David Goldman said, "well, there is a certain kind of gentile who buys Israeli dreidels in particular for good luck. I remember that from being in Jersualem. Hardcore gamblers, most of them were. And they'd keep the dreidels in their pockets and then go off to the casinos in Monaco or on Crete. They were not very pleasant people."

"No," Gregor said. "I can see how they might not be. The third one, assuming there is a third one, hasn't turned up?"

"No," David Goldman said. "A couple of other dreidels have turned up. DeAnna Kroll found one stuck in one of those plastic dry cleaning bags that were covering Lotte's clothes, but it was an ordinary one. She gave it to Lotte yesterday morning."

"Has anybody else found any others at all? Ordinary or not?"

"Oh, Mr. Demarkian. Of course they have. It's like I said. They're all over the place."

"All over the place," Gregor repeated, and then shook his head. "I don't know. It doesn't make any sense to me."

"Will you talk it over with the police detective?" David asked.

"Of course I will," Gregor said. "But I don't know what good it will do. I don't know what he can do with the information. I don't know what I can do with it."

"You can keep the dreidels," David Goldman said. "They ought to come in handy. In case they mean anything."

"Right," Gregor said.

David Goldman shrugged. "I said it was a little strange. Well, there it is, it's a little strange. And Lotte is very disturbed about everything that's been happening, of course."

Gregor picked up the two dreidels and put them in

the breast pocket of his suit jacket, looking them over carefully first, noting the anomalous letter.

"I didn't say you did the wrong thing. You did the right thing. I'd like to talk to Dr. Goldman about it later, if she wouldn't mind. I just don't know if it will lead anywhere."

"Of course," David Goldman said.

"It will lead somewhere," Father Tibor said firmly. "Everything always leads somewhere, Krekor, even if not to the place you would expect."

"I think I'm going to have another plate of sausage," old George Tekamanian announced. "Martin said something about a wonderful new kind of tofu burgers."

On that note, Gregor decided to order himself koritzov gatah.

It wouldn't be kosher, it wouldn't solve the murder of Maximillian Dey, and if Bennis saw him eating it, she'd kill him.

But at least it would be sweet.

FOUR

1

Gregor Demarkian and Tibor Kasparian were due for their lunch with Helena and Sofie Oumoudian at one o'clock. What Gregor had intended to do in the hours between the time he got back from breakfast and the time he had to meet Tibor so they could walk to the Oumoudians together was work. "Work" was an elastic concept in Gregor's life these days. He did not like to define it as doing what he had done before he retired. What else he meant by it he wasn't sure. Talking to David Goldman about the dreidels was "work" in the sense Gregor used the word now, and so was talking to John Jackman on the phone about the status of the lab reports the city of Philadelphia was running on the blood of Maximillian Dey. He wanted to push all that talk about dreidels to the back of his mind and let it ferment. Maybe it would come to something. He fully intended to call John Jackman today, but he didn't want to call him yet. It was only eight thirty in the morning when he left the Ararat. John Jackman often got to work that early, but he didn't arrive at a decent mood until at least noon. Besides, it was highly unlikely that there would be any word on the lab reports until later in the day. The Philadelphia police department was good, and it was being pushed—having a corpse turn up in the middle of a bunch of famous visiting television people from New York was practically the definition of being pushed—but money was tight everywhere, and Philadelphia was no exception.

Gregor Demarkian could remember days when money was not tight and police departments were not under-staffed, but they were a long time ago. Agents at the Bureau had a one-word answer for what had gone wrong and why everything was such a mess: cocaine. Gregor Demarkian knew next to nothing about cocaine. There were FBI agents who had enlisted as soldiers in the drug war—along with DEA agents and local police forces and customs agents and military men—but Gregor had never been one of them. The mere thought of drugs made him catatonic. Serial killers were terrible people, but at least they made some kind of sense. Serial killers might be evil, but they were at least logical. To Gregor's mind, a thirty-year-old investment banker who was blowing his mind out with free base hadn't needed drugs to make him stupid and a fifteen-year-old motor jockey who thought crack was an amusement to eat up Saturday night had a pair of parents who deserved to be shot. He had never met a single person involved in drugs who could think his way out of a paper bag. Gregor Demarkian preferred to spend his time on what he couldn't help thinking about as Real Crime, crime with method and motive, crime with passion and purpose, crime with sense.

Gregor left the Ararat right after David Goldman did. David Goldman had appointments, and Gregor didn't want to watch old George Tekamanian eat yet another plate of hash browns and yet another order of bacon. He didn't

have to worry about how old George would get home.
Tibor would see to that. He took a wad of money out of
his wallet, threw it on the table, waved good-bye to Linda
Melajian, and went back onto Cavanaugh Street. The side-
walk was crowded with children on their way to Holy
Trinity Armenian Christian School. Holy Trinity Armenian
Christian School only went up to grade eight. If it had
gone farther, he wouldn't have had to worry about Sofie
Oumoudian and Joey Ohanian could have gone back to
Deerfield. Unfortunately, even the eighth grade was a bit
of a stretch. There were only two students in it, and next
year there would only be three.

Gregor let himself into his building, checked the mail
even though he knew it wouldn't be there—half the time,
it didn't arrive before four o'clock in the afternoon—and
paused to admire Donna Moradanyan's latest extrava-
ganza, a free-standing papier-mâché menorah at least as
tall as he was, painted gold on the base, white on the candles, and hot phosphorescent pink on the candle flames. A
note attached to the mock-holder for the mock shammes
said,

> HOWARD,
>
> THIS GOES AT THE BASE OF THE CHURCH
> STEPS ON THE LEFT SIDE BETWEEN THE
> BUSH WITH THE SILVER RIBBONS ON IT
> AND THE ARMENIAN FLAG.

That was good. That meant that Howard Kashinian was
supposed to remove this menorah and put it outside in
front of the church, where presumably it would cause
fewer traffic problems than it was causing in this foyer.
Gregor wondered why Donna had asked Howard to do it
and not him. Gregor and Howard had been in the same
class all the way through grammar school, except for the
year Howard had spent in the reformatory. Lida and Han-

nah had been a year ahead of them and Sheila had been a year behind. And Howard was in no better shape than Gregor was.

Gregor went up the stairs and stopped on the second-floor landing. He could hear no movement going on behind Bennis's door, but he was fairly sure she was up. She'd been complaining all week about a copy-edited manuscript she was supposed to go over. She wasn't much of a sleeper, anyway, at least when he wanted her to be. In the middle of murder cases, he usually wanted her to be. He knocked sharply on her door and waited to see what would happen.

What happened was that there was the sound of shuffling from the foyer inside, and the door was opened just enough for Bennis to stick her head out. Her great floating storm cloud of black hair had not been brushed. It stuck out every which way from her scalp, the way the hair of cartoon characters did when they were supposed to have received an electric shock. She hadn't gotten dressed yet. Instead, she'd buttoned an oversize flannel shirt over her pale green nightgown. The nightgown looked like silk. The flannel shirt probably belonged to one of her brothers. Looking at her, it was impossible to tell that Bennis Hannaford had once had a coming-out party that cost so much money, it occasioned an editorial in the *New York Times.*

"Can I come in?" Gregor asked her.

Bennis nodded and stood back. "Believe it or not, I'm awake. Believe it or not, I've been awake for hours."

"I've been having breakfast."

"I've been smoking cigarettes. Come into the kitchen. If you haven't overdosed on coffee, you can have some more."

Gregor had, in fact, overdosed on coffee, but he let Bennis pour him a cup anyway, just to be polite. The copy-edited manuscript she'd been talking about was laid out across the kitchen table, covered with the notes

Bennis had made in bright green felt-tipped pen. Most of these notes said *"STET!!!"* in a frantic scrawl that seemed to indicate a writer at the end of her rope. One or two indicated a problematic situation Gregor wouldn't have begun to know how to deal with. *"Subjunctive mood,"* one of these read, canceling a change from "if she were" to "if she was." Gregor sat down and pushed a page with the words

designations of offices in the hierarchy of the Catholic Church, like Cardinal, should always be capitalized

out of his way.

"Bad mess?" he asked sympathetically.

Bennis looked blank for a moment. "Oh, no," she said, when she finally understood. "She's wonderful, really. I mean, she's twenty-two and her grammar is sketchy because they don't teach grammar anymore, but she's not a prig and she isn't trying to make my work politically correct, which it would have a hard time being anyway since it's set in the twelfth century or whenever, but you know what I mean. No, this one isn't any trouble at all."

"What do they look like when they are trouble?"

"A solid mass of red and they take me two months. Where are my cigarettes? You look all up and awake. I take it you went down to Ararat."

"I went down to Ararat. Would you like to hear what I was listening to at Ararat?"

"Sure."

Gregor outlined David Goldman's story about Lotte Goldman's story about the dreidels as quickly and succinctly as he could, which was considerably more quickly and monumentally more succinctly than David Goldman had. Bennis sat in a kitchen chair with her legs folded up under her and smoked. Bennis always smoked. It was the one bad habit she had not managed to give up since moving to Cavanaugh Street. Gregor was beginning to think nicotine was a true addiction—meaning a substance that took over for some other bodily function when you used it. Maybe when you used nicotine, your adrenal gland stopped producing enough adrenaline to keep you moving. God only knew, if social pressure could make someone quit, Bennis ought to be tobacco-free.

When Gregor finished talking about David Goldman, Bennis was halfway through with her Benson & Hedges Menthol. She blew a stream of smoke into the air and said, "That's interesting. Do you suppose it means anything?"

"I don't know."

"You ought to find out how easy it is to get one of those Israeli dreidels in this country. You ought to send somebody out looking for one."

"I'd have to do that both here and in New York," Gregor said. "I could probably do it here. John would send someone if I told him it was important. What would I do in New York?"

Bennis had turned away a little at the mention of John Jackman's name. Now she took another drag on her cigarette and stared at the ceiling. "Call the police in New York," she said. "After what's happened here, they can't go on treating the death of Maria Gonzalez like an ordinary mugging. Maybe they'll have somebody they can send out trying to buy dreidels."

"It's the kind of thing the district attorney's office would do, not the police," Gregor told her. "After they've already got their man in jail, to back up their case, if you see what I mean. And even if it turned out that it was impossible to buy one in either New York or Philadelphia, I don't know what it would mean. The dreidels weren't found near the scenes of the crimes. They don't seem to have anything to do with anything."

"They're just strange."

"That's right. And I don't like strange. Do you know what else I think is strange?"

"What?"

"The business with the wallet."

"What business with the wallet?" Bennis cocked her head. "You mean the fact that Maximillian Dey had his wallet stolen before the show left New York?"

"It's not just that Maximillian Dey got his wallet stolen," Gregor said, rearranging his body on the chair and stretching out his legs. Bennis had very modern, very angular, very uncomfortable kitchen chairs. She also had very modern, very angular, very uncomfortable marble sculpture in her living room. Gregor often wondered how she could stand it.

"Think back to yesterday," Gregor told her. "When we got to the studio, the first thing that happened was that we ran into Max, and he dropped—"

"Everything," Bennis picked up. "I remember. All that stuff fell out of his pockets."

"Right. Including his green card. I know his green card was there, because I picked it up off the floor and handed it to him."

"Oh." Bennis sat up straight. Her cigarette was out. She lit another. "I see what you're getting at. Most people would keep their green cards in their wallets."

"Like credit cards, yes," Gregor said. "In fact, I don't think I've ever known anyone who had a green card who didn't carry it in his wallet. Carrying it in a wallet simplifies things. People do forget their wallets at home but it's rare. They remember because they need their money. And they're careful with their wallets because they're careful with their money. And since aliens residing in the United States must have their green cards on them at all time, wallets are the logical place to keep them."

Bennis frowned. "Maybe it was just an idiosyncracy," she said. "Maybe he was just so paranoid about losing it, he kept it pinned to his underwear or something."

"It's laminated. But yes, I know what you mean. Somebody on *The Lotte Goldman Show* might know. Max might have mentioned it when he talked about getting his wallet stolen."

"I think that DeAnna Kroll woman knows everything." Bennis took another drag and blew out another stream of smoke. Gregor gave himself a measure of comfort by reminding himself that Bennis's smoking always tapered off in the afternoon.

"You know what else I'm interested in finding out," he said. "I'd like to know if that card was still on him after he was found dead."

"Why wouldn't it be? What good would a green card do anybody?"

"Maybe one of the staff on *The Lotte Goldman Show* is in the country illegally. Then a green card might do a good deal of good, if you could alter it, or knew somebody who could alter it, or knew somebody willing to trade it for a forgery."

"Would they do that? Would a forger trade it for a forgery?"

"I don't think so," Gregor said. "It's easier to forge those things from scratch. The real ones do have one characteristic the forged ones don't, though. When you run their numbers through the INS computer, they check out."

"That could be helpful in a pinch."

"Mmmm. But what gets to me, Bennis, is that I'm sure I heard somebody say yesterday that Maximillian Dey's pockets had been cleaned out. Cleaned out. Those were the exact words."

"I'd think that was the kind of thing you'd pay attention to."

"I had other problems on my mind at the time. John and I were discussing possible murder weapons. But it just doesn't make sense."

"Maybe John and you should discuss it some more," Bennis said.

Bennis still had a fair amount left of her cigarette. She stubbed it out in the ashtray anyway, then stood up and lit another. Then she turned her back on Gregor and went to the sink.

"I was thinking," she said. "I'm a little burned out, you know what I mean? I'm a little stale. I thought maybe it might make sense if I got away for a little while."

"Starting when?"

"Starting tomorrow. I made some phone calls last night. I can get Concorde tickets for the day after. Tomorrow morning I could go up to New York and do some shopping."

"Concorde tickets to where?"

"Paris."

"Bennis, it is not John Jackman's fault. If it's anybody's fault, it's mine."

"You didn't testify at the sentencing hearing."

"I wasn't asked to."

"He testified at the sentencing hearing after I'd slept with him."

"Bennis—"

Bennis whipped around. She was holding her cigarette high in the air in her right hand. It nearly set fire to her hair. For the first time Gregor could remember, she was in tears.

"Listen," she said, "I know all the arguments. I've made all the arguments myself. I mean, for God's sake, it was *my* father she killed."

"Yes," Gregor said.

"And not just my father, oh no, trust the Hannafords, we can't do anything in moderation. So there are a lot of people dead and we've had the trial and we've had the sentencing and we've had two stays of execution so far and I don't want it, Gregor. I don't want her to be executed. I don't care how many people she killed. She's mine too."

"I know," Gregor said. "I don't blame you. But it is not John Jackman's fault."

"I didn't say it was."

"You just blame him for it. *I* solved that case, Bennis. You know that. You were there. Why not blame me?"

"You didn't—"

"Testify at the sentencing," Gregor said. "Yes. I know. But John didn't exactly volunteer. He was called."

"He could have recommended—"

"He couldn't have recommended anything. That's not how these things work. You're punishing him for—"

"I'm not punishing him for anything." Bennis tapped a long column of ash into the ashtray with a finger motion that reminded Gregor of whips. "I'm not doing anything to anybody. I'm just suggesting that I might spend this Christmas someplace else."

"In Paris."

"Yes."

"Alone."

"Yes."

"Tibor will be very disappointed."

Another long column of ash had appeared on Bennis's cigarette. It was as if she sucked them into art forms. She studied the ash with fascination and took another drag. The ash didn't fall and she tapped it out.

"I don't want her to die," she said, her voice under control again. "I just don't want her to die. There has been enough dying in this generation of the Hannaford family. I am sick of it."

"It isn't up to you."

Bennis took a last drag and put the cigarette out. "Just let me go to Paris," she said. "Just don't make a fuss about it. I'll spend ridiculous amounts of money and cheer myself up."

Gregor wanted to point out to Ms. Bennis Hannaford the fact that she had been spending ridiculous amounts of money for almost three years now and she hadn't cheered herself up yet. She had spent a ridiculous amount of money buying this apartment, free and clear, for cash, the way other people bought sweaters. She had spent a ridiculous amount of money buying her little tangerine orange Mercedes sports car, also for cash. There wasn't a day when the UPS man didn't stop at her door, delivering another package from Saks Fifth Avenue and L.L. Bean and J. Crew. It was a damn good thing Bennis Hannaford got seven-figure advances for her books, because the way she'd been behaving since her father had been murdered, if she hadn't she'd be broke.

That was a lecture Gregor had been wanting to give Bennis for months, but he decided not to give it to her now. He had a lot to deal with, what with *The Lotte Goldman Show* murder and the graffiti on the synagogue and the problem of Sofie Oumoudian, but he figured he could take on one more thing if he had to. He just had to give himself time to think about it.

In the meantime, he decided to get out of Bennis Hannaford's apartment.

2

Several hours later, Gregor Demarkian met Tibor Kasparian on the steps of Holy Trinity Church, and the two of them started walking in the direction of the tenement where Helena and Sofie Oumoudian lived together. They were a little nervous. They had been invited to this lunch before Maximillian Dey had been killed. They had no idea how much a conservative old lady as Helena Oumoudian would take all the publicity that had been heaped on Gregor since Max's body had been discovered. Gregor kept thinking about Helena's thick wooden cane, its handle carved into gargoyles, its base worn down to a point. It reminded him of the lethal weapons old lady spies used to carry in British World War II movies. Helena Oumoudian reminded him of a gargoyle herself. She had a face with skin so wrinkled, it must have been pickled in brine at birth. Her temperament wasn't much better connected to sweetness and light. When they had gone to have tea there, Helena had interrogated them with as much patience as Savanarola ferreting out a heretic. Heretics were what Helena Oumoudian suspected both Gregor and Tibor of being. She didn't like Gregor's looks. She didn't like Tibor's background. She had no respect for what either of them did for a living. And she didn't trust their interest in her niece.

"She thinks we're a pair of dirty old men," Tibor had said in shock as they left the apartment the last time.

The only ray of hope Gregor saw in the entire situation was that she apparently thought they were interesting dirty old men. That was why she had asked them back to lunch.

"You're the one who should worry," Tibor told Gregor. "I'm a widower. Widowed priests cannot remarry in our church."

"Widowed FBI agents aren't interested in changing their marital status at Christmas," Gregor said. "Don't worry about it. Joey will be the perfect match for Sofie. Assuming it ever gets that far."

"It is better not to ask how far it has gotten," Tibor said. "At least, not these days."

Approaching the Oumoudians' street, Gregor saw that a few more people had made an effort to spruce things up for the holiday. Cavanaugh Street was already about as spruced up as anybody could stand. Sometime while Gregor was talking to Bennis or hidden away in his own apartment, Howard Kashinian had come and moved the menorah to its place in front of the church. Donna had been harder at work than that, however. All the light poles had been wrapped, barber-pole fashion, in red and green ribbons. Bagdesarian's Middle Eastern Import Store had a big silver bow in its plate glass window. Ohanian's Middle Eastern Food Store had a pyramid of ornate, enameled dreidels right next to the pile of karabich cookies it kept to the right of the door. Dreidels. Gregor was thoroughly tired of dreidels.

He shoved his hands into the pockets of his suit jacket—when he lived in Washington, it was customary for men to go without coats, no matter how cold the weather, because a suit without a coat was considered "more professional"—and said, "So, Tibor. Have you thought about it? What are we going to do about Bennis?"

"Of course I have thought about it," Tibor said. "I have thought ever since you called. And what we should do about it is obvious."

"Is it?"

"Of course. We must stop her from leaving tomorrow. Tomorrow is much too soon. It doesn't give us any time."

"I know it doesn't. Have you ever tried to stop Bennis when there was something she wanted to do?"

"I know, Krekor."

"Under ordinary circumstances, getting me involved in a murder investigation would keep Bennis at my side like a hangnail, but these aren't ordinary circumstances."

"In these circumstances, it is the murder investigation that is the problem."

"Not the murder investigation," Gregor corrected, "who's conducting the murder investigation."

"Which is too bad," Tibor said, "because John Jackman is a very nice man and a very good police officer and also he will do what you want him to do."

"I don't think we can do anything directly," Gregor said. "I think she'd suspect something."

"I do, too," Tibor said. "But I do not know who to ask, Krekor. I do not trust Donna Moradanyan. She would tell."

"Yes, she probably would. And Lida would be bad at it."

"And Hannah Krekorian would tell everybody in the neighborhood and it would get back." Tibor sighed. "This is a difficulty, Krekor. This is an impossibility."

"No it isn't," Gregor said.

"What do you mean?"

Gregor felt much better. He felt much better. "You do agree that the problem is that Bennis should not be left alone?"

"Of course."

"Especially at Christmas?"

"This is indubitable."

"Fine, Tibor, fine. We need about three extra days. I know just how we're going to get them, too."

"How?" Tibor asked.

They were at the building that housed the Oumoudians' apartment. They were coming up the steps just as Sofie Oumoudian was opening the front door. Sofie looked harassed.

"Quick," she said. "My aunt has been excited all day. She can hardly wait to talk to you."

Gregor Demarkian grinned. "Well, that's better than I thought we were going to get. I thought your aunt was going to refuse to have anything to do with us. Two unsavory characters. Mixed up with the police."

"*So-fi-aaaa,*" a thin high voice called from up the stairs.

Sofie looked in the direction of the noise with exasperation. "She may kidnap you," she warned. "It's all she's been talking about since last night. She's beside herself."

"She was beside herself the last time," Tibor said.

"The last time she was nervous. Please. Father. Mr. Demarkian. Please hurry. She keeps saying she wants to hear about every drop of blood."

Every drop of blood.

So she was one of those old ladies.

Gregor decided not to care.

He was too wrapped up in the thought that he'd finally hit on a plan that would fool Bennis Hannaford.

FIVE

1

DeAnna Kroll thought about violent death differently than most of the people she worked with. Murder didn't seem as unreal to her as it did to Shelley Feldstein and Sarah Meyer. For a long time DeAnna had thought that this was a result of a better than passing acquaintance with death in general. Now she knew it wasn't true. Poor people die more easily than richer ones do, even in countries with national health systems and publicly administered prenatal care. Malnutrition and disease, depression and accident: DeAnna remembered reading once about a man in Tupelo, Mississippi, who died by falling into a well he'd dug on the edge of his property. It was broad daylight, he was stone cold sober and the well was marked. Nobody had any idea why he'd fallen into it. Things like that never happened to lawyers' wives in Scarsdale or plastic surgeons in Beverly Hills. It was as if God passed out the freak accidents based on whose bank account was the thinnest. The only kind of death he allowed to be an equal-opportunity employer was death by traffic accident. Whatever it was that got a man on the highway was just as likely to kill him as it was to kill anybody else. That was why DeAnna Kroll didn't drive.

Death by deliberate murder, though, was different. Before Maria Gonzalez died—and before Max—DeAnna had thought there would be similarities between that kind of thing and what Lotte or Itzaak Blechmann had lived through. Holocaust and political persecution seemed like variations of deliberate murder to her. Now she knew that they weren't, at least in terms of the effects they had on the people who survived them. Lotte and Itzaak were both terribly upset. Lotte had been sick to her stomach after she'd seen the body of Maria Gonzalez. Itzaak had cried for half an hour after Max's body was taken away. To this day, DeAnna could remember what it had been like the first time she had been in an apartment whose windows were sprayed with bullets. It was years ago, long before drive-by shootings got to be a kind of national ghetto sport. She was sitting on the floor with both babies crawling over her feet on the worn carpet when the craziness started. It was nuts. There was the sound of a car pulling up to the curb downstairs—the wrong sound, complete with squealing brakes and a honk. Then someone with a boy-man's voice had started screaming some words DeAnna couldn't make out and somebody else had let loose with a machine gun. Whoever it was was not a very good shot. He did very little damage to the apartment above DeAnna's, which was the one he wanted. He blew out all of DeAnna's windows and cut her pendulum cuckoo clock off the wall and into shards. He killed a three-year-old girl who had been watering the flowers in the window box of the apartment downstairs. The police came later and managed to look shocked, but that didn't make them effective. It was impossible for them to be effective when nobody would tell them anything. Nobody ever told the police anything in the neighborhood DeAnna

lived in before she got successful enough to move downtown. One of the hardest adjustments she had to make
when she got the apartment in Turtle Bay was in her attitude toward the police. People in Turtle Bay called the police all the time. And the police came.

Itzaak and Lotte were upset. Shelley and Sarah were
nervous. Prescott Holloway seemed to want to fade into
the background, which was where he belonged, anyway.
DeAnna Kroll felt as if she were coming home. DeAnna
Kroll felt as if nothing had happened to her that wasn't
perfectly normal. DeAnna Kroll thought she was going
nuts. Maybe this was the flaw in the fabric of the American Dream. Maybe you could get your body out of the
ghetto and into the upper middle class, but your head always slept in the bed it had been born to. That was a terrible way to describe it, but DeAnna knew what she
meant. Maria and Max were dead and that felt just about
right, for a death rate, among the group of them, in this
period of time. Maria and Max were dead and all DeAnna
could think about was how to devise ways to ensure that
she never got left in the ladies' room without at least two
other women for company.

Now the taping was over for the day and the studio
was dark. Since *The Lotte Goldman Show* had rented not
only Studio C but the entire cluster of offices around it for
their two-week stay in Philadelphia, nobody would be
coming in to produce a game show or give the weather report between now and the time they were ready to tape the
next Lotte Goldman show, tomorrow morning. This was
the shoe fetishists show they had done today. It had come
off better than DeAnna had expected. DeAnna wasn't sure
what she had expected. The Shoe Lovers Liberation Army.
Shoe Fetishists Anonymous. It wasn't drive-by killings or
the murders of Maria and Max that made her think the entire country was going insane. She wrapped up the
paperwork she had been doing through lunch—hot pas-
trami on a roll with Russian dressing; guest roster for the

show on sex therapists who say their clients make them frigid—and put it under her paperweight for Sarah to find. She thought about leaving a nasty note under there for Sarah to find—but she thought about doing that every day, and she never did. She got up and grabbed her tote bag and went into the hall. All she had to do now was watch the tape, make sure anything that needed fixing got fixed and sign off on the show. After that, she could go back to the hotel and have a good stiff drink.

Out in the hall, she saw Prescott Holloway following Carmencita Boaz down the hall. Carmencita was telling him how they had to have six dozen yellow roses brought up at the crack of dawn tomorrow morning, it didn't matter when the flower shops opened, because roses were the only thing that would calm the sex therapists down enough so they wouldn't swear when the discussion started.

"They're very tempermental," Carmencita was saying. "They're highly sensitive people. They'd have to be, given their work."

"Right," Prescott Holloway said.

DeAnna turned a corner and saw Lotte through the door of one of the offices. Sarah was in there, too, which made things easier. Shelley and Itzaak were nowhere to be seen, but that didn't matter. DeAnna didn't need them for this.

"Come on," DeAnna said. "Let's get moving. I want to get out of here at a reasonable hour today."

"Most people would say three or four o'clock in the afternoon is a reasonable hour," Lotte responded.

"Most people don't start work at three A.M. Come on, Sarah, move your butt. And you need your pad."

Sarah made a face, which DeAnna ignored. DeAnna had suffered through her share of shit jobs. She didn't have much sympathy for a Wellesley girl who thought typing was beneath her. She went on down the corridor and stopped at a door with a big red dot on it. Just to be safe, she knocked. There was no answer.

"All clear," she told Lotte and Sarah, who had come up behind her. She opened the door and stuck her head in. The room was dark. She felt around inside the door for the light switch and switched it on.

It was a compact, crowded room with one wall taken up entirely by an enormous television screen and quadrophonic speakers. Under the television screen there was a VCR unit so small, it was ludicrous, like the mouse the elephant stood on in the illustrations to the old children's story. This was the room people came to to review the tapes they had made of their shows and decide what to keep and what to cut in them. In a minute or two, the technical man who would do the actual cutting would come along to get them started. DeAnna was in rooms like this five days a week, forty weeks a year. There was nothing about them to make her feel so nauseated.

Nauseated, however, she was. She grabbed the nearest chair and sat down in it. She put her head between her knees and felt her shoulders tremble in fluttery little spasms that reminded her of the heart palpitations you got from drinking too much coffee.

"Are you all right?" Lotte asked her.

"Jesus Christ," DeAnna said, when she was able to talk at all. "You won't believe what I just did to myself."

"Maybe I should get her some water," Sarah said, sounding as if she'd just as soon rather not.

DeAnna sat up and shook her head. The motion didn't clear it. It did come close to giving her a headache.

"Jesus Christ," she said again. "It was unconscious or something. It was weird. I turned on the light, and then when there was nothing here, I think I went into shock."

"You're not making sense," Sarah said.

"She is making sense," Lotte said. "Do you want to lie down, DeAnna, and leave this to me?"

"No, no, of course not. You can't cut a tape. You've never done it in your life."

"I've been working on this show for fifteen years of

my life. And I've been sitting in on your cutting sessions for just as long. I would do all right, DeAnna."

"Yes," DeAnna said. "Yes, you probably would. But it's okay, Lotte, it really is. I'm fine."

"Fine," Lotte repeated.

DeAnna laughed. "I'm getting soft, Lotte, I'm having visions. What do you say about that?"

"I say that I am having visions, too," Lotte said. "The day has felt all wrong from the start."

It was not, DeAnna thought, what she wanted to hear. Always before, she and Lotte bounced off each other. When one of them was depressed, the other was optimistic. When one of them was afraid, the other was fearless. It had been a good partnership that way and it had been supposed to last forever.

DeAnna hauled her tote bag onto her lap and began to go through it, pulling out papers and pens and spiral notebooks in profusion.

"To hell with this," she said. "We're letting ourselves get spooked. Nobody on earth can predict the future."

"My paternal grandmother used to do a good imitation of it," Lotte said drily.

"You only believed that because you were a child at the time."

The entire contents of DeAnna's tote bag were now on the seat of the chair next to the chair she was sitting in—except for the four kinds of makeup she always kept with her just in case, which didn't count. DeAnna grabbed her favorite pen and one of the spiral notebooks and sat back, looking busy, looking important, trusting in what she always trusted in when she was scared stiff. Besides, she told herself. She didn't have any reason to be scared stiff.

Just because she *felt* that something awful was about to happen, didn't mean it really was.

2

Carmencita Boaz also felt that something awful was about to happen. She'd been feeling it all day, and it had been making her dizzy. Carmencita always got dizzy when she was frightened. She'd been doing that since she was a child. Guatamala City had not been the calmest place on earth over the last twenty-five years. It had not been as bad as Managua or some of those places in El Salvador, but it hadn't exactly been St. Petersburg, Florida, either. Carmencita could remember hearing gunfire in the distance when she was very young and being warned against stopping for ice cream in one café or another because some political group nobody had ever heard of the day before yesterday was now threatening to bomb it. There were times when Carmencita thought that getting the United States of America out of Guatamala was the best thing that could happen, but she'd never understood how anybody was going to bring that about by blowing up cafés. That was when she'd decided that all political people were mentally and spiritually ill. She had added *spiritually* to her definition in spite of the fact that her own spirituality was somewhat suspect. Itzaak thought she was very religious. She let him go on thinking that because he was very religious himself, and she thought he might think less of her if he realized how ambivalent she had always been about Catholicism. Maria had gone to Mass every morning and made her go, too. Now that Maria was dead, Carmencita slept late or stopped at the Greek diner around the corner from work for breakfast and a newspaper or just walked slowly instead of rushing, but she did not use her mornings for church.

Back in Guatamala city, the nuns brought the children

to Mass every morning before school. The children knelt in the dark and the cool of the church and looked at the statues cradled in the niches against the walls, the Virgins and the Martyrs, the Patron Saints and Intercessors. To Carmencita, they had always looked as wooden as they really were, as dull as the plaster they were made of. The nuns were real and always holy. The nuns gave up their lives for the sake of other people. The saints stared sightless into the candles poor women had spent the milk money to light at their feet, and did no good at all.

I should have joined one of the Pentecostal churches, Carmencita thought, and almost laughed, out loud, in this temporary office with its walls of thin plasterboard. She could just see herself, jumping and dancing and speaking in tongues. She could see herself doing those things the way she could see herself bungee jumping from the Brooklyn Bridge.

She got up from behind her desk and went into the hall. The cutting room door was open. She could see DeAnna and Lotte and Sarah sitting around inside it, but no sign of the tech man. If this had been New York, Lotte would have been screaming, wanting to know why the tech man hadn't gotten there first, wanting to know who she had to fire to get the job done the way she wanted it done. Since this tech man belonged to WKMB and not to *The Lotte Goldman Show*, DeAnna apparently believed she didn't have the right to shriek or that it wouldn't do any good.

Carmencita moved off to the door that led directly into Studio C. She opened that and peered into the rafters to see if Itzaak was still at work. The rafters were empty. They echoed hollowly above her head. Carmencita pulled the door closed and went on down the corridor.

She found Itzaak in the room they called the open room, which was nothing but a small space that had been cleared of everything but a few chairs and designated for the use of nothing. It was where the people who didn't have offices ate their lunches if they didn't go out or rested for a moment or two when nobody needed their services. It was the only room in the Studio C suite that had been decorated for the season. In one corner stood a dwarf plastic Christmas tree, with a handful of tinsel on it and not much else. In another corner stood a plastic menorah with plastic candles with plastic flames on them, set off by strings of paper-doll cut-out menorahs stuck to the walls behind it. Itzaak was always saying that it didn't make any sense, the way Hanukkah was celebrated in the United States. Everywhere else in the world, it was a minor holiday. But Carmencita understood.

Itzaak was sitting at a cardboard-topped, fold-up card table, eating soup out of a polystyrene cup. When he saw Carmencita in the doorway, he got immediately to his feet and held out his hands to her.

"Carmencita," he said, "come in. I would have stopped by and asked if you wanted to eat with me, but I thought you would be working."

"I was working." Carmencita kissed him on the tip of the nose, and then pulled up a chair for herself. "I got tired of working. And besides, I was a little nervous about this afternoon."

"This afternoon," Itzaak repeated, sitting down again. "Is it this afternoon, that you are supposed to see this person?"

"Yes, Itzaak. It's this afternoon. I'm glad it could be arranged so quickly. It's an emergency. And it's not like we're in New York, where I'd know a dozen places to go."

"It still worries me, this meeting of yours," Itzaak said. "I wish you would at least tell me the name of the person you will see."

"The person asked me not to," Carmencita said, careful to keep the pronoun out of it, careful to keep sex vague. "And it's just as well, Itzaak, it really is. For your protection."

"I do not need protection. I am an old man. And I have been shot at."

"You are not an old man. At least I don't have to worry about the quality of what I'll be getting. It's the same person who got Maria her green card. I saw Maria's green card. Hers was very good."

"Yours is very good," Itzaak said, "but it's like all of them. It will not survive a check."

"Nobody's going to check it."

"That policeman in New York checked mine," Itzaak said. "It was a good thing I was legal. That is the other thing that worries me about all this. If you get caught, they will not only investigate your cousin Alejandro. They will investigate you."

"I won't get caught."

"It is a crazy situation all around," Itzaak insisted. "You should not have to have a forged green card and a dead person's social security number. The United States should be proud to have you."

"What about my cousin Alejandro?"

"I have not met your cousin Alejandro. I have only met you."

There were two unopened bags of potato chips at Itzaak's elbow. Each one was stamped with the *U* inside a circle that was a symbol of the Union of Orthodox Jewish Congregations of America, certifying them kosher. Carmencita took one and opened it.

"I'm starving to death," she said. "I haven't eaten since before we got here this morning. I'm sorry this has caused you so much trouble, Itzaak. What with the money—"

"I'm not worried about the money."

"But it really is an emergency. Alejandro has to report for work in just four days. It's not much of a job. He'll only be a janitor in Queens somewhere. But it is a start and if he doesn't have his papers when he shows up for his first day, they'll throw him out. The government is getting so picky about these things."

"I don't care about the government. I'm worried about what I told you I was worried about. And I'm worried about your going to meet this person alone, when there have been two deaths and we don't know who has been commiting the murders."

Carmencita shifted uneasily in her seat. "It's broad daylight."

"Max was killed in broad daylight."

"There will be lots of people around, lots of people in shouting distance. There will. And it won't take very long to get the business over and done with."

"So," Itzaak said. "You are worried about this person. You are not sure this person is safe."

"Of course I'm sure."

"This is why you look so sick to your stomach," Itzaak said. "It is because you are so sure."

"I just don't like to think about the things that have been going on around here," Carmencita said. "Around the show, I mean. In New York and here. I get so confused. And I hate to think about them."

"So do I."

"But I am sure about this person, Itzaak, I really am. I'm certainly not worried that this person is going to kill me. It would be bad for business, wouldn't it? Killing off your customers."

"And you won't tell me who it is?"

"No, Itzaak, I won't."

"Or where you will be meeting?"

"Of course not. You'd come."

"Or when?"

"It's much better the way it is now," Carmencita said. "Really, Itzaak, it really is. When is sometime this afternoon, and that's all you have to know. When I'm finished with it, I'll come and get you and we can have a drink at the Israeli nightclub you told me about."

"Then it will be late this afternoon," Itzaak said, and then he sighed, and put his hands up to his face, and rubbed his eyes. He looked suddenly very old, much older than he really was, and Carmencita's heart went out to him. She put her hand on the thick hairy pad of his wrist.

"Don't do this to yourself," she said. "I'll be all right. I really will. You can't protect me from everything in the world."

"I don't want to protect you from everything in the world. I only love you."

"I know," Carmencita said. "I love you too."

Itzaak put his hands on the table. "This is not how I had imagined saying it to you for the first time. In a place like this. Worried sick that you are going to get yourself killed. I saw us in a restaurant with candles and a tablecloth."

"I don't need a restaurant with candles and a tablecloth."

"I don't know what you need," Itzaak said. "Maybe this Mr. Demarkian will be the genius he is reported to be. Maybe this will all be cleared up in a few days and we can go on with things."

"Maybe we ought to go on with things now."

"Even if Mr. Demarkian is the greatest genius that ever lived, still I will not like it. That you have to do with people like this, who deal in illegalities."

"I know."

"I blame you for none of it. But Lotte Goldman is a rich and famous woman, with powerful friends. After we know who has done these terrible things to Max and Maria, you should go to talk to her. You should tell her everything. She may be able to help you."

"If she can't help me, I will have to go back."

"If you have to go back, I will go with you. Here. You can't go all day only on potato chips. Sit here and I will find you some food."

"I can find food for myself."

"No. Sit. There may not be much I can do for you, but I can at least do this. I will be right back, Carmencita. You take a rest."

Carmencita didn't want to take a rest, but it all seemed so important to him, and he seemed so sad and discouraged, she sat where she was and let him go. When he was gone, she opened the other bag of potato chips and began to nibble on them.

She had told him as much of the truth as she had dared, but she hadn't told him the whole truth. She hadn't wanted him to worry, and it wasn't as if she had anything specific to hang her uneasiness on in the first place. It was just that so many things were . . .

Out of whack, that was the phrase she wanted. Good old American slang. There wasn't anything really wrong. There wasn't any big discrepancy she had to consider. It was just that there were a few things, about Max and the things that had happened to Max . . .

Carmencita would be much more relaxed once she had Alejandro's faked green card and social security card and driver's license tucked safely away at the back of her wallet. She would be much more relaxed once she was quit of this person and quit for good. This person gave her the creeps worse than the voodoo ladies ever had at home.

Once this way over, she would think of nothing at all except for the fact that Itzaak had told her he loved her. She would leave the detecting to the police and the investigating to Mr. Demarkian and the worrying over the morality of helping illegal aliens look legal to whoever it was that wanted it.

She could see both sides of the issue herself. She always ended up making up her mind on the basis of what she wanted and needed and hoped for herself, and she thought everybody else probably did that, too.

3

Shelley Feldstein had earned a certain reputation for sub-
tlety in her life, and a larger one for sophistication, but on
this early afternoon she was employing her talent for neither. To get into Shelley Feldstein's room, Sarah Meyer
had sneaked and schemed and stolen a key. To get into
Sarah Meyer's room, Shelley Feldstein marched right up
to the front desk, said her name was Sarah Meyer, and announced that she had lost her room key. The hotel staff
couldn't have been more helpful. They recognized her as
a bona fide guest. They couldn't see any reason why she'd
be asking for the key to anybody's room but her own. A
nice young man in a crisp dark uniform got her a brand
new key card and then came all the way upstairs to make
sure the door opened with it. The door did and Shelley
tipped him a dollar for his trouble Then she closed the
door behind her and got to work.

When Sarah Meyer had searched Shelley Feldstein's
room, she had been extremely careful to keep the place
neat, to put things back where she'd found them, not to tip
her hand. Shelley took no such precautions. Shelley didn't
give a hoot in hell if Sarah knew she'd been in here
searching around. In fact, she intended to make a point of
ensuring that Sarah knew just that. She didn't give a hoot
in hell if Sarah knew something was missing, either. Obviously, there was going to be something missing. The
three letters Sarah had stolen from Shelley's room were
going to be missing, calf-love missives from an infatuated
and sex-crazed Max. Shelley had half a mind to set fire to
them right in the middle of Sarah Meyer's floor.

Sarah had a little Hanukkah display on the top of her
tall bureau. There was a little menorah and a palm-size

book with the story of the festival in it. Shelley recognized both as gifts from Lotte. Shelley had a pair herself. In spite of the fact that she wanted to smash everything in this room, she decided not to smash this. She might not be religious, but like many other people who had drifted into agnosticism for no particular reason, she was leery of the possible power of religious objects. Or she was sometimes. Maybe it was just that right now she was more than a little on edge.

She found the letters right off, in the otherwise empty center drawer of the room's desk. She pulled the drawer open and there they were. If she had been going about this logically, she would have left Sarah's room then and there.

Shelley Feldstein was not going about this logically. She knew just how much time she had—more than half an hour, now, before the cutting session broke up and Sarah was free to come back to the hotel. Shelley had all the time in the world. And she didn't want to waste a moment of it.

She stuffed the letters down the front of her shirtwaist dress, under her belt, so that they would stay put. Then she headed for Sarah's suitcases.

One real suitcase. One briefcase full of papers. One overnight bag with cosmetics and bath supples.

Shelley upended both the suitcase and the briefcase, spilling their contents on the floor. Then she took a bottle of Max Factor foundation out of the overnight bag, opened it, and poured the contents into the mess of clothes and papers at her feet.

Good, she thought, very good.

By the time she got done with this room, Sarah Meyer would have been taught a lesson. By the time she got done with this room, nothing would ever put it back together again. By the time she got done with this room . . .

What?

Shelley went into the bathroom, got Sarah's bottle of shampoo and her bottle of conditioner, and came back into the main room to dump the contents of both on the mess she'd already made.

She was no longer doing this for revenge or to teach Sarah a lesson or to strike a blow in the holy war for a right to privacy.

Shelley was doing it because pulling a stunt like this on a fat slob bitch like Sarah Meyer was *fun*.

SIX

1

It was three thirty when Gregor Demarkian showed up at the precinct where John Henry Newman Jackman was spending his afternoon, and three thirty-one when he decided that he was glad he had never been an ordinary local police officer. Why was it that local police stations were always so depressing, even when they were in the middle of big-money, low-crime districts? This one was not in the middle of a big-money, low-crime district. It was in the middle of a slum that was rapidly metamorphosing into what the cops had started to call "UFO territory." UFO territory was the bastard child of the drug wars. Poor neighborhoods were full of drugs these days. Everybody expected them to be. There was a point, however, when a neighborhood got too full of drugs. There was a moment when the nonaddicted and the uninvolved decided they would rather be homeless than live around this. That was when things started to get really bad. The buildings emptied out. The windows got broken and the bricks began to crumble. There would be a rash of fires.

Gregor had seen whole blocks burn in a matter of days and weedy vacant lots sprout from the ruins overnight. This neighborhood was not quite there yet. The blackened bricks strewn across the lumpy ground of the lot next to the station house testified to at least one fire, but the tenement directly across the street was still full of people. Gregor even saw children straggling down the pavement, probably on their way home from school. Several of them wore Catholic-school uniforms, which meant somebody around here was still trying. Gregor didn't think the trying was doing much good or that it would continue much longer. Up at the corner there was a building with shattered windows and splintered doors. Passing it, Gregor had heard the giggles and the sighs. The sounds were so soft, they might have been made by ghosts. Maybe they had been. The building was crammed full of hibernating junkies.

The glass in the station house door had a crack in it. Gregor ran his hand across it, clucking like an Armenian grandmother just quietly enough so that no one could hear him, and then went inside. He walked up to the counter and gave his name to the desk sergeant. She was a heavy woman in her forties who looked like she'd just stepped out of a raging tornado. Her wiry, salt-and-pepper hair was standing up from her scalp and corkscrewed in every direction. The collar of her blouse was pulled sideways and her rolled-up sleeves were wrinkled into accordian pleats. Her eyes were wild. Gregor stood politely in front of her and let her look him over. He didn't think much of anything about him was actually sinking in. Her mind was on an altercation taking place on her side of the dividing rail. Two cops had a young man in custody and were trying to ask him questions. The young man would sit silently for a minute or two and then leap to his feet and yell *"Bungeeee!"* at the top of his lungs. The young man was as crazy as a loon, and the two police officers knew it, but they slogged on bravely anyway, as if they had a hope in hell of getting something done. The desk sergeant turned her back to Gregor and looked at them. Then she turned to face Gregor again and sighed.

"It's like this all the time now," she said in a wondering voice. "It's amazing. Where do they get the energy?"

"Detective Jackman," Gregor reminded her.

She picked up her phone and punched a couple of buttons. Then she said, "Guy named Gregor Demarkian here for John" and waited. A second later, she put down the phone.

"He'll be here in a minute," she said. "You can take a seat, if you like."

The seats were all made of plastic and cracked. They were also filthy. "That's all right," Gregor said. "I'll stand."

"Bungeeeee!" the young man in the back said, hopping around on one foot.

One of the cops standing next to him reached out, grabbed his shoulder, and pushed him down into his chair. "Jesus Christ," the cop said. "What did I ever do to deserve this?"

"Wait a minute," the desk sergeant said. "Aren't you the one they call the Armenian-American Hercule Poirot?"

"I'm the one they call the black Cardinal Cushing," John Jackman said, coming through the propped-open fire doors to the left of the counter and grabbing Gregor by the arm. "I'm going to take this man upstairs, sergeant. If I get calls from anybody lower than the chief for the next thirty minutes, I don't want to know about them."

Gregor supposed that this meant that John Jackman did not now have a wife or a girlfriend or a lover, but that was the kind of question he should save for later, and he appreciated what John was doing for him. What John was principally doing for him was providing him with an escape from having to answer the sergeant's question about the Armenian-American Hercule Poirot. Gregor hated answering questions about the Armenian-American Hercule Poirot. He wasn't all that fond of the original Hercule

Poirot. If the newspapers had to nickname him after some character in crime fiction, they could at least have chosen one of the characters Gregor actually liked.

John Jackman was pushing Gregor through the fire doors he had come through himself, but not up the stairs. There was a door beyond the fire doors that led outside to a parking lot. John shoved Gregor through that and stumbled out into the cold after him.

"You told your sergeant a lie," Gregor protested. "She won't know where to find you."

"She can call my beeper," John said. "Come on. I want to get out of here before anybody thinks up anything else for me to do."

"Where are we going?"

"To WKMB. I've got the lab reports—I've got them on me—"

"You're not wearing a coat."

"I never wear a coat. Here's the car, Gregor. In."

Gregor got in. It was an ordinary police car, but there was only one uniformed officer in the front instead of two. The uniformed man waited until both Gregor and John Jackman were seated and John had the door pulled shut. Then he peeled out. Gregor hated peeling out. He kept getting crystal clear images of a car peeling right into the side of a building somewhere and leaving pieces of itself all over the sidewalk.

"You seen my publicity?" John asked him. "Or have you been too busy reading your own?"

"I've been too busy reading my own," Gregor told him. "What did they say about you?"

"They called me a cross between Virgil Tibbs and Sidney Poitier. And then they said that if this city had any sense, it would make me the next chief of police."

"So?"

"So they only said it because I'm black, Gregor. And at the moment, we *have* a chief of police who happens to be a *good* friend of mine and in no hurry to *retire*, for God's sake, and he isn't going to *like* this."

"He'll live with it."

"Yeah. Give me a second, here, Gregor and we'll start on the lab reports. Sidney *Poitier*, for God's sake. Virgil *Tibbs*."

Gregor had always thought Sidney Poitier was a very fine actor. This didn't seem to be the time to say so.

2

Philadelphia is ringed by highways and linked together by concrete overpasses. On a good day, this system makes travel from one side of the city to the other a snap. This was not a good day. With Hanukkah falling so late this year—practically in the lap of Christmas—the usual seasonal traffic had been doubled. Everywhere the roads were full of drivers who came into the city only one day out of three hundred and sixty-five and who didn't have the faintest idea where they were going. Everywhere the roadsides were crowded with vehicles disabled by their owners' stupidities. The traffic was maddening. Gregor tried to sit back and ignore it. He couldn't, because their driver was as tense as a cop about to break up a domestic argument. John Jackman was irritated as well. Gregor thought cops had to deal with too much frustration over important things. They deserved a break from the Almighty on side issues like the traffic. They weren't going to get it.

Stuck in bumper to bumper on one of the long curving sweeps of overpass, Gregor looked down and saw a cluster of stores with wreaths and bells and Christmas trees in their windows. He tapped his fingers against the handle of his door in impatience.

"It's started to bother me," he said. "Christmas decorations without Hanukkah decorations. It doesn't seem right."

"Why don't we just do away with Christmas and solve the problem that way?" John suggested.

"I take it you've had a bad day."

"They go nuts," John said darkly. "I'm not kidding. Say *holiday* to these people, and they go nuts."

"Which people?"

"All people. Race doesn't matter. Class doesn't matter. Sex only matters because if *he* goes nuts he's likely to beat her up and if *she* goes nuts she's likely to put a bullet through his arm, but that's the difference in size talking, that's all. I'm not talking about ordinary domestic violence here, Gregor. I'm talking about—"

"Nuts."

"You got it."

"Why don't you tell me what you've found out about the death of Maximillian Dey," Gregor said. "Maybe that will take your mind off the nuts."

John patted the front of his suit jacket, didn't find what he was looking for, and started patting his pants. Then he stuck his hands in his front left pants pocket and came out with what looked like a million sheets of computer paper compressed into a cube. The cube sprung open in his hand. It looked alive.

"These are just summaries. If you want to see the full reports, I've got them downtown at my regular office. I didn't want to drag them out to—"

"That's all right," Gregor said. "I don't think this should be too complicated. Did you contact the police in New York?"

"Oh, yes."

"And?"

"He's bent," Jackman said shortly. "The one they call Chickie. Hell, he's so bent you could use him for a paper clip."

"Ah. Well. Did you swallow your distaste long enough to get some information out of him?"

"Yeah, I swallowed my distaste, as you put it. And I got some information out of him. He tried to put me on to arresting this guy on *The Lotte Goldman Show* called Itzaak Blechmann. Did we meet him?"

"Yes," Gregor said. "He's the lighting engineer."

"Oh, that one. Well, with our friend Chickie, the clincher seems to be that Itzaak is not only Jewish, but Jewish from a foreign country, and besides he wears a yarmulke. Except Chickie didn't say *yarmulke*. He said—"

"Funny little hat," Gregor hazarded.

"Right. Christ, Gregor, I hated this guy. But I got his information. It wasn't much more helpful than our own."

The traffic had broken up just a little. They had to be doing fifteen miles an hour. Gregor leaned forward and looked out the windshield. The cars went on for miles. He sat back.

"Let me make a few guesses here," he said. "In the first place, the murder weapon in both cases was a tire iron or something like a tire iron."

"Right," Jackman said. "But that was easy enough to see from the condition of the corpse. It was the kind of case that makes me wonder what we have to bother with a medical examiner for."

"Everything was obvious from the condition of the corpse in the first case we worked together after I came back to Philadelphia," Gregor said, "and there it turned out that the obvious was not the cause of death after all."

"That's true."

"So we have to be sure," Gregor went on, "and now that we have the report we are sure. The report was the same in New York?"

"It was."

"What about the force of the blows? From what I saw, it looked like at least three sharp, powerful smashes to the side of the head, at least powerful enough to break the cheekbone—"

"And the skull," Jackman said. "On Maximillian Dey, broken bones in the head included the cheekbone, the upper and lower jaw, the nose, and the cranium in two places."

"What about Maria Gonzalez?"

"Worse. According to Chickie, her face was practically pulped."

"What about the angles?"

John Jackman shook his head. "It won't help. Whoever it was was either taller than both of them—considerably taller—or was standing on top of something when he struck. All the angles are more consistent with an overhead delivery rather than a right or left handedness."

"Don't start thinking in terms of 'he,' " Gregor warned. "There's nothing we have so far that would preclude a woman as perpetrator."

"What about the force?"

Gregor shook his head. "You've just told me that the angles are consistent with an overhead delivery. That would give the murderer leverage. And you can't discount the extra force inherent in extreme anger."

"Somebody was extremely angry with Maximillian Dey and Maria Gonzalez?"

"Yes," Gregor said thoughtfully. "I think they were."

"Why?"

"I'll have to check through a few things first. I just have a—feeling. Did you know Maximillian Dey had his wallet stolen the day before yesterday?"

"Yeah, I heard about it. Do you think it's connected?"

"Not directly, no. I mean, I believe it was an ordinary pocket picking with no broader implications in and of itself."

Jackman scowled. "You're being cryptic, Gregor. I don't like it when you're cryptic."

"Let's go back to the tire iron," Gregor said. "Have you looked around for it? Have you found it yet?"

"My people naturally looked around for a murder weapon," John Jackman told him, "but we didn't find one. And you keep saying tire iron, but we don't know if that's really—"

"It's a tire iron. You'll find it in the trunk of one of the limousines *The Lotte Goldman Show* drove down from New York. I believe they said there were two. Limousines, that is."

"How could you possibly know that?"

"Because it makes sense," Gregor said. "I take it no weapon was found in the Gonzalez case, either."

"No, no, it wasn't."

"From what Elkham told me about the Gonzalez case, Maria Gonzalez's body was moved around and nobody was ever sure where. Well, where's the most likely place?"

"You mean in the trunk of a car," Jackman said. "But Gregor—"

"No buts. Correct me if I'm wrong, but there doesn't seem to me to be anywhere else her body could have gone to. And the trunk of the company limousine is not a place the police would necessarily think of to search unless there was an obvious reason for it. You didn't search the limousines yesterday, did you?"

"No," Jackman said.

"There, then. And the wounds are consistent with a tire iron. And the thing about a tire iron is that you can just put it back where you got it—meaning in its place in the car—and you don't have to worry about it looking out of place. Then later, when you have a little extra time, you can dispose of it. You can throw it in the river."

"Fine," Jackman said. "But it's an incredible risk to take."

"So what? So this murderer just killed a man in the

men's room of a busy office suite. I don't think we can accuse him of being afraid to take risks."

"Are you sure the tire iron will still be there? In the limousine? If we look?"

"No. He might have gotten rid of it already. He might not have had time. I couldn't say."

"You're using *he*."

"It's for convenience."

"Are you trying to tell me that the murderer is one of the drivers? Do you have a reason to think—"

"Of course the murderer doesn't have to be one of the limousine drivers," Gregor said impatiently. "He—or she—just has to be someone with access to the vehicles, which means with access to the keys. The person who comes immediately to mind is that secretary, Sarah Meyer. I'll bet anything she has keys to every door, box, and vehicle connected to that show. And she's got mobility, too. She wanders around a lot. It's part of her job. People expect it."

"What reason would she have for killing Dey and Gonzalez?"

"Maybe there was a love triangle," Gregor suggested. "Maybe Sarah was in love with Max and Max was in love with Maria, and Sarah killed Maria in the hopes that Max would turn to her in his bereavement, and when he didn't she killed Max himself in a rage."

"Not bad," Jackman said. "But it sounds more like something on *Days of Our Lives* than real life."

"All right then. Try Dr. Goldman or DeAnna Kroll. Either one of them might have something in their past they don't want anyone to know about—"

"Saints in heaven," Jackman groaned, "not a deep dark secret from the past."

"Make it something in the present instead," Gregor said. "My point is that they've got access, too, and mobility. And people do have reasons."

"It helps if they have reasons that would convince a

jury," Jackman said. "What's that up there? My God. I do believe the traffic is about to get moving."

"The traffic is about to get moving," the uniformed man in the front seat said. "Look. Do me a favor. Let me run the siren."

John Jackman took a look at his watch. "Okay," he said. "Run the siren. But only for as long as it takes to get out of this mess. Turn it off as soon as we get to town."

"Right," the uniformed man said. He put the car into gear and turned on the noise, producing a whooping wail that reminded Gregor of the death throes of whooping cranes.

Gregor Demarkian hated sirens and everything that went with them. He shut this one out of his consciousness as far as that was possible and turned to John Jackman so he wouldn't have to look out the windshield at the progress they were suddenly making.

"Now let me tell you something," he said. "David Goldman came to see me this morning, to tell me all about a curious little item called an Israeli dreidel."

3

The halls and corridors of WKMB were neither more nor less busy than they had been when Gregor had first seen them early yesterday morning, but the halls and corridors of that part of WKMB now assigned to *The Lotte Goldman Show* were almost deserted. Gregor and John Jackman went in together, without bringing the uniformed man along. This was only a semiofficial visit. John Jackman wanted to check out the scene one more time, now that the crisis was over and he could investigate in relative calm. Gregor had a few questions he wanted to ask. Studio C looked forlorn. The furniture that had served for this morning's taping was still strewn across the platform.

Prescott Holloway was picking up a small round coffee table just as Gregor and John came in. He paused in his work as Gregor and John walked toward him. Gregor thought he was probably handier at this than Maximillian Dey had been. He was certainly stronger. Gregor and John stopped at the edge of the platform and said hello.

"Everybody's gone," Prescott told them. "Everybody except DeAnna, that is. She'd down in her office."

"DeAnna will be fine," Gregor told him. "We really just want to look around."

"Yeah. Well. Have a good time. I really want them to hire another set man. I want them to hire two. I was getting drafted into this shit all the time back in New York, and Max was alive and kicking then."

Prescott raised the coffee table a little higher and wedged one curved edge of it against his hip. Then he hopped off the platform and headed for the doors to the outside. Gregor and John Jackman went in the other direction, to the doors at the back of the stage, and let themselves into the corridor that led to the offices and the greenroom and the other temporary accommodations for *The Lotte Goldman Show*. Prescott had been absolutely right when he said the place was deserted. Gregor and John passed door after door, open on empty offices.

DeAnna Kroll was in the very last office at the back. Her door was open too, but what it revealed was chaos. It did not seem to Gregor to be the kind of controlled chaos very creative people were supposed to prefer to work in. It looked like an outrageous mess she had been helpless to prevent. Papers and envelopes were spilling off the desk onto the floor. Half-filled polystyrene coffee cups were balanced on chairs and arranged in a pattern on the file cabinet top. Bits and pieces of Hanukkah and Christmas paraphernalia kept popping up in the oddest places. A plastic crèche with babe in manger was nestled in the folds of a gray flannel scarf that had somehow fallen to the floor. One of those ubiquitous little plastic menorahs with nine supposedly already-lit plastic candles was coming out of the pocket of the pea jacket DeAnna had hung over the top of the office door. Gregor checked out the pea jacket and saw that it had been bought at Ralph Lauren Polo. DeAnna went on talking into the phone.

"I know it's impossible to get Marianna here from Sarajevo by Monday," she was saying, "but you have to get Marianna here by Monday from Sarajevo and that's that. . . . Well, I know they're having political difficulties, everybody over there is having political difficulties, but. . . . Well, bribe them. . . . Bribe all of them. . . . Bribe enough of them to *get* a cease-fire. . . . Wait, I can't. . . . *Shit!*" DeAnna dropped the phone into the cradle. "He hung up on me. Can you believe that? Long distance from Vienna and he hung *up* on me."

Gregor could believe it.

"What was that all about?" John Jackman asked. "Is Marianna a guest you want for the show?"

"Marianna is a show," DeAnna said. "She wrote a book called *Masturbation as an Art Form.* Now she's coming out with one called *Masturbation as a Political Act.* Lotte can do an hour with Marianna standing on her head. And with the way things have been going around here, we need—oh. You should sit down. Do you want to sit down?"

There was nowhere to sit down. All the chairs were covered with papers, or worse. Gregor tried perching himself on the arm of something that looked a little fragile, but might do. John Jackman continued to stand. DeAnna stared at the phone as if she were willing it to ring.

"Wars," she said. "People ought to give up having wars. They're a damned nuisance."

"That's a thought," Gregor said blandly. "Would you mind answering a few questions for us? Right now? We realize this is a little spur of the moment, and you might be busy—"

"Oh, I'm busy enough," DeAnna said, "but I'm not

going anywhere. I have to wait for that idiot to call back. And he will call back. He always does. What do you want to know? I don't have an alibi."

"An alibi isn't necessary at the moment," Gregor said. "Do you know anything about Maximillian Dey's having had his pocket picked—"

"Well, *of course* I know about that," DeAnna interrupted. "Everybody knows about that. He went on and on about it."

"Good," Gregor told her. "Now. When did it happen?"

"As he was getting off the subway when he was coming down to meet the rest of us so we could all take off for Philadelphia. We all came down in two cars."

"Limousines?"

"Of course limousines."

"Fine. So Max got his pocket picked. It was just his wallet that was missing? Nothing else?"

"Well," DeAnna said, "with Max, his wallet would have been enough. He kept his life in there. Pictures from back in Portugal. A fake ID saying he was twenty-one so he could drink. Everything."

"Everything," Gregor repeated. "Fine. Max was an immigrant, am I correct?"

"Yes, of course. From Portugal."

"He'd been in this country how long?"

"I don't know. A little more than a year, I think, but don't quote me. It's just a guess."

"You never asked him?"

"Well, Max didn't have what you'd call a position of trust," DeAnna said. "And we don't ask those kinds of questions. Gradon Cable Systems does that. It's just that we wouldn't mind."

"Wouldn't mind what?"

"Wouldn't mind that his English was a little sketchy and that he didn't know enough about the city to really operate," DeAnna said. "Lotte is always taking on stray kittens, if you know what I mean. Immigrants, especially, because she was an immigrant. But it isn't only immigrants. We have about six inner-city high school kids as interns on the show every summer. Lotte is like that."

"That's very commendable, but that's not exactly what I'm getting at," Gregor said. "About the contents of this wallet. Do you know what else might have been in there besides a fake ID and some family pictures from Portugal?"

"Money," DeAnna said.

"What about his green card? He did have a green card? He wasn't a citizen yet?"

"He wasn't a citizen yet," DeAnna said, "and he definitely lost his green card. He went on and on about it. About how difficult it was going to be to replace."

"That was the day before yesterday?"

"Yes."

"You're sure?"

"Of course I'm sure, Mr. Demarkian. What are you getting at?"

"Well," Gregor said, "when I arrived here yesterday morning, I walked into Studio C to find Max lifting a chair into the air and the contents of his pockets falling on the floor. I picked up a number of the things he dropped and gave them back to him. One of those things was a green card."

"It was?" DeAnna looked confused. "Maybe he was wrong, then. Maybe he had it someplace else and didn't realize it, and then he found it later."

"Maybe he did," Gregor conceded, although he didn't believe it for a minute. "What about after he left me? I know we went over this yesterday—"

"And over it and over it." DeAnna was irritated. "I can't tell you anymore than I already have told you. He brought the chair downstairs and put it in the truck. We know that because the chair was in the truck and Prescott saw him at the truck. After that we just don't know."

"That's right," Gregor said. "We don't know. Between yesterday and today you haven't remembered anything else on this score? Nobody has come to you and said, oh, by the way, I forgot, but—"

"No," DeAnna said. "There's been nothing like that."

"You haven't found anything anywhere that might have belonged to him in an unexpected place? The back stairs? Another bathroom? Somebody's office?"

"I haven't found anything that belonged to him, period."

"Has anybody else?"

"No."

"What about messages? Did Max ever get any? Just before you came up here? On the trip? Since you got here?"

"People like Max don't get messages," DeAnna said. "Not on a regular basis. If they do, they get fired."

"Meaning you would have remembered if he had gotten a message."

"Meaning I would have and so would anyone else, and somebody would have made a remark about it."

"Fine," Gregor said. "No messages."

"Gregor?"

John Jackman's voice sounded oddly strangled, and it came as a surprise. Gregor had been so intent on questioning DeAnna Kroll, and thinking about Maximillian Dey, he'd forgotten John was there. Now he felt a little guilty about it. John was the professional. This was his case. Gregor was only along for the ride.

"I'm sorry," he said, turning to John.

But John wasn't looking at him. He was staring in the direction of the office door. As Gregor turned to see what John was looking at, he realized DeAnna was staring in that direction, too.

Itzaak Blechmann was standing right in the middle of the office doorway, his hands wrapped around his bloodstained chest, his legs shaking, his face covered with tears.

"Come and see," he said, in English so heavily accented it would have been hard to understand, except for the intensity of the emotion behind it. "Come and see. Carmencita is—Carmencita is on the floor, and she is dead."

PART THREE

*Lady Chatterley's
Demarkian*

ONE

1

Carmencita Boaz was not dead. There were times in the next half hour when Gregor and John Jackman both thought she was going to die. There were times when they even thought she had, slipping away from them as they did all the frantic things people do when they have been trained in first aid so long ago they don't remember most of it. God only knew, she ought to have been dead. Gregor couldn't remember seeing a face in a worse mess than this one on a live person. He had to keep reminding himself about the peculiarities of head wounds. Head wounds bled. He had to keep reminding himself that nothing terrible had happened to Carmencita's eyes. Eyes were the most vulnerable place, except for the softnesses inside the ear. Carmencita's eyes opened every once in a while, when the pain pierced her shock and made her twitch, and they were a beautiful, shiny blue that made Gregor think of polished lapis lazuli.

Carmencita was lying on the floor just beyond the

fire door next to the elevators that went down to the lobby and opened on this floor to the reception desk for WKMB. It was a utility area and not much frequented by WKMB staff or casual visitors. It wasn't much frequented by anybody except the cleaning people, and they weren't likely to show up in force before six or seven o'clock. Even so, it was a risky place for whoever it was to have pulled this sort of stunt. There was always the chance that something would need to be fixed, sending a janitor up from the basement offices of the Maintenance Department. There was always a chance that some hotshot on the rise who wanted to get in shape was taking the stairs as a form of aerobic exercise. There were all kinds of chances, including the one that had come to pass. Itzaak had been worried. Itzaak had opened every door he could find.

Itzaak was covered with blood. His shirt was a sodden mass of it and his pants looked as if they had been splattered with ketchup and vinegar. He had lost his yarmulke and didn't seem to have noticed.

"We have to find a priest from her church," he kept saying. "We have to find a priest from her church."

Gregor and John Jackman were most interested in finding a doctor from the hospital. Itzaak was useless. The only reason he hadn't collapsed from shock was that the fact of Carmencita's being alive had given him a last jolt of energy. As soon as they had Carmencita in competent hands and he no longer had anything he might be called on to do, Itzaak was going to collapse. It made more sense to rely on DeAnna Kroll.

"Make some phone calls," Gregor instructed her, as soon as John Jackman had leaned over the body and pronounced it alive. "St. Elizabeth's Hospital. We need an ambulance. We have a—no, don't tell them that. Tell them we have a woman who's been hit with a tire iron and her skull's caved in—"

"But—"

"I know it's not strictly the truth," Gregor said, "but we want to get them here."

"Shouldn't I call nine one one?"

"Nine one one serves the entire city. St Elizabeth's will be faster. John, do you want to call in to your people yourself?"

"Yeah, I'll do it."

"Good," Gregor said. "That will be faster, too. Go on now, Ms. Kroll. We don't have a lot of time."

DeAnna Kroll looked in the direction of Carmencita Boaz's body, which meant she looked at John Jackman's back, because it was blocking her view.

"Is she going to die? Is she—"

"She is if the ambulance doesn't get here soon," Gregor said.

"The ambulance," DeAnna said. "Yes. And I have to call Lotte."

Gregor didn't know what good Lotte was going to do. DeAnna probably didn't know either. She hurried off. Gregor went over to John Jackman. He was doing all the right things for head wounds and concussion. Hard as it was to believe, what had happened to Carmencita Boaz was going to be technically called a concussion. To Gregor, concussion was what boys got playing sandlot baseball when they came from families too poor to afford helmets.

"Go," Gregor told John. "Let's get this moving. I'll take over here."

"Right," John Jackman said. He turned Carmencita Boaz over to Gregor and straightened up. Gregor was relieved to see that the woman was breathing more regularly now, and more deeply, if still not deeply enough. When they had first arrived on the scene, Carmencita had had the hitching, shuddering breath of someone in the throes of tachycardia.

John Jackman disappeared through the fire door.

Itzaak moved in beside Gregor and looked into Carmencita's face.

"She is breathing," he said, and even though he must have known she would be, he sounded awed.

Gregor found himself wondering how long it would be before they could calm Itzaak down and question him.

2

Having the most famous homicide cop in the city and the Armenian-American Hercule Poirot on the case had its advantages. The ambulance responded with alacrity, and four pairs of uniformed cops showed up at the scene in one and a half minutes flat. Gregor was glad to see every one of them. Being an FBI agent is a manner of being a policeman. The Bureau as federal police force was a concept much stressed when Gregor was training at Quantico. The first time Gregor had ever been present at an actual crime scene, he had discovered the difference. The FBI was always coming in after the Sturm und Drang was over: after the kidnapping had happened and somebody was needed to set up and monitor a ransom drop; after six local police forces in three states had racked up a string of seemingly related killings and needed someone to coordinate an interstate hunt. When the FBI wasn't doing that, it was dealing with paper crime. The FBI was very good at paper crime. A well-trained Bureau agent to track the course of a million dollars in drug money from the streets of New York to the bank vaults of the Cayman Islands. Of course, he couldn't actually get his hands on any of it. International banking regulations would keep him from doing that.

The first time Gregor had stumbled onto a real crime scene, he had been astounded. All the blood and confusion and mess: How did they work under such conditions? He had also been a little embarrassed. There he was, the expert, the country's most famous specialist in murder, with his picture on the cover of *Time*—and he hadn't known a damn thing. That the murders he was an expert in were the serial kind—or that his expertise in solving them depended heavily on computers—hadn't seemed to absolve him. He had thought he ought to know something. He had thought he should at least not feel out of place.

The first crime scene Gregor had stumbled onto had contained the body of Bennis Hannaford's father. The investigating officer had been John Henry Newman Jackman. It had all happened in Bryn Mawr three years ago.

Carmencita Boaz was going out into the foyer on a stretcher. She was not conscious, and Itzaak, walking along beside her, wasn't exactly conscious either. Gregor saw one of the stretcher men turn to say something to Itzaak and decided to intervene.

"Let him go with you," Gregor said. "If you don't, you'll have two cases of shock on your hands besides the concussion."

"It's against regulations," the stretcher man said.

Itzaak looked like he was going to cry. At that moment, DeAnna Kroll came up to him, put her arm around his shoulder, and whispered in his ear. Itzaak brightened immediately.

"Watch that woman get a limousine to bring the two of them to the hospital," John Jackman said. Behind him, uniformed cops and techies and a lot of other people were milling around, taking samples, trying for fingerprints. There was no sign of the murder weapon and Gregor didn't expect there to be any. He didn't expect there to be much physical evidence, either. It wasn't that kind of crime and it wasn't that kind of crime scene.

Gregor drew John Jackman away from the scene and the cops and the techies and into the foyer near the elevators. In the few seconds that he had had his head turned, the crowd around Carmencita Boaz had disappeared. Gregor found himself wondering how the stretcher had fit into the elevator. It was a slightly oversize elevator, so maybe the crush hadn't been too bad. It was only very slightly oversize, so maybe it had. Obviously, Gregor thought, he wasn't doing any better at thinking straight than anyone else.

Gregor shut the fire door on the techies swearing at each other—they did it so well, Gregor sometimes imagined they had to take a test for it; if you couldn't think of thirteen ways to use the *F* word in one sentence, you had to give up your dreams of being a techie and go into library work—and said, "Well? What do you think?"

"Itzaak Blechmann walked in on it," Jackman said. "Either that, or he did it."

"He didn't do it," Gregor said. "Our friend got lucky."

"You mean because Itzaak didn't see him? Maybe. But he got unlucky, too. The woman's alive."

"Alive and unconscious," Gregor said. "And there's nothing to say she saw her attacker. And even if she did, she may not remember."

"Gee, Gregor. Don't work too hard at making me feel good. I might get overconfident and think I was having a good day."

"Don't be facetious," Gregor said impatiently. "Look at our situation here. In the first place, I think this time we may be able to find the weapon."

"Why?"

"Because there wouldn't have been time to get rid of it. Our friend is in a bind. The plan was to kill Carmencita Boaz in a place where she was unlikely to be found for several hours, therefore making time for all the housekeeping details so necessary to bringing off a successful homicide. But there wasn't any time. Our friend lifted the tire iron—"

"Are you really sure it was a tire iron?"

"I'm positive. Our friend lifted the tire iron and be-gan to bring it down on Carmencita's head. Then our friend heard Itzaak, not passing across the foyer to the el-evators but coming closer, or maybe our friend heard Itzaak's hand on the knob of the fire door—"

"That would have been close," John Jackman said.

"Whatever our friend heard, it was enough. Enough to interrupt the blow. Enough to leave Carmencita Boaz alive. And then what?"

"What?"

"Well, John, there would hardly be time for our friend to go tearing off to throw the tire iron in the river, especially since our friend is not a resident of Philadel-phia and doesn't know the city well. Our friend might, but there's no reason to suppose it's so. And with Carmencita found, of course, we're in the middle of an emergency."

"So?"

"So our friend's services are going to be required. Have you noticed that everyone we've met who works on *The Lotte Goldman Show* carries beepers?"

"Yeah," Jackman said. "Even the chauffeurs carry beepers."

"People carry beepers when they're expected to be on call. Which our friend is. Which means there is no time for our friend to go chasing around the city, getting rid of the murder weapon."

"So where is it?"

"In the trunk of one of the limousines, I would ex-pect. Tire irons go in trunks. The limousines are parked right downstairs where anybody can get at them. I'll bet half a dozen people have keys to the trunks, too. DeAnna Kroll. Sarah Meyer."

"Why Sarah Meyer?"

"Because secretaries are always being asked to carry things. Of course, this is the third murder. If our friend didn't start out with a set of keys to those limousines, by now—"

"Do you know who 'our friend' is?" John Jackman demanded. "Do you have a name?"

"I know who it must be," Gregor said. "That is, if one last speculation of mine turns out to be right. Then there's only one person it could be."

"Good. Why don't you give me a name?"

"Why don't you send somebody to find that tire iron? It won't be much use to you. It won't have any fingerprints on it. Our friend is not a fool. But it would be good to have."

"Gregor—"

"Then we'll go to the hospital and talk to Itzaak Blechmann," Gregor said. "There are a few things he may know that nobody else would. Then we'll figure out what to do. We're going to have to do something. We can't just wait for Carmencita Boaz to open her eyes. She may not have the information we need. And once our friend realizes she isn't going to die, our friend may bolt."

"If our friend is so damned smart," John said, "why doesn't our friend bolt right this minute? Why doesn't he or she or it just hit you over the head for all this 'our friend'—"

"When I give you pronouns, you get ideas," Gregor interrupted patiently. "Go send somebody for that tire iron. You may have to chase it to the hospital. What was that we were saying about how DeAnna Kroll was going to get Itzaak there? Whatever. And then let's go. It doesn't make any sense for us to be standing around here. We've got work to do."

"Work to do," John Jackman muttered. "Sometimes I think I'm crazy ever to talk to you."

Then he stalked back across the foyer, opened the fire door, and stuck his head through.

"Pilsudski! Estavez! Get over here. I've got something I want you to do."

3

One of the things Gregor always forgot between murder investigations was the media, by which he meant the *Philadelphia Inquirer* and the local television news. He didn't forget that the media were there. He got the paper every morning and he watched the evening news at least once or twice a week. What he forgot was the way they behaved when they scented blood, and how much worse they were when the blood they scented had a tinge of celebrity in it. A murder and an attempted murder among the staff of *The Lotte Goldman Show*—with yet another murder, back in New York, to use for atmosphere—was just what these people liked the best. By the time Gregor and John Jackman got to St. Elizabeth's hospital, the place was literally coated with reporters and photographers and stringers from the wire services with connections to the suburban weeklies. Gregor wondered how they had heard about this, who had called them. Monitoring the police band all by itself wouldn't do. Monitoring the police band, they would have known there was an attempted murder. They would not have known there was *this* attempted murder. Gregor saw a young man in black sweats and black sneakers with a badge on his chest that said CBS. Whether he was really from CBS or just trying to crash the party, there was no way to know. Gregor saw a thin young woman with a half dozen cameras slung over her shoulders get knocked against a lamppost by another thin young woman with a notebook in her hand. A third thin young woman got out of the second thin young woman's way before she could be knocked to the side herself.

"Wonderful manners these people have got," Gregor commented.

John Jackman grunted.

They had come down to the hospital in a patrol car with the siren blasting. The siren was still blasting, but nobody was paying any attention to it. The entrance to St. Elizabeth's parking garage was blocked by people. No amount of extra beeping and blooping would get them to move. They were stuck almost directly opposite St. Elizabeth's front doors. The front doors were at the top of a long flight of shallow marble steps that led down to a gently curving drive that made a kind of smiley face in the road it came off of. Smiley face. Now Gregor knew he was losing it. A young man leaped onto the top of the police car and plastered himself against the windshield, peering inside. Even with the heater going and the siren wailing and the cop behind the wheel honking his horn to get the young man off, Gregor could hear what the young man had to say.

"It's Demarkian!" he was shouting at the top of his lungs. "Right in here! It's *Demarkian!*"

"Maybe I'll get out and fire a warning shot," John Jackman said.

Gregor sincerely doubted that a warning shot would do any good. Not a single person in the crowd would believe John Jackman meant it. Killing somebody would do some good or even wounding them a little, but neither of those things was a politically viable alternative. Moving the police car into the parking garage wasn't a materially viable alternative. Now that they knew who was in it, the crowd would never let it pass. Gregor had never in his life felt so much in need of the National Guard.

"I think we're going to have to make a run for it," Gregor said.

"Run where?"

"Right up to the front doors. They won't push too

hard, John. These are not people who are used to getting hurt."

"Maybe we could get them used to it."

"On the count of three, I'm going to open this door and bolt. Be ready."

"Why? Nobody is interested in me."

"Three," Gregor said.

So many people were leaning against the door, he almost couldn't open it. Then someone out there realized what was happening and stepped back. Gregor shoved hard with his shoulder and the door sprang open. Gregor stuck his legs out into the street and a young woman fell into his lap.

"Excuse me," he said, lifting her off.

"Mr. Demarkian!" someone in the crowd yelled. "Have you caught the murderer? Are you going to make an arrest?"

"I can't make an arrest," Gregor said. "I'm not a police officer."

"Get out of the way," John Jackman said. "Get out of the way. If you don't get out of the way, I'm going to fire this thing."

"Get a picture of the cop with his gun in the air!" somebody else yelled.

"Mr. Demarkian," the first someone yelled. "Is it true that Lotte was on the scene when the attack on Carmencita Boaz occurred?"

"As far as I know, Lotte Goldman was visiting relatives on the Main Line when the attack on Carmencita Boaz occurred. Will you please get out of my way?"

"Get a picture of Demarkian going up the stairs," somebody else yelled.

It was like swimming in molasses, except that molasses wouldn't have been hostile, and Gregor definitely felt some hostility in this crowd. They kept pulling at him. People grabbed at his suit jacket tugging and crushing. Somebody tore his jacket pocket on the left side. Somebody else got hold of his tie and nearly strangled him. It suddenly struck Gregor that he was extremely glad that none of these people were liquored up.

"Hey Mr. Demarkian," somebody yelled. "Look this way and *glower*."

Glower. He was at St. Elizabeth's front doors. He pushed on one and couldn't make it budge. He pushed on the other and couldn't make it budge either. He looked through the glass and saw that there were a set of keys in the lock on the other side.

"Knock," John Jackman said, coming up behind him.

Gregor knocked. An older woman in an abbreviated nun's habit—full-body white apron over a pale blue dress; tucked-back white veil starched into immobility and falling just below her shoulders—came to the door and shook her head. John Jackman leaned past Gregor and held out his badge.

The nun hesitated, looked worriedly at the crowd, and then nodded.

"They can't lock a hospital," Gregor said. "What will happen to the sick people?"

"The ones who want to get in will just have to go down to Quaker General. Here we go. Be fast."

Gregor was fast. The door opened a very tiny crack. John Jackman pushed him from behind. Gregor stumbled through the doors and past the nun into a large blue-carpeted lobby. In fact, from what he could see, everything at St. Elizabeth's was blue. Then he remembered. Blue was the color of the Virgin Mary. St. Elizabeth was supposed to have been Mary's cousin and John the Baptist's mother. Catholics didn't make any more sense to him than television people did. The nun was locking the doors behind them with a series of sharp clicks that seemed to give her limitless satisfaction. She turned around to them when she was done and said, "You two gentlemen will want the fifth floor, north wing. That's where we put her. And enough police officers to start our own department."

"They're no better than reporters sometimes," John said.

"You're Mr. Gregor Demarkian, aren't you?" the nun said. "I'm Sister Mary Vincent. Sister Scholastica Burke is my second cousin."

"Oh," Gregor said.

"I've heard a great deal about you," Sister Mary Vincent said. "I think you must be quite an unusual man."

"He is," John Jackman snickered.

Sister Mary Vincent didn't seem to have heard the snicker. She was marching to the elevators. She was pushing the call button to get them a car. Gregor looked across the lobby at the desk and saw a crèche on the counter there, with the manger empty. Catholics always left the manger empty until Christmas day.

"You may hear differently when you get upstairs," Sister Mary Vincent said, "but the reports that have come down to me have all been very encouraging. She seems to have arrived here in time and mendable. Good luck."

"Wish Carmencita Boaz good luck," John Jackman said.

Sister Mary Vincent sniffed. "I am *praying* for Carmencita Boaz," she said.

Then the elevator doors popped open, and Gregor and John Jackman stepped inside. When the elevator doors closed again, Gregor realized that the elevator walls were hung with the story of Hanukkah in words and pictures. Mattathias of Modin and his five sons were painted in earth tones and beards, the way characters from the Bible were always painted these days—except that Gregor couldn't remember if this story was in the Bible. Mattathias of Modin was the man who had led the uprising against Antiochus Epiphanes when Antiochus had attempted to prevent the Jews from practicing their religion. It was at the successful conclusion of this uprising that the Jews had been left with oil enough only for one day when they needed much more to keep the light lit in front of the Torah, and God had sent along a miracle to let that one day's oil burn for eight. Gregor didn't know if he believed in miracles or not, but as miracles went, this was one of his favorites. He wasn't surprised to see it on the walls of an elevator in a Catholic hospital, either. He had heard stories about the intolerances of nuns, but he'd never actually met a nun who was religiously intolerant. He was fairly sure he would find a nun up on the fifth floor somewhere, searching diligently for something to replace Itzaak's yarmulke.

He looked over at John Jackman and asked, "What are you thinking about?"

"Carmencita Boaz," Jackman replied.

Gregor felt the elevator car bounce to a stop and sighed. "Of course you are," he said. "Of course you are."

4

Up on the fifth floor, everyone was thinking about Carmencita Boaz. Nurses went back and forth, in nun's habits and traditional uniforms and less traditional but still blindingly white trousers and tops. Doctors popped in and out of the room at the center of the corridor where all the action was. Police officers milled around, looking useless.

"I'm going to have to break some of this up," John Jackman said. "They can't just stand around and sightsee. You got something to occupy yourself with for the next ten or fifteen minutes?"

"I've got somebody I want to talk to."

"Good. See you later."

John Jackman took off, rounding up cops as he went.

Gregor moved closer to the door where everyone was congregating. DeAnna Kroll was there, looking frustrated and giving orders to Prescott Holloway. Gregor wasn't surprised that she was looking frustrated. She was a woman used to being able to get things done, and now she was being forced to wait without doing anything at all.

"Go out and get Lotte and bring her back here," she was saying. "And when you get back I want you to come right up and find me because I'm going to have something else for you to do—"

"I can't go out and get Dr. Goldman," Prescott was saying patiently. "The police just took the car."

"Well, she's got to get out here."

"Well, she can call a taxi. I can't get her if I don't have a car."

"Excuse me," Gregor said, moving up between them. "Could you tell me—"

DeAnna Kroll's fingernails were long and red and clawlike. She waved them in the air in front of Gregor's face, as if she were trying to dispel a mist, as if she couldn't quite remember who he was. Then she seemed to come to.

"Oh," she said. "It's you. You want to know about Carmencita."

"Carmencita is coming along very well," Prescott Holloway said. "At least, that's what we've been hearing."

"Her cheekbone is cracked, but it isn't really caved in. That's what they told us. And if her cheekbone isn't caved in then—"

"There's less chance that a bone fragment will get into her bloodstream," Prescott said.

DeAnna Kroll looked relieved. "I knew it was something like that. I'm sorry, Mr. Demarkian, we're all in a mess here, nobody knows what's going on and Lotte is going crazy out there at David's house, trying to get in and see for herself and *this* idiot—"

"It's not my fault," Prescott Holloway said.

"How is Itzaak?" Gregor asked. "Have you seen him around?"

"Itzaak? Oh, Itzaak. He's around somewhere. He's—"

"Over there," Prescott Holloway said solemnly.

Prescott Holloway was pointing not toward the door, but away from it, at the nurse's station with its counter and its small row of black vinyl-covered chairs for visitors. Itzaak was slumped in one of those chairs, his head in his hands. He was wearing a beautiful yarmulke, pushed far to the back of his head. It was made of raw silk and bordered with embroidery so fine, Gregor could practically see the perfection of every individual stitch. Gregor wondered where the nuns had found it.

"Excuse me," he said to Prescott Holloway and DeAnna Kroll.

He crossed to the row of chairs and sat down next to Itzaak. Itzaak raised his head and then lowered it again. For the moment, Itzaak was only interested in talking to doctors.

"Mr. Blechmann," Gregor said gently, "I know you are very upset at this time—"

"Not so upset," Itzaak said. "Not so upset as I was. She is not dead."

"No," Gregor agreed. "She is not dead."

"The doctor says to me there will always be something different now about her face. I mind for her because she will mind, but I do not mind for myself. She will always be beautiful to me."

"That's very wise, Mr. Blechmann," Gregor said, wondering what he meant by that. Itzaak didn't challenge him, but Itzaak wasn't listening to individual words. "I know your mind is with Ms. Boaz for the moment—"

"Miss," Itzaak said. "She never liked that other thing. Ms. She is from Guatamala. It is a conservative country."

"Yes. I know. Mr. Blechmann, we do have to talk, you and me. We have to get a few things straightened out. Because if we don't, Mr. Blechmann, the person who did this to Carmencita is going to go free."

"Free." Itzaak Blechmann shook his head. "I don't care if he goes free. I care only about Carmencita."

"Fine, Mr. Blechmann, fine. But how about this? I was for many years an agent for the Federal Bureau of Investigation and later a very high level administrator there. I still have a great many friends in the Bureau, and on Capitol Hill, and—possibly more pertinent to the present discussion—in the Immigration and Naturalization Service. If you will talk to me, and tell me everything you know, I give you my word that I will make a few phone calls about Carmencita. And about you, too, if that happens to be necessary."

"No," Itzaak said. "That isn't necessary."

"That's good."

"Why do you have to ask me questions if you know everything about it already?"

"Because I don't know everything about it already," Gregor said, standing up. "I only know the bare outlines. And I don't know enough to give the police an excuse to put this idiot out of business. There are also something called rules of evidence, and whether we like them or not, we must follow them. There's a coffee machine down at that end of the hall. The coffee will be terrible, but we could both use some. Shall I get you a cup?"

"Yes," Itzaak Blechmann said.

"Good. Will you talk to me?"

"Yes," Itzaak Blechmann said again.

"I'll be right back."

Gregor meant it, too. He had no intention of letting Itzaak Blechmann get away.

TWO

1

To Lotte Goldman, the principal problem with this tail end of the twentieth century was softness. Everyone and everything had melted just a little in the heat of luxury. Instead of men and women with firm identities and ramrod backbones, there were—what? It was hard to put it into words. The people who came to be in her show were often colorful and frequently outrageous, but at the core of them there was nothing in particular. It wasn't that they were hollow, the way shallow people are supposed to be. Most of them meant well and most of them felt as much as it was possible for them to feel. The problem was, it wasn't possible for them to feel much. It wasn't possible for them to know much, either. They were adrift in a sea of indeterminacy. Lotte had never been able to make herself a religious woman—although she had tried from time to time, for David's sake—but every once in a while, sitting on the platform next to some woman in bright green silk and twenty-two-carat solid-gold hoop earrings, she would want to claim the history of her religion for her own. The woman in the green silk would be going on and on about how terrible her life had been, about what life had been secretly all about behind the pretty facade of her middle-class suburban American home. Her mother had praised her brothers' good grades and only praised her when she was looking pretty. Her father let her brothers ride their bikes all over town but told her girls were only safe when they stayed in the yard to play. Lotte would sit on the platform with her hands folded in her lap and her teeth clamped down firmly on her lower lip, wanting to say: When I was twelve I lived with my brother in the hills outside Jerusalem, in a hole dug out of the ground to keep us safe from rain and gunfire; when I was fourteen I had one dress to wear to school and every night I had to come home and wash it; when I was sixteen a bomb went off under the bench at a bus stop I had just left to get on the bus, and through the bus windows I saw four people blown into pieces of blood and skin and bone on a city street. Lotte wanted to say these things, but she never did, because she knew what answer she would get.

She wanted to say something similar now to the reporters stationed outside the front doors of St. Elizabeth's hospital, but if she tried she could just imagine what answer she would be reported to have given. What she did instead was to stand on the front steps and give a little press conference, filled with all the correct expressions of horror and sympathy and all the expected resolutions to urge the police on to greater tenacity of commitment in the doing of their duty. Privately, Lotte thought the police had about as much tenacity in the doing of their duty as anybody could reasonably expect. The people who were not reasonable about it did not spend their working lives wondering if someone was going to shoot them.

What had to be said and done here was a script, written by God only knew who God only knew when, and now as surely engraved in stone as any one of the Ten

Commandments. Lotte performed her part in this script well. Because of that, her clothes were not clutched at, never mind ripped or torn, and not one person in the mob screamed directions in her face to get her to look at the camera. She said her piece. She answered a few questions. She explained that she was anxious to get upstairs and check the situation out. Then she knocked for Sister Mary Vincent to let her in and escaped into the silence of the lobby. Sister Mary Vincent had been warned that Lotte was coming. There was no time-wasteful checking of identification.

"Mr. Demarkian said you were to be sent directly up," Sister Vincent said, locking the door again. The reporters hung back and smiled at her. "It might relieve you to know, everything seems to be all right. The doctors don't believe there will be brain damage or anything like that. I'm afraid she will need some plastic surgery on her face."

From what Lotte had heard from DeAnna Kroll, this was something of an understatement. She looked at the cross on the wall behind the reception desk and wondered what it would be like to belong to a religion that encouraged you to go to God with every little thing in your life, that promised that God would answer all your prayers and protect all His children. But she didn't want that. She didn't even want the God of the Covenant. She only wanted herself.

She went up in the elevator, got out on the fifth floor, and looked around. It wasn't as hard to find the north wing as she'd thought it might be. All she had to do was follow the trail of doctors and nurses and police officers. She passed another crucifix and thought of what David had told her once, that his friend Father Ryan had said: *God answers all our prayers, but most of the time He says no.* The next thing she saw was a little menorah on display, just inside the door of a room where an old woman was sitting up in a chair, reading Barbara Tuchman's *The*

Zimmerman Telegram. In all the other rooms Lotte had so far passed, the space on the wall over where this woman's head was was occupied by a picture of the Virgin Mary on a cloud. In this one, that wall space was blank. Lotte wondered whose decision it had been to take the picture out of there.

She stopped at the nurse's station. The woman there could be identified as an RN only by the plastic name tag above the breast pocket of her white polyester tunic. Otherwise, she could have been a surgeon or a waitress.

"Excuse me," Lotte Goldman said. "I am looking for the room of Miss Carmencita Boaz."

The nurse looked up, blinked and blushed. "Oh," she said. "Oh, Dr. Goldman. You shouldn't have been left waiting. Have you been left waiting? You should have been brought up right away."

"I just got here," Lotte said. "I would like to see—"

"Never mind," DeAnna Kroll said, emerging from a knot of people farther down the hall. "Hello, Lotte. I'm glad you're here. The doctor's still in with her."

"Still?"

"They have to make sure the wound is entirely cleaned out before they can bandage it. I've had hell's own time keeping Itzaak out of there. He gets hysterical and the doctors just want him gone." She looked around. "Now he seems to have disappeared."

"He was talking to Mr. Demarkian," the nurse said politely, "but now Mr. Demarkian is over there with that police detective and I don't see Mr. Blechmann."

DeAnna sighed. "I've got it all arranged with the head nun downstairs that Itzaak can spend the night sitting beside Carmencita's bed as long as there's also a police officer in the room—"

"A police officer?"

"Well," DeAnna said, "they have to take precautions. You and I may know better, but they don't have any other choice but to suspect—"

"*Itzaak?*"

"Lotte, calm down. It's only a precaution. Even Mr. Demarkian doesn't actually think—"

"Let me talk to Mr. Demarkian," Lotte said.

Mr. Demarkian was away from the clutch of people at Carmencita's door. He was standing at the end of the hall looking out a window onto Lotte didn't know what— probably a parking lot, in this part of Philadelphia—and talking to John Jackman. His clothes were rumpled and one of the pockets on his suit jacket was torn. Beyond him, the gray day Lotte had come out of only a few minutes before had turned nasty. Something that looked like sleet was falling in slanting lines from black clouds that looked as heavy as bowling balls. Lotte strode over to the two men and grabbed Gregor Demarkian by the shoulder. Since he was over a foot taller than she was, this was not as dramatic a gesture as she wanted it to be.

"Mr. Demarkian," she said, "would you please tell me—*me*, not DeAnna and not that silly man Itzaak Blechmann—what you can possibly be thinking of to even conceive of the idea that Itzaak might do anything to harm Carmencita? Itzaak, of all people."

"I agree," Gregor told her politely. "I don't think Itzaak Blechmann will harm Carmencita Boaz."

"Well," Lotte said. "Well."

"I don't think he will, either," John Jackman said. "I just know how easy it would be to get lynched if he happened to. If you see what I mean."

"No," Lotte said.

"I don't blame you," Gregor said, and Lotte found herself thinking that he was a very attractive man. Not physically attractive, exactly—he could take off some weight—but attractive in his person. "Are you going to go in to talk to the doctors now?" he asked her. "Do you have a couple of minutes to talk to us?"

Lotte looked back at Carmencita's room. She would, of course, have to talk to the doctors. She would have to see Carmencita and comfort Itzaak. She had always hated hospitals. She had always hated sickness, too, and she had a positive phobia about death. Maybe that was why she did a television show about sex. She was old enough to be of that generation that still connected the act of sex with making babies. Making babies was the ultimate commitment to life. She turned back to Gregor Demarkian.

"I don't have to go there now," she said. "What is it you wanted to ask me? When Carmencita was hurt I was—"

"At your brother David's," Gregor said. "I know. It isn't about Carmencita I wanted to talk to you. It's about Maria Gonzalez and Maximillian Dey."

"I don't think the police are really looking into the death of Maria Gonzalez," Lotte said. "DeAnna and I have been very disturbed about it. We were going to ask you—"

"To investigate?" Gregor nodded. "That probably would have been impossible, you know. It took place in another city. The police would have been hostile to any intrusion from me—at least from what I've heard."

"The policeman in charge of the case is a bigot and a fool."

"Yes," Gregor said. "Well. Let's not worry about that for a moment. Were you told anything at all about the police investigation into the death of Maria Gonzalez?"

"A little."

"Were you told whether anything was found in her pockets? Driver's license. Social security card. Anything—"

"It was all gone," Lotte said. "We were told all about that. Her purse was gone. It was in the papers."

"They never found anything of the sort that normally goes into a wallet? Social security card? Green card?"

"Oh, no. We would have heard about it, I think."

"All right," Gregor said, "now think for a moment about Maximillian Dey. I have heard from several people that on the night you all left New York, he had his pocket picked."

"Oh, yes. He was complaining about it nonstop."

"He had his wallet stolen."

"Exactly."

"Would you know if his green card was in that wallet?"

"Of course I would know," Lotte said. "Anybody would. Max complained bitterly about all the expense and fuss it was going to take to replace it. I even offered to loan him the money for the service fees. What was expensive to Max would not, of course, have been expensive to me. But he only wanted to complain. He was not truly interested in seeking help. Which was of course his privilege."

"Of course," Gregor agreed. "But you're sure. His green card was in that wallet?"

"I'm positive."

"Fine. Let's look at something else. You came to the United States from Israel. Do you ever go back?"

"Oh, yes. Every other year or so. I have friends there."

"Has anybody else on your staff been to Israel in the last, say, two or three years?"

"Is this about the dreidels?" Lotte asked him. "I've been very worried about those dreidels. They aren't the kind of thing I buy. Although I have a dreidel. A big one. It's enameled. I keep it in my apartment in New York."

"I'm a little worried about the dreidels," Gregor said. "But I'm not yet sure in what way. *Had* anybody on your staff been to Israel in the last two or three years?"

"DeAnna came with me about three years ago," Lotte said. "She met a man. DeAnna will be the first to tell you that men are useless, but she always meets a man. She's that kind of women. Men are attracted to her. Her daughters came with us."

"Anybody else?"

"Sarah Meyer," Lotte said hesitantly. "I'm not sure, though, when it was. It might have been more like five years ago. She went with her mother. If you want my opinion, Sarah would be a much more pleasant person if she never went anywhere with her mother."

"Itzaak also came here from Israel," Gregor said. "Has he been back?"

"Not that I know of."

"What about the others? What about Shelley Feldstein?"

"Shelley went in 1973. War broke out right in the lobby of her hotel and she swore she'd never go back."

"Prescott Holloway."

"Prescott Holloway." Lotte blinked. And then she laughed. "Oh, dear. I don't think he's gone, but with Prescott you never know. He's our mystery man, you know. We speculate about him."

"Why?"

"Well, he hardly seems the kind of man who would end up being a chauffeur. He's too intelligent and too sophisticated and too—I don't know what. DeAnna thinks he was an executive somewhere once and lost it all due to drink. Sarah Meyer thinks he gambles, but Sarah will say anything if she's in the wrong mood. You mustn't take all this seriously. It's probably just the army."

"The army?"

"Prescott was in the army, yes," Lotte said. "For a good long time, if I remember correctly. The army will put a veneer of sophistication on a certain kind of man. It'll give him an air of authority. It's just that Prescott looks like Jack Palance, so he's intriguing."

"Let's go at this from another angle," Gregor said. "Money. Do you know roughly what the people on your staff make?"

"Of course."

"Is there any one of them who has more money to spend than he should have? More money than you pay him?"

"But of course they do," Lotte said, surprised.

"Shelley Feldstein is married to a very successful man. And Sarah Meyer's parents are rich people. I think Sarah still has an allowance. And Sarah's mother sends her things, too, of course. Like the cashmere snow hats last December. Six of them in six different colors, seventy-five dollars apiece at Saks. I saw them."

"What were you doing on the night Maria Gonzalez died?"

"I was home in bed," Lotte said, with some amusement. "Alone. I have reached that time in my life when I am allowed to retire from the sex wars, and I have."

"I find it very interesting," Gregor said, "that there is no one—no one—who seems to have a verifiable alibi for the time of Maria Gonzalez's death. It's as if the woman was killed at high noon on Fifth Avenue."

"I don't find that odd at all," Lotte said. "We were taping. That's the way things always are when we're taping."

"Do you tape five days a week? All year?"

"We tape five days a week for thirty-nine weeks a year. The rest of the time, the show is in reruns. And we all need the rest. Let me tell you."

"There's a doctor up there with DeAnna Kroll. I think they're trying to get your attention."

Lotte turned around and saw that it was true. DeAnna was standing with a man in a white coat and waving at her frantically. The man in the white coat was just waving. He looked too exhausted to make any more effort than that. Lotte felt her stomach turn over. She really did hate hospitals. She really did.

"I hope it isn't bad news," she said.

"They wouldn't be behaving like that if it was bad news."

Lotte hoped he was right. She said good-bye and started walking away. She got halfway down the corridor to DeAnna and her white-coated companion before she stopped. Crises always got like this for her, stuck in a

groove of feelingless efficiency. She wondered how long it
would take, this time, for her cool control to collapse into
headaches and insomnia and a second martini before she
went to bed.

She turned around to get another look at Gregor
Demarkian—whose cool control seemed to her to be the
kind that would never collapse at all—but he was gone.

2

Shelley Feldstein's take on Gregor Demarkian hadn't
changed a whit since she'd first seen him after the death
of Maximillian Dey, and it wasn't going to change now,
when she was in a bad mood and tired to death and wish-
ing to be home in New York instead of stuck out here in
the boondocks with some kind of nut. That was how
Shelley was explaining the deaths of Maria Gonzalez and
Maximillian Dey to herself, and the attack on Carmencita
Boaz—although on that last she had alternative theories.
That a nut was responsible for Maria and Max, though,
she had no doubt. Shelley had tried very hard, earlier today, to find some proof that that nut was Sarah Meyer, but
she had been unsuccessful. She had torn up enough cashmere to build her own goat. She had poured enough perfume on enough carpet to stink up that small corner of the
Sheraton Society Hill until the coming of the Messiah. She
had ripped the covers off enough paperback books to become a one-woman rack jobber. She had found nothing
that would convict Sarah Meyer of plotting or executing
two violent deaths.

Shelley had not, however, come out of Sarah's room
empty-handed. She had had a stroke of luck, the momen-
tousness of which she never expected to be repeated as
long as she lived. The fact that she had never even suspected the existence of such a thing made the luck even

better. She wouldn't have found it if she had gone looking for it. She had simply opened the zippered compartment in Sarah's suitcase where Sarah kept her underwear—Sarah was just the sort of person who wouldn't unpack her underwear—and there it was. Black. Leather-bound. Stamped in gold. Bought at Mark Cross.

A diary.

Shelley was at the hospital now half because she was supposed to be, but half because she had this book to carry around. DeAnna had called her, as DeAnna had called everyone else, expecting a great convergence without wondering why it should happen. Under any other conditions, Shelley would have stayed at home and made her excuses afterward. DeAnna would never notice who had come and who had not—and if she did, in the cold light of sweet reason, she would realize it made sense for Shelley not to be there. But Shelley had the diary. And she wanted to get a good clear look at Sarah Meyer's face.

Gregor Demarkian was standing with his friend the black policeman when Shelley came down the hall. Otherwise, she would have passed him by without a greeting. The policeman made her feel compelled to do something polite. The compulsion made her angry. Farther down the corridor, she could see Lotte and DeAnna with their heads together, looking more relieved than grave. So Carmencita would be all right. That was good. Shelley had nothing against Carmencita. She did wonder about Itzaak, though. Usually when a woman was battered, it was her husband or boyfriend who had battered her.

Gregor Demarkian and the policeman had fanned out from the wall, blocking her path. Shelley nearly told them to get the hell out of her way. Then she thought better of it. No need to antagonize the police, no matter how much she would like to antagonize Gregor Demarkian. She hated to look at anyone who was so obviously fat. She put her hand in the pocket of her trenchcoat and felt the patterned leather cover of Sarah's diary. It made her feel better.

"Well?" she said.

The black policeman looked about ready to explode. "Well," he said. "*Well.* What am I supposed to do with *well.*"

"Nobody has asked you to do anything with it," Gregor said.

"We want to ask you a few questions," the black policeman said.

Jackman, Shelley thought. That was his name. Something Jackman. She looked up the hall again, but there was no sign of Sarah, and Sarah was all she wanted to see. She knew that Sarah would be here, because Lotte and DeAnna acted like infants whose formula had been taken away any time they had a crises and Sarah wasn't in attendance to be ordered around. Lotte and DeAnna would have thought of a million things they wanted Sarah to write down in her notebook and a million people they wanted her to call, and then when all this was over they would forget all about it. That, in Shelley Feldstein's experience, was the way all bosses behaved. It was a psychological abnormality that was conferred by the board of directors along with the title.

There was still no sign of Sarah anywhere in the hall. Shelley shifted from foot to foot and said, "What do you want?" She said it directly to Mr. Jackman. She didn't look at Gregor Demarkian at all.

Even so, it was Gregor Demarkian who spoke. Shelley resigned herself to it. The policeman called Jackman was spineless. He'd behaved just like this after Max's body was found. He let Demarkian do all the talking.

"What we want to know," Gregor Demarkian said, "is whether or not you were aware of the fact that Maria Gonzalez was in the United States illegally."

Oh, shit, Shelley Feldstein thought. She touched the cover of Sarah's diary again.

"If I did know that Maria was an illegal alien," she

said crisply, "I'd hardly tell the police, would I? I could get in trouble."

"This is a murder investigation," Jackman said. "I don't care what kind of trouble—"

"You couldn't get in trouble," Gregor said. "Whoever hired her might."

"Lotte?"

"Or the personnel department of Gradon Cable Systems."

"I didn't *know* she was an illegal alien," Shelley said. "I *suspected*."

"What about Maximillian Dey?"

"With Max I knew, yes."

"That he was in the United States illegally?"

"Yes."

"What about Carmencita Boaz?"

"Was she really?" Shelley looked up the corridor again. "I suppose it figures. They all know each other. It's like an underground community. Is Itzaak illegal, too?"

"Not as far as we know," Gregor said.

"Well, maybe that figures, too. Max was Portuguese, of course, and not Spanish. You never call a Portuguese person Spanish. He's likely to want to hit you. Still. They tell each other, I think."

"Tell each other about what?"

"About where they can get hired without too many problems," Shelley said. "I'm not saying personnel doesn't check. I'm sure they demand to see a birth certificate or a green card or something. But I'll bet they don't run a computer check."

"You never thought it was odd? That Max was in the country illegally and Maria might have been? It wasn't a coincidence that disturbed you?"

"I never thought it was a coincidence," Shelley said. "It's like I was telling you. They tell each other. They bring each other in."

"All right," Gregor said. "Are you aware of the fact

that Maximillian Dey had his pocket picked just before *The Lotte Goldman Show* left New York?"

"Of course I am. The desk clerk at Max's hotel was probably aware of it."

"Are you aware that among what he lost when his pocket was picked was his green card?"

"Oh, yes."

"Would it surprise you to hear that on the very next day, before six o'clock in the morning, he had a green card?"

"No," Shelley said, sighed. "It wouldn't surprise me. I saw that one, too."

"You saw the new green card Maximillian Dey was carrying on the morning he died," Gregor said.

"Yes, I did. Max showed it to me."

"Do you know where he got it?"

"No."

"Do you know who he got it from?"

"No."

"Did he say anything at all that might indicate anything at all about who might have supplied it to him?"

"Not exactly," Shelley said. "He told me he'd found a new source, better than the one he had used in New York when he first came to this country. This source was cheaper and faster and more accommodating about the money."

"Was this a source in Philadelphia? Or someone connected with the show?"

"I don't know. But Max had never been to Philadelphia before. I don't see how he could have known where to find a person like that here."

"Maybe somebody else told him," Gregor suggested. "Maybe Carmencita Boaz had a source in Philadelphia."

"She'd never been to Philadelphia before either," Shelley said. "She said so just before we left New York. She'd been on staff longer than Max had, but she'd only been Maria's assistant. Maria's assistant didn't travel with us when we did the road shows."

"Mmm," Gregor Demarkian said.

Shelley Feldstein was still looking at the policeman called Jackman, still looking away from the round softness under Gregor Demarkian's belt. Now she turned all the way around and looked again at Lotte and DeAnna. Lotte and DeAnna were no longer alone. Sarah Meyer was standing between them, holding her steno book and pouting.

She hasn't been back to her room yet, Shelley thought, and knew it had to be true. If Sarah had been back to her room, there would have been a fuss big enough so that even the attack on Carmencita Boaz couldn't have stopped the staff from talking about it. Surely DeAnna would have said something when she called Shelley to come to the hospital.

Sarah Meyer caught sight of her and smiled. Shelley smiled back and touched the cover of the diary one more time.

"Mrs. Feldstein?" Gregor Demarkian said.

"I'm sorry," Shelley said. "I really do have to talk to Lotte and DeAnna now. Can the rest of this wait until later?"

"There really isn't any rest of this," Gregor said. "I was just a little worried about you. You've gone pale."

"I'm tired, that's all. Excuse me."

Gregor Demarkian or his friend the policeman may have said something in response, but Shelley didn't hear them. Sarah had closed her notebook and begun to move off. Shelley picked up speed to close the gap between them. Sarah walked into Carmencita Boaz's room and disappeared.

If Lotte and DeAnna had stayed where they were, Shelley might have been held up. But they didn't. They drifted off themselves, never realizing she was on her way. She let them go and went up to the door of Carmencita's

room, pushing her way gently between the nurses and policemen who were standing there. Inside she could see
only the foot of Carmencita's bed and the backs of the
doctors that stood around it. She pushed in a little farther
and caught sight of Sarah Meyer, listening to a white-
coated woman and taking it all down in her notebook.

Sarah Meyer saw Shelley Feldstein and smiled.

Shelley Feldstein reached into the pocket of her coat,
pulled out the diary, held it in the air and smiled back.

Sarah Meyer's jaw dropped open far enough to let
Dumbo the Elephant crawl into her mouth.

THREE

1

Bennis Hannaford was waiting at the top of the front steps, outside in the cold, when Gregor Demarkian and John Jackman drove up. They were riding in a standard city of Philadelphia police car, but without the siren running. John Jackman had let the siren rip once on Cavanaugh Street. Gregor had threatened to tell the papers something cute about him if he ever did it again. He even threatened to invent the something cute. *Philadelphia Homicide Detective Wears Dinosaur Pajamas to Bed.* Right. It would be beautiful. Gregor looked out the window at Bennis with her arms wrapped around her knees and her breath blowing white in the cold. It was already dark. Up and down Cavanaugh Street, amber lights glowed steadily in curtained windows. Streetlights cast harsh circles of white on the icy pavement. It was hard-cold and nasty, without gentleness. Gregor didn't think there would be snow for Christmas. He looked up at the facade of his building and saw that the lights in his own living room were on. He

checked out the Christmas wreaths and Hanukkah menorahs arranged in clusters near his front door and saw that
they were backlit with tiny Christmas lights. He wondered
where Donna Moradanyan had found an outlet to plug
them in. The police car braked to a full stop, causing him
to bounce against his seat belt. John Jackman leaned
across him, saw Bennis sitting on the stairs, and said, "Oh,
shit."

"The sentiment is probably mutual," Gregor told him
drily. "Come on. Let's get it over with. We've got work to
do."

"We don't have any work to do that couldn't be done
at my office."

"Come *on*."

Gregor got his door open, thanked the uniformed
driver, and got out onto the pavement. Bennis stood up
and started to come down the stairs to him. A few seconds
later, she saw John Jackman and stopped.

There was nothing to do about this but bull through
it. Gregor had bulled his way through meetings with J. Edgar Hoover himself. He'd even bulled his way through a
couple with Richard Nixon. Why did dealing with Bennis
always seem so much harder? He walked up to the stoop
and started to climb the stairs.

"Bennis," he said. "I thought you'd be gone by now.
I thought you were going to be on your way to New York
or Paris."

"Tomorrow," Bennis said vaguely. She was looking at
John Jackman. "I was supposed to leave tomorrow."

"Hello, Bennis," John Jackman said.

"Hello, John." She turned away and looked toward
Gregor for the first time since she had realized that Jack-
man was with him. "Except now it seems I'm not.
Maybe."

"Maybe?" Gregor took her by the elbow, turned her
around, and moved her up the stairs. Her skin felt thick,

like gelatin congealed. She was that cold. "I thought it was definite," he said. "I thought you wanted to get away."

"Well, I do." Bennis was letting herself be pushed. "I even called the travel agent. I even started to pack."

"So what's the problem?"

"Problem," Bennis repeated. "Well. Do you know a woman named Helena Oumoudian?"

"Oh, yes. She's Sofie Oumoudian's aunt. Sofie goes out with Joey——"

"Ohanian. Yes, Gregor, I know. Well, she's in my living room."

"Why?"

"Because Sofie Oumoudian and Father Tibor put her there," Bennis said. "She's got a fractured hip."

"She's got a fractured hip and she made it up to your apartment? Up the stoop flight and then to the second floor?"

"No. She broke her hip this afternoon. At old George's place. They sent for the doctor."

"That was good." They had reached the front door. Gregor tried the knob, found that the door had been left unlocked—again—and stepped back to let Bennis go in before him. He tried to let John Jackman in before him, too, but John wasn't having any. John wanted to take up the rear. "I don't understand," he said to Bennis. "If she broke her hip at old George's place—*how* did she break her hip at old George's place?"

"She and George were doing the tango. George was, you know, lowering her down to the floor."

"How's George?"

"Contrite."

Gregor checked the mail table and noted that his mail had been retrieved already—Bennis was always doing that, so that she could check the return addresses—and that the space where the huge menorah had been was now taken up by an equally huge Santa in his sleigh. Fortunately, the reindeer were not along.

"So," Gregor said, "that still doesn't answer my question. Why is Helena Oumoudian in *your* living room?"

"Well, for one thing, everybody agreed—in my absence, by the way, I was not a witness to this tango—that taking her up one flight of stairs to my apartment made more sense than taking her down the stoop flight and across a few blocks and then up I don't know how many flights to her own apartment."

"All right."

"And I wouldn't have minded that," Bennis said, "because I was going to be leaving anyway and if they wanted to use the apartment for the old lady, who cared, except that isn't all they wanted. They wanted somebody to take care of the old lady."

"What about Sofie Oumoudian?"

"Sofie Oumoudian is leaving tomorrow on a three-day class trip. Sunday school class. You know. They're going to Washington to sing Carols on the steps of the capitol. As if that would help."

"I should think Sofie would just have to stay here instead."

"It would break her heart. According to Tibor."

"Then there must be someone else," Gregor insisted. "Lida. Hannah. I don't suppose Sheila Kashinian would be any use. Howard would have a fit. How about Donna Moradanyan?"

"Donna Moradanyan has a child to raise," Bennis said in exasperation. "And she's busy. I took her into New York last month to show her portfolio and now she's working on a book cover for some mystery novel Bantam is publishing. And it's her first job and she's got a deadline."

"How's the cover?"

"It's a cover painting," Bennis said, "and it's wonderful. I wish they'd assign her to me. Sheila Kashinian is never any use."

"What about Lida?"

"Lida and Hannah are preparing to go on a trip," Bennis said. "Together, I presume. Anyway, they're much too busy."

"I take it they've annoyed you."

"Everybody's annoyed me," Bennis exploded. "Tibor won't help because besides doing all the Christmas stuff he has to for the church—and there is a lot of it, really, this year, there's too much—anyway, on top of all that he's helping David Goldman do a library reading for the first day of Hanukkah for the Bryn Mawr library and he spends all his time walking around his apartment rehearsing his little speech. So he won't help. And the only good news in all this is that I haven't already paid for the Concorde tickets."

"You absolutely have to stay?"

"Of course I have to stay. Somebody has to stay. The old woman has to be helped out of her chair and back into it again."

"Maybe you could hire a service. A practical nurse. That sort of thing."

"A service would take me at least two days to set up. I might as well wait for Sofie Oumoudian. But I don't want to wait, Gregor. I want to get out of here."

"Don't look at me," Gregor said. "I'm in the middle of a murder investigation."

Bennis gave him the kind of look that suggested he'd invented this murder investigation just to keep her from setting off for Paris and went stomping up the stairs to the second-floor landing. She was wearing her classic hanging-around-the-apartment clothes and draped in her classic hanging-around-the-apartment disarray. Her great cloud of black hair had been inadequately pinned up with bobby pins and was now half falling down. The knee-sock clad feet emerging from the legs of her jeans were wearing no shoes. She must have been freezing out there.

They got to the second-floor landing and stopped. Through the open door to Bennis's apartment, Gregor could see past the foyer and into the living room. Helena Oumoudian was sitting in Bennis's favorite black leather club chair, a tiny queen on an oversize throne, an Empress of the Universe whose diminutive size only underscored the force of her personality. She was dressed in the head-to-toe black lace Gregor remembered from their first meeting in the Oumoudians' apartment. She was holding her black cane in front of her like Queen Victoria about to chastise Disraeli. Her spine was straight. Her head was held high. Gregor was sure that if he went closer, he would find her eyes as clear and sharp and bright as an evil imp's.

"There she is," Bennis said, looking around Gregor to see inside. "It's intolerable, Gregor, it really is."

"Miss Hannaford?" the sharp old lady's voice called from inside. "Is that you now? There's something wrong with the television set."

"She can make the cable go out just by looking at it," Bennis hissed into Gregor's ear. "What am I supposed to do about this?"

"Wait a couple of days and leave for Paris," Gregor said.

Bennis made an extremely rude gesture and said, "Thanks a lot, Gregor. That's just what was required in my hour of need."

"What else am I supposed to say?"

"Miss Hannaford?"

This time the voice was accompanied by a sharp crack, so much like a gunshot that John Jackman jumped.

"Jesus Christ," he said. "What was that?"

"That," Bennis said, "was Miss Oumoudian's cane. I'm expecting to find out she's got a whip hidden in the folds of her dress somewhere and she's only waiting for a chance to use it."

"Now, now," Gregor said. "It can't be that bad."

Bennis shoved her hands into the pocket of her jeans and glowered.

"Yes it can be that bad, Gregor, yes it can. Trust me."

Then she marched past him and into her apartment, slamming the door behind her. Both Gregor and John Jackman winced at the violence of the sound.

"Well," John Jackman said after a while. "This Miss Oumoudian isn't one of the people I've met, is she?"

"You'd remember," Gregor said. "She's new. Not in the neighborhood but around the block. She and her niece immigrated from Armenia just after the collapse of the Soviet Union."

"Immigrated," John Jackman said. "That's nice. No wonder you know so much about green cards."

"She goes out with one of the boys from the family that owns the Middle Eastern Food Store," Gregor said. "No, of course she doesn't. I'm tired, John. It's her niece—"

"The one that's going on the class trip," John supplied helpfully.

"Exactly. The niece is Sofie. She was going to high school down the block here and having a little trouble."

"A little?"

"A lot. Tibor and I have been helping to set up a scholarship fund to send her to Agnes Irwin. The problem is convincing old Miss Oumoudian that it wouldn't be taking charity."

"And did you?"

"Not exactly," Gregor said. "She thinks the money is going to be paid out for services rendered."

"What?"

Gregor was still staring at Bennis's closed door. Now he turned away from it and headed up the stairs, shaking his head.

"Come on," he said. "Let's go get some work done."

"I think it's really too bad Bennis has decided she hates me," John said. "I don't hate her in the least."

That was a can of worms that Gregor Demarkian had

no intention of opening. He climbed the stairs to the third-floor landing and let them both in to his own apartment.

2

In the beginning, when Gregor Demarkian had first moved to Cavanaugh Street after the death of his wife, the floor-through apartment whose streetside living room window faced Lida Arkmanian's upstairs living room window on the other side was mostly bare. Moving in, Gregor had bought the minimum amount of furniture and no decorative elements at all. Coming home one night it had struck him that his apartment looked very much like the apartments of the serial killers he had spent so much of his time tracking down. At least, it looked like the apartments of the neat ones. There was a certain kind of serial killer who liked to imitate a pack rat. He collected the memorabilia of everything, from cereal-box tops to human body parts to string. This kind of serial killer was almost always psychotic. He saw visions and everybody he knew thought he was strange. The neat kind of serial killer was something else again. He was more normal than most of the people he knew, and better adjusted, and better organized—at least on the surface. He was a pathological liar but a meticulous one. His apartment was as antiseptic as the waiting room of a cancer ward. Gregor's apartment had been antiseptic in that way, too. His foyer had been empty. His living room had contained one couch, one coffee table, and one chair. Women who had visited his kitchen had felt compelled to rearrange it, as if there were something you could do to a bar table and four plain chairs to make the arrangement look more human.

Gregor Demarkian had made this observation about his apartment three years ago. He had not rushed right out and done anything about it. What he had done instead was to open up another barren part of his life, and one that seemed much more in need of immediate attention: his lack of connection to other human beings. When he came back to Cavanaugh Street and moved into the apartment, he was friendless, in any substantive definition of the term "friend." Eight months later, he had Tibor in his life and Bennis Hannaford and Donna Moradanyan and Lida Arkmanian and God only knew who else, and curiously enough, there was an entirely different feel to his apartment. It wasn't that he had made any changes. Gregor was the kind of man who took six months to buy himself a new Jet-Dry bulb when the one in his dishwasher wore out. It was the rest of them who had changed his apartment. Donna Moradanyan had drawn pictures and had them framed and hung them in his foyer, along with everything else she hung in his apartment from time to time, the glowing menorah in his living room window not being the least of them. Bennis had bought him a living room full of house plants, which she watered for him. If she didn't, they would die. Lida Arkmanian and Hannah Krekorian had stocked his kitchen with equipment he never used (he didn't know what it was all for) and pretty place mats and bright yellow kitchen curtains that at least made the place look less like the utility room at a group home.

John Jackman noticed the difference as soon as he walked in, and approved. He walked from foyer to living room to kitchen and around again, nodding his head.

"Not bad. I take it you're in a better mood than you were during—ah—during the Hannaford case."

"Sit down, John. Don't worry about the Hannaford case."

"I try not to."

John Jackman sat down on one end of the couch, and Gregor went into the kitchen to do his usual bit with the coffee. Since discovering instant, he no longer made a brew that could be used to clean sewer pipes and probably did when his guests dumped his stuff down the drain. He

set the water on to boil and propped open the swing door
from the kitchen to the living room, so he and John could
talk while he fussed with spoons and cups. He looked into
the refrigerator to see if anything had appeared in it while
he was gone and saw he was in luck. A plate of mamoul
cookies was sitting right next to the only other thing in
there, a bottle of Perrier water. The Perrier water belonged
to Bennis. The mamoul cookies had a note stuck in with
them that said,

> Buy something to eat, Krekor,
> this is not good for you.

Gregor took the plate out and put it next to the cups.

"So," he said to John through the door. "Did you
check out the things I asked you to check out?"

"Yesterday. I told you I checked them out yesterday."

"I know. I just want to make sure. I've made a great
many really stupid mistakes in my life, going with my instincts without making sure."

"Yeah. So have I. What do you want to be sure
about?"

"First, about Maria Gonzalez. This would all be a lot
easier if you got along with the New York police. . . ."

"I get along with the New York police," John Jackman said. "I just don't get along with Chickie baby."

"Right. About Maria Gonzalez. They searched her
apartment."

"They did. It was a wreck."

"I understand that. Did they find anything missing?"

"Nothing but what they already knew was missing.
Her purse was missing, the one she'd been carrying at
work that day. That was it. Of course, that isn't the most
accurate sort of finding. She could have had a stash of
Bacarat crystal nobody knew about. She could have had a
stash of dope."

"But there was never any suggestion that she was involved with dope," Gregor pointed out.

"There was evidence to the contrary," John conceded. "The New York police talked to her neighbors. She went to Mass every morning before work. She baby-sat for other women's kids. All they seemed to have against her was they thought she was a little too flashy in the way she dressed. Welcome to the big city."

"What about things that weren't missing that should have been? Did they find money in the apartment? Jewelry?"

"I see what you're getting at. A thief would have stolen what he'd found, and the apartment was enough of a mess so he'd have found what was there. No, there wasn't anything like that. Not on the lists I read."

"That's too bad. That means there's no way we can know for sure."

"Do we ever really know for sure, Gregor?"

Gregor thought *he* knew for sure often enough, far more often than he could prove it. He got down the pewter tray Howard and Sheila Kashinian had given him for Christmas last year and piled it up with cups of coffee and milk and sugar and mamoul cookies. At the last minute, he noticed the spoons he had left on the table and put them on too. He usually kept the pewter tray on top of the cabinets next to the refrigerator, which made it something of a stretch to get. Now he flexed his back where the reach had strained it a little. Then he picked up the tray and went into the living room.

"I don't suppose it's information I really need," he said, "but I like to have everything I can get."

"Don't we all. You going to tell me what this is all about, finally?"

"Of course," Gregor said. "We've got a serial killer on our hands."

"What?"

"A serial killer," Gregor said. "A—"

"Yes, I know," John Jackman said, "but what is this guy? Bisexual? There are two corpses and a near corpse and one of them is—"

"Why do you think this has to be sexual?"

"Isn't it always? The two I worked before were sexual."

"There's usually a sexual element," Gregor conceded, "but it isn't always so obvious. And why do you think it's a man? Women have been serial killers in a number of well-known cases. Geneen Jones, for instance, who murdered all those infants because she liked the high that came from responding to a code blue."

"Wonderful," Jackman said. "What in the name of God makes you think this—this person—is a serial killer?"

"There's the correlation in the methods reports, for one," Gregor said. "I've looked at your methods reports on the death of Maximillian Dey. I have also looked, although more briefly, on what you got from the NYPD on the death of Maria Gonzalez. The methods in those two deaths were not similar. They were identical. You could have used one report for the other and nobody would have known the difference."

"So?"

"So," Gregor said, "it's true that ordinary murderers repeat their methods. What they do not do is repeat them this closely. In order to repeat this closely—to smash just the same teeth, just the same part of the jaw, just the same place on the cheekbones; the accuracy is astounding for a pair of deaths effected with a blunt instrument—in order to do all that, you'd have to plan. I'd be interested in knowing if New York has any unsolved cases sitting around with identical methods. I would guess they have several."

Jackman still looked skeptical. "The third one wasn't so exact," he pointed out. "Carmencita Boaz is still alive."

"With Carmencita Boaz, he was interrupted," Gregor said. "I'm telling you, John, there can be no other explanation. It has to be a set of serial killings."

John grabbed a mamoul cookie and chomped down on it. His coffee was getting cold, untouched.

"What about all this business with the green cards," he asked. "What does that have to do with anything?"

"The green cards are how this serial killer finds his victims."

"I don't get it."

"Selling forged IDs that make illegal aliens look legal is big business," Gregor said. "It's also easy business, if you know what you're doing. And it's fast. I saw a report on *60 Minutes* once—it might have been *Inside Edition*—where someone pulled up to a curb somewhere, asked for ID, and got it in less than half an hour."

"Got a green card," John Jackman said.

"And a social security card."

"So what you're saying is that this serial killer of yours supplies forged IDs to illegal aliens and then bumps off his customers?"

"Exactly."

"Why?"

Gregor shrugged. "There isn't any *why* with these people. Not the kind of *why* you and I would understand, anyway. We'll find out once he's arrested. Assuming he's the kind who talks."

"What if he isn't the kind who talks?"

"Then our problem is going to be just a little bit bigger."

"Gregor, if you really know who this person is, and if it's really a serial killer we're talking about here, then I think you've screwed around more than enough. I think you should provide me with a name and let me arrest this person."

Gregor sighed. "Could you? Could you arrest, with what you have now? What do you have now?"

"Nothing," John Jackman said reluctantly.

Gregor took a long drink of his coffee and picked up a couple of mamoul cookies.

"This is what happened," he said. "Maria Gonzalez was killed at the Hullboard-Dedmarsh building, at work or just after work, and her body was stuffed somewhere for safekeeping. In the basement of the Hullboard-Dedmarsh building, maybe. Someplace temporarily safe but not safe enough. It was covered with a blanket or a plastic garbage bag. Then our killer took Maria's keys, went up to her apartment, and ransacked the place."

"Why?"

"My guess is that that forged green card wasn't on her," Gregor said. "The killer went up there to find it. Maybe he got angry when he was working. Maybe he just thought he'd put on a good show. At any rate, the status quo was acceptable until DeAnna Kroll sent out a hue and cry for Maria Gonzalez, and then the hiding place wasn't safe any more. So our murderer brought the body upstairs—"

"How did he do that without getting seen?"

"It would have been very unlikely if the murderer had been seen," Gregor said. "This fuss started between three and four o'clock in the morning. There wouldn't have been that many people around. Besides, if the murderer had been seen, so what? Carrying something big and bulky wrapped in plastic—while *The Lotte Goldman Show* was setting up for a tape? Nobody would have noticed."

"Maybe not," John Jackman conceded.

"The murderer then put the body of Maria Gonzalez, minus her covering, into the storeroom. It must have been a blanket or something like that that Maria was wrapped in. Otherwise, why not just leave it with the body?"

"What did happen to it?"

"It probably went down the incinerator. Now we come to Maximillian Dey. Max was carrying chairs and other furniture for Shelley Feldstein. He went downstairs and was never seen again, until he was dead. Was he killed in that bathroom?"

"I think so, yes. I haven't had time to read the report in any heavy duty way, but from what I remember, there were splatters on the wall behind him, which would indicate—"

"I know what it would indicate," Gregor said. "That means there's nothing we can do with Max. There's no way to prove anything there. And the same is true of Carmencita Boaz, of course. It's exactly the same situation. We're going to have to rely on Maria Gonzalez."

"Rely on her how?"

"Well, what I had in mind was—"

That was the phone ringing. It was actually two phones ringing, because Gregor now had one in the kitchen as well as in the bedroom. He picked up another mamoul cookie and headed into the kitchen to pick up.

"Just a minute," he told John Jackman. "I'll be right back."

He picked up the phone with one hand and stuffed mamoul into his mouth with the other. He said hello through a mass of crumbs and waited to see what would happen. He was absolutely convinced that what he was about to hear was a phone solicitation. What he got instead was, "Excuse me? I'm looking for Gregor Demarkian."

"This is Gregor Demarkian," Gregor said cautiously.

"Oh, good." The voice sounded relieved. "You didn't sound like yourself for a minute there. Hello, Gregor. This is Ira Ballard. I got that information you wanted."

"Information?" Gregor was drawing a blank.

Ira was either used to this sort of thing or not inclined to carp on it. "I've got the information you wanted on the White Knights, Defenders of Race and

Faith," he said. "You know. The jerks who are bothering the synagogues."

Synagogues, Gregor thought, straightening up.

In all this fuss, he'd forgotten all about them.

His life was getting totally unmanageable.

FOUR

═══════

1

Philadelphia was not a small town, but Cavanaugh Street was a small town in a large city, and people there often talked and thought in ways that were more rural than urban. Ira Ballard had spent all his life in the great urban centers of the East Coast. He'd come into the Bureau about five years after Gregor had, landing on kidnapping detail at just about the time Gregor was getting himself out of it. [He had landed in the job of tracking nutcase organizations the way most Bureau agents landed in out-of-the-ordinary Bureau assignments: in a concerted attempt to have nothing at all to do with drug investigations.] Gregor had known him for what seemed like forever. Gregor had forgotten how easy it was to slip back into all that, too. The patterns of speech. The habits of thought. Three years on Cavanaugh Street and he was nearly human. Two seconds on the phone with Ira Ballard, and he was sliding back into a place where the White Knights made much more sense than Lida Kazanjian Arkmanian.

For Gregor Demarkian, for years, *Ted Bundy* had made much more sense than Lida Kazanjian Arkmanian. That was why Gregor was so determined to stay on Cavanaugh Street.

Ira Ballard was smoking a cigarette. Gregor could hear the puff and drag. There had been a lot of pressure in Gregor's last days at the Bureau to get all agents to quit smoking. Gregor had been spared because he had never smoked, except in the army, which didn't count. Considering the intensity of that pressure, Gregor thought Ira must be much better at resisting authority than he had ever given him credit for.

"All right," Ira was saying, as Gregor paced back and forth across the kitchen. "Let's start at the beginning. The White Knights, Defenders of Race and Faith were founded in St. Paul, Minnesota, in 1983. At the time, they were calling themselves the White Knights, Defenders of Our Heritage. According to a press release they sent out at the time—"

"A *press* release?"

"Everybody sends out press releases these days, Gregor. Survivalist organizations hiding out in the hills of South Dakota have contacts at the *New York Times.* Yes. They sent out this press release, and according to it they were formed to provide the first line of resistance to the— and I'm quoting here, this is not my prose, 'the de-Americanification of America.' End quote. The chief agent of the de-Americanification of America, by the way, was supposed to have been Ronald Reagan."

"Ronald *Reagan*?"

"Well, they didn't like Jimmy Carter, either, Gregor. They aren't to the left. They're just so far to the right, they make David Duke's biography look like the history of the Cuban Communist party."

"I understand that," Gregor said, "but even so—"

"They thought Ronald Reagan was a shill," Ira explained. "They thought he was a plant. As part of a plot by Planned Parenthood, Ted Kennedy, and the National Education Association. To take over the country."

"That wasn't Ronald Reagan," Gregor said deadpan. "That was Dan Quayle."

"Let's not get into Dan Quayle." Ira Ballard laughed. "Okay. So they sent out this press release and for a while nothing much happened. They seem to have died out in Minnesota. They resurfaced again in Markdale, Arizona, in 1985. This was apparently the result of a move. The founder of the White Knights was a man named Robert Waltrek. He moved to Arizona."

"And restarted the organization," Gregor said.

"If it needed to be restarted. He might just have decided to go public again. There were never too many people in the White Knights in Minnesota—four or five—and none of them has resurfaced on the lists of any other racialist organization. In Arizona, Robert did better. He got a group of about thirty people from Arizona and New Mexico."

"Where did he find that many?"

"Survivalist conventions. Meetings of other organizations. That kind of thing. In 1987, he decided to do something smart—at least, smart for an organization like this looking to add new members. He took out classified advertisements in six different survivalist magazines. They were classics. Our educational system is a mess, Gregor, trust me. Our educational system is doomed."

"I know," Gregor said. "What did these advertisements say?"

"They said. 'WHITE MEN, DEFEND YOUR SKIN.' In capital letters. And then they went on from there."

"Wonderful. Then what?"

"Then," Ira said, "came the convention. The first one, I mean. I told you about the one last April—"

"In Kisco, Oklahoma."

"Right. Well, they've only been holding them in Kisco since Waltrek moved to Kisco. They held the first one in Markdale, Arizona, because that's where Waltrek was living then. They got a hundred and fifteen people."

"Not bad."

"Not bad, and not as good as it was going to get. But close. The thing is, it was right after the convention in Markdale that the trouble started."

"What kind of trouble?"

"The usual kind. On day three of the convention, a bunch of them got drunk and went throwing rocks at the house of the only known black person in Markdale, who turned out not to be black after all but native American. He also turned out to be a Harvard lawyer. They got caught."

"Did they get prosecuted?"

"Oh, yes. Prosecuted and sued," Ira said. "The next year they held their convention fifty miles south, in Hornby, just to stay away from the sheriff. The year after that, they moved to Kisco."

"How many people did they get in Kisco?"

"A hundred fifty-three," Ira said. "And that was it, by the way. The first convention in Kisco was in 1990. Every convention since has drawn fewer people. Last April they were back down to double digits."

"There's hope for the human race yet."

"Most of the human race at least knows a loser when they see one," Ira said. "And these boys are losers, Gregor, it's pitiful. Anyway, to get to the part you want to hear about. At the Kisco convention in 1991, it was decided to form local chapters in various parts of the country so that White Knights could meet on a regular basis and try to do something about the mess the country is in. One of these chapters was formed by two young men from Philadelphia, Ricky Calverness and Ted Gressom."

"Wait a minute," Gregor said. "Let me get a pen."

What he got was a pencil and a scrap of paper with "Hogrogian Bakery" written on one side of it. John Jackman was still sitting in the living room, eying his coffee suspiciously and looking bored. Gregor waved to him and then sat down at the kitchen table, so that it would be easier to write.

"Give me those names again," he told Ira Ballard.

"Ricky Calverness," Ira said, "and Ted Gressom. Calverness is twenty-four. He was jailed last year for three months for punching some guy out in a bar and doing it so well the guy ended up in the hospital for six weeks. That was in West Virginia. Gressom has a somewhat more interesting history. He's twenty-six. He did two years at the Colby Work Farm for beating the girl he was living with into a coma. And I do mean girl. She was fourteen."

"They sound like pleasant people," Gregor said. Colby was the most notorious work farm in all of Georgia—maybe, in law enforcement circles, in all of the United States. Gregor couldn't remember another person who had been sent there on a domestic violence case. This must have been one hell of a case. Either that, or at least one judge in this system was finally waking up.

"When did these two get to Philadelphia?" Gregor asked.

"They've been in Philadelphia on and off for years," Ira said. "But both of them attended high schools on the Main Line—Calverness in Wayne and Gressom in Paoli. They must have been the token poor people. Neither of them graduated. Did I need to say that?"

"No. Are they living in Philadelphia now?"

"They're living on the outskirts. I've got addresses here, Gregor, if you want to take them down."

Ira gave them. Gregor took them down. They did not look familiar. Somewhere out in Bucks County, Gregor thought, and then marveled anew that there always seemed to be pockets in rich places where poor people lived.

"All right," Gregor said. "Are you sure these two are meeting? Are they meeting with anybody?"

"They're meeting with one of my agents," Ira Ballard

said. "After we talked I made a point of it. But there isn't anybody else."

"Well, that's a relief. What does your agent say?"

"Eight fifteen," Ira said.

"Eight fifteen?"

"That's right. Eight fifteen. They're going to hit the B'nai Shalom Synagogue on West Benverton Street at eight fifteen."

"Eight fifteen *tonight*?"

"Of course eight fifteen tonight, Gregor. What do you think I've been talking about?"

"But that's only." Gregor checked the wall clock. It was in the shape of a teapot and had been given to him as a housewarming present by Sheila Kashinian. It had come from Lord & Taylor and probably cost the earth. It looked surreal. "That's only an hour and ten minutes from now," Gregor told Ira Ballard.

Ira was not sympathetic. "I have been trying to get you all day, Gregor. You've been out. I did call the Philadelphia police department and tip them off. They'll be staking out. The eight fifteen is a gift. The White Knights don't usually operate that early, but according to my agent the neighborhood around the synagogue isn't very good and they're a little nervous. Some white knights."

"Is the neighborhood likely to be deserted?"

"Not of cops. Listen, Gregor, I've got to go. It's late and I want to get home. This ought to at least get you started on your way to solving your problem."

"Yes," Gregor said. "Yes, Ira, this is wonderful. Thank you."

"Glad to help. Every little bit counts. Only, after the Philadelphia police catch these guys, you could take my agent out to dinner or something. He's getting that tone in his voice my guys get when they have to spend too much of their time around morons. Say hello to your lady friend for me. And keep in touch."

Ira Ballard was out of touch. The phone was buzzing in Gregor's ear.

Gregor replaced the receiver and walked into the living room, thinking. John Jackman had eaten all the mamoul cookies. It was late and neither of them had eaten dinner and Gregor didn't blame him. Jackman sat up as soon as he realized Gregor was in the room and stretched his legs.

"I've been thinking," he said. "Why don't we go to that restaurant down the street that Bennis took me to. If it's still in business."

"It's still in business. It's been in business since 1938. It's called Ararat."

"Good. It was great. Let's go. I'm starving."

Gregor sat down on one end of the couch and rubbed his face with the palms of his hands. "John," he said, "if I wanted to sit in on a stakeout, could you arrange that for me?"

"A stakeout? When?"

"Tonight. At eight fifteen, to be exact."

Jackman checked his watch. "You've got to be crazy."

"I don't want to sit in with the official presence," Gregor said patiently. "I just want to be on hand and out of sight when the arrest is made."

"You're worse than crazy."

"Tom Reilly could do it for me."

"Gregor, what are you talking about?"

"I'm going to call Tom Reilly," Gregor said. "I'll be back in a minute."

John Jackman was staring at him, half-angry and half-astounded. Gregor turned his back on the living room while he dialed. If he got what he wanted, John wasn't going to get any dinner any time soon, and it was just too bad.

John didn't even know what all this was about.

2

Gregor Demarkian had never liked stakeouts. He had never even liked the idea of stakeouts. Something in him—the Aristotelian, logical part of his soul—said that stakeouts shouldn't be necessary. There was a crime. There was a criminal. There was evidence linking the criminal with the crime. Surely that evidence was out there, somewhere, if they were only smart enough to find it. Surely they should be able to think their way through problems instead of attacking them with frostbitten fingers and brute force. It just never worked out that way. Gregor couldn't count the hours of his life that had been spent on stakeouts. Especially in the beginning, when he was assigned to kidnapping detail, his time in cars had seemed to him to be endless. There was a crime. There was a criminal. There was evidence linking the criminal to the crime. The problem was, the way the jury system was set up, nobody would believe it.

The stakeout that had been organized in the hope of catching Ricky Calverness and Ted Gressom in the act of committing vandalism at the B'nai Shalom Synagogue had been set up inside the synagogue. As the two uniformed officers in charge of freezing their butts told Gregor and John Jackman—after Gregor and John Jackman had been foisted on them by the chief of police, forget what they thought about it—there really wasn't any place else in the neighborhood to hide. They couldn't park an unmarked car somewhere and just wait. This was an act that was supposed to take place outside. Ricky and Ted might be jerks, but the officers had to assume that were not such monumental jerks as to fail to check if the cars parked around their crime scene were occupied or not. Then, too, there

was the safety factor. Saying that this was not a good
neighborhood was putting it mildly. One out of every three
buildings on this block was abandoned. An abandoned
building could sometimes be very good news for a stakeout. Cops could go into one and set up all kinds of fancy
equipment as well as themselves, and nobody would ever
be the wiser. People used to neighborhoods like this one
don't expect abandoned buildings to actually be unoccu-
pied. There are hordes of junkies and homeless people
who want to use the space. The two uniformed officers
had checked out the abandoned building across the street
from the B'nai Shalom Synagogue and come to a hasty but
well-founded conclusion: If they tried to set up in that
place, the whole neighborhood would know they were
there in three minutes, and they would never come out
alive. This was not a neighborhood that looked kindly on
the presence of cops.

B'nai Shalom Synagogue was an Orthodox synagogue, the last vestige of what had once been one of the
most thriving Jewish communities in Philadelphia. Now
the neighborhood belonged to nobody—black or white,
rich or poor, Christian or Jew, European or Asian or Hispanic. For all the apocalyptic pictures painted in the press
and in the kind of murder mystery of which Bennis did not
approve, Gregor had never seen poor neighborhoods as
breeding places of nothing but pathologies. They were
simply residential areas for people who needed more
money, and since quite a few of the greatest men on earth
had had no money at all, he wasn't about to dismiss the
residents of Harlem or Watts as being no damn good at all.
The real problem, for Gregor, came in places like this,
places that weren't really places anymore at all. He wasn't
sure what they were, besides dangerous. Being in them after dark made him feel as if he were standing in the Gar-
den of Eden, listening to the serpent creep.

Because B'nai Shalom Synagogue was an Orthodox
synagogue, there were none of the bright Hanukkah deco-

rations Gregor had seen not only on Cavanaugh Street but on synagogue lawns in other parts of town. There was just the plain brownstone facade of the place, looking dignified and old in the cold and dark. The uniformed policemen had taken up positions on either side of the front doors. For this one night, the doors had been left unlocked. The uniformed policemen were able to see out because they were standing next to tall thin windows that flanked the doors. In keeping with the best Jewish practice, these windows were not adorned with pictures in any way whatsoever. They were, however, stained glass. They were glass stained just dark enough so that nobody from the outside looking in could tell that anybody was standing beside them.

Gregor and John Jackman were supposed to stay out of the way on the second floor, looking out through a great round window that blossomed over this disintegrating street with all the startling exuberance of a meteor shower. Gregor wondered what it looked like in the daylight, or lit up from behind. It had been designed for celebration and display. Now it was dark and still magnificent, but muted. Everything here was muted.

Gregor and John Jackman got to the site at two minutes to eight. It was close enough to the possible take-off time to make the uniformed men nervous. Neither Gregor nor John was interested in doing a song and dance about rank, although John would have been allowed to. They did what the uniformed men told them and climbed the stairs to the second floor. Then they lay down and put their heads up to look through the bottom-most petals of the scalloped window. Neither of them had any idea if they could be seen from the outside if they were standing up. It was better not to take any chances.

The floor under the window was dusty. John Jackman brushed a matted ball of gray off the front of his suit and muttered,

"If they were that good, we wouldn't be here."

"Yes," Gregor said. "But you wouldn't want to ruin everything just by giving them a chance to get lucky."

"If we'd done what I wanted us to do, we wouldn't have to worry about giving them a chance to be lucky. We'd be tucked in at the Ararat, eating dinner."

"I'll buy you dinner when this is over."

"When this is over, you'll think of something else to do."

Out on the street there were the sounds of footsteps. Gregor could hear them clearly through the thin panes of the window. For the first time, he realized he was cold. Terribly cold. He didn't think the heat was on up here. He knew the window provided nothing in the way of insulation. He listened to the footsteps and said, "Hobnail boots."

"Or spike cleats," Jackman agreed. "Doesn't it figure?"

It did, but Gregor had never understood why. He strained his eyes to see in the dark. There was street-lamp pole right in front of the synagogue's front door, but the street lamp shed no light. There was no telling how long it had been since the bulb had been shattered by a flying rock. There were no lights anywhere else on the street. The only light there was came from the moon, and that was feeble.

"Here they come," John Jackman said.

Gregor pulled himself closer to the window and nodded imperceptibly. Two young white men were swinging onto the block from the north, dressed in heavy boots and thick jackets and jeans that looked painted on. Their hair was hidden under dark knitted caps. They brought their own light in the form of cigarettes. Gregor looked again and decided that what he was seeing was joints or else home-rolled. He would bet on joints.

"High," he whispered to Jackman.

"As kites," Jackman whispered back. "How much

you bet, they get arrested, turns out they got stewed before they ever started on the marijuana?"

"Are they singing?"

They were most definitely singing. Like Sioux warriors or members of the old East Indian militia, they were strengthening their resolve at the start of battle with music. Since they were young men of the twentieth century in the United States of America, every once in a while they would accompany their music on the air guitar. Gregor shook his head again and sighed a little. They were slight, these young men were, small and fragile. Their bones looked as fine as the bones of birds. Gregor was not a believer in the kind of pop psychology that said that all members of racialist groups would be men like this, puny and weak and yearning to satisfy an impossible standard of masculinity. He had met too many who were big enough and strong enough to give long hard pause to Muhammed Ali. Personally, he thought men joined racialist groups when they were too damn dumb to think of any other form of recreation and too damn mean to go to Walt Disney World. As an explanation, it fit just as many cases as the pop psych one.

What the two young men were singing was "Sympathy for the Devil." Even sitting where he was, and knowing as little as he did about rock music, Gregor could tell they were doing it badly.

"Tone deaf," John Jackman said. "And with the sense of rhythm of an Eskimo Pie."

"You have the sense of rhythm of an Eskimo Pie."

"I know. But I don't sing except in the shower and I don't even do that when I have a lady over."

Gregor didn't even sing in the shower. When he did, odd things happened to the water. The two young men had reached the front steps of the synagogue now. They were fumbling around in the pockets of their jackets. One of them came up with another joint, lit it, and tried to pass it to his friend. The other pushed it away and found a joint of his own. The one who had had the joint first was wearing a red scarf. The other one was wearing a pair of bright blue gloves. Neither of these details had been clear when the two were still across the street. Since they were clear now, Gregor used them for identification: the first one was Red Scarf; the second one was Blue Gloves.

"Don't you know anything about AIDS you dumb jerk?" Blue Gloves demanded. "You can get sick to death sucking on somebody else's joint like that."

"Nah," Red Scarf said. "You can't get AIDS like that. You can only get AIDS letting some faggot pork you up the ass."

"You can get it by being anywhere near a faggot," Blue Gloves said. "You can get it just by breathing some faggot's air."

"If that's true, then everybody in town is going to get it. Cause this city is full of faggots and we're all breathing the same air."

"Everybody in town is going to get it. That was the plan. The Zionist Underground put the virus in the water and they're just sitting back and watching the rest of us die."

"Yeah," Red Scarf said, "them and the Catholic church. They're in it together."

"And the niggers."

"And the Spics."

"It's a worldwide conspiracy," Blue Gloves said. "I wish I was smarter about all this shit. I get to thinking about it and I get confused."

"How can you tell?" John Jackman muttered under his breath.

"They certainly aren't being quiet about it," Gregor pointed out. "They have to be audible in Delaware. That ought to help the case down the line."

"Here comes the paint," John Jackman said.

Red Scarf had taken a can out of his jacket pocket. He turned it over a couple of times and then shook it in the air. Blue Gloves dropped the roach of his joint onto the street and stamped what spark there was left in it under his boot. Then he reached into his own jacket pocket and pulled out a spray can of his own.

"Do you think they believe any of the things they say?" Gregor asked idly, watching them begin to pace back and forth in front of the synagogue's facade.

"I think they have a hard time remembering it from one day to the next," John Jackman said. "Except that they think they've been screwed. They remember that."

"Maybe they have been screwed," Gregor said.

John Jackman snorted. "Their mothers should have screwed up the courage to give them a few good spankings. That's the only way they've been screwed."

Out on the street, Red Gloves had raised his arm in the air and aimed the spray can at the synagogue's front face. He set it off in a blur of white and yelled, "Die, you Jew bastards, die!"

He was very loud, but to Gregor he did not sound convincing. Blue Gloves leaped in next to him and raised his spray can in the air, but with less dramatic flourish.

"We will not be destroyed!" he shouted, but he didn't sound convincing, either.

This was as far as the two uniformed cops had ever intended to let it go; just far enough to get the conviction they wanted, and no farther. Gregor and John Jackman heard the double doors beneath them slam open. A second later, the uniformed cops were on the street and the two white boys were in custody, handcuffed and secure, swearing away in language so foul it would have got them bounced from the Marine Corps.

"Let's go." John Jackman leapt to his feet and heading for downstairs.

Gregor couldn't leap. It had been twenty years since he even tried. He got up in a much more dignified manner. The foyer was now brightly lit. Either John Jackman or one of the uniformed cops had had the good sense to turn the lights on. The two young men were hopping and jumping and shaking in custody.

Gregor arrived just as the one he'd been calling Red Scarf caught sight of John Henry Newman Jackson. Red Scarf froze. His body went rigid. His eyes seemed to bug out of his head. He seemed to have stopped breathing. Then he started to wail.

"Ricky!" he shrieked. "Ricky! Look at this! It's the Head Nigger himself come down to do us in!"

"Oh, *fine*," John Jackman said. "Sidney Poitier, Virgil Tibbs, and the Head Nigger. It's been quite a week. Let's go eat, Gregor. I can't stand it anymore."

"We can't go eat," Gregor said.

"Why not? I'm starving. Of course we can go eat."

"We've got to go back to the hospital and see Carmencita Boaz again," Gregor said. "We've got to go right away."

FIVE

===

1

DeAnna Kroll was good in a crisis. In fact, she was best in a crisis, which was part of the reason she was not still living in Harlem and all of the reason she had so many nights like this one, pacing back and forth in front of blank windows and wondering what she was supposed to do next. What she was expected to do next was go home: back to the hotel, back to her room, back to the usual routine, assuming she had a usual routine. Instead, she was walking back and forth in front of the windows in the waiting area of Five North, wanting a cigarette so desperately it made her chest ache. Five North was very quiet. It was after nine o'clock at night. Visiting hours were over. Patients were medicated and put to sleep. The nursing staff was reduced to a skeleton force, and would remain that way until the morning. DeAnna looked down on the parking lot and the street and the light and dark of Philadelphia and realized she was about to have One of Those Moods. Lotte had Those Moods, too. In fact, she'd had one just this afternoon. Maybe she was having it still. One of Those Moods was a time when you just couldn't stand it any more, the senseless triviality of everything, the endless posturing of people who wanted to feel important without going to the trouble of doing anything of consequence. That was the trouble with television talk shows. In no time at all, they made you think your fellow human beings were no better than grapefruit with delusions of grandeur. Unless, of course, you were a grapefruit yourself. DeAnna had met a certain Very Famous Talk Show Host, one of those people with near-saintly reputations for Sensitivity and Courage, and he not only had been a grapefruit but had been from the planet Mars. Or maybe it was the planet television. Had she always been so cynical about what she did?

Lotte had gone off to the bathroom fifteen minutes ago. She still wasn't back. DeAnna cast another look at Carmencita's door—what for? Carmencita was asleep. Itzaak was in there talking to her as if she could understand every word he said—and then headed down the hall for the bathrooms. The ladies' room was in the elevator lobby, on the right side of the elevator bank. The men's room was on the left. DeAnna stifled her perennial impulse to go into the men's room and see if she could use a urinal and went into the ladies' room instead.

"Lotte?"

"I am here, DeAnna. I am smoking a cigarette in a toilet stall, like the girls in that movie you gave me about the convent school."

"The Trouble with Angels."

"What?"

"Never mind. Come out of there and I'll light a cigarette, too."

"What will happen if they catch us?"

"They'll ask us to put it out. And then they'll ask for your autograph."

The door to the last stall on the far end opened and Lotte came out, looking diminutive and furious.

"This is a crazy situation in this country, DeAnna, the way it is with smoking. It is one thing to be concerned about health. It is another to turn your country into a health police state."

"Now, Lotte. Don't exaggerate."

"I am not exaggerating. There are three places where smoking should never be prohibited. In hospital waiting rooms. In psychiatrist's offices. And at tax audits."

"I'll give you the tax audit." DeAnna reached into her pocket for the pack of cigarettes she had taken off Lotte earlier in the day and lit up. "God, I'm feeling tired. Do you suppose Mr. Demarkian has a clue to what's been going on around us?"

"I don't know," Lotte said soberly. "I will tell you, DeAnna, he is not what I expected him to be."

"What did you expect him to be?"

"I thought he would be more like Sherlock Holmes," Lotte said, "or like Columbo that I watch late at night when I can't sleep."

"At least that's a range," DeAnna said.

"Range or not, Mr. Demarkian is not like either of them. He does not seem to do anything but ask the same questions, over and over again. I do not think he is very intelligent."

"I do."

"Do you? Well, DeAnna, maybe you are right. I do not have any expertise in these things. Today I have been feeling that I do not have any expertise in anything."

"Yeah, I know," DeAnna said. "I've been having the same kind of night."

Lotte's cigarette was out. She leaned back, dumped the butt in the toilet, and reached for another.

"I think about Hanukkah," Lotte said. "About David and Rebekkah and their children and the way Jews in

America have taken a very minor holiday and turned it
into a wonderful occasion for families, a wonderful occasion for children, because families and children are
what are in the end important. I mean, DeAnna, what
else is there? Does it really matter if I get a forty share
next week? A hundred years from now, who will remember?"

"Oh, my, my, my," DeAnna said. "You've got it even
worse than I do."

"I haven't *got* anything," Lotte said. "I'm just at the
end of my rope. Carmencita is lying in there half-dead,
and tomorrow morning what are we going to do? We're
going to go into the studio and tape a show on five
women who are suing Saks Fifth Avenue for having
caused their shopping addiction with the mail-order cat-
alog."

"Oh, that show," DeAnna said. "I'd forgotten that
one."

"I had not forgotten that one, DeAnna. It is impossible to forget. Why do these people expect us to take them
seriously?"

"Because they know we want that forty share."

"Why do we want that forty share?"

"Because my last bonus from Gradon Cable Systems was a million five and your residuals statements
look like the miscellaneous expenses section of a Penta-
gon budget."

"Money should not be the point, DeAnna."

"But it is, Lotte. It is always the point."

"The point should have some sort of cosmic significance. I am not a theist, DeAnna, you know that. I do
not want angels and fairies and a God on a cloud. But
still."

"Still what?"

"Still there should be some point to it all. There
should be some reason why we do the things we do. There

should be more to going on with life than listening to privileged women whine."

"'Oh, dear," DeAnna said.

"I have been having a very bad day," Lotte told her. "I have come to one of those points where I think it is time to terminate my contract and retire to Jerusalem."

"You can't retire to Jerusalem. You hate Jerusalem. You hate the heat."

"No Jew hates Jerusalem, DeAnna. It is a matter of principle."

"It is a matter of mental disturbance. It is about time I took you out for a little kosher wine."

"Getting me drunk won't solve my problems, DeAnna. It will just make one of our guests accuse me of having a secret addiction."

"None of your addictions are secret." DeAnna's cigarette was out. She pitched the butt where Lotte had pitched hers. Then she got out another cigarette and lit up. The heat of her Bic lighter shot up too far and licked the tip of her nose. The smoke she blew out after her first long drag made her eyes sting. She was going to have to quit smoking again as soon as she had a chance.

"Listen. I know how you feel because I've been feeling that way too, but I've got a better idea than retiring to Jerusalem."

"What kind of better idea?"

"'I Can't Help It, I've Got to Have Two Husbands—At the Same Time.'"

"The polyandry show?"

"Exactly."

"But we have discussed it," Lotte said. "We have talked to those women. They have sex lives Hugh Hefner couldn't have dreamed of in a vision. And they talk like—"

"I know. They've always promised to bring videotapes. Of, you know, marital sessions."

"No videotapes."

"Maybe not," DeAnna conceded.

"Even without the videotapes," Lotte said, "we would never get away with it. We would be replaced in every market from Wilmington to Las Vegas."

"Actually, I don't think so," DeAnna said. "That's why I brought it up. I think I've found a way around that."

"Like what?"

DeAnna waved her cigarette in the air, realized that wouldn't do any good and stuck it in her mouth for safe-keeping. The smoke got in her eyes, but she didn't care. She rummaged around in her tote bag until she found a pen and a piece of paper. Then she laid the paper out on one of the sinks and bent over it.

"This is what we're going to do," she said.

DeAnna felt much better, and she could see Lotte did, too. That just went to prove something she'd always believed. There were no real cosmic questions. There was no honest impetus to discover the meaning of life. There was only boredom, and the answer to boredom was really kinky sex.

Not, of course, sex in the flesh.

Sex in the flesh was messy.

What you really needed was sex in the abstract.

Somebody else's sex.

Sex so weird it made you dizzy.

To hell with Aristotle.

2

For Carmencita Boaz, time was a river, just like Stephen King had said it was in the one long novel she had ever read in English, but for her it was a river of pain. The pain was almost a headache but wasn't quite. It started in that flat place at the side of her eyes and traveled across her

cheekbones to her jaw. They had given her Demerol half
an hour ago. She knew the pain should be on one side of
her face and not the other, but couldn't make it feel that
way. She was very tried but couldn't sleep. Itzaak was
half-sitting and half-not in a plain, armless plastic-covered
chair at the side of her bed. Every once in a while, he
would jump up and pace across the room. Carmencita
wondered if someone had told him that it helped patients
when you talked to them. If nobody had, this was a sign
of nervousness beyond any she would have imagined him
capable of. She wished she knew all those things Gregor
Demarkian was hoping she knew: what her attacker looked
like, who her attacker was, what had happened and when
it had happened and why. All she remembered was standing there in that stairwell next to the elevators, waiting to
buy the green card and thinking about Itzaak. After that
she had nothing but the face of the doctor staring down at
her and a voice saying: *You have to hold very still.* It was
ridiculous. It was like telling a ship's barnacle not to take
a vacation to the North Pole.

There was only one light on now in this room she
was in. It was a light on a metal arm like a drafting board
light, that could be moved back and forth depending on
where you wanted it. Itzaak had pushed it down low to the
floor and turned it so the bright bulb faced away from
them. It caused shadows and movements on all the available walls. On the table next to the bed was a vase with
a dozen red roses in it. As soon as Itzaak had heard she
was all right, he had ordered them for her.

He took her left hand into both of his and held it
tightly. He got up and sat down and got up and sat down
again, probably unaware that he was moving at all.
Carmencita wished she wasn't so very tired. She wished
she could do something to soothe his soul and put an end
to his misery.

"It will be all right," he said to her now. "I have
thought the whole thing through. I have told you Mr.

Demarkian has promised to talk to the people at the Immigration and Naturalization Service?"

Carmencita tried to nod, but it made her head hurt. She lifted up her hand and let it drop instead.

"Mr. Demarkian is a very powerful man," Itzaak said, "and it is likely he can do what he has said he can do. But it is not a hundred percent certain. Nothing is a hundred percent certain. I do not like to take too many chances."

Carmencita raised her hand and dropped it again.

"If Mr. Demarkian cannot do what he says he can do, then we have a number of possible courses of actions. In the first place, we should get married. In my opinion, we should get married even if Mr. Demarkian can do what he says he can do, because I love you. But I will understand, Carmencita, if you do not wish to marry me."

This required more than a hand raised and dropped. What was she supposed to do? Her jaw was wired shut. Moving her head in any direction at all made her feel ready to explode. She raised her hand and dropped it again, raised her hand and dropped it again, raised her hand and dropped it again, over and over, as quickly as she could. At least it got his attention.

"You mustn't do that," he said, frowning. "You will hurt yourself. The doctor has said it. For the next two weeks or so, you will be very fragile."

Fragile, Carmencita thought. If she was going to be here for two weeks like this with Itzaak babbling nonsense about how he'd understand it if she did not want to marry him, she was going to be a raving lunatic before they ever took the wires out of her jaw. She raised her hand in the air and made writing motions. She did her best to compose her face into a mask of sternness and resolve. She didn't think she succeeded. Demerol made everything so—squishy. Squooshy squashy. Squirt.

Itzaak was still frowning at her. "Something to write with," he said. "You want something to write with. But you cannot write, Carmencita. You do not have the strength."

Carmencita made writing motions in the air again. Itzaak got up and started to look around the room.

"I have talked to Lotte," he said, "and we have talked to the doctors, and we have talked to Rabbi Goldman and his wife. That is where we will take you, when you are released from there. That will be the week after next. I will not go on with the show, Carmencita, I will stay here and take my vacation time. I have much vacation time due to me because I have never taken any. So, you will be released just in time for the first night of Hanukkah. You will like it, Carmencita. Especially at Rabbi Goldman's house. The rebbitzin is a wonderful woman."

Carmencita was sure that Rebekkah Goldman was a wonderful woman. She was also sure there was a pen stuck into the medical chart hanging at the foot of her bed. She had seen a doctor put it there. She tried to think of a way to tell Itzaak and just couldn't.

Itzaak was looking through a tray of gauze and bandage tape. Why did he think he was going to find a pen there?

"It is a beautiful ceremony," he said. "There is the menorah with the shammes in the middle, to light all the other candles. And there are blessings. One is in praise of God who commanded us to light the Hanukkah lights, and one is in praise of God who did the miracle that we want to commemorate. And on the first night of Hanukkah there is a third one, in praise of God who has kept us—has kept the Jews—a people from that time to this, still alive and together. Which, considering some of the things that have happened to us, may be more of a miracle than a day's oil that lasts for eight. I just realized, Carmencita, there is a lot of praising God with us. Maybe there is also a lot of praising God with you. I do not know much about Catholicism."

I don't know much about Catholicism, either, Carmencita thought, not in the way he means it. Itzaak had moved away from the medical tray and gone to search through the small bureau. Carmencita would be very surprised if there was actually anything in it. She hadn't had any clothes brought to the hospital from her hotel room yet. The hospital didn't supply courtesy stationary and a room service menu.

"Later on, after the candles are lit, there is a song," Itzaak said. "It's called 'Ma'oz Tzur.' It is a song about all the times God has saved us. It has six verses, but it could have a hundred and six. Or a thousand and six. And it stops with Frederick Barbarossa, who was emperor of Germany in the twelfth century. Maybe no one has had the heart to do an update since then. It is a melody you may know, Carmencita, it was not written just for this song. I have heard several Protestant Christian hymns with the same music."

The only Protestant Christian hymn Carmencita could think of at the moment was "Oh, What a Friend We Have in Jesus." Itzaak was now searching the little night table next to her bed. That at least had a few things in the drawer. A tongue depressor. A laminated 1987 pocket calendar from Hazelbury's Body Shop. A small pad of plain white paper with a cardboard back. Itzaak snatched the pad from the drawer and held it up in triumph.

"Here," he said. "Here is the paper. Now we have only to find you a pen. Should I go to ask the nurse for a pen, Carmencita? You don't seem to have one here."

I'll give it one last try, Carmencita thought. She concentrated very hard. She willed her left foot upward. To her surprise, it went. It fell back to the bed again almost as soon as she'd got it up, but it went.

"What?" Itzaak said.

Carmencita did it again. It hurt.

"I don't understand," Itzaak said. He went down to

the foot of the bed and looked at the lumps under the blankets where her feet were. She did it one more time and startled him so much he jumped back.

"I don't understand," he said again, and then stopped. "Oh," he said. "Carmencita. You are very intelligent. I always knew you were very intelligent. Here is a pencil."

Good, Carmencita thought.

Itzaak extracted the pencil from under the clip and brought it up to the head of the bed.

"Are you sure you want to do this, Carmencita? It will be much too much of a strain, I think. You are supposed to be getting your rest."

Carmencita raised her left hand and let it drop again. Itzaak gave her the pencil and brought over the pad. Carmencita was right-handed, but that was much too complicated a problem to go into at this point. She couldn't sit up to see what she was writing, either. It hurt too much to move her head in any direction at all. She felt the pencil in her fingers and brushed against the paper on the pad with the side of her hand. Then she gave it a try.

Si, she wrote. She couldn't remember the English word for it. It was a perfectly simple word. She'd known it since she was two. She just couldn't remember it.

Itzaak picked up the pad and looked at it.

"S. I." He shook his head. "This is the beginning of a word, Carmencita? Do you want me to try to figure out what it is?"

She gestured and he gave the pad back to her. He held it down under her hand to help. She wrote, *si,* again, and then, in a burst of brilliance and energy she wouldn't be able to match for several days, she followed with NOT NO.

Itzaak took the pad. "S. I. Not no. Oh. Oh. I see. *Si.* Not no. Yes."

Carmencita got the pad back and wrote, *SI* in the biggest letters she could make. She wondered what they looked like.

"Yes," Itzaak said happily. "You mean yes. But yes what? That you will like Hanukkah?"

If the human race had to rely on the perceptive intelligence of men, Carmencita thought, it would have been extinct a couple of million years ago. She gestured for the return of the pad and got it. She got a grip on the pencil and tried one more time. She was really very tired. Exhausted. It was difficult to keep this up. She got out some semblance of *M A R*— she really wished she could see what she was doing—but that was as far as she could go. Her hand felt numb.

Itzaak looked worried. He took the pad away from her but didn't look at it. Instead, he stared into her face.

"You should not put yourself to so much effort. You will make yourself more sick than you already have to be. It is not something I would like to happen."

It wasn't something Carmencita wanted to happen, either. She raised her left hand and lowered it again, doing her best to point to the pad.

Itzaak got the message. He looked down at the pad and read. "M. A. R." He looked thoroughly bewildered.

"Yes, not no. And mar. Carmencita—"

Carmencita Boaz had heard often enough about light bulbs going on over people's heads. She had seen enough animated movies and read enough comic books to know it was a popular culture cliché. She had never seen anything in real life that might equate to it. Itzaak's face at this moment did. His eyes were brighter. His smile was wider. His face glowed as if he'd been hit by a hot pink spot. He was ecstatic.

"Carmencita," he said. "Carmencita, this is wonderful. You will marry me. You will marry me."

Carmencita raised her hand and lowered it again.

"Of course," Itzaak told her, "this is no place for a woman like you to receive a proposal of marriage. We will go out as soon as you are better and do it all properly, in a restaurant, with candlelight. I will start at the beginning and tell you I love you and go right on to the end. And in a year, Carmencita, I will be an American citizen. Do you understand?"

Carmencita raised her hand, wobbled it back and forth, and lowered it again. She didn't understand much of anything at the moment.

"The wife of an American citizen can also become an American citizen," Itzaak said, "it is more complicated than that but less more complicated than you think. It will be fine, Carmencita, you will see. It will all be just the way you want it to be."

I wish I could tell him that I'm willing to convert, Carmencita thought, feeling herself drifting away. I wish I could tell him I am at least willing to keep a kosher home. I wish I could tell him *anything*.

The floating feeling was really awful now. The bed felt like water. Carmencita's eyelids felt like stones.

Itzaak was fussing around at the side of the bed again, holding onto her hand, stroking her fingers. The skin of his hand was rough and yet soft at the same time. That didn't make sense but she knew what she meant by it. If he would just go on doing that for another sixty seconds, she would be asleep.

Asleep.

Darkness and peace. Silence and the light of dreams.

Way on the other side of the room there were three sharp raps, and Carmencita thought: Death always knocks three times.

"Just a minute," Itzaak told her, letting go of her hand. "There is someone at the door, Carmencita. Perhaps it is the nurse and it is time again for your medication."

But it wasn't the nurse and it wasn't time for her medication. Carmencita knew that. She knew it as certainly as if she could see who was standing outside that door.

It was just that she was much too weak to get a warning to Itzaak before it was too late.

3

For Sarah Meyer, Shelley Feldstein's theft of her diary would have been enough on its own to provide cause for launching thermonuclear war. The state her hotel room was in was—well, she didn't know what it was. She didn't know what to think of it. She didn't know what to do about it. She was going to have to do all the usual things, like get in touch with the hotel staff and swear out a complaint of some kind. Whether anybody would believe her if she said Shelley had done this, she didn't know. She wasn't sure that was the way she wanted to go about it in any case. She wasn't sure what she wanted to do, except sit down and think.

Sarah had come back from the hospital dead tired and in a foul mood. Shelley had made such a point of reading that diary whenever Sarah could see her, it was a form of abuse. That diary was damned dangerous, and Sarah knew it. It was the only place on earth she ever allowed herself to be herself. Making that sort of thing public would be a disaster. At least, it would be a disaster for Sarah. Sarah suspected that Shelley would think the consequences were just fine. Sarah knew what that was about. Shelley hated the idea that she had ever been one-upped by a fat person.

Sarah locked the door to the room, considered opening it again to put out a "do not disturb" sign, and decided against that. She wanted it to look as if she'd come right into the room, seen the mess and called the desk, right away. She also wanted to give herself enough time to take her revenge. She went over to the desk and opened the drawer. This was how she could be sure the mess was Shelley's doing, if she hadn't been sure already. Her own clothes and perfume and papers were all over the floor, destroyed forever, but the red leather address book, which was the property of *The Lotte Goldman Show*, was still in the desk intact. Which was good. Sarah took it out and flipped through it until she found Feldstein, Shelley. Then she sat down to puzzle this out.

There were four phone numbers under Shelley's name in the red leather book, next of kin to call just in case. Two of these were identified as belonging to "Robert." The other two were identified as belonging to "Stephen." Two of these were the phone numbers—at home and at work—of Shelley's husband. The other two were the phone numbers—at home and at school—of Shelley's oldest son. It was such a pain when parents gave their children their own private telephone lines. Sarah's parents would never have done any such thing.

Husbands come before children, Sarah told herself, and home comes before work. She punched in the number and her phone credit card and waited. She heard the phone picked up in New York and a deep bass voice say,

"Hello?"

"Hello?" Sarah could do breathlessly upset very well over the phone. The only thing she couldn't make convincing was her face, and she didn't have to. "Is this Mr. Robert Feldstein I've got hold of? Husband of Shelley Feldstein?"

"If you're some kind of a reporter," Robert Feldstein said, "I have already made it perfectly clear—"

"Oh, I'm not a reporter, Mr. Feldstein. I'm Sarah Meyer. I'm an assistant on *The Lotte Goldman Show*. Do I have the right Mr. Feldstein?"

"Yes," Robert Feldstein said reluctantly. "Yes, you do. Has something gone wrong? Is Shelley all right?"

"Oh, Mr. Feldstein," Sarah said. "I don't know what to do. Let me tell you the story from the beginning."

Sarah Meyer then proceeded to tell Robert Feldstein the story from the beginning, complete with names, dates, times, places, and preferences in romantic restaurants and out-of-the-way sexual venues, like the roof of the Hullboard-Dedmarsh building.

By the time Sarah was through, Shelley Feldstein's life sounded like a chapter from *Peyton Place*.

SIX

==

1

At just about the time Carmencita Boaz was listening to Itzaak Blechman explaining the ceremonies of Hanukkah—before she was able to tell him "not no," significantly before there was a knock on the door and everything began to get nasty—Gregor Demarkian was getting out of a police car on the far side of the street from St. Elizabeth's south-side door, so tense with impatience he felt as if his muscles had turned to glass. It would have been quicker to go in through the front doors, or the north-side entrance, but he didn't have access to either. The north-side entrance was on a side street now blocked entirely by eighteen-wheel tractor trailer trucks, bringing in supplies for the hospital and the few businesses that surrounded it. St. Elizabeth's was in one of those parts of Philadelphia that looked as if it had stopped being part of a city and started being part of the interstate highway system. What was going on around the front doors was bad. Stuck at the corner, realizing what it all meant, Gregor almost longed for the return of the reporters. Reporters only stabbed people with their rapier wits, which were far less sharp than they liked to think. Whoever had stabbed the two men now bleeding into the steps leading up to St. Elizabeth's front doors had either used a very sharp knife, or gone at his victims over and over again. The rescue effort now taking place in the curving drive was a full-scale object lesson in emergency mobilization. Maybe whoever had done the stabbing was up there, too, half-dead on the ground. Wherever he was, Gregor and John Jackman were not going to be able to go through St. Elizabeth's front doors.

"It might be different if we could claim an emergency," John told Gregor, "but not much. We have other options."

"Let's use them," Gregor said.

The other options turned out to be the south-side door, a gray metal slab with a tall rectangle of glass in the upper half of it that opened onto a small staff parking lot. The parking lot was deserted and the security light that was supposed to shine right at the door's knob and keyhole was broken. At least half the lights in the parking lot were broken, too. Gregor looked into the deserted space and grimaced. Staff parking lot. Nurses' cars. Aside from serial killers, there were animals known as serial rapists. Gregor had run across one or two. This was just the sort of place they liked. It was infuriating. It was so easy to fix a situation like this. It was cheap, too. A couple of the right lights, a fence—

He was always doing this. He had someplace to go and something to do. John Jackman was already at the fire door, rattling the lock.

"There's a buzzer," he called out. "I rang it."

"Fine," Gregor said.

He lumbered up to the fire door and looked through the rectangular window. The window was composed of two panes of glass with wire edging pressed between. Beyond it there was a deserted hall with doors opening off it on both sides, dimly lit. The far end wasn't lit at all. Gregor thought this place ought to have a sign on it that said:

> *REALLY BAD SEX CRIME*
> *TROUBLE EXPECTED HERE.*

At least it would give the women who were forced to use this passage a shot at informed consent.

Out of the dark spot at the back of the hall came a middle-aged woman in a nun's habit, carrying too much weight on too short legs and looking as if she were getting winded. Bennis said so many nuns got heavy because they weren't required to do anything to make themselves attractive to men. If women ever got feminist enough, a lot of them would get heavy. Considering the fact that Bennis could eat her way through four pounds of yaprak sarma and a foot-tall mound of halva and never gain an ounce, Gregor didn't think he could trust her opinion on this.

The nun stopped at the door and peered out. John Jackman raised his identification to the window. The nun began to open up. There were a lot of locks on this door, a bad sign. It would take a woman a good two or three minutes to open up, and two or three minutes was more than an attacker would need.

The door swung open and the nun peered out. "Yes? Didn't you want to go in the front door?"

"There's a medical emergency going on at the front door, Sister," John Jackman said politely. "We couldn't get through."

Sister made a face. "Stabbings. Always with the stabbings. Two or three times a week."

"Right at the hospital doors?" Gregor asked.

"Father McCormack came and talked to us about it. It has something to do with where we are. The neighborhood to the north is controlled by one gang, and the neighborhood to the east is controlled by another, so—"

"Never mind," John Jackman said. "We get the idea."

"It causes everybody no end of problems when they do this," the nun said. "And they get terribly hurt and somebody always dies. How do you talk people out of behaving like that?"

"If I knew the answer to that, ma'am, I could retire to Miami."

"Oh, I wouldn't go to Miami," the nun said. "Miami is worse. I know. The Sisters always watch the reruns of that show on television."

"Nuns who watch *Miami Vice*," John Jackman said into Gregor's ear. "I think that makes my week complete."

Gregor ignored him. The hall was not only dimly lit but much too well heated. It was so hot, Gregor thought steam was going to rise from the floor beneath his feet.

"You come right this way," the nun told them, padding off down the hall into the dark. "The elevators are right over here. Just push the button for lobby and get off when the elevator stops. Unless you're looking for a room on the south side. Are you looking for a room on the south side?"

"North side," Gregor told her.

"Oh. Well, then. You get off at the lobby and use the other set of elevators. They'll take you right up. And there'll be a Sister on duty at the desk to give you any other directions you need."

"Thank you," John Jackman said.

They were at the elevators now. They had passed into a lightless place. Then the Sister had flicked a switch and an entire ceilingful of overhead fluorescents had come on.

"Saving on electricity, you know," she said. "Looking out for the environment."

Gregor punched the call button and looked at the whitewashed concrete walls. Somebody had gone to the trouble of putting up candles cut out of construction paper and a bright silver tin foil star.

"Take a little advice from me, Sister," Gregor said. "Stop worrying about the electric bill. And leave the environment to somebody else. Keep the lights on."

"But—"

"Sister, you're in a very bad place in the middle of a very tough part of Philadelphia, and in the dark the way you are you're asking to get hurt."

The elevator bounded down to them. The doors slid open. Gregor and Jackman stepped into the car.

"But," Sister said again.

"Trust me," Gregor told her.

Then he pushed the button marked "L" and the doors slid closed.

2

The lobby was almost as deserted as the hall downstairs had been. There was one Sister at the reception desk. She recognized them and nodded them past. There was a policeman on duty in front of the north side elevator bank. He was sitting in a chair reading *The Body Lovers* by Mickey Spillane. It was an old paperback falling apart at the spine. Its cover was a 1950s hard-boiled cliché, complete with shapely high-heel-clad leg coming out of nowhere and snaking up into the cover. It was the kind of cover Tibor disguised by pasting it over with brown paper cut out of grocery bags. Tibor loved Mickey Spillane.

When they came up to the cop, he put down his book. When the cop saw who he had in front of him, he stood up.

"Hello," he said. "I didn't expect to see you here."

"I didn't expect to be here," John Jackman said. "Anybody go up?"

"Not for over an hour. There was a big rush between seven and eight. That was because of visiting. Since then it's been dead. You could ask Shecker upstairs."

"Shecker's on duty on Five North?"

"That's right. But I don't think anything's happened up there, either. I mean, except for what you would expect."

"What would you expect?" Gregor asked.

"People from the show," the cop said. Then he looked a little worried. "That was what I was told. They could come and go as they liked. I wasn't supposed to stop them—"

"No, no," Jackman said. "That's absolutely right. We don't have anything to stop them for. I just want to keep an eye on them. Which of that crowd has been up?"

"Well, it's like I told you, nobody's been up for at least an hour. Before we got a flurry or two, during visiting hours, you know. There was that black lady, you know, with the hair—"

"DeAnna Kroll."

"Yeah. Shecker says she gives him heart palpitations. And he's white. I mean, excuse me. I didn't—"

"Never mind," John said wearily, "who else?"

"Oh, the two crazy ladies. You know. Shirley and Sheila. Susan and Sandra—"

"Shelley and Sarah," Gregor said.

"Yeah, them. They're nuts. First one of them goes tearing up, then the other one does. Then one of them goes tearing up, then the other one does. I think they're following each other."

"Which was it the last time? Up or out?" Gregor asked.

"Up," the cop said. "The tall thin one—"

"Shelley Feldstein," John put in.

"She went up. That was just around eight o'clock."

"What about the other one?" Gregor asked.

"The short fat one. I didn't see her."

"Had she gone out previously?" Jackman asked.

"Oh, yeah. But that doesn't mean anything. You have to go through the lobby to get to the cafeteria, so she may have never left the building."

"Wouldn't you have seen her when she came back?" Gregor asked.

"Not if she went across the bridge on eleven. It's a weird way around but some people—"

"That's why we have a man on Five North," John put in. "Because in a building this big there have to be half a dozen ways to get to any one place. It's inevitable."

"Mmm," Gregor said.

"You want to get going?" Jackman said.

Gregor got going.

He hadn't noticed it before, but this part of the lobby was decorated with all the feverish intensity Donna Moradanyan brought to Cavanaugh Street. There were Hanukkah candles and Stars of Bethlehem. There was a life-size statue of the Madonna cradling her Child. There was a tall wicker basket full of hard Christmas candy with a sign that said

> "TAKE SOME"

on the side. Leave it to the nuns. Not "take one," "take some."

"Wait a minute," Gregor said. "Let me work this out. DeAnna Kroll is in or out?"

"In," the cop said.

"How about Lotte Goldman?"

"Also in."

"Sarah Meyer?"

"Out, I think."

"And Shelley Feldstein is in?"

"That's right."

"I suppose that leaves Itzaak Blechmann," Gregor said. "He should be in."

"He should be in all night," John Jackman said. "That Kroll woman went to no end of trouble to get permission for him to stay with Carmencita Boaz for the night. The nuns were a little uneasy because the two of them weren't married, but Señorita Boaz is in no shape to engage in any hanky-panky, so they relented. It would be odder if he had come down and gone out."

"All right," Gregor said, "but it still doesn't add up."

"Add up to what?"

"There are too many," Gregor said. He punched the button to summon the elevator, but he didn't have to wait. The cars were all at lobby level. The doors opened as soon as he put his finger on the button. Gregor stepped into the nearest car and beckoned John Jackman to follow him.

"There are too many people upstairs," he said. "You've got to add the cop into the equation. Our murderer is not a stupid person."

"Maybe our murderer is waiting for the day after tomorrow," Jackman said. "If nothing happens between now and then, we'll pull our cop off. And there's no reason not to wait until then. Even if Carmencita Boaz knows who hit her, she's not going to be able to say a thing about it for at least two weeks."

"She's going to be able to write."

"Not for a couple of days," Jackman said. "Right now, she can't sit up in bed without giving herself a headache the size of Godzilla and totally impervious to painkillers. She's out of the game for the next good little time now."

"She's going to be able to point."

"Right. This is pushing it, Gregor."

Gregor sighed. "She doesn't know who hit her. I'll practically guarantee it—"

"You didn't ask, did you?" Jackman sounded alarmed. "The doctors practically said we'd kill her if we asked to—

night and I told all my people to keep their mouths shut until tomorrow—"

"I didn't ask," Gregor said. "I just know. She didn't see who hit her. But she does know who promised to sell her a forged green card. And that's all we need."

"You mean if we can't get a murder charge to stick, we can go to the Feds and let them charge forgery and conspiracy and all that? That'll get our murderer five years in Danbury and he'll be out in eighteen months."

"The Feds couldn't make forgery and conspiracy stick," Gregor said. "We'd have to get some physical evidence to go along with it. Carmencita Boaz's unsupported word won't do it, especially since Carmencita has a forged green card of her own, and our friend didn't get it for her."

"Then why does it matter if she knows who promised to sell her the green card? Why is that all we need?"

"Because we can use it."

"For what?"

To be sure, Gregor thought, but he didn't say it, because the doors had opened on the fifth floor and as soon as they had he could sense something off. Not wrong, not really. Not flagrantly out of place. Just *off.* He stepped out of the elevator car and looked around. They had ridden in the car with Hanukkah decorations again, but Gregor hadn't paid attention to them. Now he saw the Christmas decorations around the elevator bank and decided to ignore those, too. Whatever was bothering him had nothing to do with any of that.

John Jackman stepped out of the car behind him and looked around.

"It seems quiet to me," he said to Gregor.

Too quiet, Gregor thought, but he didn't say that either, because it was too much like what one of the detectives in the mystery novels Bennis was always giving him would say. Instead he looked around and then down the short corridor to Five North proper. There was nobody and nothing to be seen. Even the nurses' station seemed to be deserted.

"Where would your cop be, if he was where he was supposed to be?"

"Not here," John Jackman said. "Too much could happen behind his back, and he'd bother too many people who have a right not to be bothered."

"Where?"

"Down by Carmencita Boaz's room."

Gregor looked down the corridor again. "He isn't there."

John Jackman came to stand behind Gregor and looked, too. "Don't panic," he said. "He could be *in* Carmencita Boaz's room."

"That's true. He could be in the bathroom."

"If he goes to the bathroom, he's supposed to get someone to take over while he's gone. You know that. You've been on stakeouts."

"On the kind of stakeouts I was assigned to," Gregor said, "there was nobody to take over for us when we were gone and no place to go anyway. We used to carry these little plastic jars . . ."

"I don't want to hear about it," John Jackman said. "This doesn't feel very good, does it?"

"No. But still—"

"Still?"

"Itzaak Blechmann is in the room with her," Gregor said.

"Would that make a difference?"

Gregor didn't know. He went a little farther down the corridor, being as quiet as he could, making no noise. He went past the door of the woman he had seen propped up in a chair earlier in the day. Her lights were out and she seemed to be asleep. He walked up to the edge of the nursing station and looked around.

It really was quiet. And empty. There was no sign of anything or anyone. He looked behind the nurses' station counter and found nothing. He looked through the glass window in the door to the head nurse's office and saw that the office was empty. What did I expect? he asked himself. Blood stains on the floor? Maybe that was exactly it.

Jackman came up behind him. "This is weird," he whispered.

"There isn't any need to whisper," Gregor whispered back. "By now, anyone who isn't asleep knows we're on the ward."

"Anyone who isn't asleep or dead."

"There should be at least one nurse somewhere on the floor," Gregor said, "they can't all have gone to the bathroom."

"Maybe there's just one nurse and she's in with a patient. I think I'm going to go into Carmencita's room now, Gregor. I think I have to."

"Wait," Gregor said.

For once, the "wait" had a substantive reason behind it, not just hunch and not just emotion. Gregor felt like he'd been saying "wait" now for hours, and always on the basis of some nebulous concept. But this was no nebulous concept. This was a leg.

"In the laundry bag," Gregor said, pointing.

John Jackman followed the direction of Gregor's finger and saw it. The laundry bag was one of those tall, rough white cotton ones hospitals always seem to use, stretched over a metal frame to facilitate the collection of dirty linen. It came about chest high on Gregor and higher than that on John Jackman. And there was most definitely a leg in it, stuffed down among the sheets.

"Jesus Christ," Jackman said, when he realized what he was seeing. He strode over to the bag and put his hand around the ankle. "Nothing in the way of a pulse. Not the best way to check. Help me get her out of here."

"Don't do that first," Gregor said. "She's dead."

"Maybe she isn't." Jackman tipped the laundry bag over and let the linen fall onto the floor. He pulled at the leg and the woman slipped out, small and crumpled. The left side of her face had been smashed to pulp.

Jackman put his fingers on the woman's wrist, tried again in a different place, and then stood up.

"Dead," he said.

"Your cop is going to be around here somewhere," Gregor said.

"Also dead?"

"At least badly hurt."

"I've got to go into that room now, Gregor. I can't wait another minute. I can't go looking for my cop first."

Gregor Demarkian sighed. "I know," he said. "But don't go in. Just call out. Just in case he doesn't realize there are two of us here."

"He?" Jackman said.

He didn't have time to go into it. He went out into the corridor in front of Carmencita Boaz's door, took out his gun and assumed firing position.

"All right," he called out, "I want whoever is in Room 507 to come out now with your hands in the air. Any and all of you. Right now. Or I'll rush that door."

Too late, it occurred to him that the room might be occupied by no one at all but Carmencita Boaz herself.

3

Too late, it occurred to Gregor Demarkian that it was not going to work. They were not going to catch a murderer in the act. They were going to be left in the worst possible position. The only consolation they might have was that Carmencita Boaz might not be dead.

This was intuition on a scale to rival the Oracle of Delphi, but it was true. To Gregor, John Jackman seemed to be standing for endless hours with his gun cocked and pointed at the door, but it was only forty-five seconds.

Then a deep voice called "I'm coming out" and the door began to open.

"Hands in the *air*," John Jackman repeated.

Prescott Holloway had his hands in the air. Prescott Holloway was not now and had never been a fool. Prescott Holloway was convinced that he was about to get away with a great deal of murder.

"Itzaak's in there lying on the floor," he said in a reasonable voice. "I think someone hit him on the head. Don't you think we ought to call a doctor?"

"Why didn't you call a doctor?" John Jackman asked him.

"I just got here. It's weird. There isn't a soul around anywhere. So I went in to check on Carmencita and there was Itzaak, on the floor."

"How is Carmencita?" Gregor asked.

"I don't know," Prescott Holloway said. "Sleeping, I guess. I never got a chance to look."

"You look," John Jackman said.

Gregor walked around Prescott Holloway to Carmencita's door, being careful not to blunder into the line of fire. He looked Prescott over as he passed. The verdict wasn't good. A quick once-over was never conclusive. The techies had a lot of equipment and they might find something in the end. In Gregor's experience, however, a suspect who looked clean usually turned out to be clean. Prescott Holloway was clean. There was no blood on him anywhere. There was no mud. There were no signs of strain of any kind.

Gregor went into Carmencita Boaz's room. Carmencita was sleeping peacefully, her body limp, her breathing regular and deep, the gift of Demerol. Itzaak was lying on the floor just inside the door with an enormous welt on the side of his head. Gregor took his pulse. It was too rapid but not impossibly so. Would he remember who had hit him when he woke up? Would he have seen? There was no way to tell. From the way Prescott Holloway was behaving, the probable answer to both of those questions was no. But there was no way to tell about that either.

Gregor stepped back over Itzaak's body and into the corridor again. "Blechmann needs a doctor," he told John Jackman, "but Carmencita seems to be perfectly all right."

"I think I got here just in time," Prescott Holloway said.

John Jackman ignored him. "Gregor?" he said. "There are a pair of handcuffs in the inside pocket of my suit jacket. Will you please take them out and use them on Mr. Holloway."

"It always amazes me where police detectives can hide handcuffs."

"I've been caught short before," Jackman said. "Just do it."

Gregor did it. He got the handcuffs. He got Prescott Holloway's hands behind his back and secured. Prescott Holloway cooperated and the whole operation took less than one and a half minutes.

"I can understand what you guys are thinking," Holloway said. "But I didn't do anything. I just came up to see where everybody was and found Itzaak in there lying on the floor."

"Put him in a chair," John Jackman said.

Gregor escorted Prescott Holloway to the chairs beside the nurses' station and sat him down. Prescott did some more cooperating and ended up with his legs stretched out across the vinyl floor, twisted into that strange body kink that is the only way to sit comfortably in a chair when your hands are cuffed behind your back. Gregor made a note of the fact that it was a maneuver Prescott Holloway seemed perfectly familiar with. He didn't have to fumble around and he didn't have to be told.

John Jackman was behind the nurses' station counter and on the phone. Gregor could hear him giving directions in his patented police command bark.

"Tell the nun at the desk we need some doctors up here. We've got at least one person dead and at least one person seriously hurt and I want someone to check out Carmencita Boaz just in case. And get up here yourself. Shecker's missing. And get me some uniforms and the techies and the mobile crime unit and do it in the next ten seconds because I need help up here and I need it right away."

Gregor left Prescott Holloway where he was sitting—it was not easy to get out of a chair from that position; it took work—and went around to John. He watched Prescott Holloway every second of the way. The bland smirk on the face. The smooth fall of rep stripes under the perfect knot of the tie. The little bulge in the pocket of his shirt where it looked as if he'd stuffed one of the nuns' hard candies. The brass buckle on his good leather belt. Gregor had heard people describe Prescott Holloway as someone who had "seen better days," but that wasn't accurate. Prescott Holloway was a man whose days were pretty good right now.

Gregor came to a rest beside John and looked down at the back of Prescott's head. John was staring at the phone, looking morose.

"Come here," he said, gesturing toward the head nurse's office. When they were out of Prescott Holloway's way and had a decent chance at not being overheard Jackman went on.

"It isn't going to work is it?" he asked Gregor. "We're going to arrest him. And they're going to prosecute him. But we're not going to get him."

"I don't know what they have in New York," Gregor said, "but here you've got Herbert Shasta to contend with. Herbert Shasta was a known serial killer and he was found standing right next to the body. That's reasonable doubt."

"Right," Jackman said, "and unless Carmencita saw him hit her—which she probably didn't—the defense is just going to say she would testify to anything to get out from under being deported, and if we don't get her out from under being deported, she might not be here to testify. God, this is a mess."

"I know," Gregor said. "I know."

"Sometimes I think I want to go into the army, Gregor, I really do. Get a rifle. Shoot the sons of—"

"Skip it," Gregor said. "Shouldn't we be looking for your cop?"

"I can't leave *him*. You could look."

"Maybe I will. Just in case we got lucky and we don't have another dead body on our hands."

"Good luck."

"I hope your uniforms get here soon," Gregor said. And then he stopped. He stopped dead in his tracks. He ran the memory of his last look at Prescott Holloway through his mind one more time, and he nearly laughed.

"What is it?" John Jackman demanded.

"It isn't hard candy," Gregor said.

"What are you talking about?"

"Good luck charms."

Gregor went back around the nurse's station counter and stood in front of Prescott Holloway again. He looked at the bulge in Prescott's shirt pocket and smiled.

"Excuse me," he said, reaching in and taking out the dreidel. "I'm making a note to Mr. Jackman here that I removed this dreidel from your shirt pocket. That's for the chain of evidence report."

"Chain of evidence for what?" Prescott Holloway demanded. "That's a plain ordinary wooden dreidel. It's practically Hanukkah. I work for a Jewish woman. Why shouldn't I have one?"

"No reason at all," Gregor said. "Except that this isn't an ordinary dreidel."

"What's that supposed to mean?"

"This is an Israeli dreidel," Gregor said. "It's of a kind that can only be bought in Israel, not in the United States. See? You can tell. Dreidels sold in the United States have

the letters *nūn, gīmel, hē,* and *shīn* on them. For the first letters of the Hebrew words that make up the sentence 'A
great miracle occurred there.' But in Israel, instead of the
last *shīn,* we have *pē*—for the Hebrew word for *here.* 'A
great miracle occurred here.' Do you see the difference?''

"I don't see what difference it makes."

"Have you ever been to Israel, Mr. Prescott?"

"I've been to Israel. I was stationed in Greece when
I was in the army. Everybody on the show has been to Israel."

"Not everybody on the show was found standing over
the body of an attempted murder victim with one of these
dreidels in his possession."

"So what?"

"So these dreidels are sold in packages of three. And
we found the other two."

"Where?"

"Where do you think, Mr. Holloway? We found one
next to the dead body of Maximillian Dey. The other was
picked up next to the body of Maria Gonzalez. You've
been very careless, Mr. Holloway."

"Bullshit."

"It isn't bullshit at all. I would suggest you have exactly two choices. You can either have a nice long talk
with Mr. Jackman here, or he can use this dreidel," Gregor
held it up and spun it by its handle, "to put you right into
the electric chair."

"Bullshit," Prescott Holloway said again, but he
sounded different now. Gregor could hear the waver in his
voice.

They're all stupid in the end, Gregor told himself.
That's why we win as often as we do. They're all stupid
in the end.

Gregor tossed the dreidel in the air, and caught it, and
smiled. Then he tossed the dreidel in the air again, and
caught it again, and smiled again. That was when Prescott
Holloway lunged.

It turned out that it was easier to get out of a chair from that position than Gregor thought.

Fortunately, Prescott Holloway was not only hand-cuffed, but a victim of very bad timing.

Just as he made it to his feet, the elevator doors on the other end of the corridor opened and let out a crowd of white-coated young doctors on the run.

That was when all hell broke loose.

Epilogue

*Another Friday
(Fortunately Not the Thirteenth)
This Time in Philadelphia*

1

"But it wasn't true, was it?" Bennis asked later. "About the dreidel? The dreidels weren't found with the bodies at all."

They were sitting in the first row of audience seats in Studio C at WKMB, waiting to be told that Gregor could go home and Bennis could be off to New York to take the Concorde. The whole mess had been over for days, and Gregor had just taped the show Lotte Goldman had wanted him to do from the beginning. He did not think it had been a very good show. Herbert Shasta had not been available for a repeat performance. His warden had understandably felt that *The Lotte Goldman Show* was not capable of taking very good care of him. DeAnna Kroll had dug up a much better prospect—if by better you meant both more attractive and more murderous. This was John Stewart Pell, the twenty-six-year-old executioner of eight women in Pennsylvania, New York, Delaware, West Virginia, and Maryland, the one all the papers had called "The Choir Boy." To Gregor's mind, Pell did not look like a choir boy. He looked like a cross between James Dean and the kind of tenth-string Hollywood actor who made most of his contacts at the beach. He looked smarmy as hell. Gregor couldn't understand what any woman would see in him. That only went to prove he knew nothing at all about women. A great many women had seen a great deal in John Stewart Pell. At least eight had been willing to go off alone with him on no acquaintance at all.

John Stewart Pell's particular perversion was anal sex with dead bodies. His position on *The Lotte Goldman Show* was that dead bodies had nothing to do with it. He liked anal sex, but society had stigmatized the practice to the point where he had repressed it. And you know what repression leads to. Repression always leads to violence.

John Stewart Pell had been handcuffed to his chair throughout the taping of the show. He had been handcuffed by a single ankle, made invisible by the placement of a cedar block coffee table, but he had been handcuffed. This was good, because every time he talked to one of the younger women who asked questions from the audience, his hands clenched and unclenched at his sides, compulsively. Gregor had seen them.

John Stewart Pell now had his hands handcuffed behind his back and his legs free. He was standing up at the back of the stage, talking to Lotte Goldman and DeAnna Kroll. He was being very charming. From what Gregor could tell, Lotte and DeAnna weren't buying it.

"Gregor," Bennis said.

"Of course it was a lie," Gregor told her. "Why shouldn't I tell a lie?"

"It isn't usually your kind of thing."

"You try solving a murder case on nothing but logic and then wondering what you're going to do about it. Do you know how I knew it had to be Prescott Holloway who was committing those murders?"

"How?"

"Because Maximillian Dey was dead," Gregor said. "I told John Jackman this—don't wince, for heaven's sake, he isn't here—anyway, I told him, just after Dey's body was found and we were looking back at the death of Maria Gonzalez. The key to this whole thing was that whoever was committing those murders had to be able to move the body of Maria Gonzalez to that storeroom after she was dead. In the first place, it's not easy to move dead bodies around. They're heavy and they don't cooperate. That made the murderer more likely to be a man than a woman. Though DeAnna Kroll could probably have managed it physically."

"She wouldn't have to," Bennis said. "She'd say 'move,' and the body would get up and walk. It wouldn't dare not."

"The more important aspect," Gregor went on, "was that he had to be able to move that body through the halls of the offices and studios of *The Lotte Goldman Show* in New York without anybody remarking on how odd it was that he was wandering around carrying a big unwieldy thing on his shoulders. Of course, as it turned out, nobody saw him. But think about it. You have a body. You wrap it up—it turned out to have been wrapped up in plastic garbage bags, by the way, that was in his statement; he was trying to make it look like a length of stage carpet—anyway, you wrap it up and you throw it over your shoulder and then you go marching into a place that isn't crammed full of people, but isn't empty, either. If you're Sarah Meyer, for instance, and somebody sees you, what do you say?"

"Oh, I see," Bennis said. "Even if you have a decent explanation, it would be odd, and once the body was found someone would remember."

"Exactly. Even if someone had seen Prescott

Holloway carrying his load, though, he wouldn't have thought anything of it. Prescott Holloway often got called into service to move props and furniture when there was an emergency. And there was an emergency. They'd just discovered that the people who were supposed to be the guests on their show were not going to make it, and they were in the middle of putting together a new show to tape on the spot."

"Well," Bennis said. "Then why didn't you just arrest him?"

"On what?"

"But—"

"But nothing," Gregor said firmly. "I'm not one of those people who think the police ought to have proof good enough to establish the existence of God before they arrest anyone, but they have to have *something*. I sent John Jackman's people out looking for the tire iron. We got nothing. He'd disposed of it already. That's why Itzaak is alive, by the way. He was using a prop block instead of his usual thing. A tire iron is always metal of some kind, if not iron. A prop block is wood."

"It killed the nurse," Bennis pointed out.

"True, but it only wounded poor Shecker. In fact, in spite of the fact that it knocked him out, he barely gave him a decent concussion. Itzaak was a little worse off, but not by much. Prescott Holloway wasn't used to using it, you see. He wasn't prepared for the kind of force he'd have to use or the angle he'd have to take to do what he wanted to do with the prop block."

"Is Shecker the cop who was found in the utility closet?"

"That's the one."

"That must have been embarrassing," Bennis said.

"It was all embarrassing." Gregor sighed. "What else we were supposed to do, though, I just don't know. You really can't arrest someone on the kind of speculation I had. You really can't."

"I know," Bennis said. "Did your lie with the dreidel work? Did he talk?"

"For six hours," Gregor said. "You should have heard him. And I thought he was going to be one of the minority who keep their mouths shut."

"He talked about killing illegal immigrants," Bennis said.

"Oh, yes. About how they are the cause of all the trouble. They come here and expect us to wait on them. They take good jobs away from American working people because they are willing to work for nothing. They are trying to turn us into some kind of primitive culture instead of an advanced Western one and that's why they want the schools to teach Spanish instead of English and on and on—do you really have to hear all of this?"

"No. But why was he supplying them with fake green cards and social security numbers if he hated them so much?"

"So that he could find them."

"What?"

"I got caught by this in the beginning," Gregor said. "When I realized that Max Dey had managed to replace his green card in much less than twenty-four hours— never mind the weeks it takes if you go through INS—I knew that Max's card had to have been forged and that what had happened was that he'd gotten himself another forged one. I also knew he had to have gotten it from someone on *The Lotte Goldman Show*, because he didn't know anybody in Philadelphia and also because the card was replaced in the dead of night. Would you go wandering around a strange city looking to buy something like that? Never mind the fact that if you got it from someone you didn't know, you'd also have to supply cash on the barrelhead, and we know that Max didn't have any cash. His wallet was stolen and his cash was in it. Not only his green card."

"Okay," Bennis said slowly, "but—"

"You've got to turn it around," Gregor said. "It wasn't that Prescott Holloway happened to work in a place with an unusually large number of illegal immigrants. It was that an unusually large number of illegal immigrants were on staff at *The Lotte Goldman Show* because Prescott Holloway worked there. With the exception of Carmencita Boaz, he brought them in."

"Who brought Carmencita Boaz in?"

"Maria Gonzalez. They lived in the same neighborhood and were friends. That's how Carmencita knew where to go for a forged green card when she got word from her family that one was needed in a hurry. We've got the cops in New York checking the staff lists for *The Lotte Goldman Show* going back to when Prescott Holloway started working there. We're expecting to find a number of abrupt disappearances with Spanish names attached to them."

"Max Dey wasn't Spanish. He was—"

"'Portuguese. I know," Gregor said.

"And there's one more thing," Bennis told him. "Why did he wait? Why didn't he just kill them when they came asking for their forged green cards?"

Gregor was astonished. "Because he wanted the money," he said. "He was making a very good thing out of his little business. He wasn't making himself a millionaire, but he was doing all right. His ties were more expensive than mine."

"A Bowery bum has ties more expensive than yours," Bennis said.

"There was another way you could tell it had to be Prescott Holloway," Gregor said, ignoring her. "He was the only one who had the mobility. Maria's apartment was trashed. Maria's body was moved from one place to another. Who else could have gone tearing around town like that without it becoming obvious?"

"I think it's all very depressing," Bennis said. "The

only thing that isn't is that Carmencita and Itzaak are getting married, and I can hardly get a thrill out of that because I've only just met them. Never mind. At least I get to get out of the country at last. I was beginning to think I was going to lose my mind."

"Mmm," Gregor said.

Down on the stage, John Stewart Pell had disappeared—in the direction of further incarceration, Gregor truly hoped—and Lotte and DeAnna had gathered the staff on the stage in what seemed to be a sort of celebration. Carmencita and Itzaak were not present, of course. Carmencita was still not well enough to leave and Itzaak spent all his time at the hospital. Shelley Feldstein was there, though, and Sarah Meyer, and a few other people Gregor recognized as minor support staff. On the coffee table that had hidden the handcuff on John Stewart Pell's leg, there was a cake.

DeAnna Kroll came to the edge of the platform and waved. "Come on down," she said. "We're celebrating Carmencita and Itzaak. Or something. Lotte's got little menorahs all over this cake. Come eat some."

"Do I have time?" Bennis asked Gregor.

"You've got fifteen minutes," Gregor said. "I ordered the car for you for eight o'clock."

"Cake for breakfast," Bennis said. Then she got up and went over to the platform.

Gregor Demarkian watched her go. So far so good, he thought. Now if he could only get himself through the next fifteen minutes.

2

The first signs of trouble came when Bennis Hannaford was halfway through her piece of cake, sitting cross-legged on the club chair nearest the coffee table and jabbing rhythmically at the wisps of hair that kept escaping from the pins she had put it up in. She was talking to DeAnna Kroll, as she had been for the last three minutes. She was playing with the plastic menorah that had been on her piece of cake and talking about high-heeled boots and whether they inevitably hurt your toes. That was when DeAnna Kroll asked, "What about that old lady you were telling me about last week? Is she still holed up in your apartment?"

Gregor backed away instinctively and held his breath. Bennis put down her cake fork.

"It was the oddest thing," she said. "Day before yesterday, she just got up and walked away. At least, I assume she did. I went to the grocery store and when I got back she was gone."

"Did she leave a note?"

"Oh, yes. Her niece came and got her. Her niece had been away, you see, on some sort of class trip or something. I don't know. Anyway, I called and the niece said the old lady was all right and safely home, but I don't really understand it. Maybe I would if I'd talked to the doctor."

"I thought you did talk to the doctor."

"I wasn't home. It all happened in the apartment directly underneath mine, you see, but she couldn't stay there because the man who lives there is in his eighties and he couldn't take care of her. They brought her up to my place while I was out. Do things like this happen to you?"

"Constantly," DeAnna Kroll said.

Bennis nodded. "I got the impression this place was like a floating Cavanaugh Street. I don't mind, you understand. I mean, she was a really terrifying old lady and there were times I thought I could use a chair and a whip, you know, like a lion tamer, but in the long run I didn't mind. But I'm glad to be able to get off. I really need this trip."

"Which of the old ladies is she?" DeAnna Kroll

asked. "The tall one with the black hair or the short round one with the gray hair and face like Moondog Kelly?"

Bennis looked confused. "The short one with the gray hair and the face like Moondog Kelly sounds like Hannah Krekorian. But how could you have met Hannah Krekorian? She didn't come to either of the tapings."

"She's downstairs in the car," DeAnna Kroll said.

"In what car?" Bennis asked her. Then she turned around to look at Gregor Demarkian and Gregor Demarkian winced.

Bennis put her feet down on the floor and her plate of cake on the coffee table.

"Gregor," she said warningly. "What car?"

"A black stretch limousine from Society Hill Rentals."

"Wonderful, Gregor. And what's Hannah Krekorian doing in this car? And who else—Lida?"

"Well," Gregor conceded, "Lida, too."

"Who else?"

Gregor sighed. "Donna Moradanyan and Tommy. Sheila and Howard Kashinian. Mary Ohanian. Oh, and old George will be coming too, but in another car with his grandson Martin and Martin's wife."

"Coming where?" Bennis demanded.

"To the airport," Gregor said.

"Gregor, the airport is in New York."

"I know."

"Isn't that a bit of a drive for all these people to take just to see me off?"

"They're not just going to see you off. Neither am I."

"Oh," Bennis said. "You're in on it, too. And where are you going?"

"We're all going the same place you're going. To Paris."

"To Paris," Bennis repeated. "Why?"

"We didn't want you to be lonely."

"You didn't want me to be lonely . . ."

"It's going to be all right," Gregor told her, "really. Lida rented the entire fifth floor of the Georges V—I think there was a problem with that, but one of Lida's sons is in the diplomatic service, so it got worked out—anyway, we have the entire floor and Lida wants to go to Notre Dame for Christmas Eve Mass and I think we've rented some restaurant for Christmas Eve dinner. Tibor wanted to come, by the way, but he has to be at Holy Trinity for Christmas Day."

Bennis took a pack of cigarettes out of her pocket, took a cigarette out of the pack, took her matches out of another pocket and lit up. She did all this very, very slowly, so that Gregor got the impression that it was only manners that prevented her from braining him.

"Gregor," she said finally, "if all you wanted was to make sure I wasn't lonely, why didn't you just ask me to come along yourself?"

"Yes. Well—"

"Why did you bring along all these other people? I mean, I love them, I don't mind, but this is going to be a circus."

"Yes," Gregor said. "Well."

"I mean, for God's sake, Gregor, what are we going to do with them all?"

"They're going to serve a very useful purpose."

"As what?"

"Chaperons," Gregor said grimly.

He said it quickly, before he thought of the trouble it might cause, and as soon as it came out of his mouth he got ready to take a body blow. It was just the kind of thing Bennis got ready to kill him for.

Fortunately for Gregor's physical well-being, that was when the real trouble started. That it came from an entirely unsuspected corner—at least unsuspected by him—made it all that much better.

This is what happened: Just as Bennis Hannaford was about to start ripping Gregor Demarkian up one side and down the other, Shelley Feldstein walked over to Sarah Meyer and punched the younger woman in the nose.

ABOUT THE AUTHOR

JANE HADDAM is the author of eleven Gregor Demarkian Holiday mysteries. *Not A Creature Was Stirring*, the first in the series, was nominated for both an Anthony and the Mystery Writers of America Edgar Award. She lives in Litchfield County, Connecticut, with her husband, and two sons, where she is at work on a Birthday mystery, *And One To Die On*.